Fake it for the Billionaire

In the playroom...

Lana Stone

The Billionaires of New York 2

Copyright © 2023 by Lana Stone

All rights reserved.

No portion of this book may be reproduced in any form without written permission from the publisher or author, except as permitted by U.S. copyright law.

Dedication

As always, I dedicate this book to the love of my life.

Chapter 1 – Aurora

Snorting, I shook my smartphone as if a shaken battery could solve my problem. Again, I only reached Maxine's voicemail. I took a deep breath and swallowed all the curses and insults I had at the ready.

"Hey Max, it's me. Again. Aurora, your best friend." I paused meaningfully before continuing. "I know I wasn't supposed to get here for a few days, but my whole family is freaking out right now. I've already explained that to you in detail in the last few messages. Anyway, I hope you ignored the last five messages and aren't waiting for me at the airport now, I'm at your front door. I still have the keys to it, so take your time."

After I hung up, the large entrance door of the luxurious high-rise building swung open as if by itself, and I stepped inside. I felt strangely observed as I pushed my small suitcase through the magnificent hall and headed straight for the elevators. Quickly I scurried through the high room, whose marble floors echoed my footsteps. There was no one here but me, except for the man standing at the reception looking at me expectantly. I smiled at him without changing my direction, because I had only one destination left: the huge bathtub in Maxine's penthouse suite, with whom I was about to have a date. A very hot, sudsy date!

Sighing, I ran my fingers through my wet blond hair, which was sticking to my back from the sudden midnight rain. Without looking, I knew I had to spend hours combing out all the little and big knots.

What a day.

The older man from the reception desk appeared behind me, clearing his throat, as I rummaged through my handbag in front of the elevator. With every second that passed, the damp cold crept more into my bones.

"Can I help you, miss?"

"No," I replied, smiling politely. When he made no move to leave, I looked up at him as my hand continued to rummage through the bag. He was wearing one of the uniforms that all the receptionists here wore, but I had never seen his face before. His name tag read *Sebastian* in Helvetica letters. Not that I define people by their name tags, but his stiff, stern demeanor would be more suited to Arial or Times New Roman. Yep, Sebastian was more the *Times New Roman-I'm-the-rules-police type* and just looked at me like it was a crime to stand in front of the penthouse suite elevator.

"You know this elevator only goes to the top floor?"

I nodded. "I know, that's exactly where I want to go."

"Is that so? No one was announced to me."

Even though I was jet-lagged to death, my legs hurt like hell, and the freezing rain shower had completely soaked me, I tried to remain friendly.

"I wasn't supposed to be here for another week either, but now I'm here early."

"I'm afraid there's nothing I can do for you without notice. I'm very sorry, miss." Sebastian looked at me businesslike and without expression of regret. The only thing he regretted was the time he had, in his opinion, *wasted* with me.

"Sebastian, I had a really terrible day. My flight was delayed for four hours, my entire suitcase was cleared out at the airport, and because of a traffic jam I had to walk the last five blocks here. In the rain! And all that just because I had to run away from my family because everyone just committed to the collective madness. It's late and I just want a hot bath and then bed, okay?"

The receptionist didn't make a face. "I still can't give you a key card."

"You don't have to, I have my own."

It felt almost like a small triumph when I finally found the card among a brush and a dozen old bills and raised it in the air like a trophy.

"You have a card?"

"Yep." Admittedly, I was a bit grumpy, but I was at my wits' end.

Now Sebastian looked at me in surprise, it was the first emotion I recognized under his professional expression.

Almost as if I had to prove to him that I was innocent, I placed the card on the electronic recognition field and the elevator doors opened silently.

At first I wanted to ask if there was a problem with Max handing me a key card on my last visit, but then swallowed the question. The way Sebastian was looking at me, he definitely thought of a problem that kept me away from the huge bathtub with massage jets.

I got on the elevator and saw Sebastian also suppressing saying anything or preventing me from my bathtub date.

"Have a nice day," Sebastian said, still irritated, and turned back.

"It can only get better," I replied with relief as the doors finally closed. I leaned against the wall to rest my feet when my cell phone vibrated.

"It's about time, Max!" I exclaimed euphorically, because there was finally a sign of life from my best friend. But my jubilation died away when I looked at the display and accepted the call with a sigh.

"Hey Mom."

"Aurora, sweetie, did you get here okay?"

"Yep, I am, that's why I called your house earlier when it wasn't the middle of the night."

"But New York streets are dangerous, especially at night! You could have had an accident, or worse, a mugging!"

I held my breath to suppress all reflexes that were fighting for dominance. Of course, my heart went out to my mom for worrying about me, but she was doing it – again – for the wrong reasons. Not to mention, the area around Central Park was worlds away from Hell's Kitchen and the mafia-like structures there.

"Don't worry, Mom. I'll be back in Seattle in time for Maggy's wedding, healthy. I promise."

"I hope so, it's your little sister's big day!"

"I know."

And I also knew that my mom was afraid that I would steal Maggy's thunder if I had to show up with a cast on my arm or in a wheelchair. Well, my mom expressed her affection for her children in a very special way. If I had found a husband before Maggy – God forbid – our roles might have been reversed. But I had written off a husband as well as my studies at the University of Technology.

Silence. Neither of us dared to say anything. Lately, this oppressive silence was a frequent guest when Mom and I talked.

"Is there anything else, Mom?" I asked so the silence wouldn't smother us.

"You really need to think about that dress!"

I rolled my eyes because my mom was again throwing our biggest bone of contention from the past few weeks into the room.

"I promised you that Max and I would do some shopping!"

"But it has to be orchid, not raspberry, not magenta, orchid! You know we have a great dress here, you'd just have to lose a little weight. Anyway, it wouldn't hurt you."

Cursing inwardly, I put my head back. "I'm a size ten dress, and I'm comfortable in it, how many times do I need to say that?"

I didn't want to say it out loud, but Maggy's wedding had turned my mom into a monster.

"It's okay, it's okay. I just don't want you to stand out from the other bridesmaids," my mom replied so dryly that my stomach tightened briefly but painfully.

"Of course not, I'm just the sister of the bride," I replied cynically.

"Don't get all huffy, you know how I meant it."

"Yes, that is, exactly as you said it."

I wonder if my mother would make such a mess if Ben Goldberg wasn't a rich lawyer but a salesman, handyman, or unemployed long-term student?

Bing.

"Hold on, Mom."

The elevator doors opened, and I entered Maxine's luxury loft, which had an extravagant panoramic view of Central Park when it wasn't pouring down rain that restricted my view to ten feet. I put the phone to my chest for a moment so that my mother wouldn't get an earful.

"Max? Are you there? Hello?" Silence. I looked around and had to admit that I remembered the apartment differently, much more colorful and much less depressing. Sterile black and white didn't match my best friend's style at all. Anyway, as long as the bathtub was still where it always was, I didn't care about my best friend's architectural experiments.

"Mom, I need to hang up now so I can get out of these wet clothes."

Crap! Actually, I had wanted to keep my involuntary rain shower to myself, but the jet lag had made me tired.

"Make sure you don't catch a cold! It would be terrible if you catch a cold during the wedding, or worse, infect Magnolia!"

"Mom, I'm not going to get a cold. And if I do, I'll have cured it at least three times before the wedding," I reassured my mother.

I heard a quiet discussion in the background, then the receiver was passed on.

"Aurora?" My sister had grabbed the phone. "Don't let Mom drive you crazy, okay?"

"Too late. But it's not too late for you to escape to New York, too," I joked. Heedless of the sterile order that reigned here. I tossed my heels off, followed by my unbuttoned sweater, which I wore over my summer dress.

"Aurora! I can't leave our mom alone with the wedding preparations!" Maggy replied, horrified. I wasn't sure if Maggy was afraid of her wedding escalating because our mom couldn't be left alone or if my little sister had secretly switched sides.

"I have to hang up now, the bathtub is calling," I said goodbye, because I was too tired for further conversation.

"All right, sis."

Just as Maggy was about to hang up, Mom stole her phone back.

"Stop, not so fast!"

"What else?"

"You're going to have chicken soup delivered."

"All right, Mom, I'm hanging up now."

"And you get yourself cod liver oil, that's good for the immune system. Best of all, you also make yourself ginger-lemon tea with honey!" My mother threw one home remedy after another at me without me being able to stop her. "But it would be best if you had a husband to take care of you! Speaking of which ..."

"No, Mom. *We don't* talk about it, only you do."

"All right, fine. I just don't want you to be all alone at Magnolia's wedding with everyone looking at you pitifully." My mom spoke of me as if I were a pitiful street kitten with huge, hungry eyes.

"I'm sure you'll make sure everyone will only have eyes for the bride and the beautiful wedding," I replied sugary sweet.

"Or you could meet Silvia McKinney's son Steve, she raves at every Pilates class we take about what a talented surgeon he is. If you'd like, I could also set up a date with Oliver and Jada Rosenberg's son, I'm sure he'll be a senator in years to come!"

I had hoped that Maggy's wedding and the imminent prospect of grandchildren would put the brakes on my mother's matchmaking attempts, but the exact opposite had happened. Now that my mother was hooked, she couldn't wait to get me hitched, too. The wedding mania had visibly gone to her head.

"Mom, the reception's getting really bad," I lied. "Hello? I can't hear you anymore. Maybe the phone system is breaking down right now because it's storming. I'll call back later, kiss."

After that, I hung up and exhaled with relief. Of course I loved my family, but they could also drive me up the wall, especially in exceptional situations like weddings or Christmas parties. I don't know why, but my mother had an innate weakness for putting her foot in her mouth, and the way she showed her motherly love was sometimes highly questionable, but I knew she really only meant well. Otherwise, my dad certainly wouldn't have been going through this mess for thirty years; he was the only *normal one* in my family, and I was a lot like him. I had inherited not only his patience, but also his green eyes and his talent for craftsmanship.

I peeled myself out of my wet summer dress that was sticking to my body and dropped it on the floor. Because I couldn't get rid of the cold, wet fabric fast enough, I also *lost* my underwear on the way to the bathroom.

Relieved, I noticed that the bathroom had hardly changed, and I let steaming hot water into the huge, free-standing tub. I took a bath bomb from a decorative glass and threw it into the water as well, which immediately got a blanket of foam.

Oh, why be so stingy? After such a day, I had earned a generous bubble bath, so I immediately took two more scoops and threw them into the tub.

Before I climbed into the cozy warmth, I snapped a photo of my perfect bubble bath and sent it to Maxine so she would know where to find me when she got home and my breadcrumb trail wasn't enough.

Immediately, when I dived into the steaming water, it displaced the cold that had nested in my bones. Incredibly, all the stress, all the anger and frustration were washed away. Maxine's bath bombs had put an end to my impending burnout, and the floral-scented, crackling foam immediately enveloped me in tender comfort.

I allowed myself to close my eyes and enjoyed the comforting warmth that enveloped me. No idea if minutes or hours had passed, but when I opened my eyes again, I got the shock of my life, because I was no longer alone in the bathroom. Directly in front of me was a man who looked at me with interest and put my soaked clothes on the dresser.

A damn handsome man, his face was mercilessly beautiful and could grace the cover of any Beautiful People magazine.

As if stung by a tarantula, I jumped up, but instead of calling for help in panic, I got lost in his dark brown eyes. God, those looks! Millennial looks definitely. On top of this millennial looks package, there was also the sexy-as-hell upgrade. Even though he was wearing a suit, I recognized the outline of his dominant abs.

The stranger had taste, for his suit was made of fine, wrinkle-free fabric and definitely tailored. Off-the-peg suits would never fit over those broad shoulders.

On his lips was a half, seductive grin. That grin must have broken dozens of hearts, I caught myself melting away.

Who was this *Mister Universe*?

It wasn't until I finally broke free from my stupor that I realized the situation and the fact that the glitter foam on my body was slowly, but surely, slipping down.

No matter! The guy could still be so attractive, he was at best a pushy visitor with whom Max was friends, or at worst a burglar. Either way, he was definitely dangerous, because in his presence my heart beat faster.

"Jesus Christ!"

"Caden will do," he replied with a smile. Madness, most women would kill for a smile like that, I was sure of it. Under other circumstances I would have been one of those women, but not here, naked in my best friend's bathroom!

"What are you doing?" I asked.

"I guess I should be asking you that, huh?"

He approached me as if it were the most natural thing in the world. Without a doubt, Caden was a man who not only knew exactly what he wanted, but also just took it.

"Please?" I looked at him challengingly.

"I think you heard me perfectly, little mermaid."

Unbelievable. Caden had somehow gained access to my best friend's apartment, stormed the bathroom, and now took the liberty of hitting on me?

Shamelessly, he let his eyes wander over my – still – moderately foam-covered body.

"Are you flirting with me right now?" I asked in shock.

"Could be." He came closer and looked at me even more closely. Slowly, but surely, the foam no longer offered any privacy.

"Do I have to call the police first?" My voice shook with anger.

Caden raised a brow questioningly. "So you can turn yourself in? I think I'd prefer other methods that suit us both better."

Shaking my head, I tried to ignore the flirting attempts, which I found dangerously seductive.

"Why should I turn myself in? You're the one who broke in here!"

"No, I live here, but I'm dying to know how you made it past security and the alarm systems."

He said it so convincingly that I almost believed him. But only almost. After all, I knew exactly that Maxine had bought this apartment the year before last - and had extensively remodeled it. Here Maxine and I had danced off the heartache of the time, my failed studies and the rest of the frustration of the world!

"I came in with my key card."

I would have loved to show him the card as triumphantly as I did the reception guy down in the lobby, but the card was on the floor somewhere between my dress and my heels.

Caden came even closer to me, and I held my breath because otherwise his masculine scent would have robbed me of the rest of my willpower.

"I would remember such a beautiful face," he murmured.

His fingers brushed my cheek, and I didn't resist as he gripped my chin with his thumb and forefinger and gently turned my head left and right. I could feel the heat of his skin, which sparked a longing for *more in* my body.

"What does that mean?" I asked. Was he still going to play the you-are-the-burglar game? Did he really think I was that naive?

By now Caden had a perfect view of my naked body but putting me back in the tub would have been a sign of weakness, and I certainly didn't want to admit that to him. I didn't give up, and that's exactly what Caden should know.

"It means I didn't give you a card, little mermaid."

"So you stand by your assertion that this is your loft?" I crossed my arms provocatively in front of my chest, as if I were a six-foot-tall bouncer whom nothing could shake.

"Yes."

And now? We were in a stalemate, even though I felt Caden was telling the truth. He was far too charismatic for a burglar.

"What's your name?" he asked me.

"Aurora."

A smile flitted across his lips.

"Aurora," he repeated softly. "What an unusual name."

He had no idea how unusual. *Aurora Winter*. At first glance, the name game was quite nice, but when you're subjected to twenty-four years of repeated mediocre word jokes, the charm of the name eventually gets used up.

"I'd like to get out of the tub now," I said promptly.

"Go ahead, Aurora."

He skillfully ignored my hint to leave, which angered me.

"If you're going to break in here, at least show some respect!" I ruled him.

"I respect you and all other beautiful women who stray here, even if in an unconventional way."

Wow. A small part of me would have liked to figure out right then and there what Caden meant by *unconventional*, but the rest of my mind beat that small part senseless. This was no time for flirting!

Still, I couldn't help but feel perhaps a little jealous of the women who knew Caden's methods.

I rolled my eyes, snorting, which caused Caden to give me a serious look. Something about those looks told me he was really dangerous, in a rough, heartbreaking way. He wanted to say something, but then let it go.

The tension in the room grew, as did Caden's attraction.

Was this actually still salvageable? A strange guy stood in front of me while I was naked in the tub and the only thing I could think of were his incredible brown eyes!

A muffled buzz cut through the silence, and it took me a moment to understand that it was my smartphone humming away at the edge of the tub. Maxine – finally!

It was a huge weight off my mind that my girlfriend could finally give me support, even if only mentally. Today was really not my day.

"Maxine, I ... " I began, but she interrupted me in a shrill voice.

"Aurora! Get out of the bathroom!"

"What?" My relief turned to horror because I guessed what Max was about to say.

"This isn't my apartment anymore, Aurora! I sold it a few weeks ago."

"I know," I replied automatically.

Oh. My. God.

"What, from where? Aurora?"

"The new owner is facing me right now."

I couldn't say more because Caden's amused grin threw me completely off track. I ended the call. Geez, today really wasn't my day at all. It felt like I had all my negative karma paid off at once, and in the most sadistic way possible. Because still my biggest problem was that Caden was the most attractive guy in the universe, I had broken into Mr. Universe's apartment and then called him a burglar.

Today was officially the second scariest day of my life right after my first day of college.

Caden moved around me like a hungry wolf on the prowl.

"What are we going to do with you now, huh?"

There were two things that came to mind.

First, he did what any normal person would have done, which was to call the police.

Or else, Caden delved into the *unconventional methods* he had spoken of earlier.

Fact: Caden had managed in an instant to awaken desires in me, of which I had known nothing until now. I had to get out of here as soon as possible, otherwise I would have much bigger problems, I was sure of it!

Chapter 2 – Caden

I watched with amusement as Aurora's facial features slipped when she realized that she, not I, was the intruder. At the same time, I let my gaze continue to roam over her flawless body, from which I simply could not detach myself.

What a pleasant surprise, and when I looked at it soberly, I had been damn lucky to have met Aurora at all, because I had been sort of living in my company for the last little while.

Under other circumstances I would have simply accepted Aurora's invitation, bent her over and fucked her, but I had rules I had to follow.

"What are we going to do with you now?" I asked. But actually I wondered why I was suddenly questioning the rules I had set up, which had proven themselves over the years.

"I think it's best if I leave now and we both just laugh at this stupid coincidence, okay?"

None of us laughed. She was embarrassed, and I was overwhelmed by the strange feelings she aroused in me.

Aurora got out of the tub, smiled shyly at me and reached for her clothes, which I had put on the dresser. How multifaceted the little mermaid was. Just a moment ago she had almost fought me like a lioness, and now she was as mild as a lamb.

Every fiber of my body wanted to possess Aurora.

Jesus, I really couldn't help but lay claim to her.

Just thinking about how submissive she could look at me with her emerald eyes almost blew all my fuses.

Remember the rules, Caden.

My subconscious urged me to be calm, because I could not be responsible for a loss of control. I should have let her go, but I could not.

"What are you going to do now, Aurora?"

"I'll go."

"And go where?"

Aurora shrugged her shoulders but didn't dare look at me directly. "To a hotel."

I looked at my one-of-a-kind Rolex. "It's getting late, no hotel is going to let you check in now."

Off the top of my head, I could think of a dozen hotels that received guests around the clock, but I was selfish. Of course I stuck to my damn rule, but just the thought that we were breaking the rule had an invigorating effect that I desperately needed.

"Then I'll just go to my best friend's house."

I clearly shook my head. This time I did not agree with her proposal for other reasons.

"At this hour, a girl like you shouldn't be getting into cabs alone and driving around New York."

"A girl like me?" asked Aurora innocently. Did she really have no idea what effect she had on men? Her scent alone was the purest drug for men like me. One that, once you had taken the first shot, you could never escape.

"We both know what I'm talking about," I murmured as I pushed a strand of her long, blonde hair behind her ear. She sighed softly as my thumb grazed her silky soft skin. Aurora wanted to say something, but then fell silent.

Damn, she really didn't know what I was talking about, which only made me want to possess her even more.

"You have a special effect on men like me."

"Men like you?"

Aurora looked at me questioningly with her big green eyes.

"You should stay away from men like me. You're lucky, I'm a gentleman, I stick to my rules."

Instead of answering, she only exhaled audibly. Then she made an effort to put on her soaked clothes, which I took from her. Instead, I stripped off my jacket, unbuttoned my shirt and gave it to her.

"You're going to catch a cold wearing those wet clothes and running haphazardly through New York at night."

She gratefully accepted my shirt and slipped it on. It was much too big for her, but she looked damn seductive in it.

I smiled with satisfaction as Aurora was longer than decent, admiring my trained upper body. Admittedly, I enjoyed it to the fullest.

Her gaze traveled further down, to my belt and a little further.

You have no idea who you're getting into ...

Caden Saint - Successful businessman, dominant alpha and definitely no saint!

"You can sleep here tonight," I said seriously.

"That's very nice, but ..."

"You'll sleep here tonight, too." My penetrating look made it clear to her that I was serious. Damn serious, even. Just the thought of this small, delicate creature struggling alone through gloomy, dangerous New York drove me half mad.

"I don't think that's a good idea. We're still doing things we might regret."

I knew exactly what Aurora was alluding to, but she was lucky, my rules prevented us from doing things we both wanted to do. A single rule protected Aurora from what I really was.

"We won't."

"What makes you so sure?"

I led Aurora out of the bathroom towards the bedroom. I stopped in front of a closed black door.

"Because you're not in this room. And I advise you to stay out of this room."

"I don't understand."

I grabbed Aurora by the shoulders and pushed her against the wall so I could breathe in her sweet scent. My lips slid along her neck, she tasted as sweet as she smelled.

"I told you I was a gentleman, and I keep my word. But behind this door, I am no longer a gentleman. Beyond that door, not even your big emerald eyes can save you. Please, Aurora, never open Pandora's box."

Reluctantly, I detached myself from her and took three steps back. Her scent pursued me anyway.

"Don't stop!" whispered Aurora in a weak voice, but I had to stop. If I didn't slow down now, I'd drag us both down into the abyss.

"Yes, I'm going to stop now and you're going to go to my bedroom, call your girlfriend and tell her you won't see each other again until tomorrow."

Aurora shook her head.

"But I can't just hog your bedroom like this."

"I have more than one bed."

Actually, there was another bed, and it was in the room that Aurora was supposed to stay as far away from as possible. I hadn't slept in that bed once, that had been the prerogative of my subs who were too exhausted to go home at night.

I allowed myself just a single second to think about how graceful Aurora would have looked in my playroom before I dismissed the thought again.

My work has been taking up so much of my time lately that I haven't had time for a sub, not to mention Aurora surely had her own plans.

Hell, she was a born sub, I saw that at first glance, but whether she saw it the same way was another question.

Damn, why had she had to stray into my apartment of all places?

"Okay." Aurora gave up, albeit reluctantly. Something flashed in her eyes that I had never seen before in the eyes of my subs – resistance.

Damn it, Caden, she's not your sub!

Still, I couldn't help but get to the bottom of the resistance; whether Aurora was mine or not.

"If you sneak out of the penthouse tonight, I'll hear about it."

Her cheeks flushed slightly as I caught her trying to make a break for it.

"You don't know me, but you can believe me that I would put you over my knee without hesitation if you were so careless with your life."

"Jesus, this isn't Hell's Kitchen! Besides, I can take care of myself very well. I have no idea why I always have to justify myself because of that!"

I had definitely hit a sore spot, which is why I got her concentrated anger. Normally I didn't let anyone talk to me like that, but I was curious about her further reactions, so I stayed calm.

"Obviously you can't take care of yourself if you act so carelessly."

"We're in the middle of Manhattan, there are no crazies or criminals here, at least not any more than in Seattle."

I growled softly, because on the one hand I found her naive view of the world quite cute, but on the other hand she was also setting a direct course for small and large disasters.

"Believe me, the whole city is full of danger."

I knew this better than anyone, because I had been pushed by my closest confidants into the deepest abysses a person could fall into. Paradoxically, I had been trying to suppress these thoughts for years, but it felt like it was yesterday.

"You also claimed you were a danger to me."

Aurora crossed her arms in front of her chest and looked me in the eyes with confidence.

Kind of cute, but also further proof that I was right. Aurora had no idea who I actually was and what I could do to her if she was reckless enough to let me.

"That's right," I replied.

"If that were true, you wouldn't have stopped."

Damn, the conversation was going in a direction I didn't like at all.

"You better watch what you say or do now."

I was about to break the only rule I had.

"And what do you think I should do?"

It didn't help, I had to give Aurora a taste of the danger that surrounded me.

"I want nothing more than for you to throw caution to the wind and walk through that damn door, Aurora. And that's exactly why you should stay as far away from that door as you possibly can. Do you understand?"

Aurora looked at me with her eyes wide open. I had shocked her, no question, but she was nowhere near as afraid as she should be.

Why did I only feel that the danger surrounding me aroused her curiosity? She flew unsuspectingly to her doom, like a moth attracted by candlelight and diving straight for the flame.

Chapter 3 – Aurora

Caden's scent hung in his sheets, in his towels, and in my hair. All morning I had tried to wash away his scent and everything I associated with it, but I couldn't do it. Caden was everywhere, even in my thoughts he was omnipresent.

Pull yourself together, Aurora!

Relief and tension came over me in equal measure when I heard noises coming from the kitchen. Should I stay here and pretend that I was still asleep? No, I wanted to go to him.

Okay, I definitely needed a strategy for that, because I could do without embarrassing small talk. But what should I say to the man who had first turned my head and then suddenly dumped me?

Good morning, Caden. Remember me? You dropped me like a hot potato yesterday.

A bit provocative, but not bad to read him the riot act today.

Clad in his shirt, I plodded toward the kitchen as the closed door caught my eye, the one I'd been racking my brains over all night. I wondered what was hiding behind it and why Caden only ever spoke of this place in a lowered voice. Yes, I wanted to find out what was behind that door, but I was also afraid of it.

I didn't know Caden, he could be hiding anything else behind that door. Corpses, nuclear bombs or even worse: model trains.

Caden had given me a choice, and I had chickened out because I was too afraid of heartbreak. Because his deep brown eyes definitely had the potential to break hearts, I had recognized that at first sight.

Sighing, I went into the kitchen and watched Caden prepare a French omelet. I was disappointed to see that he was not naked, but wearing a tailored suit, under which I could nevertheless make out the contours of his muscles. Heavens, that body! Just thinking about his divinely trained upper body made me drool again.

"Good morning," I said. I stifled the rest of my sentence.

"Morning!" he greeted me without looking up.

"Is this not a *good* morning for you?"

"Every morning is the same."

"With your pessimism, definitely."

Caden looked up and gave me a seductively serious look.

"Sit down." He pointed to one of the chairs that stood in front of the cooking island, which was about as big as my entire kitchen.

"That's nice, but I don't eat breakfast."

"No?"

I shook my head. "No."

"Then you should sit down more than ever. Breakfast is the most important meal of the day."

"I prefer coffee with an extra shot of milk. That's the breakfast of champions."

Grinning, Caden placed a cup of steaming coffee in front of me, and I immediately sipped the strong hot beverage.

Caden eyed me from top to bottom.

"You should still eat something."

"Later," I waved it off.

"That wasn't a request."

Wow, Caden's eyes got all dark and it took all my strength not to avoid his gaze. There was something about his raspy voice that made me want to obey all his commands right away. But I wasn't that kind of person, I had my own head and didn't let anyone tell me what to do, not even Mr. Universe.

Just as I was about to say something back, Caden turned away from me and left me alone with my thoughts.

"You can't just turn your back on me," I protested.

"Yes, I can. And in case you haven't noticed, I already have," Caden replied coolly.

One moment my blood froze in my veins when Caden's dark looks brushed my skin, and the next moment, I almost boiled over with rage. What was it between him and me? We wanted each other, we wanted *more,* and yet we both did everything we could to keep it from happening. Caden pushed me away, and I contradicted him at every turn – perfect ingredients for something that was doomed to fail.

"I thought you were a gentleman?" My pointed question gave him pause for a moment.

"You better shut up now."

"No."

"No?"

Yes, it was dangerous and I was on very, very thin ice, but I couldn't help it. We probably never saw each other again after this breakfast, so I might as well get rid of what I still had to say.

"I don't know you, Caden, but I think people far too rarely talk to you the way I do."

"So rude and provocative? That's right, no one has ever spoken to me like that." His voice became a deep rumble of thunder that dwarfed even the summer storm yesterday. My treacherous abdomen quivered expectantly, but I tried to ignore the feeling that was clouding my senses.

"Then it's high time someone contradicted you for once."

"I must confess that I'm a little disappointed that you stayed away from the forbidden door, but that's been your damn luck."

Caden turned around and his gaze captivated me. They were no longer Caden's eyes, they were those of a hungry wolf that had found its prey.

"Why?" I asked quietly.

"Regrettably, I don't think we'll ever find out."

I slid off the chair. "Yes, we can. Right now, if you want!"

"Sit down!" His harsh commanding tone made me cringe. "We're going to eat breakfast now, then I have to go."

I wanted to rebel, I really did. Every fiber of my body wanted to fight Caden's command, but instead I silently sat back in the chair and sighed softly.

"Good girl."

Caden set a plate down in front of me, and though it smelled delicious, I wrinkled my nose.

"I'm really not a breakfast person." It took all my effort not to sound provocative or dismissive. I really wasn't a breakfast person, no idea why. Okay, actually, I knew exactly why I could do without the breakfast table with my crazy family since junior school, but that was another story.

"You're not from around here, are you?"

His question surprised me, yet I nodded.

"I'm from Seattle," I said proudly. New York had 5th Avenue and Central Park, sure, but we had the Seattle Seahawks and the Space Needle in our portfolio. "Why?"

"Because you don't survive long in New York without breakfast."

"Don't worry, I'm not about to starve to death."

Caden smiled at me as if I had said something rather naive. "Don't worry, I'll make sure you don't find out what I'm actually talking about."

He took a fork, picked up some omelet and held it to my lips. I took a deep audible breath of indignation, but he literally stifled my revolt by putting the fork and omelet in my mouth.

"Oh. My. God!" it escaped me as I finished chewing. Not just because Caden had simply fed me, but rather because it was the best omelet I had ever eaten.

"Good?" asked Caden, grinning, because he already knew my answer.

"It's perfect!"

"Of course it is, I don't do things by halves."

"I hadn't pegged you that way either."

No one could afford such luxury suites on *half measures*, that much was clear, but his looks alone were enough to know that he always got what he wanted.

His looks also said, *I want you, Aurora*. At least, deep down I wished that's what his expression meant.

"What else do you think of me?"

"Huh?" To stall for time, I took his fork and stuffed my mouth to think. Of course, I had understood his question perfectly, but I didn't know how to answer.

"What kind of person do you think I am, Aurora?"

Caden had pushed me into a corner from which I could no longer talk my way out. What a bummer, but that's exactly what I had planned if the roles were reversed!

"You're a gentleman."

"And you know very well that's not an answer to my question."

"Actually, that's an answer, it's just not one you wanted."

I took another omelet bite, this time not to stall, but because I couldn't get enough of the deliciousness.

"Okay, fine by me. I'm a gentleman. And what else am I?"

"Successful, I suppose." I pointed to his expensive-looking, tailored suit.

"Right. And what else?"

Caden was going for something specific, but I didn't allow him to go any further in that direction. I was pretty sure I had blown my chance with the mysterious door. Caden was certainly not a man who believed in second chances.

"You can be pretty persuasive." This time I clarified my statement by eating the rest of the omelet.

"Do you want to know what kind of girl you are, too?"

"No."

"You're cheeky, but not at all naive. Behind your emerald eyes is a clever little mind, and somewhere deep inside you know exactly what effect you have on men like me."

Why had I guessed that Caden would just ignore my request not to say anything about me?

"I guess this is the first time I've met a man like you," I admitted honestly. Because I really didn't know what Caden was talking about all the time.

Caden gave me a frown.

"Really?"

"Why would I lie?"

His irises turned darker. "I'd better go now."

"You haven't had breakfast yet," I replied. I didn't care about his breakfast at all, but I wanted to continue to be near Caden, especially now that our conversation was heading in a direction that seemed excitingly unfamiliar.

"Never mind."

"No, not indifferent!"

Before he could march past me, I got in his way.

"Get out of my way."

"Do I seem like a girl who's avoiding you just because you want her to?"

"No. And that's what makes it so dangerous."

"What's dangerous?"

"Me, damn it. I'm dangerous. I'm full of darkness that could swallow you whole if I wanted to."

"What if I want it too?"

Caden looked at me urgently. "You should never say something like that lightly."

"I didn't decide this lightly."

Basically, I had been thinking about it all night. Actually, my whole life, except that I didn't know what I was missing until just now – I had only known that something was missing. I was more than ready to let Caden's darkness swallow me, he just had to push me into his abyss.

Caden's hand brushed my cheek and pushed a stray strand back behind my ear.

"I would be your downfall."

"Maybe not."

"Besides, I don't have time right now."

"There's always a moment to be found."

"It would never work with us."

"Possibly so."

His lips came closer and closer, I could already feel the heat of his skin. His masculine-harsh taste was already on my tongue when Caden forced himself to retreat.

"You should be gone by noon, there are some reporters coming from the Times."

"Okay," I replied quietly. I was not a person who gave up easily, but I knew I had lost this battle. No matter how good my arguments were, as long as Caden kept his mouth shut, I didn't stand a chance.

Before I knew it, Caden was gone. He just left me alone in this huge, stifling apartment.

"What a big ass!" I snorted loudly to vent my anger.

Be gone by noon – what glorious last words. Shaking my head, I gathered my seven things and was about to storm out of the loft myself because I was so angry, but then I paused. I had quite a bit of time to kill before lunch with Max. Besides, Caden still owed me a bubble bath.

If I remembered correctly, there was a Jacuzzi on the roof terrace one floor up, with a perfect view of Central Park.

I went into the bathroom, grabbed a handful of bath balls, and stomped upstairs. With each step I took, some of my anger dissipated.

Was it really possible that Mr. Universe was also my Mr. Right and I had simply let him go? No! He had let me go, that's how it had been, and that's why I told myself that he didn't deserve me at all. Period.

I threw the bath bombs into the Jacuzzi, turned the jets on the strongest setting and tried to enjoy the luxury for a while.

At first it took a while for my heartbeat to calm down, but at some point the massage jets had such a soothing effect that my eyes fell shut.

I wonder if such jets were also available to *go*? On long-haul flights or boring birthdays of distant relatives, these parts would be worth their weight in gold!

The ringing of my phone jolted me out of sleep. It took me a moment to get used to the bright sunlight, then I took Maxine's call.

"Hey Max."

"Aurora? Where are you, I'm getting worried!"

"Wait, what?"

Only now did I notice how the position of the sun had changed and jumped out of the Jacuzzi. Geez, there was a curse on this house that drove people out of their tubs as soon as they allowed themselves to relax!

"Max? What time is it?"

"A little after twelve. We had an appointment half an hour ago."

"Oh. My. God."

That was all I could say. Not because I had stood Maxine up, but because I had perhaps exaggerated a bit with the bath bombs.

"It's okay, Aurora. I just want to know if you're okay."

"I'm screwed. I am so definitely screwed, Max!"

"Yes, it was a missed dinner at *Tasacorte*, all right, but that's just a small end of the world."

"This is the absolute total apocalypse!"

Gasping breath set in when I realized the extent of the disaster I had conjured up. The entire roof terrace, on which a football game could have taken place, was full of foam. In places, the white stuff was even overflowing the railing.

"Aurora, calm down, it's just dinner!" my best friend tried to reassure me.

"That's not the problem!"

"On a scale of one to Maggy Winter's wedding, how bad is the problem?"

"I would say the winter family celebration from three years ago."

"Oh, God." Now even my best friend understood the extent of the disaster.

"Hold on."

I paused the call to send Max a photo of the mess.

Carefully, I climbed out of the tub and descended the completely foamed steps. The foam had pushed through to the kitchen and fought its way forward piece by piece.

Heavens, I had forgotten to turn off the Jacuzzi's massage jets, which were continuously producing more foam.

"Oh, wow," Maxine said, impressed.

"Yep. What am I going to do?"

"The matter is out of your hands. Just hope his cleaning company will clean up the mess."

"He has a press appointment at the apartment now. I can't leave Caden's place like this."

First of all, I went to the bathroom and put on my summer dress. Caden had to show up any moment and I didn't want to embarrass him any more than necessary.

"Caden? No formal Mr. Saint?"

"Caden Saint? That name means something to me," I answered thoughtfully.

"Oh, from where? He's only the most successful tech entrepreneur of the last twenty years and about the hottest billionaire ever! All of New York is billboarded with his smile and the stuff he produces."

"You know I'm from Seattle!" I defended myself.

"Yeah, okay. With villages, it takes longer for the stagecoach to arrive, I get it."

"Max!" I couldn't help but take her teasing seriously. "Jimi Hendrix was born there, Nirvana was founded there, and the largest online mail order company in the Western world has its headquarters there. Just like nearly eight hundred thousand other people, by the way!"

"All right, all right *Miss Seattle-is-great*. You better figure out how to get your foam massacre under control."

"Foam massacre pretty much sums it up." I put my head back. "Caden is going to kill me if his article paints a false picture of him."

"But look on the bright side, you're definitely leaving a lasting impression on him!"

"Thanks," I replied cynically. "Anyway, I'm going to try to do some damage control now, and then I'll get back to you, okay?"

"You got it. But remember your new code word: Candy."

"Candy?" I repeated questioningly.

"Yes, Candy. Because you're so cute when you're about to have nervous breakdowns."

"No, why a code word!"

"So I know you're okay when Caden Saint has you cleaning up the foam mess forever."

"Wow, thanks for your encouragement."

"I'm your best friend, but that also means that sometimes I have to confront you with harsh reality."

"Well, I'm going to hang up now and confront the harsh reality."

"Okidoki, I love you!"

"Me too."

Heart racing, I grabbed the biggest pot I could find and tried to scoop the foam outside, but my progress was slow.

Sports had never been my thing, and today was the first day I regretted not wearing a shirt with a *sports-is-my-life patch*.

The foam wasn't even halfway out again when I fell to my knees, gasping.

What a bummer! My body needed a break or Caden would have to explain to his press people right away why there was an unconscious woman lying in the middle of the bath foam. Desperately, I buried my face behind my hands.

Perhaps Caden and the journalists from the Times were stuck in traffic? After all, they were supposed to arrive half an hour ago.

Oh, who was I kidding? Even if I had a whole hour left, I couldn't sweep the evidence of my massacre under the rug.

"Oh God, only a miracle will help me now."

Admittedly, I rarely sent out push prayers, but maybe God liked my frugal ways and was helping me out now?

I listened in the silence and waited for a magical miracle. A click echoed through the room and my heart almost stopped. Unfortunately, it wasn't a miracle, but the electronic lock that had opened. Footsteps followed by Caden's raspy voice echoed through the room.

Crap, crap, crap!

If God really existed, he had a rather absurd sense of humor.

Chapter 4 – Caden

Not a second after the elevator doors of the top floor opened and I walked toward my office, I was surrounded by no less than three employees. They pounced on me like hungry hyenas, looking as if they were waiting for a juicy piece of meat.

Actually nothing new, but today I had no head for it. My thoughts were only about Aurora, who had left more of an impression than I would have liked.

When the babble of voices wouldn't end, I stopped and raised my hand, silencing everyone.

"One at a time," I grumbled annoyed, while I took the coffee from my personal assistant's hand. I don't know if it was even meant for me, but I needed it more. "Coleman first."

He was my chief engineer and oversaw our multi-billion investment, with which we soon made history.

"There are a few technical challenges that still need to be worked out." To avoid looking me in the eye, he adjusted his perfectly fitting glasses.

"Meaning specifically?"

"That we might have to push back our release schedule," he replied meekly.

"No, we don't." That was the end of the conversation for me. "Alastair, what's up?"

"But Mr. Saint!" I raised my hand, thus interrupting him, while looking expectantly at my accountant.

"I just need a few signatures from you."

"Otherwise, everything's going well?" I asked.

"Everything is fine."

"Good, you see that, Coleman? That's news I want to hear."

The relief that Alastair didn't have any more bad news for me was written all over his face. Nodding, I took off his file.

"Janice?"

"There are a couple of press appointments we should still talk about."

"Why?"

"The best place to talk about this is in your office, sir."

All right, the way she called me *sir*, it wasn't about press appointments, it was about sex.

"No need."

Janice was quite attractive, no question, she had been submissive and a good sub for a short time, but that between us was over since the last contract had expired. It just hadn't clicked. Maybe because she was too submissive or maybe because I was bored.

Shrugging my shoulders, I continued walking to my office.

"But Mr. Saint, I can't guarantee I'll find a solution to the technical setbacks!"

"You studied engineering, so you and your team should also find a solution. Alastair should provide you with all the resources you need. All the press appointments are in place, we've invested millions in the campaigns to show the world we're the most revolutionary company in the world."

"Okay." My engineer gave up, albeit with a dissatisfied expression.

"If anyone can get it done, you can," I said, patting him on the back and then leaving the saturated hyenas behind.

I wasn't lying, my team included the best engineers in the world, but they only developed their full potential when they were under pressure to perform, just like me.

Stupidly, the pressure to perform has just been supplanted by another pressure that is much harder to control.

Aurora, Aurora, Aurora. Why can't I get you out of my head?

No woman – or any other human being – had spoken to me like she did for a long time. Refreshing, but that was exactly what had driven the urge to put her over my knee for it almost to infinity. But without her signature on my contract, Aurora was untouchable for me.

As I entered my office, I looked in surprise at the upturned office chair directly behind the panoramic glass from which one could see all the way to Jersey, weather permitting.

"There you are at last," Jackson murmured, sitting in my chair and spinning around diabolically like a James Bond villain. I didn't even ask how my best friend had managed to sneak past security and staff again, or who he had bribed. Jackson could get in anywhere with his thick skull, even through miles of concrete.

"It's my company, I decide when I'm on time and when I'm not."

"Come on, Caden. When was the last time you were in the office after nine?"

Without looking at the clock, I knew Jackson wasn't supposed to be here right now either.

"Wouldn't you have to rescue little kittens from tall trees or throw yourself death-defyingly into flames now?"

"I have a few days off. And what's your excuse?"

"I didn't sleep well," I grumbled.

"Does this have something to do with the unknown blonde beauty?"

"How do you know about Aurora?" I asked seriously.

"Who doesn't know about it?"

I leaned against the table and crossed my arms.

"Jacks, cut the crap. I don't need that kind of press at all right now, okay?"

"All right, all right." He raised his arms placatingly, took momentum, and spun boredly in the office chair a few times. "Sebastian told me about her."

"Sebastian?"

"The guy in the lobby. In the building where your giant penthouse is, you know."

"I know who you're talking about. I'm just surprised you're talking to him about this."

Of course, Sebastian was always polite, but he didn't strike me as a guy who liked to make small talk.

"We're not just talking about you."

"Oh yeah, so what else do you guys talk about?" I asked curiously.

"We talk about Eagles games, senators' missteps, subsequent firehouse budget cuts and your loves. He really has a sense of humor."

"Are we talking about the same Sebastian? Or am I just meeting his evil twin?"

Jackson grinned at me. "So, what's going on with Aurora now? I thought you didn't want a woman at the moment."

"It's a long story with Aurora."

"It's okay, because I have a lot of time."

"Does this have anything to do with the budget cuts at the fire station, perhaps?"

Jackson looked at me in irritation, knowing I was an attentive listener.

"It may be, but it doesn't matter."

"Jacks, I'm drowning in work. You know how much I hate press appointments. Not to mention almost every single department has some kind of problem I don't even want to know about."

This wasn't my first *we-have-new-innovations rodeo*, but I felt like I kind of missed all the missing hustle and bustle ten years ago when Saint Industries was a one-man company.

"All the more reason to get out with me and clear your head."

Jackson's offer was tempting, and I was almost willing to fold.

"The Times is in my loft today. I can't show up there sweaty."

"Don't be." Jackson pulled a key card out of his pocket and waved it in my face.

I squinted my eyes. "Did you really ...?"

"Hell, yeah. Wasn't cheap to bribe the security guard, but we won't get in trouble with the cops this time. Besides, there's an employee washroom we can use with this."

"I hate you, Jacks."

"Are you going to accept my offer now? Or are you thinking about it?"

It was a deal I couldn't refuse, but immediately I had to think about Aurora again, who was just one deal away from my playroom.

Not now, damn it!

I was up to my neck in work, not to mention my last sub was still clinging so badly that I didn't want to risk another issue.

"All right, I'll go with you. But only if you admit that your day off is not entirely voluntary."

"Fine, fine by me. I may have had a small but heated discussion with the captain."

Grinning, I put my hands in my pockets and leaned against the wall.

Jacks had his heart in the right place, but sometimes, when his fuses blew, he was quite the hothead.

Jackson walked past me to one of the closets and took out two large gym bags.

"We're not going to talk about the details of this conversation," he admonished me.

"You got it. You and I won't say another word about Aurora, either."

Jackson swallowed what he was about to say and nodded, then we headed for the docks.

Breathing heavily, I rushed through and over the large overseas containers stacked quite high along the docks. Outside the playroom, there was only one other way for me to clear my head - free running. The riskier, the better. I was an adrenaline junkie with a need for control, and I made no secret of it. Jackson shared my passion, so we often pursued our daredevil adventures together.

We were cut from the same cloth, seasoned, totally screwed-up guys who boxed our way through life.

"Caden! Take it down a notch!" Jackson ordered me.

"What, I can't understand anything because I've lost you!" I teased him, running a few more yards and coming to a stop just before a gap.

Gasping, Jackson stopped in front of me and propped his hands on his knees.

"You're an idiot."

"And you're not on point."

It usually took more than that to bring my best friend to his knees.

"You certainly don't charge ahead wrecklessly!"

Touché. Of course he was right, but I had made it clear that Aurora was a taboo subject.

"What's going on at Seventeenth?" I asked in a conciliatory tone. Actually, we spared ourselves talking about details from work, but it seemed more than appropriate today.

"Our old captain left us with a bunch of problems and more shit. That's what's going on."

Frustrated, Jackson kicked one of the containers next to us, which vibrated tinny.

"Shouldn't the new captain bring order to the chaos?"

"No, he's too busy kissing the board's ass. We can't even get enough funding to maintain our most important stuff, when we desperately need a new truck with a aerial ladder. It's just a matter of time before that thing breaks down."

"Want me to ask around?"

"No way, Caden."

I patted him on the shoulder placatingly.

"Was just an offer."

"I know, thank you. But that would only lead to more chaos."

"The chaos thing must be the weather. As if I didn't have enough problems with Saint Industries, all of a sudden Aurora had to show up in my loft."

Jackson frowned at me for even bringing up a subject that I had actually forbidden. But there was no other way, I had to talk to someone about Aurora, in the hope that I would then get her out of my head.

"I thought we weren't going to talk about Aurora?"

"Well, we don't usually talk about work either, and we haven't done anything else today."

"Right again. So how did she talk you into giving her a key card?"

"So you can get one the same way?" I asked with a grin. My loft was the only place Jackson's burglary talent had failed so far.

"Probably your conquests and I have entirely different strategies and intentions," he replied with a grin.

"We didn't sleep together." There was regret in my voice, even though it was I myself who had rejected Aurora.

"No?"

"No. I'll only tell you more if you hang with me in the next stage."

I looked at him challengingly, and Jackson ran off without warning, which I didn't blame him for. At least now one of us was getting other ideas.

My best friend and I were in a neck-and-neck race. Although the containers were stacked only maybe twenty feet high – Jacks and I also had duels on rooftops in the Bronx – it was difficult to maintain speed because the containers were swaying slightly. Only about an inch, but it was enough to throw my sense off balance.

"Man, you really want to know what happened last night, don't you?" I shouted to Jackson, who was right on my heels.

"Yeah, damn! Maybe my hundred bucks will be safe with Sebastian after all!"

"What hundred dollars?"

Although I was rarely irritated by anything, Jackson's bet had set me back a bit, so we were now running level.

"A little bet, nothing more," Jackson replied, gasping.

"Next time, you let me pay into the pot with you, all right?"

"Can't, you're part of the bet."

"So?"

"You might have personal interests in the outcome."

"As if I needed the trouble," I replied glumly.

"They don't, but you're the kind of winning guy who always wants to be the best."

"It's possible."

We interrupted our conversation for a series of containers, between which there were many gaps and crevices that needed our full attention. That's exactly why I loved this sport. Nowhere did I feel more clearly in control of my body than here. One wrong step and I could break my neck or worse. Although my heart was racing, my thoughts always came to rest. In free running, it was just me and my goal. And sometimes Jackson, with whom I could compete on friendly terms.

This time we reached our intended destination at the same time, and because I was a man of honor in such matters, I decided to give Jackson a few details about my last evening.

"Aurora didn't get the key card from me, it was from the previous owner."

"There was no lock changed?"

I shook my head. "No, why would I? We just changed the code for the entrance and the alarm system."

"Hmm, maybe you should have the lock changed because of precedents like that."

I grumbled softly, not knowing what to answer.

"If it wasn't for that stupid coincidence, I probably wouldn't have found Aurora in my bathroom."

Jackson let out a whistle. "In the bathroom? And then what happened?"

"She called me a burglar and got out of the tub."

I began to grin, and Jackson burst out laughing.

"Wow, she really had *cojones* talking to you like that while standing naked in front of you."

"Hell, yeah. I haven't seen fire in the eyes like that in a long time."

Maybe Aurora had no idea how the dominance-and-submission thing worked within my four walls, but I was sure it would have been pretty exciting with her. I wonder if she would have gone for it. Well, I would probably never find out, because I had more or less kicked her out of my loft this morning.

"And when are you going to see her again?" Jackson asked me the question, which was almost painful.

"Not at all."

"Not at all? Are you out of your mind, Caden?"

"I don't have time for a woman, damn it."

"There is always time for beautiful women. And the way you talk about her, I've never heard you talk about women before. She seems to be something special."

Yes, damn it, she was, and I wondered if I could figure out what made her so special. Was it her lovely, sweet scent? Her sparkling eyes? Or was it her bewitching smile?

"She definitely made an impression. I can say that much. Still, right now is not a good time, now that all eyes are on me."

"That's exactly why the timing is perfect! Imagine your project goes wrong," Jackson began.

"Thanks for your confidence, best friend," I growled, but Jacks just ignored me.

"Imagine missing some silly deadline, but all the world talks about are the bikini atoll vacation photos of you and your lovely fiancée."

"Why does it have to be a fiancée?" I eyed him critically.

"Because a wild marriage is not for a serious businessman like you."

"Says Jackson Washington, fire department lieutenant, image consultant and wedding planner."

He punched me hard in the chest, but his punch barely shook me. "I'm serious about this, Caden. There's no better press than an engagement party. Yes, there is, exactly one, and that's the wedding articles."

Even though I was happy for Jackson's newfound optimism, I had to put the brakes on him.

"And you know what's really bad for PR? A divorce. No, wait. A really messy divorce with a war of the roses and all the trimmings."

"You can contract out, like you always do," Jackson suggested, shrugging his shoulders. "Anyway, you should think it through. The right articles in the right papers and you'll still have stock prices going through the roof even with minor disasters."

"So you're a shark on Wall Street, too?" I teased Jacks.

"Go ahead and joke if your pride can't take it any other way that I was right."

He had hit the bull's eye, because I knew for a fact that Jackson was right. Things were going well with Saint Industries, but the more good press, the better.

And whether I wanted to admit it or not, it would please me only too much to show the whole world that Aurora was my girl ,... but for that she had to become my girl first. Sighing, I exhorted my thoughts to return to reality, for I had made it clear to Aurora more than once that she should stay away from me – because I could not.

The realization that Aurora would not be in my apartment later when I returned was like a punch to the pit of my stomach. I knew only one way I could stop the pain and the tormenting thoughts. Run. Running. Climbing. As high as I could, as fast as I could. I looked at the clock.

"We can do one more lap before I have to go back."

Then I ran, hoping I could outrun my thoughts and knowing I wouldn't make it.

Chapter 5 – Aurora

I had screwed up. Really bad shit, which on a scale of one to ten was somewhere between apocalypse and the end of the world. Suddenly I longed for the chaos that reigned in Seattle and from which I had fled, which was nothing compared to this problem here.

Footsteps echoed through the halls, and I heard Caden talking to a woman. By now I had given up trying to shovel the foam outside, it was an impossible task.

When Caden stood in front of me and looked at me in irritation, I smiled awkwardly at him.

Wow, he looked pretty darn seductive when he looked so business-like serious. Next to him was a reporter whose face I knew from the evening news, and behind them was a photographer who could barely contain his grin.

"Hey Caden. What are you doing here?" I asked with a trembling voice.

Did I really just ask what Caden was doing here? Oh man, I was really screwed. My brain had switched into the kind of survival mode that could only lead to natural selection.

"I happen to live here," Caden replied calmly, eliciting a giggle from the reporter next to him. "I guess the more important question is, what *are you* doing here?"

"We're talking about this foam massacre, right?" I tried to delay the inevitable.

Breathe, Aurora, breathe.

"You have no idea how burning my interest is in what has happened here in the last two hours." There was an amused smile on his lips.

The reporter, whose name I couldn't think of, cleared her throat. "So, to me, it's pretty clear cut."

"Yes?" asked Caden and I, as if from the same mouth.

"But of course, there's a foam party!" She sighed loudly audibly and then dropped her stern posture. "I must confess, I'm relieved. Don't get me wrong, Mr. Saint, but I was rather expecting a dry, mind-numbing interview."

I stretched out my arms and tried to smile confidently, as if I had intended this chaos.

"Surprise!"

"Surprising indeed," Caden murmured. His eyes got all dark and I wondered what he was really thinking right now.

"Wait until you see the foam on the roof deck," I muttered sheepishly.

"Wouldn't you like to introduce us to each other, Mr. Saint?" the reporter asked curiously.

"But of course." Caden winked at me. "Aurora, this is Jelinda Cherry, a reporter for The Times." Smiling, I shook her hand as Caden continued to introduce us. "Jelinda, this is Aurora, my fiancée."

"Pleased to meet you, Jelinda," I said with a smile. When Caden's remaining words reached me, I was speechless. *Had I just misheard him?*

"You two are engaged?" Jelinda looked at us in turn. "What a surprise!"

"You can say that again," I replied. Although I couldn't see my face, I felt myself getting paler and paler.

Caden pulled me tightly against him, apparently he had a good eye for women whose knees became soft as jelly.

"Just play along!" he whispered so softly that no one else could hear.

Unbelievably, Caden just expected me to play along with his charade. But the worst part was that I wanted to play along. Against all better knowledge, I liked that the most beautiful man in the world wanted me. But whether I wanted him or not, he couldn't just expect me to claim to be his fiancée at a press conference! What was Mr. Universe thinking? Probably that the world was at his feet – and not only the world …

"Caden, can we talk for a minute?"

"But of course, darling. Have you gotten the alcohol for the cocktails yet?"

I shook my head.

"There are cocktails? This interview just keeps getting better!" cheered Jelinda two octaves higher than her actual speaking voice.

"What's a pool party without cocktails?" asked Caden charmingly. He had been able to adjust to my foam massacre much more quickly than I had. Still, he couldn't shock me with a lightning engagement after sending me to the desert – twice!

"I could really use a strong mojito right now," I heard myself say.

"Please excuse us for a moment, go ahead and make yourselves comfortable on the roof deck," Caden said, then pushed me up to the walk-in pantry behind the kitchen, where not only food was stored in refrigerators, but also wine and other alcohols, I noticed.

When Caden closed the door behind me, I blew the last fuse.

"Caden Saint, how dare you introduce me as your fiancée? Are you out of your mind? They're professionals, they'll figure out that's a lie within the next five minutes!"

What was wrong with me? Actually, I should complain that he had patronized me and that he had decided over my head to put on such a farce. Instead, I was worried that his lie would be exposed sooner than either of us would have liked.

"I improvised," Caden replied calmly.

"So you weren't serious?"

"I didn't say that."

"You should know a few things about me before you present me to the world as your fiancée," I said in a trembling voice. There were things I was not proud of.

"Are you a terrorist?"

"Heavens, no!"

"Did you torture cute little puppies?"

"No! Caden!"

"Are you vegan?"

"No!" With each question I became angrier because he wouldn't let me get a word in edgewise.

"All's well, then."

"Good? God, Caden, I want to strangle you for getting us into this situation!"

Although I provoked Caden to scream, he remained calm. How could he remain so calm while I was almost hitting the ceiling? It was not at all my way to freak out like that, but the circumstances were anything but normal.

Instead of saying anything, Caden grabbed me by the shoulders, pushed me backward until my back was against the door, and rubbed his well-groomed beard against my cheek.

"You could have been gone by now, Aurora, but you're still here."

"Because I was trying to save your press date."

"No, you're still here because you couldn't get me out of your head."

My whole body shook, and a soft, approving sigh escaped me. Caden was right, he had nested in my mind, he and this spicy, exciting secret that was behind his closed door.

"And so what, Caden. You should have asked me to be your fiancée."

"Will you be my fiancée?"

Yes, what woman could say *no* to those dark brown eyes, his raspy voice and the muscles of steel? Caden had turned my head, he had long since pulled me to his side, even if I could not yet fully admit it to myself.

"That's not right," I replied, sighing. "A promise like that should be something valuable."

"I can lay the world at your feet, Aurora."

Knowing his lips were so close to mine and still not kissing him was the hardest thing I ever had to do.

"I know, but I don't even want the world to kneel before me."

I wasn't looking for someone who could buy me the world, but someone with whom I had my own place in the world. Of course, I wished that Caden could be that person, but I wasn't sure. He had pushed me away, twice – just because he was the one for me didn't automatically mean I was the one for him.

"Would you rather kneel yourself?" asked Caden, his eyes twinkling.

"What?"

"Anyway. Tell me, Aurora, how can I convince you to play along?"

"I'm happy as a clam," I replied as my hips stretched toward him. I sensed that Caden was making every effort to restrain himself.

"No one is happy without a wish, Aurora. I will now make you an offer you should not refuse. You will become my fiancée, I will dance with you at the most beautiful balls in the world, I will fulfill your every wish, and I swear on my honor as a gentleman, I will not touch you."

"Caden, I don't know ..."

He gave me that *I-always-get-what-I-want* look again, and what could I say? It worked. Yes, I may come out of this with a broken heart, but I would hate myself forever if I didn't take him up on the offer.

"Okay, I'll do it on two conditions."

"You're making demands?" Caden looked at me in surprise. "Interesting, let's hear it."

If I was going to seal my doom, I could at least make it as pleasant as possible. Not to mention, Caden was my best chance at a truce with my mom because I would finally no longer be the eyesore of Maggy's wedding.

"First, you will accompany me to Seattle in a few weeks for my sister's wedding. There, we'll dance together and every now and then I'll tell you bad jokes that you'll laugh at – audibly, but not too loudly. We'll have fun there, but we won't have too much fun there, because that's reserved for my sister, all right?"

Caden grinned at me.

"And your second demand?"

"I'm earning your gold Mastercard by working for you. In your business. Hire me as your assistant."

"You want to be my personal assistant?"

"Yes. And for that, I'll play your fiancée for as long as you want."

Caden gave me a serious, thoughtful look.

"You're a really tough negotiator."

"I know," I answered proudly, because my knees were still shaking, and I felt anything but confident. Just now I was negotiating with Mr. Universe about my future. Exciting, yes, but also a little scary.

"Then I have just one last question before I have the contract drawn up."

"And that would be?"

"Can you mix cocktails?"

I nodded. "It's been a while since I've worked at a bar, but I think so."

"Perfect. I guess the outcome of our interview depends on your skills then."

"Just no pressure to perform, Caden."

To help pay for my bachelor's degree, I had been mixing cocktails at a less-than-glorious club and doing other things that I wasn't exactly proud of today. I felt terrible because Caden didn't know about it yet, and I felt I owed it to him to tell the truth, even if it might cost me our deal.

"What are you waiting for?" he asked.

"There's something you should know before you present me to the world." I took a deep breath and hoped my castle in the air I had just built didn't collapse. "I mixed cocktails at a strip club."

Caden grinned broadly at me.

I slammed my clenched fist against his chest. "This isn't funny!"

"Yes, it is."

"Why?"

"Because you're more worried about what other people think than you should be."

"So that's okay? Not only did I work the bar there, but I also danced a time or two." I bit my lips and looked down at the floor in shame.

Caden lifted my chin. "Look at me, Aurora."

I could not help but obey. The authority in his voice made me long for more orders.

"I assume, as your future husband, I get a private screening?"

His reaction surprised me, because I had actually expected an immediate kick out, not a request for a dance.

"Is that a requirement of our contract?" I asked, trying to look as businesslike as possible.

"Possibly."

"And what about the room behind the black door?"

Caden's eyes darkened.

"The same rules still apply to that."

"What happens when I walk through that door?"

"Then there are no more rules for you."

It should have frightened me, but my abdomen tingled treacherously, and I could barely contain my curiosity.

"Just for you?"

"Which rules apply to you then, you'll have to find out first, willy-nilly," Caden murmured so seductively that I had to stop myself. I almost kicked in the closed door, only to find out what temptations were waiting there.

"Maybe I will."

"Maybe." Caden brushed one of my strands back behind my ear. "I've warned you often enough about the consequences, Aurora. I keep my promises, but I don't do things by halves either."

"Me neither," I replied.

Wow. What an announcement. I knew there was something dark behind his perfect, beautiful facade. An abyss from which there was no escape, but I was willing to take the risk. Either I fell and fell and fell, or Caden's darkest shadows gave me wings.

"Even though we don't have a real relationship, I expect you not to let anyone touch you. You belong to me alone and no one else."

Normally I would have protested because I didn't think I belonged to anyone, but when Caden said it, I wanted to. I wanted to belong to him, all of me...and my heart.

"Roger that."

"Say it, Aurora. I want to hear it from your mouth."

"I'm all yours."

"Good girl."

He leaned forward toward me, and my heart stopped for a moment when I thought he was going to kiss me, but at the last moment Caden changed his mind and pushed away from me.

I saw in his eyes how he struggled for control, just as I fought my desire to touch him.

"We should go to our guests now," I whispered.

Caden nodded and got dangerously close to me as he opened the door behind me.

"And we should pretend this conversation never happened, *darling*."

"Okay."

Easier said than done, as Caden's dark, murmuring side haunted me to my darkest thoughts.

Heavens, I'm Mrs. Universe now and, in a few days, the whole world will know about it!

Chapter 6 – Aurora

As the doors of the private elevator opened, Sebastian came running toward me with a serious face. "Good morning, Miss Winter. Would you perhaps like to use the back exit?"

"No, why?" I asked irritated, but continued heading for the main exit.

"If you change your mind, I'll be happy to show you the way."

Sebastian didn't say it, but his expression screamed: *You will ask me for directions*. That was a silent promise that somehow frightened me.

As I opened the door, millions of lights flashed on, temporarily blinding me, while incomprehensible murmurs of voices filtered through to me.

What's going on here?

I slammed the door as fast as I could.

"Paparazzi have some things in common with sharks, Miss Winter."

Sebastian tried to hide it, but the *I-told-you-so* was seeping out of his every pore.

"Maybe I do want to go to the back exit," I said after I had collected myself a bit.

"This way, please," Sebastian answered and led me through a long corridor that lay behind the elevators. Actually, I just wanted to see my best friend, but that seemed an almost impossible task. What if I disappeared out the back exit?

The *Hazlenut Temptation* was on the other end of Manhattan, I needed a cab, but to do that I had to get back on the main street where dozens of paparazzi lurked.

Sighing, I pulled my smartphone out of my pocket and dialed my best friend's number. She picked up after the first beep.

"What's up?"

"We need a plan B, Max."

"A plan B for what?"

"For the huge horde of sensation-hungry press outside my door."

"Press people? I thought the article doesn't come out until tomorrow, or did you contact them even before you wrote me on WhatsApp?"

"Yep. Someone spilled the beans on the engagement, I guess."

Maxine squealed joyfully. "I still can't believe you're going to be married to Caden Saint soon!"

"Back to the topic at hand, Max. Are you coming to get me?"

"Sure, I'm on my way."

"I'll wait for you at the back exit."

Sebastian cleared his throat.

"With your key card, you can also use the private underground parking."

"There's underground parking?"

"Yes. The lowest deck is reserved for Mr. Saint only."

I was speechless. Caden had his own deck for the underground garage? Yes, I knew he owned billions, but I had a hard time comprehending that number and the luxury that came with it. Not to mention, what did one need more than one car for?

"Didn't Mr. Saint offer you a car?"

"Yes, he did, even including the driver," I replied. "But I don't need a chauffeur."

Interestingly, Sebastian looked at me with the same look that Caden had when I had told him the same thing.

Yes, I loved big bathtubs and good food, but just because I was now engaged to a billionaire didn't mean I needed my own chauffeurs, spooned caviar nonstop, or to run around in thousand-dollar flip flops. I was still me – and I was a free, independent woman who didn't need a chauffeur. Period.

Fortunately, the back exit and the street leading to it were deserted, so I was able to wait for Maxine in peace until her little limousine was honking at the end of the street, waiting for me. Max got out, and when she saw me, she waved at me bouncing.

"Let me know when to see you back here," Sebastian said formally.

"I hope by the time I get back, the press mob has backed off."

Although no one was in the alley and even the sidewalks of the cross street looked empty, I stalked on quiet soles to Maxine's black sedan. I felt a little like I did when I used to sneak out of Mr. Fisher's gym class to dust off both on *burger-and-lasagna day*.

Giggling, Max and I fell into each other's arms.

"Awesome, it's been way too long since we last saw each other, Max!"

"You can say that again. Speaking of which, you still owe me a whole lot of detailed narration from the last two days!"

I put on a serious face and poked Max against the ribs with my index finger.

"I think you owe me more of an apology for not telling me about selling your apartment!"

"You know I buy, remodel and resell new apartments every few weeks. Between Caden Saint's penthouse and my current apartment, there's an old apartment in Brooklyn, a mansion in the Hamptons and two apartments in Rockefeller Center."

"Maxine Lancester," I said seriously. "You might as well have sold the loft to a career criminal or serial killer!"

"I'm not selling my apartment to serial killers!"

Max covered her mouth for a soundless scream, playfully shocked.

"That was no excuse," I grumbled.

"You really want an excuse to live the dream of all single women? My goodness, Aurora! You're engaged to Caden Saint, all thanks to me!"

"Max, you're impossible."

"I know."

I tried to keep my serious face on, but Maxine's big grin was just too infectious.

We hugged a second time, and as we pulled away from each other, my best friend yanked open the back door of the car.

"Reporter at three o'clock."

Sighing, I threw myself into the limo and made room for Max, who sat down next to me.

"Is it always like this now?" I asked.

"I don't know," Max replied, shrugging her shoulders. "I guess a little press is part of it."

"You call that *a little press*?"

The reporters had surrounded our car and were desperately trying to snap a photo through the opaque windows so they could sell the image.

From my small handbag I pulled out a small box.

"A little souvenir from my last trip to Canada with my family," I said, handing it to Maxine with a smile.

"Oh, how sweet of you!"

Curious, Max opened the small box and pulled out a snow globe with shining eyes. The snow inside was raging around the moose and the miniature trees inside.

"She's perfect!"

Satisfied, I dropped my shoulders. "You have no idea how long I searched for the perfect snow globe for you."

Max not only had a walk-in shoe closet, but also a room that held all her snow globes that she had collected over the years.

"Where do you want to go, ladies?"

"Into *Hazlenut Temptation*, please," I gushed. I had been longing for the hazelnut cake with chocolate filling for months, and I would kill for it!

"Um, do you want to go to *Biscuit Paradise* instead? They have new cupcakes there. You have to try them!"

"What?" I asked, horrified. It felt like my best friend was stealing my long-awaited piece of cake from under my nose.

"Well, there will probably be quite a few paparazzi lurking there."

"But don't they all lay siege to the penthouse?"

"Oh, Aurora, you're really cute sometimes."

"And how would they even know we were going to eat there?"

"Maybe because you told Facebook, and therefore the whole world?"

Max waved her smartphone in front of me, and I grabbed my forehead.

"Oh God, I didn't think of that at all! I'm never going to eat hazelnut cake with chocolate filling again, am I?"

Max shrugged her shoulders. "Wait and see, in a few months, two years at the latest, the press frenzy will have died down."

"You're supposed to build me up, not frustrate me more. That's your job as a best friend!" I snorted.

"And sometimes my job as a best friend is also to confront you with reality."

"Do you really think they're going to chase me for that long?"

She started to laugh, but I felt anything but like laughing.

"Sometimes it's my job to put you through the ringer too, Aurora."

"Through a hazelnut caramel cocoa?"

Grinning, Maxine leaned forward toward the driver.

"Tuck, take us straight to *Hazlenut Temptation*."

"Will do, Miss Lancester."

"So there aren't paparazzi there after all?"

I didn't understand anything anymore, sometimes Maxine's humor was so subtle that there was only confusion.

"Yes, we do, but we'll figure it out. And next time you want to share something with the world, share it after you've done it, okay?"

"As long as I get my cake, I'll do anything you say," I joked. Then I got more serious again. "Tell me, Max. Do you ever drive yourself?"

"Why? After all, I have Tuck to get me safely to my destination while also telling the best jokes on the entire East Coast."

"I'm flattered," Tuck replied with a grin.

They both exchanged meaningful glances before Max turned back to me.

"Why do you ask?"

I shrugged my shoulders.

"No reason. Caden had actually insisted that I take one of his cars."

"And why didn't you want to?"

"If I'd known about the paparazzi at the door, I would have accepted his offer," I assured Max, "but just because I'm his fiancée now doesn't mean I'm going to be patronized."

"Speaking of the engagement: I want to know every single detail from the foam massacre on!"

"You know I can't tell you everything," I began and faltered.

"Fiddle-dee-dee, I can figure out for myself what the confidentiality agreement covers. So give me the details!"

"There's this tension between us that I can hardly describe."

"More details!"

"I don't know how to explain it, but the closer we get and the more we want it, the more Caden pulls away."

"So you have yet to *deepen* your relationship?"

"Max!" For this expression, I punished my best friend with stunned looks.

"Yes, the confidentiality agreement, I know."

"It's not about whether I signed something or not, that's too private!"

I used to be able to talk to Max about everything, like a sister, but it wasn't just the confidentiality agreement that bothered me, but also the indirect threats that Caden had made.

Max raised her arms placatingly. "It's okay, I'll row back a little bit. You'll have to tell me more about your proposal in return!"

"Actually, he presented me with a fait accompli by calling me his fiancée in front of a reporter. And then after that, in the pantry, talked me into actually agreeing," I spoke my less-than-romantic engagement as quickly as I could.

"And what about the ring?"

"No ring," I sighed.

"What a shame."

"It is what it is," I replied. "Surely I can't expect Caden to know how I always imagined my engagement."

"In the most fabulous, snowy winter forest you can find in Seattle, while snowflakes swirl around you and you dance to Elvis Presley's *Can't Help Falling in Love*? As your best friend, I know what makes you tick, so should your fiancé."

"You know what, Max? Even though there's no engagement ring and we didn't dance in a blizzard, it feels right."

Max smiled with satisfaction. "That's exactly what I wanted to hear. I think you two are a perfect match, you just have to find the right way."

Yes, the only question was whether I was made for this path – behind the door.

If Caden thought I wasn't ready, he never would have made me this offer. He tried to hide it, but he had watched me, stared at me, analyzed me, and seen right through me, that much was clear to me. He believed I was the one, but could I trust that feeling? What if I wasn't the right one for the Playroom, then there was no turning back.

"Hello, Earth to Aurora," Max said, snapping her fingers in front of my face.

"Sorry, my mind was racing."

"With Caden's dreamy dark eyes? At his seductive looks? Or did you start drooling over his six-pack?"

"I wasn't thinking about his six-pack!" I protested, but reflexively wiped the corners of my mouth with the back of my hand.

"Gotcha!"

"You're imagining things," I replied, shaking my head.

I looked out the window, and my pulse quickened when I saw that the *Hazlenut Temptation* was almost ahead of us.

Tuck parked the car across the street, and Max slipped him a one-hundred-dollar bill.

"Two pieces of hazelnut cake, a box of Sprinkle cupcakes, and two cocoas with extra vanilla syrup and whipped cream."

"My cocoa with chocolate drops, too," I added.

"Will do, ladies."

"And you should try the glazed donuts with brittle, my brother is all about the new flavor."

Grinning, Tuck got out of the car and fought his way through the crowd of reporters standing outside the entrance, hunting for me.

"And suddenly I want the Seattle wedding drama back," I said, shaking my head as I stared in bewilderment at the lurking people.

"What, you'd trade Mr. Universe back for your runaway, completely insane family?"

We looked at each other seriously before we started giggling because we both knew my answer.

"We don't know each other very well yet, he's dominant and bossy, a little cryptic sometimes, but I really like Caden."

"And he likes you, too, or the most eligible bachelor on the East Coast wouldn't have asked you to marry him."

"Or I was just in the right place at the right time."

Of course, I wanted to indulge in these romantic illusions, but I forced myself to keep an eye on reality. That was the only way I could protect myself from heartbreak.

And from the frustration that Caden had kept his word and hadn't touched me once, even though my whole body craved it.

"Going back to my question earlier, would you like to deepen your relationship?"

I nodded without thinking. "Yes."

"Then tell him, he is your fiancé after all." Max winked at me.

I knew very well that just saying it was not enough. If I wanted more, I had to jump over my shadow and open the black door.

I wonder if my best friend knew more. After all, she had lived there before him.

"Say, what was in that room across from the bedroom anyway?"

"A gym, but I should put the equipment in another room and soundproof the walls."

I looked at her in surprise.

"Sound insulation?"

"Yes. Why? What's in the room now?"

If I only knew ...

Chapter 7 – Caden

"So, you're officially engaged now?" Jackson asked me with a big grin.

I ignored him, moved past him and took a running start to jump to the next steel beam.

"Fine, don't thank me for the best advice of your life," Jackson exclaimed, following me.

There was hardly a more beautiful sound than hearing the hammering of one's own heart in one's ears while the adrenaline rushed through my body. Yes, I was not normal in the head, but I had my reasons – everyone who knew them understood that.

Everyone was somehow trying to survive in this sick world, and everyone was doing what they had to do to survive.

"You'd better concentrate on our target," I ordered Jacks, pointing to the construction crane at the far end of the half-raised hall.

We were balancing on damn high steel beams, on which the roof of the large warehouse would later rest. One false step and I fell over sixty feet into the depths. This thought didn't worry me. If there was one thing I didn't want to think about, it was Aurora. As long as she didn't fall completely for me, I had no control over her, and that made me damn angry.

Had I known she really wasn't claiming my driver, I would have spanked her, contract or no contract. There were rules that were non-negotiable and using my limos was one of them.

It would be better if Aurora quickly gave in to her urge to belong to me, otherwise she would drive me even further mad. And the longer I was exposed to madness, the harder it was for me to control myself.

Great. Now I was also thinking about the other damn thing that I had not been able to control. That was the only reason I danced with death so often, confronted the limits of my body and risked life and limb for it.

"Caden, take a breath," Jackson ruled me from behind.

"I'm breathing," I growled back. Still, I paused. Jacks was right, if my head wasn't in the game, every little step was a danger.

"The new captain really followed through on the budget cuts," Jackson said glumly.

"So there's no new aerial ladder for Station Twenty-three?"

"No. There aren't even new shoes, dammit. Not long now, and our soles will be stuck to the ground when we vent the roofs."

"What a load of crap," I replied, sighing. What we were doing right now was reckless too, yes, but this and the Twenty-third were two very different things. If I myself decided to put my life on the line to give myself a sense of control, fine, but if a captain decided to put the lives of his men and women on the line to cut himself off more of the pie, that was just negligent.

"You can say it out loud. I have no idea what to do."

"I'd punch the board in the face," I replied without thinking.

Jackson grinned. "No, you wouldn't. Neither would I if I wanted to keep my job."

"I assume you want to keep it."

"Hell, yeah! Who else is going to pay me money to run into burning houses?"

Jackson tried to hide it, but actually Jacks wasn't running into burning buildings because of the fire, he was running to rescue people trapped in the flames. My best friend was one hell of a brave person, even though some might call him too hot-headed or arrogant.

"I know you don't want to talk about Aurora, but I need you to answer one question," Jackson said, giving me a questioning look.

I exhaled loudly, because Jacks would not let up until he finally had an answer, or else I plummeted into the depths.

"And that would be?"

"Is she worth it?"

"Who?"

"Aurora. I was serious about the engagement, but not the fact that you put the ring on the next best finger."

"You're the one who gave me this stupid idea!"

"I know. And probably God will never forgive me for that."

"Leave God out of it," I growled. God, if he existed at all, could stay away from me since he had left me sitting alone when I needed him most.

"I know you well enough to know that you don't actually act that lightly. So, is Aurora worth it?"

Although I hardly knew the girl with the long blonde hair and golden eyes, I felt that I could rely on my gut feeling.

"Could be," I replied with a shrug, trying to look as unconcerned as possible. Deep down, I still couldn't admit to myself that Aurora had me wrapped around her finger from the first second.

Jackson grinned at me, shaking his head. "You've never made a thoughtless decision before. It certainly has my blessing."

I looked at him in surprise. "You don't even know her."

"I don't have to. If she made such an impression on you, she must be the one, no doubt about it."

"What makes you think that?"

"Because Aurora is the first woman you've really talked to me about."

"The other women just weren't worth talking about," I growled.

"Exactly."

Jacks had caught me stone cold. And he was also right, but I didn't want to give him the satisfaction.

My last subs had been exclusively in the playroom, not in my bed, not in my thoughts and in my heart they had no place at all. They had been a means to an end and for that they had idolized me. But Aurora was different, she didn't adore me just because I was rich, good looking or my charm had wooed her. I had to earn Aurora's approval and that made it interesting – it made her interesting.

"However Aurora may be, I like her already," Jackson said with a grin.

I gave him my *fuck-you* smile, of which he knew exactly what to think.

"Just tell me what we're going to do about the forty-two, okay?"

"As I said before, Caden. We're going to have to handle this on our own."

"It would probably be easier with a donation."

Not that I threw my hard-earned money around, but there were people – like Jackson and his comrades – to whom I would give millions without hesitation because I knew they would do the right thing with it.

"And then the donations go into the pockets of the higher-ups. You know how the damn game works. And we have to come to terms with austerity somehow."

"All too well."

Austerity. Just hearing that word made me want to smash walls. In fact, austerity had destroyed my life. Not that I was coming to my father's defense, but under different circumstances, we'd still be living in suburban Jersey. *Peace, joy, pancakes.* Well, and then came the austerity measures.

The bang haunted me to this day, as did the terrible screams that ate through my marrow.

Focus, Caden. I took a deep breath, left the past behind, and sprinted across the steel beams as fast as I could. It was the only way I could leave my thoughts behind. Jackson, who was struggling with his very own problems, followed me silently.

Breathing heavily, we reached the crane from which we could leave the hall construct again.

"What a run," I gasped breathlessly.

"It's definitely a change from sprinting across the rooftops of Brooklyn," Jackson replied breathlessly himself.

"Damn right."

"Again to Aurora ..."

"Shit, you should get yourself a woman again, as often as you start about Aurora," I grumbled annoyed. For five fucking minutes I had been able to forget that Aurora wasn't my sub yet. Of course, I had no doubt that sooner or later she would enter my playroom, but every single second of knowing that she wasn't mine was hell. The only thing that didn't make me go crazy was the deep certainty that Aurora craved me and what I wanted to do to her. There was no mistaking her desire.

We could not keep our hands off each other, neither could we deny it.

"I'm at least as relationship-disturbed as you are, Caden," Jackson replied, snapping me out of my thoughts.

"Well, well, well, the relationship dysfunctional one of us is now engaged," I replied with a grin. Then I climbed the ladder that led down from the crane.

"Wow, your mood has improved abruptly."

"You could say that, yes."

"And what is the reason?"

"That at home, my fiancée is waiting for me."

I looked at Jackson meaningfully. He knew exactly what I meant.

"And I don't want to keep her waiting any longer than necessary," I added. Possibly Aurora was already waiting for me. Maybe even in the playroom. On her knees. As soon as Aurora entered that room, she knew what the rules were. Even if she had only looked into the room for a split second, I would know, because her thoughts were an open book to me, which was both a curse and a blessing.

Chapter 8 – Aurora

Exhausted, I let the front door close behind me, leaned against the closed door and took a deep breath. How could celebrities stand this paparazzi gauntlet? Although my cocoa with hazelnut syrup, extra cream and lots of chocolate drops was the best in the world, it had only tasted half as good in the car.

"I'm back!" My call echoed through the empty loft before my voice faded and silence returned.

Who would have thought that overnight I would be living in one of the most beautiful apartments in New York and my fiancé would be waiting for me there?

Stop! Caden is not your fiancé!

Of course he was my fiancé, but only on paper. If I wasn't careful, I would get caught up in fatal desires faster than I would have liked. So I had to stop myself and hope for the best.

"Caden?" I called a second time, just in case he had overheard me in that rambling apartment. Silence again.

I threw off my shoes and sighed with relief when my bare feet touched the cool marble. By afternoon, the sun had become quite oppressive, and I longed for a refreshing shower.

No sooner said than done ... almost.

On the way to the bathroom, my gaze once again lingered on the mysterious black door. I stopped in front of it and examined it closely. The door handle was polished to a high gloss and shimmered gold, as did the black lacquer with which the door was painted.

Of course I knew better, but I just couldn't resist the temptation. Caden wasn't here right now, so he would never know that I had peeked behind the door.

I wanted Caden, I really did, but I wasn't sure I wanted what was behind the door.

Carefully, I put my hand on the cool metal, and the handle was pushed down without resistance. But before I opened the door, I paused briefly.

"Do I really want this?" I asked myself. Then I nodded resolutely and opened the door a crack. To my surprise, dim light shone towards me, and I was about to back out, but it was too late for that now. Pandora's box had been opened; you couldn't just undo something like that.

Close your eyes and see this through.

I opened the door even wider, stepped inside, and winced as I looked directly into Caden's dark eyes.

"I suppose you do," he replied. There was a satisfied smile on his lips. He was sitting in a black leather armchair that faced a blood-red wall. The entire room was stylishly decorated, but I only had eyes for Caden.

"I thought you wouldn't be here," I said thoughtfully.

"And that's why you thought you could take a peek into this room without any of the consequences that follow?"

"I thought, if I don't like what I see ..."

"You thought wrong, darling. You entered my *playroom* and now my rules apply."

Caden stood up, stalked around me, and closed the door, which was covered in leather upholstery on the back, behind me.

"Now you belong to me. You decided that for yourself, and there's nothing to change."

His dark, raspy voice made me shudder as he spoke the words that triggered – and quenched – unimagined longings in me.

"Look around," he commanded, and I obeyed.

Next to the black leather chair, which was in the middle of the room, was a black dresser. Above it hung a wide variety of crops and whips. On the other side, there was a St. Andrew's cross, and chains and carbines hung all over the room, the meaning of which I was probably still to learn.

At the end of the room was a black four-poster bed, which also had chains and carabiners on it.

"What do you think, Aurora?"

"I am relieved," I answered honestly.

"Relieved? I show you the room where you are completely at my mercy, where I can drive you to madness or bliss, as I please, and you are relieved?"

I nodded. "Yes."

Caden went to the crops and picked up a short one with a wide leather patch hanging from the tip.

"Do you have any experience with it?"

"No."

He pulled open the drawer and took out two metal clamps connected by a chain.

"And how about that?"

Again I shook my head. "No. I have no experience with *any* of that."

"And what about sex?"

Well, there it looked just as bleak as with the rest of my non-existent BDSM expertise. Strictly speaking, you could say that Caden had freed me from my virginal slumber, with just one look. I couldn't and wouldn't deny that Caden had pleased me from the very first second, and that I had wanted nothing more than for him to pull me into his bedroom and finally show me what worldly pleasures I had previously foregone.

"No." I clearly felt my cheeks turn red.

"How many men have you had sex with?"

"None."

Wow, Caden's look had become even more somber and even though he tried to hide it, he seemed to like my answer. Caden grabbed my shoulders, pushed me against the padded door and let his hands wander over my body.

"No one has ever touched you like I have?"

"No."

"And then you get involved with a man like me?"

I didn't say it out loud, but I knew Caden was perfect, even if he claimed otherwise.

"I want you," I whispered.

"Oh, Aurora. You have no idea how much I want you."

His tongue left goosebumps where it passed over my neck.

"You taste delicious and so sweet I almost lose my temper."

"I opened the door, Caden. You can finally lose your temper," I replied.

"Not yet."

Caden pushed himself off me and walked back to the dresser.

"What do I have to do now?" I asked, sighing. Perhaps there was also some anger in my voice because I had done what Caden wanted me to do. I was here, and in exchange, I put up with him making the rules. What more did he want? "Do you want me to beg? That I fall to my knees before you and beg for you to finally take me?"

Actually, it was anger that drove me, but curiosity had also played its part in getting me on my knees in front of Caden, hoping that I would finally get what I wanted.

Caden smiled. "Believe me, you will soon enough – and we'll both enjoy it – but for now, I need something else from you."

"What?"

"A signature."

I frowned. "I've already signed the confidentiality agreement."

Caden handed me the paper, and I tried to get up again, but Caden pushed me back to my knees by the shoulder. "Stay down. You seem to like it pretty well on your knees."

I answered nothing, but punished him with defiant looks, which he noted with a smile.

"Your signature is needed for another document, specifically for the Playroom, even though the rules will go beyond the room."

I took the paper and read it through. Some passages were formulated in such a bureaucratic way that I had difficulty understanding the core of the statement. On the other hand, other paragraphs were so clear that nothing was left to the imagination.

"Did you get it all?" asked Caden as I looked up again.

"If I sign this, I'm yours. I can't tell anyone about it, and if I break any rules, there will be consequences," I summarized the contract briefly.

"Exactly. Do you accept that?"

"Yes."

In no possible world could I have refused Caden to become his girl. The attraction between us was far too strong for that.

"I can tell by the look on your face that there's another *but* coming. Out with it, Aurora. Once the contract is signed, there's no turning back."

"There are some rules that irritate me."

"Like what?"

"The chauffeur thing. I don't need anyone to drive me around New York, I like to be in cabs or on the subway."

Before I could explain, to my astonishment, Caden cut me off.

"That's not negotiable." Something flared in his eyes that I couldn't quite define. Anger? Hatred? Whatever it was, these emotions were not directed at me.

"Okay," I replied, irritated.

"Anything else?"

"No."

Admittedly, there was another section that made me wonder — absolute prohibition of alcohol. I was not allowed to drink alcohol, ever. Not that I drank a lot, and it bothered me, but this rule seemed somehow ... out of place in such a contract.

"These rules are very important to you, aren't they?" I asked.

"Yes. Otherwise they wouldn't be written there."

"Why aren't those rules in our first contract? You didn't mind me having a cocktail during our interview either."

"Because those rules only apply to *my girl,* and yesterday you weren't my girl."

"I see."

Caden's expression softened again.

"We still need to talk about your safeword."

"My safeword?"

"A word I hope you will never need to use to slow me down."

"And it can be anything, any word?"

"Yes. But you shouldn't abuse it. I know how far I can push your limits, and I know when you're lying to me. The safeword is not a free pass for unpleasant situations, the safeword is strictly a lifeline."

"Okay. Then Seattle is my safeword," I said firmly.

"I thought you were from Seattle."

"True, and I kind of love my home state, but I still haven't managed to break out of the vicious cycle I'm in."

I had been born in Seattle and my family lived there, but it had never been a real home for me, nor had I found a person with whom I wanted to spend my life. After graduation, I hadn't even managed to work at the same job for more than two months.

Caden took my hand. "You left the vicious circle when you said *yes to* me."

All at once, I realized that Caden had really set me free. I hadn't thought once about the chaos at home since we first met.

"Thank you," I replied quietly. "So, where do you want me to sign?"

"Right here," Caden replied in a raspy voice, pointing to the line on the last page. From his jacket he pulled out an elegant fountain pen and handed it to me.

"How appropriate that you're already kneeling," he added before handing me the pen.

I did not hesitate for a single second but put my curved signature on the paper. It was official, I was now Caden's property.

Chapter 9 – Caden

I couldn't suppress my growl when Aurora signed the document. I would have loved to grab Aurora and fuck her as hard as I had wanted to do for the last few days. But after I learned that Aurora was still a virgin, I discarded all plans.

Damn, I was the first man who could show her everything. I was the man with whom she would have her unforgettable *first time*.

She was inexperienced, no question, but she knew exactly what she was getting into with me.

"Take off your dress!" I ordered in a gentle tone. Probably no other man had seen her naked before me.

Aurora slipped her summer dress off her shoulders, hiding seductive black lace underwear underneath.

"For never having had sex before, you sure are laying it on thick, huh?"

Aurora smiled at me. "I just wanted to be prepared in case."

I grabbed her feminine hips and pulled her to me.

"Is this the case of the cases now?"

"I hope so." Her answer was no more than a moan, in which genuine longing resonated.

"I'm going to fuck you," I replied softly. Then I pushed one of her blonde strands back behind her ear and nibbled on her earlobe. "But you'll have to earn it first."

"What do I have to do for it, Caden? Believe me, I'll do anything for you, really anything, if you don't stop touching me in return!"

I smiled with satisfaction. Aurora said so without thinking about it, but in an hour at the latest she would really do everything for me. She was still inexperienced, and I took that into account, of course, but that didn't mean I had to handle Aurora with kid gloves. No, Aurora had the unique chance to discover her preferences with a man who knew exactly what he was doing.

"Before I fuck you, I should make a few things clear."

Aurora nodded and bit her lower lip expectantly.

"All rules apply not only in the playroom, but always."

"Roger that."

"Once we are in the playroom, you will kneel on the floor in front of me and wait for my orders."

Jesus. My pants were getting tighter and tighter, and I was far from finished. Knowing that Aurora was finally mine was an incredible feeling.

"Besides, a little more respect for authority figures wouldn't hurt you."

If Aurora knew how close I came to putting her over my knee the first time we met, she probably wouldn't have acted that way.

"Roger that, sir."

"Say you're mine!" I commanded softly.

"I'm yours, Caden."

"Good girl."

Aurora's entire body was electrified, for her the situation was at least as tingly as for me.

Granted, I had never felt as powerful as I did at that moment, but Aurora was also the first one I really wanted to have as a sub. She was the first I wanted not only to fuck, but to really own. And if Aurora knew that, suddenly she would be the one with power over me. I could never let it get that far.

"We should also talk about our first meeting again."

"Should we?" asked Aurora, and when she saw my look, she cleared her throat. "Of course we should talk about it, sir."

"You broke into my loft," I began.

"Actually it wasn't a burglary. I had a key card and no idea the penthouse had changed owners."

"You were rude, you cut me off, and on top of that, you insulted me."

"Oh, that's what you were getting at," Aurora replied meekly.

"Yes, that's exactly what I was getting at," I replied seriously. Even now, Aurora was foolhardy enough to run her mouth over mine. We would no doubt have a hell of a lot more fun in the Playroom.

"Sorry."

"I'm afraid an apology alone won't do," I replied with genuine regret.

"Sorry, sir."

Smiling, I had to conclude that Aurora understood the rules faster than I realized. Nevertheless, her devoted *sir* was not enough for me. I wanted screams and looks of longing. I pointed to the wall where my considerable collection of crops and whips hung.

"Pick what I'm about to punish you with."

Aurora obeyed, stood up and examined each of them carefully.

"For how many strokes?"

"You'll find out soon enough." I said no more, for the number of strokes depended on which percussion instrument Aurora chose. Her long fingers ran through the leather straps of a cat o'nine tails. From the looks of it, she had a natural feel for what I had in mind for her, or better yet, we had the same preferences.

After a moment's consideration, Aurora actually decided on my favorite whip, but instead of handing it to me, she paused and looked fascinated at the nipple clamps I had pulled out of the drawer earlier.

"What's this?" She lifted the clamps on the chain.

"Would you like to try it?" I asked, taking the nipple clamps from her. Normally I didn't ask my subs questions. I didn't give them a choice when I had specific ideas, but I already knew Aurora's answer.

"Yes."

"You're more curious than is good for you," I murmured. Then I stalked around her one more time until I stopped behind her and slowly unclasped her lacy bra. I couldn't wait to see her full breasts from the front, but first I wanted to know if Aurora's neck tasted as sweet as it looked. When the tip of my tongue touched her skin, she moaned softly.

Damn, each time Aurora tasted even more seductive. How sweet her lips tasted first? I had a hard time detaching myself from her, but I was slowly reaching my limits with my restraint, and we hadn't even started yet.

"You have a beautiful body, Aurora," I said as I continued to walk around her, looking her up and down. "Has anyone ever told you that?"

She shook her head, and her silky, smooth hair fell over her body like a waterfall. "No, never."

"What a shame. But believe me, you'll hear it from me plenty more times."

For the fact that I was about to fuck Aurora for the first time in her life, she remained quite relaxed.

"Is this how you imagined your first time?"

"No."

"How then?"

"I didn't think anyone could trigger this strong desire that burns inside me. There's this feeling inside me that I can barely describe, I just know it feels right. Right and beautiful, even though I'm about to burn if you don't finally touch me. You know what I mean?"

"I know exactly what you're talking about."

At first Aurora smiled at me, but then her smile faded.

"Will it be over then?"

"What do you mean?"

"After. Did that feeling go away after the first time?"

Smiling, I let my thumb wander over her cheek and turned her face toward me.

"I can promise you that this feeling will get stronger every time."

As long as the desire gets stronger, we both functioned together. Only when Aurora stopped getting goosebumps when I breathed something into her ear and her eyes stopped shining, it would be time to look for a new sub for me, but I didn't want to think about that now or later.

Aurora is mine. She is my girl.

I couldn't hear it come out of her mouth enough, but the best part was that tomorrow the whole damn world would know Aurora was my girl. Any guy who lingered on her beauty would know she was mine.

"Take a deep breath!" I commanded before attaching the nipple clamps to her erect buds.

"Oh," Aurora gasped, almost disappointed, as she felt the gentle pressure.

"Were you hoping for more?"

"To be honest, yes."

Aurora amused me. I never thought that an inexperienced sub would fascinate me the way Aurora just did.

"With each breath, you'll feel it a little more clearly. I promise."

Actually, it was not a promise, but a warning I had given, but Aurora would realize that soon enough.

There was a satisfied smile on Aurora's lips. Still. From behind, I grabbed her hips and pulled her so tightly against me that she could feel my hardness pressing against the fabric of my pants and her buttocks.

Be a good girl and take off all your clothes."

Aurora slipped her lacy panties down until they fell to the floor.

Her body was beautiful, and the soft light of my playroom flattered her flawless skin.

To make the lashing a bit more exciting, I pulled a black silk scarf from my pants pocket, with which I blindfolded Aurora's eyes. By taking away her sight, all her other senses intensified.

I hugged her from behind and pushed her straight ahead, at the same time gently pulling the chain of her nipple clamps. With careful steps she went forward until I had her where I wanted her.

Noisily I let the door fall into the lock. The back of the door was covered with leather upholstery, just like the rest of the wall.

"No one will hear you scream, Aurora. Your screams belong only to me."

I watched in fascination as my warm breath left tingling goose bumps on the back of her neck.

"I'll do things to you that you'll hate me for, but that's what it's going to take to get to the point where you love me for just that, too, and beg for more. There is no clear line between pleasure and pain, it depends on the dose of both."

After my hands stroked her silky, smooth skin one more time, I took her hands and placed them above her head on the wall in front of her.

"I know it's hard the first time, but I want you to hold this position until I order you to do something else."

"Yes, sir."

On the first stroke, the leather hit her upper arm to test how high Aurora's pain threshold actually was. Impressively high for a girl who had never been in a game room before. Good. So I just had to show some restraint until Aurora got more confident.

I aimed at her other arm, then slowly and pleasurably wandered down her back to her calves. Aurora seemed to be most sensitive on her thighs. *Good to know.* Murmuring, I grabbed between her thighs and pushed her legs even further apart.

The view drove me half-crazy and surpassed anything I had imagined in my fantasy by worlds.

"How many more strokes?" asked Aurora impatiently. Her whole body trembled with pleasure and her voice resonated with a kind of cry for help, begging me to finally steal her virginity. But Aurora had to be patient a little longer, because dragging out pleasure and pain was one of the things I was best at.

"I told you I would decide that, Aurora."

"I didn't disagree with that either, Caden. I just want to know how many more beatings I have to take before you ..."

"Until I fuck you?" I asked. Actually, I didn't let my subs interrupt me, but Aurora's excitement was simply delicious. She didn't know that she had just dragged out the time until I finally released her, but she would soon be able to guess.

"Yes."

Even though her face was in shadow, her flushed cheeks were hard to miss.

"Say it. I want to hear you beg me to fuck you."

"Please take me already, Caden!"

"Say the word," I demanded of her one more time.

"Please fuck me," Aurora whispered so softly that even my steady heartbeat was louder.

"Next time I ask you a question, you should answer loud enough for me to really understand you."

"Yes, sir."

"And next time you should think twice about making demands on me in your impatience."

"What do you mean exactly?"

"That you got yourself twenty more strokes than you planned."

"Oh. Sorry, sir." Her apology sounded heartbreakingly genuine, but my punishment still remained. Where would we go without educational measures?

I reached out and aimed at her shapely backside, but Aurora stretched so seductively that I slowly became too tight for my pants.

With each blow she silently accepted, I gave Aurora a taste of what would happen if she continued to contradict me. And I hoped that this was exactly what tempted her to continue contradicting me.

Aurora was doing well, so after each stroke I put a little more energy into the next. The soft jingle of the chain from which the nipple clamps hung and which resonated with each stroke was music to my ears. Her entire backside glowed seductively red when I was done with her.

No question, Aurora almost didn't care about the strokes. The fact that I decided when to finally redeem her was much worse, because she knew that I enjoyed torturously dragging out her pleasure.

I embraced Aurora's hips, turned her around and pressed her back firmly against the wall. Her mouth was slightly open and after one look at her seductive, full lips, I couldn't help but press my mouth onto hers. *Delicious.* Aurora's soft lips tasted like cinnamon. As we broke away from each other breathing heavily, I was addicted to the taste.

"Finished," I growled softly. I would have loved to work Aurora even more with my favorite whip, but I wasn't willing to give up her seductive body any longer.

"Finally," she gasped. A soft but reproving clearing of her throat was enough for her to add a quiet, "I mean thank you, sir."

"Ready?" I asked seductively.

"I've never been more ready!" replied Aurora with relief.

Another time I pulled the chain that hung between her breasts. This time Aurora bit her lips to suppress a moan.

"I promised you that the nipple clamps would be even more exciting."

"Maybe too exciting," Aurora admitted meekly.

I shook my head. "No, you're still a long way from your real pain threshold." She was much tougher than she thought. I knew exactly how far I could safely take her.

One last time, I examined the artwork of red welts and pale, flawless skin. *Beautiful.* Then I took Aurora's hands and led her to the large bed at the other end of the room. She had bravely endured her punishment, and I gave her credit for that. Therefore, and because I wanted to leave a lasting impression on Aurora, I would ensure an unforgettable first time.

Just the thought that I was branding her thoughts, her desires, and her expectations drove me crazy.

As commanded, Aurora lay down on her back, her whole body reacting to the smallest stimuli, even my breath could bring her to orgasm now.

"How did you actually know I was going to enter your playroom?" asked Aurora quietly.

"The attraction between us is so strong that neither of us can resist it."

This was not a feeling, but a fact that no one could deny.

I got rid of my clothes and knelt between Aurora's legs, which she had spread so invitingly that I would have loved to throw myself on them. I realized at first sight how wet and ready Aurora was for me.

My hands slowly moved from her ankles up to her thighs, eliciting a soft moan from Aurora. As I leaned forward, Aurora's sweet cinnamon scent enveloped me.

With pleasure, I rubbed my hardness on her most sensitive spot. Immediately Aurora stretched her hips towards me. Damn, she was more than ready for me and ready for whatever I had in mind for her.

"Tell me what you want," I murmured in her ear.

"You!" Her answer turned into a seductive moan. That was exactly what I wanted to hear. Aurora would still have had a chance to change her mind, but now it was too late. Her virginity was mine, just like the rest.

With my thumb, I massaged her clit until her breathing became irregular and announced an orgasm. Just before Aurora came, I pushed my erection into her. When I felt how tight she was, I began to growl like a hungry wolf.

"Oh God," Aurora gasped as I gave her time to adjust to the enormity of my hardness.

"Leave God out of it, if he knew what we were doing here, I'm sure he wouldn't approve."

"You're right. What we are doing must be pure sin, as good as it feels."

Aurora had no idea how dangerous her answer was.

"Do you have any idea how much strength it takes for me to hold back?" I asked.

"Then don't hold back."

My breath caught when I saw Aurora's expression. She really meant it.

"You have no idea what you're getting yourself into."

"Yes, I think I pretty much do."

"Suit yourself, I'll give you a little taste of what's to come."

I gave in to the urge to fuck her harder. Her moans got louder and louder and, with her legs, she pulled me so tight that I couldn't help but fill her completely.

Unbelievably, Aurora still had no idea at all how she should behave as my sub, and yet she did exactly what I expected of her. She was perfect. So perfect that I would love to never let Aurora out of my playroom again.

Aurora tightened around me; her whole body vibrated. Not much longer, and she came. I pulled off her blindfold because I wanted her to look me in the eye when she came. Aurora should see who was responsible for her flights of fancy.

Just before she came, I lost all inhibitions and fucked her the way I had wanted to do all along – and what Aurora had been longing for so much.

Her eyelids began to flutter, her orgasm was only seconds away.

"Take a deep breath!" I commanded with a smile. Aurora looked at me irritated but followed my command and took a deep breath. The next moment I released both clamps from her hard, sensitive buds, and Aurora let out a scream that turned into a long moan and faded away as she came.

I knew how painful releasing the clamps was, but I also knew that it led to the most intense orgasms ever, if you knew what you were doing. And I knew that very well.

Gasping, I enjoyed the way Aurora tightened even more around me, so tight that I had no choice but to follow her into ecstasy. I pumped my gold into her and, by God, there was no better feeling than knowing that I was the first man to leave traces, visible and invisible, alike.

Chapter 10 – Caden

"Are you really sure, Aurora?" I asked one last time as we entered the elevator to the executive floor. "You're my fiancée. You don't have to work."

Aurora snorted loudly as the elevator doors closed.

"Yes, I'm sure of it, Caden! I'd feel terrible if I let myself have that luxury."

"Have you forgotten that I more or less coerced you into this? If you don't want to use my Mastercard, give me an amount, and I'll transfer it to you."

Aurora looked at me, stunned.

"Caden, it may surprise you, but I'm really not in it for the money! Money can't buy everything. Neither happiness nor true friends or … " She faltered, so I finished the sentence for her.

"Or love?"

"Yes," she answered meekly. "You may be able to buy my body, but my heart is not included in the price."

Aurora had a rather special but refreshing way of thinking. I hadn't talked to anyone for a long time who didn't care about money, but if there was one thing I knew for sure, it was that everything had a price, and everything was for sale if the price was right.

"So there's no price I could pay to buy your heart?"

"Yes, there is, but you won't find it in your checkbook."

I turned to Aurora, "Now you're making me quite curious. Out with it, what is it?"

"Well, you'll have to figure that out for yourself, Caden."

"Is that how a sub should talk to her Dom?" I asked in a raspy voice.

"Probably not. But right now I'm not your sub, I'm your fiancée giving you some good advice."

I looked at Aurora with astonished eyes. She really had the courage to talk to me like that. Our first day of work together hadn't even started yet, and I already wanted to put her over my knee; at least now I had the chance to really do it.

My God, I didn't even want to think about how unbearable my job would have become if Aurora hadn't signed our contract.

"As soon as those doors open, you'll be my personal assistant – the same rules apply to you as in the playroom. So you might want to reconsider your last answer?"

"No," Aurora replied with a challenging grin. "I am satisfied with my answer, Mr. Saint."

I pressed Aurora against the chrome elevator wall with my massive torso to steal a kiss from her.

"You should be careful how you behave, Aurora. I have absolutely no inhibitions about chastising you in my office when I feel like it."

"Roger that, sir."

Aurora bit her lips as if she wanted to say something else, but she remained silent.

"What else is on your mind?"

"Do you really want me to call you Mr. Saint in front of your employees?"

"I like how devotedly you call me *sir*," I replied honestly.

"But I'm not only your personal assistant, I'm also your fiancée."

I growled softly. When she was right, she was right. Damn, this whole fake engagement thing was as new to me as it was to Aurora. Until now, I'd only known life with my subs, who had rarely bothered me outside of my playroom. Okay, admittedly, Aurora was the first woman I really wanted to be around, which was the only reason I had agreed to her request to be my personal assistant in the first place.

"I'm sure you know when a *yes sir* is appropriate and when it's not," I replied with a wink.

"And I'm almost certain you'll find ways to punish me for appropriate behavior as well."

"You bet I will. I can't wait to see you in the playroom tonight," I murmured close to her ear.

"Me neither," Aurora replied with a smile.

One last time, I tasted Aurora's delicious lips while my hands wandered down her body, then I had to restrain myself. When the elevator doors opened, I could still hear Aurora's rapid heartbeat.

Waiting in the lobby were only my personal assistant and Erica from PR, whom I rarely got to see. As soon as we stepped off the elevator, they both rushed toward us, although Janice could barely see through the high pile of files.

"Wow, you're in pretty high demand," Aurora murmured to me. "Do you have quieter days?"

"This is a quiet day," I replied seriously.

"PR first," I said, and continued on my way to the office.

"We still need an image strategy," she began, but I cut her off.

"You've been saying that for months."

"Because – with all due respect, sir – you reject everything we propose."

"Then give me better results," I grumbled. "Or settle for what we've achieved. Tomorrow, the day after tomorrow at the latest, the rates will go up another few points, that's for sure."

It was a shame for me that an engagement brought my company more attention than security systems and machines that could save lives. Of course, I had my very own abysses, but the world around me was at least as broken.

"If we could mention that ..."

"No!" I cut Erica off sharply. "This is a private matter, and that's exactly how we're going to treat it."

"Of course, sir," Erica replied businesslike. "We'll think of something else."

Aurora, whom I could only see out of the corner of my eye, was watching us closely but kept in the background.

"Janice, now you."

She immediately pressed a stack of files into my hand.

"The bills would have to be signed off on, plus there are some inquiries there from companies that would be very interested in merging that might be relevant to the current project."

"Thank you."

"Can I ask why our stock prices will go up?" she asked.

"Haven't you read the paper yet?" I asked a counter question, to which Janice shook her head in the negative.

At one of the desks we passed, I grabbed a Times lying around and thrust it into the hand of my personal assistant. She turned white as a sheet when she saw the cover.

"Oh. I had heard about it, but I thought it was just a rumor ... congratulations?"

"Was that a question?"

Janice cleared her throat, then her gaze slid back and forth between Aurora and the newspaper article.

"Janice? This is Aurora, my fiancée. Aurora? This is Janice, she's going to brief you."

After Janice caught herself, she put on her businesslike face again and extended her hand to Aurora.

"But of course."

I gave Janice a serious look. "I'm counting on you to let Aurora take over your post starting tomorrow."

"But yes, sir ... hold on." Janice faltered. "Am I fired?"

I was almost willing to say yes, because I would be rid of my last sub for good. If she didn't do such a good job, she would have been kicked out of Saint Industries long ago, because she had overstepped her boundaries more than once. But I was not a monster, and I was sure that Janice would finally get over me when she had more distance from me.

I looked at Erica, who was still standing next to me, probably because she was making up arguments for a photo shoot.

"Doesn't the PR department still have job openings?"

"That's right, Mr. Saint. A manager position is open soon because Walter Knight is retiring, and once Alexa Morrison gives birth, a spokesperson position is also temporarily open."

I turned to Janice.

"Perfect, then starting tomorrow you'll be PR manager and deputy press spokesperson. You'll know how the company runs, what makes me tick, and hopefully make Erica suggest better marketing strategies."

"Yes, of course." The shock still hadn't completely left her face, but the distance was certainly doing her good, too. It had been ages since our last contract, and she was still clinging.

I looked at Aurora, who was still in the background. Although I couldn't point to anything specific, something had changed in her face.

"You guys can start right now. In the meantime, I'll work through the accumulated stuff and make some phone calls."

Janice nodded, turned away from me, and marched to her desk, Aurora standing hesitantly.

"There's something else I want to talk to you about, Caden."

"Go ahead." I waved her into my office, and Aurora closed the door behind her. So it seemed to be a more serious matter.

"Is there any more privacy?" asked Aurora. She pointed to the glass wall separating my office from the rest of the floor, which overlooked Janice's desk and the hallway in front of the elevators.

"Would it make you uncomfortable if I spanked your bottom in public?" I asked with a grin. Aurora sheepishly turned her face to the side to hide the fact that her cheeks were reddening. She should have known by now that her feelings and thoughts were an open book to me. I knew exactly what was going on inside her.

"Jesus, Caden! What if someone hears us?"

"No one hears us, and yes, there is a way to create more privacy."

I went to my desk and pulled out a remote control from the top drawer, which caused the glass wall including the door to turn white, making it opaque.

"Wow." Aurora watched the discoloration with fascination, then cleared her throat and looked at me seriously.

"What do you even want to talk to me about?"

"About Janice, what else?"

I frowned.

"Do you have a problem with her training you when she was my sub?"

Aurora's eyes grew huge. "She was your sub?"

"That was ages ago," I replied, suppressing a sigh.

"And then you treat them like this?"

I squinted my eyes. "How do I treat them in your eyes then?"

"So heartless. You should apologize to her."

It's getting to that point. Shaking my head, I dropped into my chair and propped my elbows on the solid wood of my desk.

"She is my employee who is now needed at another post, the end."

"That's exactly what I mean, Caden. Why are you so aloof and distant?"

Were we still talking about Janice? I didn't know. Just a moment ago, I thought Aurora was an open book, and suddenly she opened a page written in a language that was foreign to me.

Aurora exhaled loudly, then her serious expression softened.

"You still haven't put an engagement ring on my finger."

"Because, technically, you're not my fiancée either."

Of course, I couldn't deny the sparks between us, but I wasn't ready to admit that either, especially not here in my company. Here, I was in control, but that only worked if I remained as aloof as a rock against which the raging surf simply bounced, for millennia.

"But the rest of the world believes it," Aurora said softly.

"You're right," I admitted, pulling a gold Mastercard out of my wallet. "Here, pick out a ring you like. The price doesn't matter. And while you're at it, you can buy some new clothes for work, too."

Aurora smoothed out her black, wrinkle-free skirt.

"Why, what's wrong with it? In bordering probability, this outfit cost more than I've ever made in a month."

"It's a little staid for my taste."

"Conservative?" Aurora pressed her lips tightly together and snorted loudly. "It's perfectly appropriate, or Max would never have given it to me."

I knew her best friend had given her this outfit. Maxine Lancester was the new face of real estate, no question, but her name was burned into my brain for other reasons. If not for this absurd coincidence, Aurora would never have stumbled into my life.

"You are mine, Aurora. You are my fiancée, my sub, and starting tomorrow, my personal assistant. I promise you that our working time will be much more interesting if you do what I tell you."

"Yes, sir." Aurora disagreed, which she did not hide. I was wrong, our working hours today were already more exciting than the last few years' total, that much was certain.

"Can I go now?" asked Aurora. "I don't want to keep Janice waiting."

"Janice is not the angel you think she is," I said seriously.

"Are you going to dump me like that someday when I bore you? *Hey Aurora, you're working in another department now. Oh, by the way, here are the divorce papers, have a nice life.*"

"That's different," I growled.

"And will you also tell your next sub that I was not an angel?"

She was on very thin ice, that much was clear.

"You should shut up now before you say things you'll regret."

Aurora nodded. "I'm already quiet. Maybe I was a little emotional, but that doesn't change the sincerity of what I said."

"That's your definition of silence?" I couldn't help grinning.

"Not quite." Aurora bit her lips before backing away. "I won't keep Janice waiting any longer, then."

"I did not give you permission to leave." To demonstrate my authority, I stood up and walked toward Aurora until she took a step back.

"No?" She looked at me in wonder.

"No. You will now remove your panties, push your skirt up, and bend over my desk."

"Are you serious?"

"Do I look like I'm joking?"

"No, sir. I just thought here I was just your assistant."

"You are, Aurora. But I reserve the freedom to punish you if I see fit."

Knowing I was right, Aurora didn't contradict me, but took off her panties, which promptly landed in the top drawer of my desk.

Damn, when was the last time I had acted out my dominant traits outside of my playroom? I could not remember.

Aurora leaned forward seductively and waited for her punishment while keeping an eye on the door.

Chapter 11 – Aurora

Oh God. I had really imagined my first day at work differently. I thought I would be sorting some files, taking calls and getting coffee, but instead I was hunched over, waiting for Caden to punish me. Yet I was the one of us who was angry! Angry and scared and kind of desperate because I was taking the engagement of us so much more seriously than Caden was. Maybe even too seriously.

Caden walked around me, his footsteps echoing on the marble floor and making him seem even more powerful than he already was. In my eyes, Caden was the most powerful man in the world; he had power, charm, and he had me.

"You can continue to give me your opinion, but we're never going to talk about Janice being my sub again, you understand?"

"Understood, sir," I replied, although this chapter was far from closed.

I was really afraid of Caden dropping me later just as brutally as he had done once before.

Before Caden had even touched me, my treacherous abdomen began to pulsate. I thought I could still feel my orgasm from yesterday and this humiliating position triggered the most contradictory sensations in me. My anger was gone in the blink of an eye; now it was just Caden, me, and the seductive power imbalance between us.

"Why are you smiling?" asked Caden as he snapped me out of my thoughts.

"I'm thinking about what you did to me yesterday."

"So you like what I'm doing to you? Do you like this too?"

"Oh yes." My whisper dragged on and finally turned into a moan.

"Then maybe you're even more depraved than I am," Caden murmured in my ear.

"We should find out."

"I'm going to show you everything, Aurora. Pleasure, pain and all the facets in between."

"Please!" I pleaded as I tilted my head to look Caden straight in the eye.

Wow. His irises were flooded with darkness that drew me seductively. I knew about Caden's abyss and, even if I had no idea what shadows lurked there, I was ready to find out.

"Sometimes you will demonize me for what I will do to you, but just as often, you will idolize me for that very thing."

Was it just my imagination, or did I hear true awe in his voice? Deep inside me, hope grew that I was *more* than just a sub for Caden, more than the signature on his contracts.

"How many strokes do you think are appropriate for your outrageous behavior?"

"You decide what punishment is appropriate, and I will accept it without protest."

"Good answer," Caden murmured. "But how many strokes do you think you deserve?"

"Ten strokes," I replied thoughtfully. "I protested, yes. But not until we were alone." I would have preferred to confront him directly when I realized that my predecessor had been cut off because of me.

"Well, ten strokes then," Caden replied with satisfaction. "By the way, the walls here are not soundproof. So if you don't want anyone to overhear what we're doing here, you should be quiet and only count along in a whisper."

Great. Don't!

Although we were on the executive floor, it was quite busy. Directly in front of Caden's office was the table for the personal assistant. In the large lobby in front of it, dozens of businessmen were standing and sitting, presumably waiting for an appointment with Caden.

The first blow was unexpected, I gasped and bit my lips to stifle my scream. I was better prepared for the second blow, even though it was about twice as strong as the first. After the third blow, I was pretty sure I was going to spend the rest of my workday standing up if Caden kept up that intensity.

The next three blows followed closely on the same spot. My nails clawed into the wood varnish, and I gasped as quietly as I could.

"I can't even hear the number of beats," Caden murmured. "No big deal, we'll just start over."

I would have loved to insult Caden with everything I knew, but I swallowed each insult and nodded. In no case, did I want to risk that Caden could invent more reasons to drag out my punishment.

"One," I said matter-of-factly. I tried to keep my tone neutral, even though I felt like yelling, but I didn't begrudge Caden the satisfaction.

I bravely counted the next beats as well, but it was getting harder and harder.

"Will we ... " I began, but then faltered because I lacked the right words.

"I wonder if we'll sleep together after this?" asked Caden. The amusement in his voice was answer enough.

"Yes," I answered anyway.

"No."

"That would be pretty mean, though."

"I know, it will still be part of your punishment."

"How am I supposed to think a single clear thought when you do this to me?" My reproachful tone was impossible to ignore. Now that I knew how delicious sex was, I couldn't do without it. Since yesterday, I thought of nothing but Caden, his overwhelming manhood, and what he was doing to me.

"I'm sure you'll have enough to do until I allow you your next orgasm."

Caden continued his beating before I understood what he had forbidden me to do.

Wow. But the more interesting thing about it was the feelings it triggered in me, because a big part of me liked it when Caden was so dominant and decided for me.

Knowing that I had to leave his office in a few minutes – without orgasm, I enjoyed the last strokes as much as I could.

"I want you to remember with every step that you are mine," Caden said in a raspy voice.

"I will," I replied with a sigh.

"I know, because I'm going to make sure of it."

At first I thought he was talking about the spanking, but when he went around his table to get something from the drawer after the tenth stroke, he gave me a serious look.

When I saw what Caden suddenly had in his hand, I gasped out loud. Was Caden really serious? Here? Now?

"I've never done this before!" I tried to protest, but Caden would not be swayed.

"It all starts with the first time."

"What if I don't like it?"

Caden smiled at me calmly. "If you don't like it, we'll find an alternative. But I think you'll like it pretty well once you get used to it."

"Okay."

Yes, I wanted to refuse, but for Caden's sake I wanted to at least try it, because he was convinced that I might like it.

I winced briefly as the lube dripped onto my most intimate parts, then the black butt plug followed. A fairly small one, maybe as long as my index finger and about twice as thick. Excitement mixed with fear, because yesterday I was factually still a virgin and today he spanked me in his office.

Caden gave me time to get used to the strange sensation before he inserted the plug all the way inside me. The feeling was unfamiliar, but it also spread a pleasant, pulsating warmth inside me.

"You may stand after you say thank you," Caden ordered.

"Thank you, sir."

He pulled me tightly against him, I felt his erection under the fabric of his pants, and it drove me crazy. I wanted him badly!

"I actually separate my job from my personal life, but I really like making an exception for you."

"Does that mean I'm the first one you've bent over this table?"

"Yes."

My cheeks reddened. I was the first; it went down like warm honey. Caden was quite secretive and rarely revealed his true thoughts and feelings, so statements like this were all the more valuable to me.

His hand slowly ran over the fabric of my skirt, so that I could feel the plug even better.

"You shouldn't keep Janice waiting any longer, Aurora."

"All right. When do you want me to come back?"

"I'll let you know."

What a nothing statement; that could mean anything. He really had a talent for confronting me with feelings that were previously foreign to me.

"Sometimes you can be pretty sadistic."

"What was that?"

"Can I get you another coffee, Mr. Saint?" I smiled sweetly at Caden.

"Better."

"I'm happy to be of service, sir."

"Very good."

With the tip of his thumb, Caden stroked my cheek and turned my face to either side.

"Before you go, I want one more question answered."

"Yes?"

"How I can buy your heart."

"I've already said that you're going to have to figure this out for yourself, Caden."

Yes, Caden was attractive and double-yes, Caden was very rich, but that didn't mean he could buy my heart just like that. He might be able to buy my body, but he had to earn my affection. And if he was willing to bet his own heart, then – and only then – was I willing to give him my own.

"Then you really should go now, or I'll drive you out of your mind until you tell me."

"I wouldn't mind staying, but my secret remains my secret," I replied. Admittedly, I would have very much welcomed a closer stay to him.

"Get out," Caden replied, grinning but unmistakable.

"Yes, sir." I looked at him seductively and gave him my best smile.

"Oh, one more thing." Caden pressed his gold credit card into my hand. "I hope you find the time to get some new clothes and an engagement ring. And while you're at it, you can have a gift basket sent to Janice, too."

"A gift basket?" I frowned. "You more or less fired her. I hardly think the problem is settled with a gift basket."

"Two baskets, then."

I shook my head in bewilderment.

"You really believe that every problem can be solved with money, don't you?"

"Yes."

I rolled my eyes. "Then the world has never confronted you with *real* problems."

Something in Caden's eyes flashed, just for a split second, but the darkness made me shudder. Even before Caden said anything, I knew I was wrong. Whatever he had locked so deeply, possibly I had just freed it. Caden turned away from me and let his gaze wander over New York.

"There are holes you can't plug with dollar bills. But with money, you have the ability to find resources that can."

"And what about the problems that no one can fix? For which, there is no solution?"

"These are irreparable mistakes that we have to live with whether we like it or not."

I didn't need to see Caden's face, his pained voice was enough for me to know how he was feeling right now. Had I just made an irreparable mistake?

"Sorry, Caden."

Caden shook his head. "There's nothing for you to apologize for."

Yes, we both knew that, but I respected his wish not to have to talk about it any longer.

An oppressive silence had settled over us and the room. How I hated these moments. The longer the silence lasted, the more oppressive it became and the harder it was to escape it again. The ringing of my smartphone came just at the right time.

"Oh no, what a bummer!" I said, looking at the display.

"What is it?" asked Caden, turning around. His businesslike expression was back.

"That's my mom."

"Is that a problem?"

"Yes!"

Another huge problem that no amount of money could solve. In all the hustle and bustle, I had totally forgotten to tell my family about Caden.

"Answer it already," Caden calmly urged me. "She's in Seattle, she can't rip your head off from there."

"You're probably right." I took a deep breath, then answered the call and retreated from Caden's office. "Hey, Mom."

"Aurora Dawn Winter!"

She pronounced my full name, not a good sign. The last time Mom had called me *Aurora Dawn Winter* with pointed screams had been ages ago. Whereas ... the thing with the car seemed like yesterday.

"Yeah?" I asked innocently, hoping it was just Maggy's wedding stuff after all.

"What were you thinking? I almost had a heart attack when Gladice brought me the morning paper!"

"I'm sorry, I haven't had time to tell you about it yet."

"That you're engaged? Jesus, kid! I thought until yesterday you had no interest in a relationship at all, let alone a plus one for Magnolia's wedding. And then this!"

"Aren't you glad I have a date for the wedding reception after all?" I tried desperately to turn the tables, but I had little success.

"How long have you been together? You never said anything about Caden Saint!"

"Believe me, the proposal was quite unexpected for me too," I confessed, as honestly as I could. Admittedly, a guilty conscience was nagging at me because I couldn't tell my mom the whole truth. It wasn't a lie, strictly speaking, but it was also far from sincere.

"You really want me to completely lose it, Aurora. Do you?"

"No, Mom, I don't." I suppressed a snort, knowing the direction this discussion was taking.

"You didn't tell us a single word!"

"I know, and I'm sorry. I wish you had found out under different circumstances, but now the cat's out of the bag."

"You can say that again!"

I could hear a cork popping out of a bottle in the background.

"Isn't it a little early for wine?"

"After the news? Actually, we all need stronger things to digest the shock."

Oh dear, I hope my mom wasn't as resentful this time as she had been when I had let her arranged date with the Sandersons' son fall through, along with all her wedding dreams. She hadn't spoken to me in months, and the Sandersons never even looked at me again. Well, my departure hadn't exactly been glorious, but I just couldn't do anything with these sports-is-my-life sunny boys. I was more of a Netflix, pizza, and ice cream girl.

Whereby ... Caden had struck strings in me that still resonated and that I had never been aware of before. I had never been shy, but I liked my submissive side, which Caden always lured out of me.

"I'm no longer the pitiful big sister who shows up lonely and alone at Maggy's wedding – that makes up for everything, right?"

My mom faltered for a moment.

"I never said it like that, Aurora."

"But you meant it," I said bitterly. "Aren't you even happy for me?"

"Oh, Aurora. Of course we're happy! But now? So close to Magnolia's wedding..."

I grabbed my forehead. Was she serious?

"Mom."

"Caden Saint is a powerful man in New York!"

"So what?"

"It's Magnolia and Ben's big day."

I sent a silent prayer to heaven that my dad would take the phone to protect me from my mother. He would certainly have done the same if he had been at home. But a glance at the clock made me realize that he was in the workshop right now.

What I would give for gasoline fumes and welding torch sparks right now!

"It will continue to be Maggy's day. Caden is not going to steal anyone's thunder, why should he? He's my plus one, a regular guest, nothing more."

"That's easy for you to say, Aurora! You'll still be the talk of the evening!"

Was there any way at all, in my mother's eyes, that I didn't stand out?

"Really, Mom, first you're on my case about not showing up alone, and now that I'm showing up with company, it's wrong again?"

I was close to tears. When was this damn wedding finally over? I wanted my old mom back!

My mother was silent, but I could hear her pouring herself some wine in the background.

"Mom, listen to me. Yes, it's spontaneous and yes, maybe a little shock. But I'm happy, okay? For the first time in a long time, I feel like I'm where I want to be. And if it makes you feel any better, I'm going to stay here in New York until Maggy's wedding is over."

Of course I wanted to accompany my sister on the happiest day of her life, but if that was the only way to save my mother from the greatest madness, I was willing to forgo my presence.

"Oh, sweetie. Of course I want you to come! We miss you. Sorry, it's just all been so overwhelming that I haven't really had a chance to think about it."

Finally, my semi-normal mom was back on the phone!

"I miss you guys, too." That was true, except I missed the madness that had crept into our home very little. At least everything was good between us again.

"Oh, God!" I groaned and immediately turned to face Caden, whose glass front was transparent again. Judging by his grin, he knew full well that the plug was suddenly vibrating. Not only was Caden watching me, but Janice and a secretary who had just packed a stack of files onto Janice's desk looked up at me. Ashamed, I tried to hide my face behind my smartphone, in vain.

"What is it?" my mom asked.

"Oh, I was just wondering if Dad and Maggy knew yet?" I stammered.

"No, Aurora. You were the very first person I called," my mom answered in an innocent voice.

"Good, then I'll call Maggy right away. And then Dad after that."

"You do that, sweetie."

"See you, Mom."

I breathed a sigh of relief when our conversation was over. Yes, it could have gone better, but on the whole, it was going quite well. Before dialing Maggy's number, I glanced briefly at Janice, who looked at me disapprovingly. I don't know if I could salvage anything regarding this relationship, but I was sure that five more minutes wouldn't make much difference.

Surprisingly, my sister picked up right after the first ring.

"Hello?"

"Hey Maggy, it's me."

"Aurora, what a surprise!"

I had to grin because Maggy was the worst liar in the world.

"Mom told you everything, didn't she?"

"What do you mean?" she asked in the same innocent tone of voice that my mother was good at.

"I'm engaged."

"Whaaat? Wow, how surprising!"

"Maggy."

"Yeah, okay. I just got off the phone with Mom."

"Thank you."

"It's still surprising," Maggy defended herself.

"You can say that again. It all happened pretty fast."

"And how was the proposal? Was it romantic? What happened?"

Unlike my mom, who was still fixated on Maggy's wedding, my sister asked me the questions I had wanted, even though I couldn't answer anything.

"It was very romantic. Caden is great, you'll love him."

"I can't wait to meet him."

When I realized that Maggy still wanted me at her wedding, it was a huge weight off my mind.

"How did you guys actually meet? And how long has there been something going on? Did you go back to New York for him? God, Aurora, I feel like we haven't spoken in years, and you've only been in New York for a few days!"

My little sister continued to bombard me with questions to which I had no answer.

"We met thanks to Max, and we clicked right away."

"How romantic!"

"Totally," I squealed joyfully. Secretly, I wished I could see my engagement through Maggy's eyes. She had no idea how unromantic the pantry proposal really was in a hurry.

"Say, Maggy. Does Dad know yet?"

"Yeah, but he'll pretend he doesn't know anything when he calls you later. He's got a pretty important job in the shop right now."

"Will he be as *convincingly* surprised as you?" I asked with a grin.

"You know how laid-back Dad is about these things. As long as you're happy, he's behind all your decisions."

"You're right."

When I could no longer escape Janice's annoyed gaze, I sighed softly.

"Maggy, I have to go, work is calling."

"All right, we'll talk more on the phone tonight, I have to go now too."

When I stopped, the vibration rhythm of my plug also changed, which I almost forgot due to all the tension.

By the time I arrived at Janice's table, I had little thought for anything but my pulsating lust.

"Hey Janice. I know we didn't get off to a good start, but I'd be happy to ... "

"Sit down, there's a lot to talk about," Janice growled, making a clear statement about how the course of our collegial gathering was going to continue.

"I'm really sorry. If you want your job back, I can talk to Caden, and he'll just give me another post."

Janice waved it off, brushing her curly hair that cut through the air like whips.

"I know the moods of Caden, I mean Mr. Saint, pretty well. I'm sure he'll come to his senses soon."

Janice tried not to let it show, but it had really hurt her that Caden had stood her up. I wondered what had happened between the two of them, but I didn't want to rub salt in the wound, so I kept my mouth shut and let my new job be explained to me.

I had a hard time concentrating because Caden kept me on my toes. Again and again I caught myself looking into his office. Every single time, he returned my gaze with a grin. I wonder if Janice realized what we were doing. I don't know, but it was so exciting, so good, that it almost felt forbidden. Stupidly, though, it also made it hard for me to follow Janice's listlessly rattled off instructions. Of course, there was no time to answer my questions, but only for little teasing, until I interrupted her.

"I know you're upset because you're being transferred to another department, but that's no reason to be so hostile to me."

"It's okay, Alexa, I'll get over it."

"Aurora. My name is Aurora."

"Whatever."

She was just taking a breath to switch back into her lecture mode, but I wasn't going to let her get away with that, because I wasn't the problem!

"If you don't like Aurora, then Miss Winter or in the near future, Mrs. Saint."

Yes, it sucked to play the *Caden-saint-is-my-fiancé card*, but Janice had it coming. I had tried long enough to make sure there was no bad blood between us, while Janice continued to sharpen the knives.

"What music does Mr. Saint like to listen to?"

Janice had caught me cold with this question.

"What does that have to do with our work?" I asked a counter question.

"During work he prefers rock music, but in the evening he also takes his evening companions out to the opera."

"And then?" I asked pointedly, even though I had long since known what Janice was trying to make clear to me. I had to swallow this bitter pill, because she was right. I knew nothing about Caden.

"What's his favorite food?" asked Janice, continuing to pick at the open wound she had discovered. Stunned, I stared Janice straight in her beastly, ice-cold eyes.

"What's your point, Janice?"

"From the looks of it, you know absolutely nothing about your fiancé."

"I know he asked me to marry him, and I know I said yes. I know Caden has special preferences that I share with him. And I know that Caden's face is the first thing I see when I wake up."

"You sleep in the same bed?"

"Of course we sleep in the same bed," I replied, frowning. Hadn't he done that with his last subs? In any case, the plug that vibrated inside me was proof that he had already broken one of his rules for me by continuing our game of dominance and submission in the boss bed.

"It also doesn't change the fact that he will soon lose interest in you. I've seen women come and go, *Aurora*, you won't be the last."

"I may not be able to list all of Caden's favorite foods, but I know he's not a fan of reheated food."

Janice's jaw dropped as I secretly celebrated my victory.

Before she could gather herself and counterattack, the small, integrated intercom on the table rushed.

"Aurora, in my office, please."

At the same time, the intensity of my butt plug tripled.

Wow. Caden really knew how to get my attention.

Smiling, I pressed the little red button in front of the speaker box.

"I'm already on my way, Caden," I replied sugary sweet.

Then I turned my back on Janice and hoped that our situation would calm down soon, otherwise this was going to be a pretty long first day of work.

Chapter 12 – Caden

I was supposed to be working, but I was having way too much fun with this little remote that I could drive Aurora crazy with. There was no more beautiful sight than her face when the vibration changed.

In the past, it would never have occurred to me to play with my subs at work, but with Aurora I had had no choice. Her attraction was far too strong and my longing for her sensual moans far too great to do without.

Aurora tried not to let on, but I knew exactly what was going on behind her pretty face as she let Janice explain what her duties were.

Was I wrong, or did Aurora seem a little bored about her tasks?

I can change that, darling.

Now we found out together how much power was in the little plug. At some point, her sweet little ass was due, but I had to hold back, until she herself begged me to finally fuck her.

My mailbox was overflowing, but while I half-heartedly worked through my priority list, I only had eyes for my fiancée. My engineers were having trouble with the final prototype, but I preferred to keep busy with the little remote in my hand while I made a few quick phone calls here and there that I had been putting off.

Actually, I had planned to drive Aurora crazy all day to fuck her in my playroom in the evening, but I couldn't wait any longer, so I called her into my office.

"What's up?" asked Aurora between doorways.

"Come in and close the door behind you," I beckoned her to me.

"That sounds pretty serious."

"I would say that's a normal working environment."

Aurora frowned. "And part of that work environment is you reminding me all the time that I'm yours?"

I smiled with satisfaction. "Yes."

"Then you should probably expect me to make quite a few mistakes."

"Good, then I can punish each one of them."

"I didn't mean it that way, Caden."

"I know." I winked at Aurora, who gave me a shy smile. "How's your first day at work so far?"

Aurora snorted softly and her smile disappeared. "Honestly, I was expecting a little more variety."

"So you found this morning boring? I can change that."

Grinning, I stood up and casually leaned against the edge of my desk. At the same time, I pulled my remote out of my pocket and Aurora groaned softly.

"Jesus, how many steps does this thing have?"

"I don't know," I replied, shrugging my shoulders. "But if you're still bored, we can find out."

"You know very well it wasn't related to *that*, Caden!" Aurora looked at me almost reproachfully.

"Then you'd better watch your choice of words."

Aurora should know by now that I would use anything she said against her when it suited. That was part of the game whose rules I had broken more often than I would have liked because of Aurora.

"I thought I would see more practical things." Aurora looked at me expectantly. "Was that clearer?"

"It was," I replied, nodding.

"But?"

"There's no but coming."

"But something has to come, right?"

"No." My answer seemed to irritate Aurora. "What were you hoping for?"

Aurora puffed out her cheeks. "Of course there's more to New York's most innovative tech company than paperwork and phone calls – that's what I wanted to hear."

"I'm the boss of this store, Aurora. I have more important things to take care of."

Without admitting it, I was damn glad I didn't have to go to the engineers or the production facilities very often. Every single visit cost me more energy than I actually had, because with every second I spent there, I fed my anger. Every damn success reminded me of my failure. And the more I wanted to forget my mistakes, the more present they felt. The more control I wanted to keep over the situation, the easier it slipped away ... and I could never let that happen again.

"Caden?" Aurora snapped me out of my thoughts.

"Sorry, what?"

"I asked you if I wasn't distracting you too much from your work."

"What makes you think that?"

Because every time I looked towards you, you were watching me."

"I just like watching my fiancée," I replied.

"I like it when you look at me like that," Aurora admitted shyly.

"Then you'll be happy to know that I'll be looking at you like this every day from now on."

"Sounds good to me." Aurora smiled contentedly, then walked to the window and let her eyes wander over the skyline and the cloudless summer sky beyond.

"It must feel great to know all you've accomplished, right?"

I nodded. "Yes." But the triumph was only a band-aid, sparsely covering my gaping wound.

"Can you describe the feeling to me?"

I hated Aurora for asking me these questions, but I couldn't really blame her because almost no one knew about my past.

"It's hard to describe."

Aurora bit her lips thoughtfully. "I wish I had clear goals like you, Caden."

For the first time, Aurora looked lost, almost as if her soul was drifting on a fishing boat through the choppy, night-black ocean.

"Don't you have any goals? Not one?"

"No. I never got past the undergraduate level."

"You're still young, Aurora." I stroked her cheek. "Besides, I don't think you have any goals at all. Everyone needs goals of some sort, no matter how boring or irrelevant they are. It's in our nature as humans to want to achieve something."

Aurora shrugged her shoulders. I decided to turn the vibrator up one more notch to motivate Aurora to think.

"Either I get an answer, or you're going to spend the rest of the day on the highest vibration setting."

"You're a monster!" gasped Aurora. She leaned her head back and tried to take a deep breath. "I can barely think straight!"

"I don't expect much just a single goal that you want to achieve."

You could see Aurora's grey cells working as she got closer and closer to her orgasm.

"I'm still waiting," I murmured, holding up the remote. I don't know how many levels the thing had left, but there couldn't be many. So I had to be more careful with my threats, or I would run out of arguments.

"I want to survive Maggy's wedding somehow," Aurora gasped.

I grinned. "There you go, that's a start. And from the looks of it, we'll survive your sister's wedding together."

"Yeah. Ironically, my mom isn't too excited about me taking you."

"Oh yeah?" I looked at Aurora with interest. Not that I was a model son-in-law, but Aurora's choice could definitely have been worse.

"Yes. She doesn't think I'm in the spotlight now because of my loneliness, she thinks I'm in your shadow."

Aurora's soft sigh made me smile.

"That's not funny, Caden! You have to be a gentleman, but not too much. And you have to smile, but not too charmingly. We have to dance, flawlessly, but not perfectly. You and me at Maggy's wedding, it's like hitting a pot in a minefield. It's going to blow up in our faces, definitely."

"Like *hitting pots on a minefield*? I like the comparison."

Aurora looked silently at the floor, but I lifted her chin with the tip of my thumb.

"I will be a gentleman, but not too much. I will smile, but not too charmingly. And we will dance flawlessly, but imperfectly. I promise."

"Thank you, Caden."

The wedding seemed to really get Aurora down, although there was no reason for it in my opinion. Aurora was gorgeous. Period. It's a shame her mom gave her such a hard time.

"Are you feeling better?"

"Much better," Aurora replied with relief.

"Then tell me what other goals you have?"

"Stay out of Janice's way starting tomorrow."

"After tomorrow, you'll barely get to see them, the PR department hardly ever comes around."

"I'm sure Janice will find reasons, and if not her, then your PR director."

I narrowed my eyes and looked at Aurora sharply. "Do I see jealousy in your eyes?"

Aurora averted her eyes from me. "No!"

"Look at me!" I ordered calmly. Aurora reluctantly obeyed me.

"Are you jealous?"

"Maybe a little."

"You're my girl, Aurora. You, not Janice. I promised you that you'd be my only girl, and I'm a man of my word."

"How long will I be your girl?"

Although Aurora struggled to keep her voice firm, it grew fainter toward the end of her sentence. I wish I had an answer to her question, but I didn't.

"What makes you think Erica will sic Janice on me anyway?"

"Because they were talking about it in whispers earlier. I didn't understand everything, but enough, I think."

Aurora was playing around with the hem of her modest skirt, which I would love to rip off her body. Not only because it covered Aurora's beautiful curves, but also because I had been feeling this urge to spank her all morning. Not because she had done anything wrong, but because she did everything. But that would have to wait. It was more important now to find out what the PR department was up to. That the noose was tightening around my neck, despite my engagement, was inevitable. Still, I was confident that I could pull my head out of the noose if I was two steps ahead of PR.

"What exactly did you hear when you overheard Janice?"

"Erica really wants you to look at her strategy again."

"She can forget it," I growled. "And if she starts that again, I'll have her fired."

I would have liked to smash my entire office to pieces with an axe. I hated Erica for being such a good journalist. She had dug much deeper than anyone else that she had actually found some of my bodies in the basement. No matter how deep the holes I dug, the demons I buried there always came to light.

"Wow, a clear statement," Aurora muttered. "What's so bad about their strategy?"

"It doesn't matter," I waved it off. "I'm just against their strategy."

"If you don't tell me, I'll just ask Erica."

"She's not going to tell you anything, though."

"How can you be so sure?"

"Because she signed a confidentiality agreement forbidding her to talk about it."

Aurora turned pale. "Erica too?"

"God forbid, no! Not such a contract, yet she has to keep quiet about some things."

Erica wasn't bad looking and she was from a good home, but I had never seen the potential in her as my sub. Probably because she could be as stubborn as a donkey and as prickly as a hungry cat.

"That sounds pretty mysterious."

"Let's not talk any more about my past."

I made it unmistakably clear to Aurora that I was not ready to talk about it. And I probably never would be.

"Let's talk about your future instead. The fact is that you're my big PR solution. You're going to create a new stock market boom and quite a bit of hype."

"Me?" Aurora's cheeks reddened. "I didn't realize there was so much responsibility on my shoulders."

"So it is, as a future Mrs. Saint." I smiled at her. "And so far, you're playing your part pretty well."

"Actually, I don't like to be squeezed into any roles, but I have to admit, I feel pretty comfortable in this one."

"Good, because you're going to have to play her for quite a while," I said with a smile. Not only because it was already clear that our engagement was making big waves, but also because Aurora brought quite a bit of variety into my life.

"I thought of another goal that I could implement right now, provided I get full support from you, Mr. Saint." Aurora walked seductively towards me, adjusted my shirt collar and looked deep into my eyes.

"I'm all ears. How can I be of assistance, Miss Winter?"

"I want an orgasm."

Touché. What a clever move.

"You want an orgasm? Here? Now?"

"Yes," Aurora replied sensually.

"Earlier, you had your reservations."

"Earlier, I didn't know about your convincing punishments either."

I grinned. Normally I never let my subs tell me anything, but I just had to appreciate Aurora's cunning idea.

"Fine, fine by me. But it's going to cost you."

"What?"

"I don't know yet." I reared up in front of Aurora and forced her to walk backwards until she stumbled into my office chair behind her.

"But eventually you'll have to pay for my concession. Maybe a look will do it. Possibly a seductive kiss. Or else a rather long night in my playroom."

Aurora sighed softly as she continued to look me in the eye.

"This game is pretty unfair."

"I know. I made the rules. But more importantly, you agreed to them." I took another step toward Aurora. The difference in height as she sat in front of me was remarkable and I could barely contain my excitement. She had the perfect height to give me silly thoughts.

"Of course, you could wait until tonight. Or until tomorrow. Who knows when I'll fuck you next and allow you to have an orgasm," I purred into Aurora's ear in a soft, understanding voice. She made no secret of the fact that the contrast of my threat with that empathetic tone infuriated her. There was no mistaking the fire in her eyes. The sparks jumped to me even before Aurora answered.

"Okay, fine with me!" blurted out Aurora. "Please, can I have my orgasm?"

I nodded with satisfaction. "If you ask so sweetly, I will grant your wish."

"I never thought I would beg for anything."

"Is it really about begging? Or more about being amazed at how well you like it?"

"Both," Aurora confessed, her cheeks flushed.

With a button, the glass walls turned white again and I got down on my knees in front of Aurora.

"What are you doing?" asked Aurora, confused.

"Provide an orgasm or two," I replied.

"Oh." Aurora almost sounded disappointed. Admittedly, my erection felt cheated too, but if I was going to get anything sensible done today, I needed to back off.

"Trust me, Aurora, you're about to beg for more."

I pushed her terrible skirt out of my sight, spread Aurora's legs and pulled her so close to me that I had a perfect view of her most feminine part. Except for a narrow strip on her mons veneris, Aurora was clean-shaven.

Madness, what a perfect view! And I wasn't talking about the skyline that was in front of us.

"You should sit back and enjoy," I said.

Aurora obeyed me and when my tongue licked over the tender skin of her Venus mound, she moaned softly. The deeper my tongue felt its way down with circular movements, the louder she became.

I knew exactly how to drive Aurora crazy, so I wasted no time and licked over her pearl again and again. Each time a little slower and harder.

"Oh, wow!" gasped Aurora as she buried her hands in my hair.

Although she had not known what to make of it at first, she was now wild for more. Good, because I could not get enough of Aurora's delicious taste. Her whole body stretched out towards me, I felt her muscles tense and felt the heat rise in her body.

Just as I was about to allow her to come, the phone rang.

"Answer it," I murmured. Then I devoted myself again to her sensitive pearl.

"What?"

"You heard me."

Damn, I loved the way her body fought the approaching orgasm I was conjuring up.

With trembling hands, Aurora picked up the phone.

"Yes?" She cleared her throat briefly. "This is Mr. Saint's personal assistant."

She paused for a moment. "Mr. Saint is not available right now."

It amused me how Aurora struggled to be professional, so I penetrated her with one finger and massaged her G-spot to elicit another moan.

"Mr. Saint is really busy!" gasped Aurora.

"Who is it?" I asked half-heartedly, because I had my head – literally – somewhere else.

Aurora cocked her head to the side and held her hand on the phone's mouthpiece. "A Mister Coleman from the development department."

Fuck. "What does he want?"

Aurora forwarded my question, nodded, suppressed another groan, and then turned back to me. "There's a problem with the prototype. He thinks it's a bug in the programming, but if you ask me..."

I interrupted Aurora annoyed because Coleman had been calling with nothing but bad news for weeks.

"Tell him to get here in ten minutes. We'll deal with each other for that long."

Aurora looked at me conspiratorially. "Mr. Saint is expecting you in his office in fifteen minutes."

What an outrageous little girl.

"Can't or won't you implement the simplest commands?"

"I want more time with you," Aurora replied in a firm voice, almost demanding. Really no sub had ever spoken to me like that before. Refreshing.

"All right, you win," I growled. But I withheld from Aurora that the price she had to pay was higher than she thought. She got what she wanted – and I got a chance at another lesson. Sometimes wishes were something very dangerous.

When I turned my attention back to Aurora's womanhood, I moaned softly. She was so fucking tight, even without the plug, which was still vibrating at one of the highest levels. I put my foot down and it didn't take a minute for Aurora to have her orgasm. But instead of letting go of her, I just kept going ... and going ... and going. Aurora smiled seductively at me, her eyes full of gratitude as she came a second time. But after the third orgasm she understood what I was up to.

"Caden, please!"

"Please what? You wanted to spend more time with me, and I am kind enough to grant it to you. So you're getting exactly what you want. Or are you going to disagree with me?"

"No, sir." Aurora gritted her teeth and braced herself for her fourth orgasm. Her whole body pulsated when she came, and I couldn't get enough of the sight.

I took full advantage of every minute I had left to demonstrate to Aurora how much power I had over her. One minute before Coleman would come here, I let go of Aurora.

"I hope you understood the lesson?"

"Yes, sir, more than clear," Aurora replied, breathing heavily.

"Good, then there would be just one more thing to do."

I grabbed Aurora by the shoulders and bent her over the desk to pull the plug out of her. Aurora's looks, every time the level or rhythm had varied, were worth their weight in gold, but this butt plug was going to remain special.

Aurora smoothed out her skirt.

"It's a pretty memorable first day on the job."

Grinning, I noted her assessment.

"Then you should be excited about the second one right now."

"Really?" Aurora looked at me, stunned.

"A little joke. You should be a pretty good girl tomorrow so I can get to work."

"I promise, sir!"

"Good." I winked at Aurora. "Then you should go back to your desk now and listen carefully to Janice."

"I'll be double-observant. If I give the wrong answer, or take my eyes off her, will I have a knife stuck in my back?"

"I can reassure you, my health insurance also covers *company accidents.*"

Aurora looked at me in horror but couldn't quite hide a grin. "Caden! That's not what I wanted to hear."

"And I wanted to hear from my engineer that our prototype was finally working."

Thoughtfully, Aurora bit her lips. "I wonder if I could see the plans? I know he thinks it's a problem in the software, but everything I've witnessed so far suggests it's not that at all."

I squinted my eyes. "Don't worry your pretty head about it, Aurora. Leave the problems to the professionals, they're paid to solve them, after all."

"I was just trying to help." Admittedly, I didn't understand Aurora's disappointment; after all, I was running a pragmatic, innovative company, not a *make-a-wish* concert where everyone threw their ideas into a big hat, and one was pulled out by the board.

"I know. Just hang in there today, and we'll be rid of Janice, and you can fully focus on your real work."

"Well, I'll be going," Aurora said, pointing to the door and turning around. But judging by her look, there was still something on the tip of her tongue.

"Out with it!" I demanded unmistakably.

"I know you're not as heartless as you often pretend to be. And I hope to see the Caden that hides behind his heartlessness more often."

"What do you mean?"

Her honesty had caught me off guard – which shocked me, because no one had been able to do that for years.

"No, it doesn't matter. Forget what I said, it's not my place," Aurora said, waving me off and leaving my office.

No, it didn't matter? On the contrary, it mattered to me – and that's what scared me.

What the hell just happened?

Chapter 13 – Aurora

I slowly pirouetted in front of the huge mirror so I could examine myself in the dress. I was wearing three thousand dollars' worth of fabric right now. Maybe that was the main reason why I didn't feel very comfortable in the beige outfit.

"What do you think?" I asked, looking at Maxine, who was eyeing me critically.

"Too staid."

"Max!" I chastised my best friend with a reprimanding look. "Stop teasing me about it."

Maxine grinned at me. "I told you from the beginning that you should wear a different outfit that shows off your curves more."

"Yeah, you're my best friend. You're allowed to say things like that. But Caden, he's ... " Well, what was Caden exactly? "He wasn't supposed to say something like that."

Max shrugged her shoulders. "Sorry, but this time I'm on Caden's side."

She walked over to the mobile clothing rack and pulled out a red dress that was hanging among other dresses I wanted – or was supposed to – try on.

"Try this one."

Although I trusted her – and the saleswoman at the boutique, who had withdrawn – I was skeptical. After all, this was not a summer dress, but an outfit that was supposed to represent Caden's company.

"I'm his personal assistant, not his prostitute."

"You're also his fiancée, sort of. Trust me, I know this kind of fashion."

Nodding, I accepted the red dress and changed. Of course I loved going shopping with Max, but the reason still frustrated me. I wanted to look presentable, professional so I wouldn't embarrass my fiancé-to-be, but he had only made fun of me. Frustrated, I blew a blonde strand out of my face.

"So, how does it look?" asked Maxine curiously.

"Hold on." After a brief struggle between my hair and the zipper, I opened the curtain of the dressing room, which was more like a *giant dressing room tent* with fairy lights and the scent of roses. "Ta-Dah."

"Wow. That's it. We'll definitely take that!"

Maxine nodded with satisfaction and was so excited that I was afraid she would rip the dress off me so she could rush to the cash register with it.

"You think so?"

"Is Heath Ledger the best Joker ever?"

I frowned. "Um ... "

"But of course!" Maxine helped me up. "He was, is – and will forever be – the best wild card. The end."

"Okay?" It was more of a question than an answer, but my best friend didn't let that stop her.

"Anyway, this dress is perfect. It's professional, classy and you have a hell of a body in it."

I had to agree with that. This dress was made of soft red fabric and although it was high cut, I had perfect curves in it. The hem of the dress reached just above my knees, so I didn't sweat even on those hot summer days. Unlike its beige predecessor, I felt like a million bucks.

"Tell me more," I replied with a grin, lolling in front of the mirror like a top model.

"Don't have to, but Caden – Sex God – Saint will definitely have a lot to say to you."

"Max!"

"What?" she asked innocently. "Isn't he – as you quoted, *one of the hottest men in the universe?* End quote – Aurora Winters, ten minutes ago."

Admittedly, when I talked to Max about Caden, I couldn't stop raving. He was a gentleman and yet so ... wild and unpredictable that my stomach fluttered. But then there was this other, heartless side that I couldn't quite place and that, whether I wanted to admit it or not, scared me.

"Yeah, okay. He's Mister Universe."

"Sounds like a *but*."

"Never mind." I waved it off, grabbed the next dress and disappeared behind the curtain again.

"You're not getting away from me that easily!" threatened Maxine, shamelessly opening the curtain while I covered my body in a makeshift manner. "What's that *but*? And I don't want a *but that's not Heath Ledger*, it's a real *but*, got it?"

"Not until you pull the curtain back!"

"Okay, okay."

"And you take three steps back," I continued to demand, so she couldn't pull the curtain open right away.

"Since when did you become so demanding?"

"Since you're so shameless."

We both giggled as I peeled out of the red dress and traded it for a light blue silk dress. It was beautiful, but looking at the price made me dizzy. Four thousand dollars! During my undergraduate studies in college, I had worked for more than three months for that much money, including overtime and night shifts.

"Well, Caden is ... " I began, then faltered. "It's ... "

Sighing, I opened the curtain and leaned forward conspiratorially to Maxine.

"Max, I can't talk about it here. I don't want anyone to hear me."

"No problem." Confident as Maxine was, she pushed me backwards and closed the curtains behind us.

Bummer. Actually, I had wanted to stall for time by suggesting we continue our conversation in our limo, but I had underestimated Maxine's pragmatism.

"Wow, real campfire atmosphere here," Max said as her gaze followed the strings of lights along the wall behind me.

"Totally," I replied, trying to smile away my defeat.

"Back on topic!"

"Oh yes, please." I made no secret of the fact that I didn't want to talk about it, but Maxine was like a bloodhound. Once she got a scent, she didn't give up until she snatched her prey – in this case, inside news from Caden Saints and my love life.

"So, out with it. What is Mister Universe hiding from the public?"

Frankly, I was glad that Caden's contract forbade me to talk about our love life, but this secret did not stand between us, on the contrary, it brought us closer. There was something else that gave me a headache.

"Is he not a gentleman?" whispered Maxine, trying to do more justice to the campfire atmosphere.

"Sure. He can be very charming," I defended Caden. "But sometimes he's pretty tactless, too."

"I see, so we're getting closer." Maxine nodded with satisfaction. "And you wonder which side of the coin he actually is?"

"He's both sides. I just don't know which one comes out more often." I sighed. "I'm afraid of him dropping me just as heartlessly as..." I almost said *my predecessor*, but at the last moment my tongue had understood what my brain wanted to kick off. "Like his last personal assistant."

Maxine shrugged her shoulders uncomprehendingly.

"He's the boss, it's nothing new for a boss to look for new staff. I change companies all the time too, no big deal."

"They were very close, Maxine. So really, really close. And now he's saying goodbye with a gift basket that I am to get for her."

"Ouch. A gift basket is really bad."

"I said the same thing!"

Because Maxine made no effort to leave the dressing room again, but we still had a few stores to visit on our tour, I continued to change.

"I'm afraid he's going to send me packing with a gift basket, too," I confessed as I surveyed the blue dress on me.

"No shit. He got down on his knees in front of you - nobody does that on a whim if there were gift baskets in the room."

But normal people didn't sign a contract that obligated them to remain silent. Would my best friend still think that way if she knew the rest?

"What if it was? If it was a spontaneous decision?"

"Spontaneous decisions are often the best. Trust me, if you knew how little I plan in my work, you'd be curled up on the floor crying."

I nudged Maxine against the shoulder. "You can hardly compare my engagement to a change of scenery."

My best friend burst out laughing.

"Isn't that exactly what just happened to you?"

Well, she was right ... New York was a change of scenery. Caden was an even bigger change of scenery. And the playroom? He tore down the entire wall and pulled it up again!

When Max looked at me expectantly, I rolled my eyes. "Yeah, you're right."

"And now loud enough that I can actually understand what you said."

"You're right! If you want, I'll have it printed on a mug for you, okay?"

"I insist!"

After we agreed with glances that the blue dress was a definite *no,* I threw on an emerald-green dress that looked better on me. I smoothed out the wrinkles and tilted my head.

"Hot piece," Maxine said, impressed.

"I think it's magical, too." Although I expressed myself more selectively, Max had nailed it. The simple cuts were elegant and accentuated my shiny blonde hair.

"Bought!" said Maxine in a serious tone.

"And what about the price?"

Max waved it off. "Don't worry about it. Mister Universe is paying."

"Money is money," I replied.

"The price is worth it, Aurora. You look fabulous. And when I say that Caden Saint is making more money in the second than you'll ever spend, that's not an exaggeration."

Maxine was right, yet I felt I could do better with the money than go shopping. Somehow I had to calm my guilty conscience.

Next, I decided on a dark gray skirt that I liked right away.

"Wow, I never thought this outfit would look so good," Maxine said with surprise.

"What, because it looked so staid?"

"That's exactly why!"

I shrugged my shoulders. The black, high-necked skirt was tight on me and emphasized my curves. I did without the blazer of the same color, because a thin white blouse for the summer months was already enough to shrink in poorly air-conditioned rooms, like a houseplant in student dormitories.

As I was changing, Maxine swooped down like a vulture on the dark gray skirt, dashed out of the dressing room, and shouted to the saleswoman, "That skirt again in size five!"

Then she ignored my privacy one more time to continue our campfire conversation.

The next dress I put on also fit pretty well.

"Couldn't you have told me earlier that stores like this *always have* the right clothes?" No matter how long I looked in normal malls, there was always too much fabric somewhere that was missing in other places.

"Told you, but you never wanted to come."

"Yes, because those stores were always too expensive for me."

"I would have paid for them after all, Aurora."

I shook my head significantly.

"You're my best friend, not my piggy bank."

Maxine sighed. "You really are a great best friend. And that includes letting your best friend buy you a drink once in a while."

"I'll keep that in mind, okay?" I replied with a grin. Fortunately, however, I no longer had to take up this offer, because now I could shop with my own, because I worked for this money quite legitimately.

Thoughtfully, I blew a blond strand out of my face.

"What is it?" asked Max, noticing my change in mood.

"Do you think Caden thinks I'm stupid?"

"What? No!"

"What makes you so sure?"

Maxine crossed her arms in front of her chest.

"What is thirty-seven times twelve."

Although her question irritated me, my brain could not help but settle the score in my head.

"Four hundred and forty-four. Why?"

"No normal person can work out such calculations in their head!"

"Yes, you do!" I defended. "You just have to ... "

Max raised his hand. "Spare me the math lesson, Aurora. But what was the name of the capital of Malaysia?"

"Kuala Lumpur. What's with the questions?"

"And how do you spell desox ... deoxi ... um. You know, DNA spelled out."

"Deoxyribonucleic acid?"

"Yes!"

"D-E-S—" I began to spell until I shook my head in bewilderment. "What is this?"

"Well what do you think? Proving to you that you didn't fall on your head and that Caden certainly doesn't think you're stupid. What makes you think that?"

"Because there's a problem with one of the prototypes, but Caden wasn't interested in my proposed solution." I looked to the floor in frustration. "He just cut me off, saying he had experts in that sort of thing."

"Okay." Maxine looked at me conspiratorially, and if I didn't know better, I'd say her eyes were flirting with me. "Then you should make sure Mr. Universe has nothing left to listen to but Mrs. Universe."

She pulled from the packed clothes cart a two-piece lingerie that I was seeing for the first time.

"Max!"

"What? Now that your slumber is surely over, you should be armed."

At first I thought Maxine's suggestion was terrible, but the longer I thought about it, the better the idea seemed. I took the hanger from her and held the two-piece set in front of my body. The black ornaments on red fabric looked classy and seductive. On the sides there were black wide ribbons that didn't leave much room for imagination.

Nodding, I put the hanger on the *buy-me* pile and got dressed again.

"Thank you," I finally said.

"Oh, not for that," Maxine replied, waving it off.

"You know what for."

"Actually, I was just teasing you about it, but it's nice that it's now becoming a valuable contribution to emancipation."

Giggling, we left the store, where I bought a handbag for Janice in addition to my haul. Of course, we wouldn't become best friends, but I thought it was more appropriate than leaving her a gift basket that she would throw away anyway. Maybe it wasn't about her at all, but just my guilty conscience and fear that Caden could dump me the same way. Maxine would catch me no matter what, but maybe Janice had no one to prevent her fall.

"Let's go to Little Italy!" exclaimed Maxine excitedly. "Trust me, you're going to love Brando Bertani! He'll make you the perfect bridesmaid dress, I promise!"

Yesterday I had been unable to think of anything but Maggy's wedding drama, but now all my thoughts were about Caden, me, and the lingerie I could use to convince him that I was more than just a number, an assistant, or a sub.

I am Aurora Winter. Best friend. Model sister. Messy daughter. And fiancée of Caden Saint!

Chapter 14 – Aurora

Thoughtfully, I stared at my screen, feverishly searching for a solution as I tried to get through this awful day. No, that wasn't quite right, basically I was still looking for the stupid problem! The records of Caden's prototypes that were available to me were not enough to put me clearly in the picture. Stupidly, however, the important data was under lock and key. In the case of industrial espionage, surely appropriate, but in my case nevertheless very hindering.

The fact that Caden didn't take me seriously only spurred me on all the more to solve his problem. I didn't have a master's degree in engineering, but I'd been wrenching on cars with my dad since I could hold wrenches, even if it didn't show at first – and second – glance. Unlike Dad, I had never felt the need to talk about engines, hydraulic and brake hoses, or horsepower all day. Yes, Caden's prototypes weren't cars, but from everything I saw, there was nothing to suggest they were rocket science.

When a pile of files slammed down on my desk, I startled.

"This all still needs to be worked through," Janice said in an icy tone.

"You got it," I replied. Discussing it was useless, because Janice had already been bombarding me with unimportant files all morning to keep me away from Caden. Probably she should have saved the files as a trump card, because Caden had no time for me today anyway. He had been on the phone all morning.

On the whole, you could say today was a shitty day.

"I'm going to lunch now," Janice said almost disappointed at my lack of response.

"Bon appétit," I replied without looking up.

I went through the files at lightning speed so that I could get back to my main problem.

"Jesus, what am I doing?" I heard myself say out loud. Whether I wanted to admit it or not, I wanted to be remembered by Caden. I wish it could be otherwise, but as of yet, I wasn't sure I'd ever get through to Caden. We acted like our relationship was boundless, but something stood between us – his cold, uninvolved nature.

My smartphone vibrated in the top drawer. Against my better judgment, I took it out and answered Maxine's call.

"And?" she asked curiously.

"Hey Max, good to hear from you too. How am I doing? Thanks for asking, very good!"

"Good, then we've settled the formalities now and can move on to the more exciting questions!"

Grinning, I rolled my eyes.

"And what would be the exciting questions?"

"Well what do you think?" Maxine snorted loudly. "Was Caden listening to you?"

"No."

"No? Why not?"

"He was busy."

"What exactly did you do? I need details, Aurora!"

Maxine didn't seem too pleased with my pragmatic answers. I, on the other hand, just didn't want to talk about my defeat when Caden had brushed me off this morning.

"He simply didn't have the time. When I asked for the blueprints for his prototype, he made it unmistakably clear to me that my job lay elsewhere."

"Ouch."

"Oh yes, please Max, put more salt in my fresh wound."

"And this is despite your persuasive arguments?"

"If by persuasive arguments you mean real arguments? Yes. If you're talking about the underwear that leaves no room for imagination, no."

"No? You didn't show it to him? There's the problem!"

I sighed softly. "I wanted him to listen to me without getting the wrong idea or agreeing because of the wrong reasons."

"Screw the reasons when you can rub his nose in it later that you solved his problem!"

For the first time, it occurred to me that maybe I couldn't solve his problem. Saint Industries employed thousands of professionals, top students and graduates from elite universities, but I had nothing to show for it beyond my undergraduate degree and a few *wet T-shirt* trophies.

"Anyway, that issue is off the table."

"No, it isn't. Besides, he can't forbid you to talk about it."

Yes, he can.

"It's not as easy as you think."

"Giving up is out of the question, that's for sure."

I don't know why, but Maxine was on fire.

"And what do you think I should do?"

"Finding a solution."

"Wow, thanks for your advice, I never would have thought of that on my own," I said sarcastically.

"What's the problem?"

"So far, that's my biggest problem. I haven't found it yet because I lack plans!"

"Then take care of the plans."

I put my head back and wished that life was as simple as in Maxine's world view.

"They're *top secret*, I can't access them."

"Hmm, that is indeed a problem."

"Yep. And it's one that I don't have a solution for."

Slowly, I had to face the fact that I might not be able to solve Caden's prototype problem. At least I was comforted by the thought that I was saving myself another embarrassment by not being smart enough for the problem.

"So, if my people or I don't have access to the plans in the cloud, we fall back on papers. No matter what we're renovating, there's a floor plan of every house, every room and every piece of furniture on paper, just in case."

I jumped up with joy. "You are brilliant!"

"I know," Maxine replied. I could hear her grin. "So, shoo shoo with you to the appropriate department."

"You wouldn't happen to know on which floor such papers are stored."

"On the thirty-seventh floor. After the elevator, the second door on the left."

My heart stopped for a moment. "Really!?"

"No. Would have been cool to know though, right?"

"Pff." I gave vent to my frustration by exhaling loudly.

Come on Aurora, pull yourself together, I said to myself, then I dug my wireless earplugs out of the drawer.

"Hold on a second, I'm going to switch to my ear pods for a second."

"Why?"

Well, Maxine. In for a penny, in for a pound. My best friend had set out to be an accomplice.

"Because you and I are now industrial spies who will sneak access to top-secret documents without permission."

"This is so cool! I feel like a secret agent. I'm the cool hacker who confidently steers you through the supervillain's corporate building, past death gyroscopes, shark tanks, and laser selfies!"

"Let's hope Caden isn't stashing documents to achieve world domination, just his prototype stuff."

I heard Maxine laugh. "Boring! Come on, Aurora, be a little more adventurous."

Admittedly, because my long blonde hair covered the ear pods, I really felt a little like I was in an action movie.

"Okay, but we'll switch roles. I'll stay here all relaxed, pining for the incredibly handsome supervillain, while you dive through shark tanks and run away from gyroscopes of death."

I especially liked the part with the supervillain crush, because I could lose myself in Caden's wonderful brown eyes for hours.

"I'm afraid I'm indisposed. Besides, I'm just *Watchman,* your sidekick, you have to get the plans, *Towerqueen.*"

"I certainly don't use code names." How had Max been able to come up with that in such a short time?

"Then you have to expect that *Operation Save-the-Universe* is going to go mightily down the tubes."

I stood up, alibi'd a few of the files, and walked toward the elevator. When Caden briefly looked up at me, my heart gave a little jump.

"Yes, all right, I'll get the plans. But you owe me for this!"

Heavens, I really had to make sure that I was remembered by him! So it was really the mission: *to be remembered by Mr. Universe at all costs.*

Maxine bristled. "Wait a minute. Why do I owe you anything? I thought you were getting the blueprints to prove to Caden that you were smarter than dozens of engineers, mathematicians, and whatever other guys with PhDs working for him."

"You don't think I can solve the problem?"

"I never said that!"

"But?"

"Well, if you fail, it's because you got caught. You've never been good at doing forbidden things."

It had been true of me before, but what I was doing with Caden was so good that it had to be forbidden! Caden had made me a *bad girl* and damn it, I loved it!

"I can do it, don't worry." Provided I knew where to look. "By the way, I'm getting on the elevator now, keep your fingers crossed."

"Both fingers crossed!"

I got on the empty elevator and decided to wait to have a casual conversation with someone. Hopefully. In my imagination, the elevators went up and down non-stop all day. In reality, however, it was a different story.

"I have to admit that I had imagined our *save-the-world mission* to be more exciting," Max said, bored.

"Tell me about it. I've been standing in this elevator for ages."

"New plan. You call me back when something exciting happens."

I yelped. "Forget it! You put me up to it, so you have to live with the consequences!"

"But Aurora, ... "

Suddenly, the elevator started moving.

"We're going downstairs!" I exclaimed excitedly. Who would have thought that I would ever be so excited about a ride in an elevator?

When the elevator doors opened, I held my breath in anticipation. *This can't be true!*

Why, among all the hundreds of people, did I have to run into Janice? It would have been wiser to leave the elevator, but I was paralyzed. Janice seemed as unamused by my presence as I was by hers.

"What a coincidence, Janice," escaped me.

"True," she replied dryly.

Within seconds, the summer temperature dropped below freezing.

"Oh my god, Aurora! Is this the Janice I think you're talking about? A silence means *yes.*" I fell silent. "Mayday! Code Red! Abort, now!"

Maxine's request to abort the mission came too late. Janice got into the elevator, pressed the button to the PR department, and ignorantly turned her back on me.

I didn't want to, but I had to get a conversation going somehow because Janice was my best chance to get the information I needed as quickly as possible. Slowly but surely, Caden must have wondered where I was.

"Where did you go to eat?" I asked.

Maxine sighed loudly. "Are you serious, Aurora? Do you want to talk about the weather?"

I knew that myself! But I could not think of anything else.

Janice looked at me, aghast. "Where was I eating?"

"Yes."

"Since I want to continue to eat there in peace in the future, I certainly won't tell you."

My jaw dropped.

"What a beast!" said Maxine in horror. I wish she would help me over the phone with good counter-sayings, but she was as speechless as I was.

"Whatever." I tried to sort out my thoughts.

"Any other questions I'm not going to answer for you?"

Okay, not ideal, but when she offered me the chance, I took it.

"Yes. I'm supposed to take these files to the archives for the engineers."

Janice looked at me in wonder. "What kind of files? Let me see."

She reached out for them, but I clutched them tightly against my chest as if they were a shield. Under no circumstances was Janice allowed to take a look at the files she had slammed on my desk an hour ago.

"You can't! They're top secret. Caden told me to stash them in storage, but I don't know where storage is."

Janice rolled her eyes. "Do you know anything at all?"

"Yes. Namely, that Caden wouldn't be happy to learn that you weren't helping me when you were supposed to be briefing me."

I tried to look as serious as possible. Lying wasn't exactly my strong point and if my plan backfired, I would have to explain a lot to my boss.

"Sixteenth floor, ask your way through there. I'm busy and can't take you by the hand permanently."

"Thank you," I said, not knowing what else to say. Janice was a bad person. I didn't think such a thing lightly, so it made it all the more clear that Janice really was a bad person. Admittedly, I didn't think it was a bad thing that my predecessor was such a beast, because if she had been the kindest, most magical creature in the world, my guilty conscience would have eaten away at me.

The air was thick to cut until Janice in PR exited the elevator. Then I pressed the button to the sixteenth floor and leaned against the wall in relief because I had survived this ride.

"Just for the record, Max, your plan is terrible."

"No, *our* plan is still good, your work colleague is terrible! Is she really good enough at her job to make this drama worthwhile?"

"I guess so," I replied with a shrug, trying to sound as uninvolved as possible because I knew details that my best friend could never know.

The way Janice moved, she was completely aware of her body. She had certainly gained a lot of experience in the playroom, unlike me. I only had the experience that Caden had given me. I wonder if I was still enough for him, even if I knew nothing.

My stomach tightened painfully at the thought of Caden comparing me to Janice during sex.

Arriving on the sixteenth floor, I peered out of the elevator.

"I have arrived. What now?"

"You have to say that. I wish it were different, but I'm not your sidekick to guide you through the departments."

"Too bad, though."

"Good luck, Towerqueen."

"Thank you, Watchman."

"Oh my god, you used our code names, I love you Auro ... um, Towerqueen!"

"With *Operation Save-the-Universe*, I could use all the luck I can get," I whispered.

Then I walked out of the elevator as if I belonged in this department and wasn't doing anything forbidden. I was pretty much the only woman here in the room, over which an eerie silence had settled after the elevator sped away behind me.

Admittedly, I was expecting a lovingly chaotic department, with somewhat absentminded men in homespun sweaters. Instead, I found myself standing in the middle of guys wearing white coats and clipboards as they watched little metal things and kept taking notes. On the other side of the room were tables and a large, crowded whiteboard around which a few men stood, discussing wildly with each other. Of course, it wasn't supervillain headquarters, it was still a department in Saint Industries, but I was still overwhelmed.

There were dozens of doors all the way to the end of the huge complex. I had no idea where the blueprints of all the prototypes were stored, so I slowly went from door to door, hoping to find one with a suitable label.

"You're so quiet, Aurora. I'm about to burst with curiosity!"

"There's nothing to say. Besides, I don't want to seem crazy for talking to myself, okay?" My voice trembled slightly as I continued to search for the right room.

"If you look like you sound, you're making yourself super suspicious right now."

"Thank you."

I pulled my head in, trying to merge with the room.

"Tell me something to calm me down," Maxine prompted. "Otherwise, this operation is going to blow up in our faces."

Without Maxine as a mental support I would never have dared to do this action!

"I spent forty-four thousand dollars yesterday."

"What, wait, where? Did you go shopping without me again?"

I shook my head reflexively. When I realized what I was doing, I tried to cover up the gesture by running my hand through my hair.

"No, but I donated the same amount I spent on the clothes."

"Oh, Aurora, you are too good for this world!"

That was a matter of course for me. Anything else would not have been accepted by my conscience.

"So, have you found the room yet?"

"No, not yet."

"Describe to me what it looks like."

"I don't think the really cool engineering stuff is here at all."

"You mean the rockets that go to Mars?"

"Yes. Or the prototypes, which is what we're here for in the first place. If you ask me, this is where the initial designs take place."

When I finally found the warehouse for the plans, I jumped for joy until I was resigned to the fact that the door was locked and could only be opened with a key card. I had one, as did every employee in the company, but apparently, as Caden's personal assistant, I didn't have the necessary security clearance for that door.

What a bummer!

Why was I constantly chased by one problem after another?

"Watchman? I'm afraid we're going to have to abort Operation Save-the-Universe."

"No way, Towerqueen! Come on, come up with a plan!"

Maxine was right, I had come way too far to give up now, so I thought feverishly about a solution while walking to the copier on the opposite side. A woman copying files on a copier didn't look very suspicious to me. Besides, the copier was in a small alcove where I could hide perfectly. Fortunately, I had a lot of files with me, because it took quite a while before anyone even entered the room. In the meantime, I had copied, sorted, and reorganized all the files twice. Just as I was gathering up the next set of papers, a few loose sheets fell to the floor – and along with the papers, the penny dropped.

"Max, I think I have an idea!"

"Let's go then!"

I took the files, ran back to the locked door and waited for the guy who had disappeared into the warehouse quite a while ago to come back outside. If I played it smart, he was my free ticket to the blueprints.

With my heart beating fast, I positioned myself near the door and practiced in my mind how best to throw the key card through the door.

I waited until the door opened, threw my useless key card into the room unnoticed. It flew in a perfect half-arc to the left and landed right next to a table with a couple of boxes on it. *Perfect!*

I took one last deep breath, then intercepted the man who was just leaving the camp. He was middle-aged, but his serious look made him seem decades older, and he was also wearing a white coat.

"Excuse me! Would you be so kind as to open the door again?"

I looked at him with my famous puppy dog look, but the man's expression did not soften.

"You have your own key card, I assume?" he asked me as I carried stacks of files up to my neck. The copies of the copies of the copies were pretty heavy, by the way, and my arms were already burning, like after gym class with Iron Man – his name said it all.

"My key card must have fallen off," I started with the truth, because I was a really bad liar. Then I hid my face behind the files I was carrying. "While I was taking care of those files."

The engineer eyed me critically, but my puppy eyes softened his heart at least enough to open the door one more time and let his gaze roam the floor. He seemed genuinely surprised when he saw my key card on the floor and picked it up as I crossed the threshold of the room.

The hardest step is done!

Sighing, I dropped my files on the table and took my key card, which the engineer held out to me.

"Aurora Winter." He read my name so strangely, as if trying to remember it. Had he seen through my act? Was I caught now?

"Yes, I am."

"Interesting name."

"My mom was pretty creative," I replied automatically. Unlike my sister, I hadn't yet found any nicknames for myself that I could half-ass my way out of.

"Anyway, have a great day."

When the engineer, who had not told me his own name, closed the door behind him, I exhaled in relief. Without further pause for breath, I stormed through the warehouse in search of the blueprints I needed. It didn't take long for me to work my way through the cataloged boxes and find the jackpot in a rather worn box.

"Towerqueen to Watchman."

"Watchman hears."

"Operation Save-the-Universe moves to the next phase!"

Maxine squealed joyfully. "I knew you could do it. Now let's get you out of here, Aurora!"

"Luckily, I had Super-Max by my side. I could never have done it without you."

"Yes, you could have, but I appreciate you saying it."

I said goodbye to my best friend, who actually had to refurnish a penthouse apartment on the Upper East Side. Then I grabbed the necessary documents to copy them. Unfortunately, the printer in the storage room only worked with a key card, so I had to switch to the printer in the hallway and hope that my I-lost-my-key-card tactic worked a second time.

But I didn't get that far, because just as I was copying the blueprints, I felt death glances at my back that belonged to Janice.

Great.

I reacted intuitively, packing the eye-catching original blueprints under my blouse and putting the smaller copies in the top file. Then I grabbed the stack of files and held them in front of my torso so that the blueprint was no longer visible under my white blouse. Without a word, I marched past Janice to the elevators. She followed me. Silently.

That was the strangest situation I had ever experienced. Even worse than the nightmarish situation when I forgot the words in my youth choir solo at the then governor's big press appearance.

"Do you want anything?" I asked, annoyed. Yes, I had folded, but I just couldn't stand the unbearable silence any longer. The trip from the sixteenth floor to the executive floor was long. Very, very, long.

"No. I'm just spying on you," she replied sweetly.

"Have fun." As best I could, I tried to keep my voice neutral as the blueprints slid further and further down. Yesterday the gray skirt fit perfectly around my hips, but today it seemed like there was enough room there to stow a small car!

"Thanks. But it doesn't get really fun until you fly out of here in a high arc."

"I'm his fiancée. He's not going to kick me out."

Janice looked at me angrily. "Whatever contract you made, I'm sure you are - and will be - his fiancée on paper only. Period. You're not even wearing an engagement ring."

Well, the engagement ring thing. Of course, I had looked at hundreds of rings at jewelers, but none of them had felt right, so I hadn't decided on any of them.

"If you say so. But no matter what you do, Caden has written you off."

"Oh yeah, did he?" Janice proudly presented me with the little red bag that had cost me two thousand dollars. "He gave it to me this morning. *Written off* looks different to me."

I shook my head. "Not to me, because I sent the bag to you."

"You're lying."

"There was a card with it that just said *thank you*." I didn't know what else to write on the card, but my point seemed proof enough, yet I decided to come clean, simply because Janice deserved it for being so awful. "Caden told me to get you a gift basket, but I thought that was inappropriate because until yesterday I thought maybe you weren't a bad person, just hurt. I was obviously wrong."

Janice narrowed her eyes. She knew I was telling the truth, even if she didn't want to admit it.

"I'm not a bad person! You don't know anything about me!" Janice finally defended herself.

"Yes, I do. I know enough to know what's real. I don't know what Caden ever saw in you, but he's too good for you."

"And even more so for you!"

"Maybe. But that's for Caden to decide."

Finally, the elevator doors opened, and I headed straight for Caden's office.

Wow. I had stood up to Janice!

"I need to talk to Caden right now!" she said angrily, trying to walk past me.

We had a race without equal, because we both wore forbidden high shoes. Stupidly, I had an eight-pound file disadvantage, plus the blueprints that by now hung somewhere around my knees. But unlike Janice, I had danced through whole nights in such shoes, I was hardened and passed Janice without any problems.

Thanks to my hothead, however, there was no turning back now, because the last lockable room was behind me. Now there was only the escape to the front into Caden's office.

When I stormed into Caden's office, he looked up in surprise. And when I slammed the door in Janice's face and yelled, "Tint the windows," he raised a brow questioningly.

"Now!" I ordered, even though I knew it would cost me more than I could pay later.

The glasses turned milky as Caden looked at me uncomprehendingly and ended his call.

"What is this, Aurora?"

My brain switched to self-preservation mode. I threw the files on the floor, unbuttoned my blouse, and let them fall to the floor along with the shrouded blueprints.

"You wanted a private demonstration from me? You'll get it now!"

Jesus. What am I doing here?

Chapter 15 – Caden

When Aurora had stormed into my office, I had just had the CEO of our largest suppliers on the phone, but for some reason I couldn't just throw her out. Before I knew what had happened, I thought it best to postpone my important conversation, so curious was I about Aurora's strange behavior.

"Excuse me, there's an emergency," I waved off my interlocutor. My demanding look made it unmistakably clear to Aurora that she'd better say quickly, which is why I was cutting off essential business.

"What are you doing?" I asked. At the same moment I saw Janice rushing toward my office, but Aurora slammed the door in her face. Outraged, Janice looked in my direction, shook her head and turned back.

At the same moment, Aurora yelled at me to color the glass walls while she threw the stack of files on the floor next to her.

What the hell?

I decided to play along with their game, but made a note in the back of my mind for this commanding tone to take hits in the triple digits.

"You wanted a private demonstration from me? You'll get it now!"

Aurora – in a somewhat strange pose – threw off her blouse before walking elegantly towards me.

She wore a seductive bra that showcased her feminine curves, covering almost nothing. Fire burned in her determined gaze; her whole body was electrified.

I couldn't define it exactly, but something in her look screamed, *I'm a bad girl* and I liked that perfectly.

The businessman in me hoped it was a one-time incident, the rest of my being wished for drama like this every day if it led to what was about to happen.

But before I could give her my undivided attention, this mess behind her had to be cleaned up. Yes, I wanted us to fall over each other, but I couldn't relax as long as everything was screaming for *loss of control.*

"Fine by me, impress me. But first, put away the files and fold your blouse neatly."

"What?" Aurora's horrified gaze shifted back and forth between the blouse and me.

"You know how I hate messes," I grumbled.

"It's not a mess. At best, it's a teeny-tiny loss of control."

"If there's one thing I hate even more than clutter, it's losing control."

Did I really have to go over the basics with her again? Or did she even go for it? That had to be it, Aurora had been looking at me all day as if she wanted to test the limits of our game.

Aurora eyed me with wide eyes. "Sometimes it can even be good to lose control."

"No," I replied seriously. Loss of control never meant anything good. Never! I knew that better than anyone, because I had experienced firsthand what it meant to have no control over a situation.

"Do I need to repeat myself?" I asked sharply.

Aurora turned pale. "No." Still, she made no effort to move.

"Do you want me to do it myself?" I stood up to add emphasis to my statement and immediately Aurora took a step back. "You have no idea how much trouble you've gotten yourself into already."

"No! I'll take care of it!"

Immediately Aurora pounced on the files, rummaged around frantically, and then folded the blouse. I had never seen such a terribly folded blouse, sometime I would give her a special lesson for folding laundry, but not today.

Aurora put the blouse on the table and to the left of it the pile of files, which was just fine with me, so that this wrinkle atrocity disappeared from my field of vision.

"There you go, there you go," I said with satisfaction.

Almost as if a switch had flipped in Aurora, the tension in her body disappeared.

"Does Mr. Saint have any specific requests?" she asked with a smile.

"Surprise me, Aurora." I grinned, because Aurora had already stunned me with her action anyway. Her combination of charming, compliant sub and unconvincing personal assistant was driving me half crazy.

"With pleasure, sir."

I leaned back in my chair and enjoyed the show that was on. Although there was no music playing that set the pace for Aurora, she moved respectably. It was as if Aurora had shed her insecurity along with her blouse. All the while, she maintained her eye contact with me, even when she turned around to present me with her perfect backside. Damn, she knew exactly how to drive me crazy.

Although Aurora's movements blew my mind throughout, I noticed how her eyes kept sliding to the closed office door.

"Do I want to know what happened between you and Janice?" I asked.

"No, you don't," Aurora replied, letting her hair whip in my direction in a sweeping motion.

"So you've been a good girl?"

Aurora leaned forward to me and kissed my neck.

"I didn't say that," she breathed against my ear. *Fuck!*

I would have loved to reach into her full, endless hair and pull her mouth to my erection, but I was curious what else Aurora had in store for me. Her expression suggested that she still had some surprises.

"You know I'm supposed to be working?" I sounded like a hungry wolf.

"Knock yourself out, I'm going to keep going anyway."

Aurora broke away from me again, turned around, bent forward and slowly slipped the skirt off her hips. I couldn't help but dig my hands into her hips. Aurora's panties, matching her seductive lace bra, also left no room for fantasy.

"Did other men touch you while you were dancing for them?" I asked.

"No, never. You're the only one I want to be touched by."

I smiled contentedly, at the same time I felt sorry for the poor devils who had not had a chance to feel Aurora's soft skin. Even I could hardly control myself, and I was a man who mercilessly controlled his life.

Damn, Aurora knew how to show off her body. Every step she took was perfect, every movement increased the desire to bend her over the table and fuck her hard.

"Why now?" I asked. "Why not tonight in the playroom? Or tomorrow?"

Aurora looked at me thoughtfully as she unclasped her bra.

"Because I want to be remembered by you, Caden."

How could this scene not burn itself into my memory?

Aurora took my hands, silently inviting me to rise from my chair. With an elegant movement, she swung her leg onto my shoulder so that she did a standing-splits move. Her agility opened up a whole new dimension of what I could do with her in the playroom.

"Will I be remembered by you?" asked Aurora with a pleading look.

My hands wandered over her tense body, down her shapely breasts to her most sensitive spot, covered only by a piece of cloth.

"You're still asking that?" I buried my face against the side of her neck, where her hair tickled my skin. "You're driving me crazy, Aurora. And madness isn't something you forget easily."

Aurora sighed in relief before making an effort to take her leg off my shoulder again. I grabbed her ankle and clicked my tongue.

"Not so fast, beautiful, I'm still enjoying."

Because the position was apparently hard to hold, Aurora wrapped her arms around my neck while my fingers kept rubbing over her pearl. Not now, but someday I would take Aurora the same way, that much was certain.

"I was trying to drive you crazy." There was something reproachful in her trembling voice.

"You do."

My grip on her ankle loosened as her body shook more and more violently. Aurora wore shoes with forbidden high heels, yet she walked elegantly in them like a queen.

Aurora swung her hips as if nothing had happened, but I felt her heart beating fast. Her heart was mine – a realization that weighed heavily on my shoulders. Yes, she was mine and I wasn't ready to let her go again, but I wasn't a man who formed attachments and probably never became a relational person.

Aurora pushed my shoulders down so that I fell back into my chair, then her incredible private show continued. There would probably be some changes regarding the playroom now that I knew her other talents and one thing was for sure, I had so many wishes and ideas that they were enough for the next decades!

When Aurora pushed her panties down right in front of me, I held my breath. Inch by inch, she pushed the silky fabric over her smooth skin, watching my reactions, which must have pleased her, the way she smiled. Hard to believe that this *femme fatale* was a virgin a few days ago!

"Say what I want to hear!" I murmured in a commanding tone.

"I'm yours." It wasn't the words, but how Aurora emphasized them, full of passion, that made me shudder.

"Good girl."

Aurora gave me a few more beautiful movements and a batting of her eyelashes that I would kill for before she nodded contentedly and smiled at me. When I said nothing, she whispered softly, "Done."

"Finished?" I asked, shaking my head. "No, we're not done yet."

Actually, I was supposed to get back to my business and somehow save Saint Industries from the impending doom of my incompetent engineers, but Aurora had a pretty convincing case for a short break.

Saint, you're losing control. Get a fucking grip!

"Shall I go on?" she asked, irritated.

"No." I felt an urgent desire that I could not postpone any longer. What a shame, because actually I wanted to introduce her mouth to my manhood only tonight. But apparently my plans rose and fell with the whims of my lovely fiancée.

I took Aurora's hand to pull her closer to me until our faces were almost touching.

"You've maneuvered yourself into quite a few problems in the last ten minutes. I'll be so kind and help you not to talk yourself into any more trouble."

"Thank you, sir."

Aurora smiled expectantly as she stared at the bulge in my pants. Even though I knew there were no restraints in my drawer, I pulled them open, hoping I was wrong. Of course, I wasn't wrong – I always kept track – but fortunately I was flexible enough not to have to rely on leather restraints.

"Give me your blouse!" I murmured.

"Why?" asked Aurora in horror.

What was wrong with that damn blouse that it kept scaring Aurora whenever I talked about it?

I raised a brow reprovingly, demanding an explanation from her as I stood up and reached for the blouse.

Reflexively, Aurora lunged at the piece of cloth like a heroic soldier throwing himself on a grenade to protect his comrades. At the same time, she had positioned herself as if I were about to spank her. I swore to God that if Aurora kept this up, all her prayers would be answered, and I would personally see to it that her ass glowed like hot steel.

"What about this blouse?" I huffed when no answer came from her.

"Nothing."

I laughed softly. "You're the worst liar I've ever met."

"I'm not lying."

"You're only making it worse, Aurora."

"I know that myself." Aurora sighed. "There's nothing wrong with the blouse. I just don't want it to wrinkle."

"Then you should probably fold them more neatly and not throw yourself at them."

Aurora shrugged her shoulders, and I heard paper rustling. "You're probably right."

The pile of files was still blocking my view of Aurora, and I was starting to get impatient.

"Give me the blouse!" I ordered in a serious voice.

"Yes, sir." Reluctantly, Aurora pushed herself up from the table and handed me the blouse.

I examined it several times from top to bottom because I suspected a stain that Aurora wanted to hide, but except for new creases, the blouse was spotless. Still, I couldn't shake the feeling that Aurora was keeping a secret from me.

"Who do you belong to?"

"To you, Caden." Aurora looked deep into my eyes and her devotional emphasis was sincere.

"Are you hiding something from me?"

She took a deep breath. "Yes."

Admittedly, I admired the courage to answer me honestly, even though I probably would have seen through a lie.

"Am I going to hear about this at some point?"

"Yes!"

"Will it break my heart?"

Not that I had ever felt this lifeless lump in my chest recently. Basically, I didn't even know what this pain felt like anymore, perhaps because I had used up all pain years ago.

"Heavens, no!"

"Good, then I'll allow you to keep your secret for now."

"Thank you."

I took Aurora by the flanks and turned her back to me. Then I put her wrists on each other and tied her hands behind the blouse as announced.

"Get on your knees!" I commanded softly. Aurora obeyed immediately, she turned around and got on her knees. She looked adorable, simply stunning, waiting with lowered, hungry eyes for me to take what I wanted.

I opened my pants, from which my manhood jumped right in front of Aurora's face. Her eyes became huge, not unusual, because I really had a considerable erection.

"Go ahead," I urged Aurora as she waited for my permission to finally take care of my cock.

Of course, I knew that Aurora had no experience, but I was pretty sure that she would not disappoint me. My gut feeling told me that she was a natural here as well, anything else I thought was out of the question.

Hesitantly, Aurora licked the underside of my erection with the tip of her tongue, and I leaned back to relax. The morning had been stressful, and this was just the thing to relax me now.

Aurora watched my every reaction closely; it didn't take long for her to know what I liked and didn't like. When her soft, full lips enclosed my tip, I growled softly. And when the tip of her tongue massaged me with circular motions, she confirmed my gut feeling. To be honest, I believed that I had never been so close to insanity during a blowjob as I was at that moment.

"You like that?" asked Aurora with a smile as she licked emphatically over my shaft.

"Yes."

"And this?" She encircled my tip again and while massaging me, she began to suck.

"Yes, damn it!"

Aurora looked deep into my eyes. She knew exactly how to drive me crazy, that much was clear. She wasn't shy about what she was doing, her movements were so natural, as if she had never done anything but serve me.

"You know what else I like?" My question was rhetorical, yet Aurora looked at me questioningly.

I gathered her long hair into a braid and pulled her closer to me until I felt her tight throat. It wasn't easy for Aurora to hold this position, but I credited her for managing it.

Madness. This sight was just pure madness. I reflected myself in her bright green eyes while I sank my erection into her mouth.

When I claimed control, Aurora let me lead her. Again and again I thrust into her and withdrew from her again. With each time a little deeper, until my manhood was up to the back of her throat. *Fuck.* Aurora's subtle makeup ran more and more as she struggled for breath. She looked perfect with my cock inside her.

When I loosened my grip, Aurora reclaimed control by setting the pace and depth herself – and she was anything but squeamish.

That was exactly what I needed; Aurora had only known this with me. Nevertheless, the noted blows remained on my list, because whether she was right or not, I didn't put up with such a tone of voice from anyone, not even from my fiancée.

"I'll have to punish you *for this* later," I gasped.

"Yes, sir," Aurora replied guiltily.

I don't know how she did it, but I wanted to fuck Aurora all day long. Aurora belonged in my playroom all day while a gag or my erection was in her mouth.

"I'm about to squirt in your mouth. After that you will get dressed as if nothing has happened. You will sit in your place and wait for me to allow you to swallow. Do you understand?"

"Yes, sir."

Still, I wanted Aurora to say my command out loud, simply because it made me furious.

"Repeat it."

"I won't swallow until you allow me to."

"Good girl."

One last time I regained control by tightening my grip around her silky, smooth hair. I pushed her head towards my thrusting hips. Again and again and again. Aurora's body was screaming to be fucked itself, but I couldn't allow her to have an orgasm, not after such an action.

The deeper I thrust, the louder I gasped, because her tight throat closed tightly around my erection. I wanted to go on, I wanted to come, I wanted everything.

A moment before I came, I withdrew my manhood from Aurora. I wanted her to see how I squirted my gold into her open mouth.

At the sight of it, I could have taken her a second time right away, but unfortunately there were other obligations I had to meet.

While I slowly caught my breath, Aurora got dressed and tried to do damage control on her makeup.

"Didn't you forget something?" I asked with a grin.

Aurora looked at me questioningly while my gaze roamed along her body. When I stretched out my hand demandingly, the penny dropped and she looked at me with a pitying look.

"Yes, really Aurora. You know I won't ask a second time."

She suppressed a sigh and took off her panties once again. Without further ado, they landed in the same drawer where the last pair of panties had already gone.

"There you go." I looked at Aurora with pride. "Well done."

Aurora had done her thing so well that I couldn't wait to lock her in the playroom and do more of those deliciously forbidden things with her there.

"Think about it until I let you," I whispered in her ear. "I want my taste to stay on your tongue."

Because she couldn't say anything, Aurora nodded and left the office with all the files, while I stared at her perfect ass, closed my pants and sat back contentedly. Just by the thought that Aurora could think of nothing else but my taste and what I had done to her, the next tingling erection was brewing.

For all I cared, every day of my future life could be like this, but before I even finished the thought, my stomach tightened painfully. Jesus, contrary to my thoughts, I knew I wasn't ready for a real relationship. Feelings were dangerous because they led to irrational decisions. At the same time, Aurora had sown doubt in me ... were losses of control sometimes not as fatal as I thought?

Chapter 16 – Aurora

Restlessly, I rocked back and forth in my chair as I waited for Caden to release me. I could think of nothing but Caden and how much I wanted him. How could I think about anything else when his salty taste was still on my tongue?

Caden was on the phone but kept giving me furtive glances while I tried to come up with a plan. The original blueprints were in the top file, but they had to be returned as soon as possible. I didn't know how long it would be before someone noticed they were gone, and I didn't want to take the chance.

If I got caught, the trouble would cost me more than I could ever pay, that much was certain. Just as certain as the fact that Caden Saint always got what he wanted.

When my intercom buzzed, I almost jumped out of my office chair.

"Aurora, can you bring me a coffee?"

He knew I couldn't answer, so he looked at me questioningly through the glass and I nodded.

"Fine, but hurry up, I have an appointment in twenty minutes that you're going to take me to."

After that, Caden turned his attention back to the phone. In that short time, I didn't know much about Caden's work rhythm, but I knew enough to know that we wouldn't return to the office after that. Caden always scheduled the long, tough appointments for the afternoon.

Bummer. After glancing at the clock, I estimated that I had a window of about ten minutes before Caden got suspicious. So I had ten minutes to sneak up to the sixteenth floor, somehow smuggle the blueprints back into the forbidden room, sprint back upstairs, make coffee in the coffee kitchen, bring it to Caden, and pretend nothing ever happened. Since I couldn't split in two, I guess it was an impossibility.

I have to at least try, I told myself, because if I did nothing, I would definitely fail. So there was a tiny chance that I could get out of this, after all I had been able to hide the blueprints from Caden, even if he had made it anything but easy for me.

Sighing, I slipped the blueprints under my blouse a second time, which by now was so wrinkled that the papers didn't stand out. I would have preferred to put them in a file, but a file folder to fetch coffee looked rather suspicious.

"Aurora? Come back to my office for a minute."

This can't be happening!

I put my head back because I wasn't going to get away with a striptease a second time – it was bordering on a miracle that it had worked the first time.

Pull yourself together, Aurora. You can do it!

The whole thing reminded me of the embarrassing attempt to smuggle a bottle of wine out of my parents' house for a high school party. I was spared the binge drinking of the century including dozens of alcohol poisonings. Instead I was grounded for four weeks and told off by death, which was no better.

I walked into Caden's office and tried to avoid his gaze because at three miles away you could still tell I had done something wrong. Caden smiled at me proudly.

What is it? my gaze asked. Subconsciously, I crossed my arms in front of my chest to protect my secret.

"Your look is literally begging for a beating," Caden said matter-of-factly.

I knew that myself, but what else could I do?

When he made an effort to pull me to his well-trained body, I bent over his desk and pushed my skirt up. To be honest, I felt sorry for my body, which already had to take the rap for my stupid ideas all day long ... and other body parts.

"Today you're really putting it on how far you can go, huh?"

I tried to look at him as innocently as possible to avoid punishment, but in Caden's world everything had a price and he demanded it. Always.

His hand touched my bare buttocks. The heat of his skin alone was enough to awaken longings in me, because unlike Caden, I had not yet had an orgasm.

"I like it when you can't talk back to me," Caden murmured. "Did you like it when you had to think of me every step of the way?"

I nodded, purring like a cat. Admittedly, it had driven me crazy, but it was also exciting. Still, I hoped Caden wanted to deal with me differently for the car ride, because I had to get rid of the blueprints somehow beforehand, and there was no way I could concentrate with something vibrating in my erogenous zones. Besides, I had to somehow manage to solve everything silently, for obvious reasons.

"I take it from the look on your face that the vibrations from the butt plug would be too violent?"

I nodded again. Such toys were better off in the playroom when no one could hear me moaning or screaming. Suppressing my lust was incredibly difficult and with the salty taste on my tongue it was getting harder.

"Luckily, I have something else for you."

Caden pulled out of his pants pocket two small balls that were connected with a thin, smooth rope. As his fingers slid over my thighs, he murmured softly as my pleasure was unmistakable. Caden massaged my most sensitive spot, using my wetness to moisten the love balls. I had seen such parts before, but I didn't know their meaning. Not yet. As determined as Caden looked, I was about to learn the function of the two little balls.

He inserted it into me, and I enjoyed the feeling of being filled. For a moment more, Caden devoted himself to my curves, then he let go of me with a sigh. "What a shame we really have no time to waste."

Just as Caden was about to say something, his smartphone rang.

I listened to the angry caller, but I did not hear the exact wording.

"What, disappeared?" asked Caden, frowning.

My heart stopped for a moment.

"Then take another look. Blueprints don't just fly away."

I closed my eyes, took a deep breath and hoped to wake up from the nightmare I was trapped in. If I was unlucky, everything would blow up now. Still lying on the table, I waited to see what would happen next.

"Grab the prepared files and wait for me downstairs, I'll be right there. If you can find a coffee somewhere..."

I nodded, stood up, and turned around before smoothing out my blouse and taking my chance to return the stolen blueprints. Now that

I was standing, I had an idea what the love balls would do to me. In any case, they wouldn't stay in place on their own and since I no longer had panties, I had to rely on my muscles alone.

Heavens, Caden really is a monster!

As ordered, I grabbed his important files, disappeared around the corner with them, and when the coast was clear, I pulled the blueprints out of my blouse and slipped them between two files. At least now I didn't have to worry about that anymore.

I created an imaginary checklist in my head.

First, go to the sixteenth division.

Second, return the blueprints to the locked room.

Third, get coffee.

Fourth, wait for Caden in the lobby.

Sounded doable, didn't it? Well, unfortunately my pragmatic plan didn't work out, because there wasn't much happening on the sixteenth floor right now. Or, to put it another way, the sixteenth floor was deserted and there was nothing to suggest that this state of affairs was about to change. Except for a man vacuuming and a single secretary sitting at a computer typing up files, there was no one else here. The secretary couldn't help me, they had the same security clearance as I did, I had learned that from the secretary at the front desk who had given me my card.

What a bummer!

How much trouble would I get into if I just confessed everything to Caden? How bad could it get? One punishment in the playroom? A hundred punishments? Whatever Caden would do to me in the playroom, I could take it. But my plan could also backfire, and I'd look like a traitor who'd stolen internal company top-secret documents without authority. God, no. I couldn't bring myself to finish my thought; after all, I felt like I belonged here for the first time in a long time. Caden made me feel *at home*. I couldn't jeopardize that!

Feverishly, I thought about what I could do in the next few minutes to get myself out of this predicament. Just as I was about to lie in wait at the copy machine, I spotted a man pushing dozens of files on a cart in front of him. I thought he looked important enough to have an access card to the locked area.

Finally a ray of hope!

Albeit a very weak one, because I couldn't just go to him and say, *hey, can you bring back the blueprints?*

Caden would notice immediately if I swallowed, so I was still not allowed to speak if I wanted to finish my mission. Too bad that I couldn't reach my accomplice right now.

Towerqueen has to do without Watchman right now. Watchman had important missions of his own to complete. I could never tell Maxine that I was using our code names even now, or there would be T-shirts, cell phone cases, and shield caps printed with the inscription by the time we next met. I knew my best friend.

As inconspicuously as possible I ran towards the file pusher, which with the increasingly heavy love balls was not as easy as it sounded. Caden really didn't make it easy for me to impress him.

When I was sure the guy was heading for the right room, I set off to wait him out. Unable to speak, I tried to put on an I'm-totally-important-and-busy face as I pulled the blueprints from the file and placed them on the file pile with a half-hearted nod before storming off.

Please, please, please! Without looking back, I walked further along the department and heard the man behind me mutter something before he pushed the entire cart into the department.

Good. That's settled.

Hopefully, I hadn't spent too much time trying to get out of it. I headed for the elevator at a fast pace, but with every movement the weight of these balls seemed to double.

Longingly I stared at the vehicle doors, because there I had the opportunity to push the love balls, which kept sliding down, back into place. I counted the floors until the door finally popped open and offered me a glimpse into the crowded cabin.

Did the whole company ride in the same elevator?

Smiling, I took a step back to signal that I was waiting for the next elevator and sent up push prayers that the next elevator was empty.

To make matters worse, my mom called me, and I pushed her away. Three times in a row. On the fourth ring, I answered because I was worried in case it was an emergency.

"Aurora! Why don't you answer the phone?"

I sighed, but answered nothing.

"Did you finally find a dress?"

I mumbled something that sounded like a *yep*.

"And it's really orchid colored?"

Good question. Maxine swore by the fashion designer we went to, but I was a little afraid of the outcome. Because with Brando Bertani, you didn't make requests, you just mentioned the occasion. He took the measurements, nothing else. The fact that I had put the color as a condition, bordered on blasphemy according to Maxine, but I took that in order not to fall into disfavor with my mom.

"Magnolia's wedding is going to be perfect! Today we visited the residence that became available at short notice and it's magical!"

What Mom actually meant to say: *Don't screw up Maggy's perfect day!*

Hopefully the stupid wedding was over soon so I could have my family back. How could Dad and Maggy stand it all day?

"Aurora, you're not saying anything," my mother stated matter-of-factly.

"Busy," I pressed out from behind clenched teeth.

Ping. The elevator door opened, and I jumped in without looking back. There were two other people riding in the elevator next to me, but I couldn't wait for a third elevator. My next destination was the ladies' room in the lobby.

"Are you still working?" asked Mom.

"Mm."

"Yes, I know it's not proper to keep someone from working. But after all, it's your fiancé's business. You can spare two minutes for your mother, can't you?"

I muttered again. What a conversation.

"When will your dress be ready? I'm dying to see it!"

"Right on time," I pressed out again from behind clenched teeth, leaning against the wall as my tense muscles nearly killed me.

Caden Saint, I hate you!

Again and again, he presented me with unsolvable tasks. Wait, actually I had managed everything he had asked of me – and if I hadn't needed a detour to the sixteenth floor, my task probably wouldn't have been as difficult as it was now.

The fact that Caden only put things on me that I could manage motivated me to persevere.

Hang in there. Breathe. Hang in there, Aurora!

"It's really inappropriate right now, isn't it?"

"Hmph!"

"Fine, but then check in with me later so we can talk about how Magnolia's wedding is going!"

What else could we talk about? Ever since the stupid engagement ring was on Maggy's finger, there was no other topic in the Winter household.

Sighing, I hung up. I loved my sister with all my heart, but jealousy gnawed at me because no one was interested in my news. I finally had a job I liked, in a city I loved, and a fiancé I had fallen in shock-love with.

When the elevator finally arrived in the lobby, my legs were shaking like aspen leaves. Every step was an endless, sweet agony. The thought of getting caught was exciting, but I definitely didn't want to get caught, so I headed straight for the restrooms, locked myself in the first stall, and sat on the closed toilet lid.

Finally! Tears of joy ran down my cheek as my muscles finally relaxed. Who would have thought that these little balls were even worse than the plug with the insane vibration levels?

At least Janice hadn't interrupted me this time, because in the meantime I had the feeling that her bad-timing radar was working perfectly. What had Caden seen in this monster of a woman?

After a brief but soothing breather, I stood back up, smoothed out my skirt, and left the ladies' room to wait for Caden in the lobby.

Because he was still nowhere to be seen, I decided to still take care of his coffee. Not because he really insisted, but because I wanted to do my job better than Janice. I really wanted Caden to know what he had in me, because I wanted to keep my job longer than Janice had.

Because I had overheard during a conversation that Caden didn't drink coffee from the lower floors, my gaze roamed the glassed-in walls, because this morning I had spotted a mobile barista stand from the car on the next street corner – just a stone's throw from Saint Industries' main entrance.

Unfortunately, there was still a gaggle of paparazzi outside the doors, just waiting for me to make a wrong move. Forest fires in Australia, the inauguration of the next U.S. president, Bonnie Buckley's world tour were just hot topics, I really didn't know why these press people had to pounce on me like vultures.

Under normal circumstances I would have just gone outside and gotten a coffee, but the circumstances were anything but normal. I couldn't speak and, with one wrong move, I might lose my love balls in front of everyone.

There were those days that were simply stupid. The sun could shine so magically, the birds could chirp so beautifully; yet on such days, nothing went right.

Caden's disappointed look when he found me empty-handed finally drove me out, though, because I had resolved to stay in his memory, and I meant it. This chemistry between us, the crackling and tingling, something like that didn't happen with just anyone, but only with one person. The right one.

In no time at all, I dashed past the press people, ordered a coffee with a wave of my hand, and ran like a world champion back into the building, straight into Caden's arms.

"Going that fast, Miss Winter?"

I nodded while he took the hot coffee from me. His gaze slid back and forth between the cup, me, the approximate location of the love balls, and the press people.

"You love living on the edge, huh?"

No! I was the exact opposite of living life to the limit. I was more interested in the *lying-on-the-couch-is-also-quite-okay* faction. Caden put his hand on my back, pushed me energetically into the nearest elevator, and waited until the doors were closed. I turned around and Caden pushed me back far enough that my back hit the cool chrome.

With his left arm, which also held the coffee-to-go, Caden propped himself up and buried me between his muscular body and the wall behind me. I inhaled the delicious scent of freshly ground coffee and Caden's masculine musk.

How did Caden manage to always make me weak in the knees? Was it his deep brown eyes? His *I'll-get-what-I-want* look or his determination?

"Open your mouth!" he murmured in my ear.

Because it sloshed dangerously in my mouth, I leaned my head back and then obeyed his command. Smiling, he let a finger slide over my lower lip, reminding me of what we had done earlier. His finger entered my mouth, roaming back and forth over my tongue. I wanted his erection back.

Wow. Caden had really gotten me to the point where I would do anything to be willingly surrendered.

"Good girl. You may swallow now."

I waited patiently for Caden to pull his fingers out before I complied with his command.

"Thank you, sir."

Of course I was grateful that I could speak again – I would never have thought that it was almost impossible to get through everyday life in silence, but at the same time, I missed Caden's taste and the associated control he had over me. The power imbalance that lay between his dominance and my submissiveness was not just symbolic after all.

"Well, let's go now. We're late."

Caden opened the elevator doors, and I followed him quickly.

"Did you think of me every step of the way?"

"Yes!"

"Are you thinking about me now, too?"

"Yes, sir!"

It was unfortunate that I couldn't tell Caden that I had run much more than he suspected. But now I realized for the first time that I had really made it.

Heavens, I had stolen Top Secret files unnoticed and gotten away with it! *Operation Save-the-Universe* – or as it was unofficially called: *Mission Mister-Universe-staying-in-memory-under-all-circumstances* had not failed. At the thought of it, I had to grin, which did not escape Caden.

"Will you let me share in your fun?"

"Oh, nothing," I waved it off. "I just had to think of an insider between Maxine and me."

Towerqueen to Watchman: Our mission is moving to the next phase.

Chapter 17 – Caden

I watched Aurora with interest as she scowled out the window. After my sessions in the playroom, my subs usually left. I wasn't used to being confronted with feelings outside of play.

"Would you like to go eat now?" I asked, even though I already knew her answer.

"No," she replied, breathing heavily.

"I thought you were hungry."

Aurora shrugged her shoulders. "I was, but I don't want to go outside. I'm too weak to smile."

I immediately understood what Aurora meant, slowly but surely the paparazzi were getting on my nerves too. They had been following us around all day while we visited conversion projects. Yesterday, one pushy guy had even made it to the executive floor. Our engagement had been out for quite a while, but other than the Times interview, we hadn't given a single interview to keep Saint Industries in the conversation. It worked, but it came at a price.

I went to Aurora, took her in my arms from behind, and inhaled her sweet scent. Unlike me, she was not used to the public pressure.

"Not long now, and the media frenzy will be over, don't worry."

Aurora tensed up, and even though I couldn't see her, I knew she was contorting her face.

"What's wrong?"

Aurora shook her head. "Nothing, it's fine."

She broke free from my embrace, grabbed her purse and ran to the door.

"Are you coming?"

I narrowed my eyes to scrutinize Aurora. She looked tired and was unconvincing about her newfound ambitions.

"Do I really have to put you over my knee to get the truth out of you?"

"It's nothing, I'm just hungry."

Aurora avoided my gaze and looked to the ground, but I didn't let her get away with that. I followed her, put on a serious face, and forced her to look at me by lifting her chin up.

"Do I get an answer now?"

"I answered you."

Women. There were moments when I just never knew what women were thinking, or if they were thinking anything at all. Normally I didn't care either, but with Aurora... I did.

"Do you really want me to beg for a sincere answer? Aurora, you know I won't do that."

After a heavy sigh, Aurora finally returned my gaze.

"I think no media hype pleases me even less than media hype."

"Why?"

"Because *I'm* just here for the media hype."

The words of her weak voice cut deep into my heart. I wish I could have shown her the feelings I had for her, but I could not. The fear of losing control was too great. I couldn't confront my past now, I couldn't.

"Don't worry, Aurora. I won't let you go that quickly." I stroked her soft cheek, eliciting a smile. "Besides, after our deal, you'll be financially independent for the rest of your life."

Her smile died and she looked at me disappointed.

"I'm not in this for the money, Caden. You really need to stop seeing life from a super-rich person's point of view all the time."

"What do you mean?"

"That money can't open every path for you, just as money can't solve every problem."

I understood Aurora, even if I disagreed. So far, money had paved every way for me.

"I bought you," I replied dryly, but Aurora clearly shook her head.

"It wasn't your money that won me over, it was your charm. I don't want your luxury or your credit cards – I just want you. I've told you before that my heart can't be bought, and I meant it. Surely by now you've figured out when you've earned my heart."

I knew all too well that we had both bet our hearts on this game, even if I didn't want to admit it. My heart would not be able to cope with another loss, it had reached its limit. But if I did nothing or said nothing, it was bound to happen that sooner or later I would lose Aurora, who had crept into my heart without permission.

"Do you want to know why I passed you off as my fiancée?"

"Absolutely," Aurora whispered.

"Because from the first second, you triggered something in me that I couldn't define. I want you around because I want to find out why I'm so attracted to you. It almost kills me that I can barely control myself around you, Aurora. And I can promise you that I won't let you go until I know all these questions are answered."

Her big emerald eyes looked at me in surprise. "Really?"

"Really."

I pulled her tightly against me and she nestled her cheek against my chest. For a while we just stood there, tightly embraced and listening to each other's breath.

"And now we should cook some food."

"Is there anything edible here at all?"

I nodded. "Just because I plug problem holes with money doesn't mean I'm an empathetic ass who doesn't get it. You haven't wanted to leave the house for days."

"Guilty." Aurora raised her arms like a caught criminal. "I didn't know you could cook."

Again, I nodded. "I can. But it's easier to just go out to eat after long days at work."

"I may not be able to meet the demands of your fine palate, but I could still serve you."

"I'd just love to see you cook for me with that elegant swing of your hips," I murmured.

Aurora giggled. Her worries from earlier were blown away, for which I was grateful. I hated to see her so frustrated, because then she lost the sparkle in her eyes. Fortunately, she had found it again.

Together we walked into the fully equipped, open kitchen that I had not used three times. I had never managed to confront the thought that I had no one to share my food with. Having to eat alone, confronted with silence and loneliness, was like a nightmare.

When Aurora opened the fully stocked refrigerator, she was speechless.

"Oh my god, who's going to eat all this?"

"Us."

"For the rest of our lives?" Aurora turned to me. "That's a doomsday supply for a football team. Heck, for the entire league!"

Grinning, I sat down on one of the stools that stood at the free-standing work surface.

"Any idea what you're going to cook for us yet?"

"You should never, ever in your life put a hungry woman in front of a full refrigerator."

"Why?"

Aurora took a long look in the refrigerator, then gradually packed meat and vegetables on the table. Quite a lot of meat. And even more vegetables.

"That's why." She let her hands wander over the mountain of food. "So you could do us both a favor by giving me some inspiration."

I raised a brow questioningly. "You want me to give you orders while you cook?"

"You could put it that way."

"No."

"No?"

Aurora looked at me in horror. "I offer to submit, and you refuse?"

"Yes."

"That's unfair," she snorted, "Why?"

"Because you belong to me. I can dominate you whenever I want."

Sighing, Aurora put some of the food back in the cupboard.

"Sometimes I hate you, Caden."

Aurora grabbed a wooden cutting board and a large kitchen knife, then began chopping vegetables.

I didn't have to ask when Aurora hated me, because in most situations, I knew right away. If she didn't look at me so sweetly, Aurora would definitely have an easier life. But I was just a man and I had needs. Her pleading looks and sensual sighs were part of that.

"Do you love me sometimes?" I asked, and the rhythmic chopping ended abruptly.

"Sometimes," she replied with a smile before turning her attention back to the fresh herbs.

"Tell me more about that."

Aurora gave me an incredibly hot look. Whatever was going on in her pretty head right now, I was almost certain that it would drive me out of my mind.

"Is that an order?"

"No orders," I murmured.

"Then it will be my secret."

Damn, Aurora played this game better than I realized. Of course, I could have demonstrated my dominance, but then I gave Aurora exactly what she wanted.

Touché, little one, touché.

I watched Aurora as, after the herbs, she also diced onions, carrots and celery. Not that I thought cooking was seductive, but as focused and elegant as Aurora was moving around the kitchen, I could pretty well imagine bending her over the kitchen counter while fucking her.

"What do you say we take a trip to the Playroom after dinner?"

"I would like that very much, sir."

"Whether you like it or not depends on how you behave the rest of the evening," I growled.

"Yes, sir."

I became hungry – and I wasn't talking about food. Aurora had this talent of driving me crazy at the appropriate moments. Unlike my previous subs, Aurora liked to rebel against me, which made our games quite interesting. So interesting, in fact, that I wanted to have her in the playroom all day. Tied up. With her legs spread. Ready for me when I wanted her.

Aurora poured olive oil into a cast-iron skillet, crushed two cloves of garlic, and put them in with a sprig of rosemary.

"How about you take care of dessert to convince me of your cooking skills?" suggested Aurora. She bit her lower lip so seductively that her message was unmistakable.

"Sounds good to me."

In my mind I drizzled her naked body with warm chocolate sauce, strawberries and whipped cream. *Delicious.*

God, if Aurora kept looking at me like that, I couldn't wait until after dinner, that much was certain. To take my mind off things, I got up and rummaged through the refrigerator for ingredients. The kitchen was big enough for a whole kitchen brigade.

When I had everything for my famous but rarely displayed *chocolate mousse,* I took a deep breath. The kitchen smelled wonderful and when Aurora took the fillets to the hot pan, my mouth watered. The song she was humming was drowned out by the sizzle of the meat.

For the first time in ages I felt at home, because for the first time there was life, love and light here, only thanks to Aurora.

When she turned the meat, she nodded with satisfaction. In the meantime, I had done nothing but gawk at her. The next time she was in the kitchen, she would cook naked, that much was certain. Maybe a custard or a cake, at least nothing where she could hurt her flawless skin with splattering grease or hot pans.

"May I help myself to your wine collection?" asked Aurora after she had placed the meat in the oven to rest.

"No alcohol!" I grumbled, because I hated this topic. If I didn't receive business people so often, there wouldn't be a single drop of alcohol in my loft.

"I only need it for the sauce, not for drinking," Aurora replied calmly, tossing the vegetables into the pan where the fillets had just been.

"Fine by me."

"Be right back."

Aurora dashed around the kitchen counter, gave me a kiss as she passed, and returned with a three-thousand-dollar cabernet. I had to admit that Aurora had a good eye, because the Lancester cabernet was one of the most sought-after wine varietals in recent years. When Aurora uncorked it, the unpleasant smell of alcohol immediately hit my nose.

Screams. Pain. Darkness.

"Caden? Are you okay?" Aurora pulled me out of the deep hole I kept falling into when I wasn't paying attention. By now, she'd loosened the drippings with some of the wine and water. The stench was getting worse. No matter how many herbs she added, it did not get better.

"Everything is fine," I pressed out from behind clenched teeth. "How can something that cost three thousand dollars smell so awful?"

Aurora turned completely pale. Her gaze switched back and forth between the bottle and me.

"Three thousand dollars?" She was suddenly holding the bottle not as if it were a normal bottle, but rather as if it were made of paper-thin eggshells. "Did I really just burn three thousand dollars?"

"Just a moment ago you thought it would be worth it."

"It is, but ... I could have gone with something less expensive. I didn't realize the Lancester was so expensive."

I waved it off and didn't even mention that there were millions of dollars' worth of beverage stored there.

"How do you know the wine?"

"Maxine and I used to cook with it a lot," Aurora replied. "The wine is from her big brother. Heavens, if I'd known how much our kitchen experiments cost!" Aurora grabbed her head. "So much could have gone wrong."

"As confident as you are in the kitchen, though, there's never been an accident, has there?"

With a nod, she agreed with me. "But that's also when I thought we were cooking up ten-dollar wine."

Suddenly there was none of her self-confidence, instead she stumbled through the kitchen like a clumsy deer.

"Relax, Aurora. If it goes wrong, you just make a new sauce."

"It's the principle, Caden! I'm not a star chef, I grew up on eight-dollar wine and mac-and-cheese. I shouldn't be cooking with such expensive ingredients." Her eyes drifted to the filets in the oven. "They cost more than fifteen dollars, don't they?"

Since these were real Wagyu filets, Aurora probably had to add one, maybe even two zeros, but I didn't want to rub Aurora's nose in it. Much more, I wanted to know why she was constantly outshining herself.

"You obviously know how to cook, so the wine is not a waste."

"It's possible." Aurora shrugged her shoulders and looked unconvinced.

"Why do you keep belittling yourself?"

"I don't," Aurora replied seriously.

"Yes, you do."

"Oh yeah, give me an example then."

"You wouldn't accept my marriage proposal because you were a fabulous dancer."

"Stripper," Aurora corrected on me.

"See, that's exactly what I mean. You're beautiful and smart. With your charm, you could wrap any guy in the world around your finger if you wanted to."

"Really?"

"Yes! Really," I affirmed one more time. Why did the most beautiful women always have the biggest doubts? And why did they need guys like me – who weren't good company – to make them realize that themselves? "All that I offer you, you deserve."

"Okay," she replied meekly.

"Say it!" I commanded.

"I deserved that," Aurora mumbled so softly I couldn't understand.

Okay, you want to play? Let's play!

I made short work of it, grabbed Aurora by the neck and pushed her upper body onto a free spot on the work surface. Then I pushed up her lilac summer dress, took a large wooden cooking spoon from the cutlery pot and slapped it on her bottom without warning.

It left a perfect red imprint. Good, because that way I hit the same spot a second time, which made Aurora cry out.

"Now would you have the goodness to repeat what I said?"

"I deserve it!"

The wooden spoon cut through the air a third time. I loved that sound.

"What do you deserve, Aurora?"

"That you punish me!"

"Damn right," I murmured. Then I turned my attention back to her shapely ass until it glowed an even red all over. "And what else?"

"What you give me."

" Aurora. Stop belittling yourself or asking for less than you deserve. Understand? You deserve the whole world."

"Roger that."

Although the lesson was over, I had a hard time detaching myself from Aurora. I just liked to fix her in any respectable positions. My fingers stroked over her sensitive skin, which made Aurora groan. By now her lust had made itself felt, I stroked the wetness and Aurora stretched out to meet me.

"Have you learned your lesson?"

"Yes, I did, sir."

One last time I patted her butt, then I let go of her.

"Good girl. Now you see to it that we can eat something."

Aurora nodded and went back to work, just like me. Together we rampaged through the kitchen, leaving behind an unholy mess that someone else would take care of tomorrow.

Could my life always be like this? So harmonious? So beautifully varied? I could not deny that Aurora awakened unknown longings in me that I had never felt before.

Again and again, Aurora looked curiously over my shoulder.

"Would you like a taste?" I asked and when Aurora nodded, I put my finger in the bowl. Willingly, Aurora opened her mouth and waited for me to feed it to her. The crackling in the air became noticeable again, until someone banged on the door so hard that Aurora winced in shock.

"Are you expecting someone?" she asked.

I shook my head. "No, not really."

"Hold on."

Aurora's mouth continued to stay open until she looked at me with disappointment as I licked the mousse off my finger myself.

"*Wait a minute*, I said," I murmured in a sharp tone. "We'll get right on with it."

"You can count on me to remind you."

Grinning, I walked to the door where Jackson was standing, the camera told me, and he did not look happy.

With a questioning look, I opened the door. "Jacks? What are you doing here?"

"Trouble," he growled. "Do you have time?"

"Sure." Actually, the timing was awkward, but I asked him into the apartment. Jackson was pretty much the only friend I had. Back when I was doing so bad, he was always there for me. Now he was having problems and I was trying to come to terms.

Together we went into the open kitchen, and Aurora looked up curiously as she cut more vegetables.

"Aurora? This is Jackson. Jackson? Aurora," I introduced the two of them.

"Pleased to meet you," Aurora replied with a beaming smile.

"Likewise," Jackson replied. "About time Caden finally introduced us to each other."

Aurora nodded and pointed a carrot in my direction. "In the meantime, I had even thought that Mister I'm-too-busy-slash-now-you was just making you up."

I cleared my throat. "Well, now you see that's not the case."

"Or he's a dedicated actor who's just pretending to be your best friend."

"Why would I pass Jacks off as someone he's not?" I asked, and Aurora looked at me meaningfully. *Oh, of course.* Aurora wasn't who she pretended to be either, and yet she was the most real thing that had happened to me over the last few years.

"Sure I'm not interrupting?" asked Jackson as his gaze roamed over the kitchen mess.

"No you aren't, we're almost done. Right?" I looked questioningly at Aurora, who was pulling two large oven mitts over her hands.

"Five minutes." She opened the oven, from which little wisps of smoke were rising, and took the two large pieces of tenderloin out of the oven. "If you set the table, it'll go faster."

"What kind of commanding tone is that, lady?" I asked with a grin.

"An appropriate tone of command," Aurora replied, winking at me.

While Aurora and I were bickering, Jackson roamed the kitchen looking for dishes. Good, because I only had a rough idea where the necessary dishes were located.

While Jackson was setting the table, I grabbed Aurora by the hips from behind and kissed her neck.

"After dinner, I'm going to drive that commanding tone out of you," I breathed into her ear.

Aurora smiled at me conspiratorially, but didn't answer anything, instead adding a few spoonfuls of strained tomatoes to the red wine sauce.

"Done. Is there anything else I can do?" asked Jackson. Seeing the half-empty bottle of Lancester cabernet, he lifted it and whistled. "A Lancester? Good wine. Expensive."

"Three thousand dollars expensive, to be exact," Aurora said meekly. Then she looked at me. "Why do you even have such expensive wine here if you don't drink alcohol?"

"Because some of my business partners drink," I replied. "I don't condone it, but I understand that it's necessary for some businesses."

Jackson patted me sympathetically on the shoulder. Unlike Aurora, he knew why I despised this devilish stuff so much.

One last time Aurora tasted everything before she gave the *ok,* and we sat down at the table together.

"It really does smell delicious," Jackson praised Aurora's cooking, and I had to agree. After the alcohol had cooked off, the scents of thyme and rosemary had filled the room. If Aurora's food tasted half as good as it smelled, she could compete with star chefs, no question about it.

While Jackson started eating without hesitation, Aurora just poked at her food. Something was on the tip of her tongue. I watched Aurora's facial expressions with amusement; she was really cute when she was so shy.

"Really delicious," I said after the first bite, and Jacks agreed.

When Aurora noticed me staring at her, she flinched slightly, as if I had caught her doing something forbidden.

When Jackson noticed the silence and our stares, he cleared his throat.

"Are you really okay with me being here?"

Aurora nodded. "Yes. It's very nice to meet you sometime. Caden talks about you a lot."

"Oh yeah, does he?" asked Jackson, looking at me.

"*A lot* would be an exaggeration, but yes, I'm talking about you."

Aurora got her attention one more time by noisily sliding some vegetables onto her fork.

"Anyway, I'm glad to finally meet people from Caden's life who aren't monsters."

"Thank you?" Jackson looked at me questioningly, and I agreed to clear up the circumstance.

"Possibly my former personal assistant is a little frustrated."

"A little?" Aurora looked at me like my statement was the understatement of the millennium, then turned back to Jackson as she pricked a piece of broccoli onto her fork. "Unfortunately, though, Caden is pretty frugal when it comes to what you guys do when you move around the house."

The conversation went in a direction I didn't like, because on this subject my former subs had reacted so emotionally that I had decided to simply withhold my extreme hobby from them. Jackson was now jumping on this subject, because I couldn't slow him down fast enough.

"Well, it's more like moving atop the houses," he replied with a grin. Heck, he was proud of his bad pun, too.

"On the houses?" Aurora furrowed her brow. "You climb around on the roofs of houses?"

"Yes, and we jump from house to house. It's not just houses. We also climb on the containers at the docks when the guards take bribes. Oh, and one time we flew all the way to Paris to jump on…"

Aurora choked, causing a small coughing fit, at the same time I interrupted Jackson.

"Okay, that's enough for now." I gave Jackson a warning look while patting Aurora on the back.

"No, it's not enough!" objected Aurora in a hotter voice. "I want to hear every detail!"

"Later," I said seriously and sat back down in my seat because Aurora was feeling better again.

"Looks like I got something going. I didn't know Aurora didn't know about our free-running," Jackson said. If there was anything more embarrassing than our current president's haircut, it was Jackson's sad attempts at apology.

"It's okay," I said, waving it off. "I was going to have to tell her sooner or later anyway."

Aurora looked at me reproachfully. "You probably would have preferred *later,* right? Why didn't you tell me about it?"

"That's why. Women always react a touch too emotionally to my hobby."

Aurora shook her head. "Possibly because you're hanging out unsecured over thousands of feet?"

"Most of the time we're out in Queens. The houses there are thirty, maybe forty feet high."

"Not helping!" I growled to Jackson. Then I turned to Aurora. "We'll talk about this later. Now is not a good time."

"Because now you have to jump over ledges with Jackson?" Aurora rubbed her temples. "That's really idiotic. Only people with a death wish do that!"

Neither Jackson nor I disagreed. Where Aurora was right...however, that gave her no right to speak to me like that.

"We'll talk more about it after dinner."

"Promise?"

"I promise."

Unsatisfied, Aurora continued to poke at the food on her plate but settled for my answer. Jackson had really done something there that wasn't so easy to sort out, which brought me back to the question of what he was doing here in the first place.

"Trouble at the station?" I asked directly.

"Remember when I said our soles were about to stick to the ground?"

"Fuck."

"I couldn't have put it better myself," Jackson grumbled in frustration. "Damn austerity measures are about to cost us our lives."

"That's terrible," Aurora said softly. "I'm sorry I called you an idiot."

"It's okay." Jackson winked at her conciliatory. "There's no denying that Caden and I are idiots."

"Back to the topic at hand. Are you desperate enough for my help by now?"

Jackson remained silent. Not a good sign. As much as I would have liked to disappear into the playroom with Aurora right now, my best friend went first. Because it was written all over his face that, if he didn't get his impulsive temper under control, he was going to smash the whole neighborhood around Twenty-third.

Chapter 18 – Caden

Although Aurora had been silent for the rest of dinner, I could see that she was a ticking bomb, just waiting for the trigger. Before I left with Jackson, I had to clear this matter with Aurora.

As I closed the door to the playroom Aurora had stormed into, she turned and looked at me angrily.

"When would you have told me about this?"

"Eventually."

Maybe I wouldn't have if I had known how it ended.

"Why all these rules, Caden?"

"The more important question is why you agreed to them if you don't like them," I growled.

"Because some of them I really like."

For a second, her features softened, and I saw that she wasn't actually angry, but hurt. I took a deep breath to reanalyze the situation, but no matter which scenario I went through, I drove it into the wall – or Aurora was at the wheel doing the same.

"You claim I shouldn't ride in Maxine's Rolls Royce but you're dancing on roof ledges isn't dangerous? Do you know what that feels like, Caden?"

"I don't dance," I growled.

"Why are you doing it anyway?" Her question didn't sound reproachful, she really wanted to know why I was doing what I was doing.

I don't know why, but when I was free-running, the noise of the world became quieter and all that mattered was my heartbeat. For a brief moment, the pain, guilt and chaos around me disappeared. The more dangerous the ridge of death was, the more alive I felt.

"If there was another option, I would do it."

"It has something to do with what Erica knows but can't say because of her contract, right?"

I narrowed my eyes and examined Aurora closely.

"What did she tell you?"

"Nothing." Automatically, Aurora raised her arms upward. "But from your reaction, I suspect it's true."

"That's a subject I'm not going to talk about, Aurora. You have your secrets and I have my secrets. End of story."

Aurora sighed softly as she bit her lips.

"But we should be able to tell each other anything. We're engaged."

For a second I wanted to agree with her, but then I remembered that it was all just a damn game, too.

"On paper."

"Whether you admit it or not, it's *more* than just a piece of paper."

She looked at me resolutely, almost challengingly.

"Not long ago, you were calling me heartless," I argued confidently.

"Now I know it's just a facade. A protection from the thing you're running away from."

Two things popped into my head. One, Aurora wasn't my damn shrink, and two, she was still right.

"Enough."

"No, we need to talk about it."

I shook my head. "We'll never talk about that."

"And what am I supposed to do while you're out collecting near-death experiences?"

"It's not that dangerous. Jacks and I have been doing this for years, we know what we're doing."

"You're a dangerously good liar."

I took Aurora's hand and placed it on my chest so she could feel my calm, steady heartbeat.

"When you lie, your pulse increases. Can you feel now that I am not a liar?"

Aurora listened to my heartbeat and gradually became calmer. Good, in this condition I could leave her alone.

"You're going to go with Jackson now, no matter what I say or what I ask you to do, aren't you?"

I pulled Aurora to me. "I'm not asking you for anything."

"Okay," she whispered, "but I won't be able to think about anything else."

Even though I had no head for games in the playroom now, I got handcuffs out of a drawer. Sometimes hunger came with food, besides I knew that it reliably brought Aurora to other thoughts.

"Get on the bed!" I ordered quietly, but Aurora stopped.

"You want to play? Now?"

"You know exactly what I want. And you also know that you shouldn't ask any counter-questions."

Snorting, and with narrowed eyes, Aurora ran towards the bed. She was just trying to get me to stay here and put her over my knee.

When she took a breath, I interrupted her.

"Not a word." I didn't give Aurora a chance to interrupt me, lest her situation deteriorate further. No matter how upset or angry or tired I was, I was always consistent.

"Kneel in front of the bed."

Aurora clenched her teeth and did as I said.

"Undress," I murmured, because I liked the hell out of the looks she was giving me.

She removed her summer dress, under which she wore no underwear, and folded it neatly before resting her hands on her thighs again.

Good girl. She carried out my orders, although I could tell she was unhappy with the situation. She played along because she trusted me. By now Aurora should know me well enough to know that I would never betray her trust.

The Playroom was not a panacea for disputes, but at least it helped shift the focus.

With the metal handcuffs I tied Aurora's arms to the bed.

"Wait here, I forgot a little something."

"How funny," Aurora replied dryly, jingling her handcuffs to make it clear that she had no choice but to wait.

I went outside, got a jar of my famous chocolate mousse and re-entered the playroom. Smiling, I got down on my knees, dipped my finger in the cream and let Aurora taste it.

She moaned softly. "Wow, this is delicious!"

"How delicious?" I echoed. At the same time, I let Aurora lick my finger one more time.

"It's the best chocolate mousse I've ever had."

I nodded with satisfaction. "Good. Then it's an appropriate punishment."

"How is that a punishment?"

I stood up and ate a spoonful of the cream.

"Caden, you're a monster!"

"Because I eat the chocolate in front of you?"

"Yes!"

"Then maybe next time you'll think better about calling me or my friends idiots."

"You're idiots!" Aurora defended her statement. Admittedly, I had almost hoped that she would contradict me.

"So that's not punishment enough for you?"

Good that I could make her stay in the playroom much more uncomfortable by placing the half-full bowl right in front of her eyes. *So close and yet unreachable.*

Aurora was silent, but she didn't have to be, because her derailed features said it all. For a moment I enjoyed how Aurora squirmed in her bonds, then I breathed heavily, because now I absolutely had to make sure that my best friend didn't reduce the city to rubble.

"Do you have anything else to say?"

"Yes."

"Out with it."

"Only if you won't punish me for it."

"That depends on what you're going to say."

If Aurora started like that, I knew I would have to punish her severely.

"No punishment!" she ruled me.

I could have just left, but Aurora had aroused my curiosity. I wanted to know what was going on in her pretty head.

"Fine, fine by me. Say whatever's on your mind."

"I hate you for tying me up here and maybe dying out there. I hate the thought that it could happen, and I didn't stop you. And most of all, I hate you for the fact that in the last moments before I starve to death, I'll be looking at your damn chocolate!"

She was on the verge of tears. *Damn.*

I crouched down to meet Aurora at eye level, grabbed her chin and forced her to look at me.

"I'm not going to die."

"You don't know that!"

"I'll be careful." Sighing, I pulled the handcuff key out of my back pocket and thrust it into Aurora's hand. "But if it makes you feel any better, there's no way you're going to starve to death here."

Aurora clutched the key with her delicate fingers.

"You're still an idiot," Aurora whispered one more time. The anger in her beautiful eyes was gone.

"I know."

"You should also know that if you crash, I will kill you myself."

I raised a brow. "Brave words for a defenseless, tied-up girl."

"Honest words. I won't be able to think of anything else until you get back."

"Hmm." I went to a drawer and opened it. "The past has shown that I can effectively take your mind off things, with these little toys."

Demonstratively, I let Aurora take a look at the vibrators in my hand.

"Stop! I think I can think of something else after all," Aurora corrected.

Good. I wouldn't have known what to do if Aurora had continued to be defiant. No idea how long I would be away, but definitely too long to be able to punish her with vibrators.

I put the vibrators back in the drawer, took one last look at Aurora, and then headed for the door.

"Don't turn anything on while I'm gone."

"No, sir."

"Caden?" I pushed the door handle down as Aurora stopped me one last time. "Take care."

"I will."

Then I left her in the playroom and entered the open kitchen. I couldn't define it exactly, but I had a sinking feeling in my stomach that didn't completely disappear.

Neither when we left the apartment, nor when we got into the car.

Because we hadn't found anyone at the docks who could be bribed, Jacks and I had agreed to try our luck at our regular Brooklyn haunt. Smaller high-rises, narrow alleys, few cops. Perfect for our goals. Plus, over time, we'd greased quite a few bouncers and security guards who let us walk down the fire escape without a hitch – not that we couldn't get back down by other means, but it was significantly easier.

"Ready?" I asked as we both stood at the first ledge looking out at the flat rooftops ahead.

"Ready," Jackson replied.

"Are we going to talk about the twenty-third after this?"

"Maybe. But for now, I want to forget about the damn firehouse."

I understood Jacks well, because I also had some things I wanted to shake off of me. That damn feeling in the pit of my stomach just wouldn't go away.

"How about a little race?" I suggested.

A little competitiveness was definitely good for both of us. We were both alphas, winners, we were men who weren't afraid of wanting to be first, and that's why we bit down on it. We had tasted blood, we wanted to be first, always and without exception.

"And what are we betting on?"

I shrugged my shoulders. "I don't know, just say what you want to give me if you lose."

"Fuck you, Caden! If I win, I want the next sneakers you buy."

"Forget it," I growled. For my semi-legal hobby, I wore only custom-made one-of-a-kind pieces. The Jordans I was wearing were even signed by Michael Jordan himself.

"Are you afraid of losing after all?"

If Jacks wanted to play that high of a poker game for all I cared, I decided to go with it.

"You owe me a favor for that if I win."

"You got it."

Jacks got ready to go, but I slowed him down to look at him urgently.

"If I show up at your door tomorrow and demand that you and the whole firehouse pose half-naked with baby kittens in front of fire trucks, you will. If I'm craving *Special Chili Cheese Nachos* at four in the morning, you'll bring them to me. And when I say take the *fucking check*, you will take the fucking check, got it?"

Jackson rolled his eyes. "I know what a favor means with you."

"Yet you're not worried? How naive."

"Not naive, confident of victory."

Focused, Jackson pushed up the sleeves of his hoodie to show off his muscular forearms. I had no idea how he still managed to climb so light on his feet with those tons of muscle. Of course, I was muscular too, but Jacks could lift small cars – really. A few years ago, he had been awarded the *Medal of Courage* by the city when he was able to free a child trapped under a car at the last second.

"Alright, first one to the roof at the Forty-third intersection wins," I said as I pressed my fingers together to prepare them for the ordeal to come.

"That short? Our route is easily twice that long."

"I want to give you a chance for a rematch."

"Fine by me. Then I'll rip off your next pair of one-of-a-kind Jordans and your record collection."

I laughed out loud, because my records were sacred to me. So sacred that I rarely listened to them so as not to wear out the wax layer too much.

"Let's finish this round first," I said, pulling a quarter out of my pocket.

"Ready?"

"Ready!"

I tossed the coin from the eaves and we both listened intently for the *ping*, which was like a starting gun, only much quieter.

Immediately we put our backs into it, and it worked. My focus was now completely on winning. My feet carried me as fast as they could, and the grips of my hands were purposeful and strong.

With each step it was only inches, but I was able to slowly increase my lead over Jackson, which further spurred me on to do my best.

The first part of the route was easy. Some of the houses were only a couple feet apart, with no major height differences. The biggest difficulties were caused by the many large fans of the air conditioners and some clotheslines hanging across our misappropriated track.

In fast, steady beats, my heart pumped adrenaline through my body, invigorating my mind. I literally flew over the edges, lightning fast, and yet I perceived every little thing. The rusted lamps cast their dim light on the garbage cans whose moss-green paint was slowly peeling off. The barking of a dog drowned out even the roaring in my ears.

The closer I got to my goal, the better I felt. I couldn't get enough of it!

"Won!" I gasped as I reached our destination before Jackson.

"Revenge!" the latter replied, breathing heavily.

"Just a second."

Of course, we had both mastered longer distances at a stretch, but we didn't have to go for it. Especially not because I had not chosen this break without reason. Directly behind us was the greatest difficulty of the route. The nearest house was quite a few feet away from us and the wall ledge was about the same distance above us. One false leap, one false grip, and I would plunge into the cramped alley, where even in summer it steamed from the manhole covers. That would be my certain death.

I stood at the precipice and for the first time I really became aware of the depth. Now I understood why Aurora was worried. Of course I knew that this sport could be fatal, but I had never really understood how I was risking my life to feel alive.

"Is it going on?" asked Jackson. Impatiently, he kicked at the humming fan of an air conditioner.

"Yeah, fine by me." I climbed off the wall and pulled another coin from my pocket to toss it to Jackson, who caught it confidently. "This time, you flip."

"Okay. I'll bet your shoes again."

"You never learn, do you?" I asked with a grin.

"Well, I already owe you a favor, so I have nothing left to lose."

"True again."

I got ready to go and waited for the characteristic sound that the coin made when it fell on the metal garbage cans or the concrete floor.

Ping.

Immediately we focused on the second part of the course. Jackson jumped without any problems to the wall, directly in front of us, grabbed the ledge and pulled himself up without any problems. I, on the other hand, stopped on the wall ledge and stared into the depths.

Fuck.

I couldn't jump, I don't know why. This had never happened to me before. Until ten minutes ago, there was no such thing as *too high, too daring, too dangerous.* There was only *more of it!*

Damn! What was wrong with me? The protrusion of the next skyscraper seemed yards away and the longer I stared at it with my gloomiest gaze, the further it moved away from me.

Cursing loudly, I jumped off the wall back onto the safe ground and took out my frustration on the door to the stairwell, banging my clenched fist against it.

In the meantime, Jackson had also noticed my absence and looked down at me in irritation.

"What's wrong?"

"Aurora happened!" I growled and banged the door two more times until my knuckles were gleaming bloody. I couldn't put it any better than that. Aurora had made me realize my mortality and suddenly I was no longer immortal.

I was no longer a superhero, an adrenaline junkie with more luck than sense. I was just a guy running away from his fucked-up past.

Jackson returned to me in which he pushed off his heel with momentum and cushioned his jump with a shoulder roll.

"What exactly happened?" echoed Jackson.

"She's worried," I replied scornfully.

Jackson frowned, thought for a moment, and then sat down on the ledge of the wall to watch the lights of the skyline in the far distance.

"Sounds really awful to have your fiancée worrying about you while you're climbing from skyscraper to skyscraper."

"Have you forgotten that I'm relationship-disordered?"

I sat down next to Jacks on the wall and let my feet hang down.

"Welcome to the club. This, by the way, would be a classic *we-toast-with-beer* moment."

"I know," I growled. He knew about my abstinence from alcohol, even though he kept trying to defuse my unhealthy hatred.

Jackson patted me on the shoulder. "It's nice to sit here with clear thoughts and look into the distance, though."

Silently, because we both didn't want to know about our problems right now, we watched the tiny lights of the cars crossing the East River over the Brooklyn Bridge.

"Jacks?" I looked at my only friend because I wanted to see the reaction to my question.

"What? The way you're looking at me, we're about to have a pretty serious conversation."

I nodded and looked at Jackson struggling to suppress one of his stupid, cynical sayings, but he managed.

"Do you sometimes find me heartless?"

"Is that a trick question?"

Jackson eyed me, irritated. That was absolutely not the reaction I had hoped for.

"No," I replied dryly. "I'm as serious as it gets."

"Well, sometimes you could be a little more sensitive. But what do I know? I'm at least as messed up as you are, though somehow different."

I sighed. "So I'm heartless?"

Jackson shook his head resolutely. "No. I know you, and I know you're not a monster. But those you don't let get to you think you're heartless, yes."

"But I don't let anyone get to me."

"Yep."

So things were worse than I had initially suspected. Yes, I knew that I put a lot of distance between myself and others, but did aloofness equate to callousness?

"Where did you get that idea, anyway? Did Aurora say that?"

"Oh, what does Aurora know," I waved it off.

Only now did I realize how deep in the shit I was. I had fucking broken my own rules. The thing with Aurora felt right - and therefore it was wrong. More wrong than wrong!

Jackson cleared his throat.

"She also said we were both idiots and she was right about that too."

"And because she said she was worried, I can no longer ... "

I did not dare to say that I felt something like *fear*. My attitude toward death itself had not changed, but the attitude of others confronting my death had.

"Stop painting the devil on the wall. Ten minutes ago you were beating me."

"Well, and then I realized that Aurora had robbed me of my immortality."

Jackson looked at me, stunned. "Today you're really going out of your way to seem heartless! Did it ever occur to you that maybe Aurora is the reason your life is suddenly worth living?"

At first I wanted to laugh out loud because Jackson brought up something like *love*, but then the whole world around me went quiet and I knew his words were true. I could neither deny nor shut down my feelings for Aurora, and the more I focused on that feeling, the stronger I felt it. And suddenly adrenaline rushed through my body, completely without exposing myself to any danger, just at the thought that Aurora might feel the same way about me.

"Fuck, Jacks, I think you're right."

Chapter 19 – Aurora

"Done," I said proudly, but also a little disappointed, and put the last papers on Caden's desk.

"Thank you," he replied without looking up. His gaze was focused on one of the letters I had gone through for him this morning. When I didn't leave, but continued to stare at him expectantly, fiddling with the hem of my dress, he did give me a look.

"What else is there?"

"Nothing," I replied.

"Good, then you can go. I still have to work through this."

He sounded annoyed, not good. Somehow Caden had seemed tense for a few days, and I had the feeling that our dinner with Jackson had something to do with it.

Admittedly, I had not reacted very positive, but who reacted positively to such news?

Will you marry me? Oh, by the way, I like to run while juggling chainsaws.

Well, at least it was never boring with Caden, his personality was way too interesting for that.

"Aurora? Are you sure it's nothing?"

I shook my head. "*Nothing* is the problem. I have nothing more to do."

That was an understatement. In fact, I had already worked ahead for the next two days, even though we wouldn't be here, but in Seattle. Unfortunately, there was nothing I could do now to distract myself.

"Then do what everyone else does non-stop when I'm not looking. Facebook, solitaire, whatever."

"Okay," I replied more hotly. Because slowly, but surely, I was completely losing it. Work had been able to distract me from the fact that my sister was getting married tomorrow, but now I was feeling firsthand what my mom had been going through for weeks. I couldn't quite renounce the female *Winter genes* after all.

"Take it easy, Aurora. We'll be on time, I promise."

Caden said what I was most afraid of. I could not, under any circumstances, miss my sister's wedding. It was Maggy's day, but I really wanted to be a part of it. Not to mention, the relationship between my mom and I couldn't take another incident.

"What makes you so sure?" I probed.

"Because the private plane we booked won't leave without us."

Caden winked at me, and my heart lightened a bit.

"Why doesn't *Saint Industries* actually have its own planes?" I asked. Caden had booked a private airline's plane, which made me wonder. I thought multibillion-dollar companies had their own planes.

With a serious expression on his face, Caden leaned forward, intertwined his hands, and suddenly looked like the most powerful man in the world.

My stomach tingled because I realized that I was engaged to this very man. I belonged to Mister Universe – and he also belonged to me a little bit.

"Why don't I own private planes? Because people come to me when they want something from me."

Wow. This gloomy look triggered things in me that I'd better not think about now. I could not use a remote-controlled vibrator to my burgeoning panic. My heart was pounding as it was, like a jackhammer. *Although ...*

When Caden got up from his desk and gave me a hug, the world became a little calmer. And the fact that he interrupted important work to comfort me also made the world a little better.

"I know you're worried, but I've got it all sorted. Every little detail, believe me."

"I believe you."

I wasn't just saying that; I really believed him.

"Good girl."

I suppressed a sigh and snuggled tighter against his well-toned chest. Although it should have been my job to take care of the flight and accommodations in Seattle, Caden had taken care of everything himself. Admittedly, it had frustrated me because it felt like Caden didn't trust me with anything in that regard. Of course, I knew his preferences and I would have found us the perfect hotel and flight. Maybe it would have even calmed me down to know exactly what was coming up, but Caden kept what he thought were *unimportant* details to himself.

Caden stole a kiss from me, then looked deep into my eyes.

"Now let me finish these things so we can get going, okay?"

"Yes, sir," I replied seductively.

I couldn't put my finger on what it meant, but that glint that Caden had had in his eyes all day was telltale. I don't know what, but I was pretty sure he was up to something. And by something, I meant some kind of toys he was carrying in his back pocket that would take my mind off things for the entire flight.

I liked the view. Even if some fear resonated that I misinterpreted his looks, and he had nothing special prepared.

I left the office with such a phenomenal swing of my hips that Caden was literally forced to look after me. But in this black one-piece I didn't make it easy for Caden either. Although the fabric was high-waisted, it was tight and accentuated my curves perfectly. The words Maxine had found for the outfit hit it perfectly. *Charming. Professional. Hot as hell!*

I wish Max would go to the wedding with me, but she had business in New York - and no one had ever been able to get her on a plane.

Once at my desk, I slumped down in the chair with a sigh because I had no idea how I was going to kill time until we finally left for Seattle.

Although I only turned to my stolen documents when Caden had visitors in his office – because it massively reduced my risk of being caught – I pulled the blueprints out of the drawer. I was quite a bit further along, or at least I imagined I was. I didn't have a PhD in physics, but the experience I had gained in Dad's workshop was now paying off.

I understood the basics on which Caden's new drones were to be built. For some things I had to brush up on my basic knowledge, which was no problem thanks to YouTube, and so I fought my way through the plans bit by bit.

Unfortunately, I had not found out much in the last few days. At first glance, everything seemed to fit - and that's exactly why the scientists despaired, because theoretically everything was right, but practically the drones flew together quite a mess.

I really had to ask Caden about what these drones were going to be used for when I got the chance, because that played a huge role. The location alone had different implications - drones flew differently in Antarctica than in the Sahara.

Yes, I had done my homework, but I was still missing some info that I had to squeeze out of Caden as well, in order to be able to completely put the pieces of the puzzle together. So far, unfortunately, I had not found the right moment, either Caden had talked about other business things, or we were in the playroom.

The intercom connected to Caden's office buzzed briefly.

"I like it when you're so focused," Caden murmured.

"Shouldn't you be more focused?" I asked with a grin.

"Yes, I should, but I am burningly interested in what thoughts elicit such seductive looks from you."

Bummer. I had no idea what to say – the truth was out of the question, but lying wasn't an option either. Sometimes I had the feeling that Caden could read my mind, because he knew immediately when I was hiding something from him.

"I'm just thinking about a problem," I said with a shrug.

"And what kind of problem?"

"How to get some secrets out of you." Basically, I hadn't told Caden a lie.

"Well, I can think of a way."

"I'm sure you do," I replied with a smile. "But let me worry about that."

"Have I still not been able to teach you that you should never refuse my offers?"

"I'm afraid there will be some lessons to be learned."

"I'm afraid so."

With his intense brown eyes, Caden saw right into my soul at that moment. I returned his gaze, even though it was much harder for me to see behind his facade. All I knew was that he needed time to open up. Whatever Caden had experienced, it had hurt him deeply.

Thinking about the look on his face when I held the wine bottle, my heart still ached a little. For a second, Caden had dropped his ice wall, and I saw how lost he felt. The pain had to be unbearable, and I wished I could take some of it away from him. Whatever Caden had experienced, it was so terrible that he never talked about it.

"I'd love to give you another lesson right now, but I'm afraid you'll have to be patient." He pointed to his phone.

"I will wait patiently, sir."

I wonder if Caden's heart was hurting too. He seemed so self-confident, as if nothing could upset him, and his eyes had that fire in them that I usually only saw in the playroom. But how did he really feel? And what did he feel for me?

It was hard for me to interpret Caden's feelings and true intentions, but I hadn't given up yet. However, since I knew that Caden was pursuing his death wishes with Jackson, something had changed between us. Caden seemed even more closed than usual. He brooded more, and I had the uneasy feeling that something was changing between us, even if I didn't let on.

I didn't want to be complicated, I didn't want to constantly bug him with my feelings, and I certainly didn't want to give him a reason to get rid of me, because that was the last thing I wanted. My feelings for Caden were no longer deniable.

As I continued to ogle Mister Universe, I continued to think about his project and how messed up it made Caden that the prototype fabrication wasn't taking shape.

Of course, I was still hell-bent on solving this problem that his engineers were failing at, but no longer to rub his nose in it, but to help him.

My perfect view of Caden, who was staring at his keyboard with a serious look on his face, was blocked by Janice, who was looking at me snootily.

"What can I do for you?" I asked politely. Just because Janice was a sore loser didn't mean I had to be a bad assistant.

"I need to talk to Caden."

"He's busy and doesn't want to be disturbed."

I pointed emphatically to the closed door, which was a clear sign to all staff that Caden wanted his rest.

"It's urgent." I was almost grateful to her for avoiding eye contact with me; it saved us both an exhausting fake smile.

I pulled out a pen and paper. "What do you want me to tell him?"

"Nothing. I need to talk to Caden himself."

I took a deep breath before looking at Janice seriously.

"Just tell me what you want me to tell him. We both know what happens if you walk out that door now."

Janice pressed her lips together so tightly that they deformed into a thin line.

"Make an announcement, I'm not leaving here any sooner."

"Fine, fine by me. It's your funeral," I said, rolling my eyes. "What's it about?"

"About the PR appointment that Caden canceled. He can't just postpone or cancel appointments like that."

I looked at Janice. "He's the boss, of course he can."

Janice snorted in annoyance, and I pushed the button to Caden's office. She wouldn't hear anything different from Caden than from me, but she just wouldn't let up.

"Caden? Janice from PR is here," I said professionally. Of course, Caden knew who Janice was, but I couldn't help rubbing her nose in the fact that she was now just *Janice from PR*.

"Not now," he replied curtly.

"They're not happy about you canceling appointments," I replied, so Janice finally left me alone.

"I'm the boss, I can agree or disagree whenever it suits me."

"See?" I asked Janice. "I told you that in the first place."

Janice crossed her arms in front of her chest and looked at me angrily. This time I hadn't given her any basis on which to insult me. There probably wasn't any more, because by now I knew almost everything about Caden, it was as if I had known him all my life.

"Yeah, yeah. Just save it, okay?"

I brought the paper and pen back into focus and put on my professional face.

"Is there anything else you want me to tell Caden?"

"Yes, Erica wants to talk to him tomorrow about upcoming press events."

"He won't be here tomorrow."

"Day after tomorrow, then."

I shook my head. "Not then either."

"Caden has never missed two days as a result. How do you know he won't be here?"

I couldn't help but look at her with a triumphant smile.

"Because he's going to accompany me to Seattle for my sister's wedding."

"What?" Janice's jaw dropped. "You sure?"

"He's my fiancé, of course he accompanies me on such occasions," I replied, as a matter of course.

Yes, it was mean, but after all the bullying and unnecessary punitive work, it felt good to finally be able to rub her nose in it.

"I'll believe that when I see it," Janice muttered, staring at my bare ring finger, which I covered with my other hand.

"I can show you pictures once we get back from Seattle," I offered Janice with a sugary smile.

"That was rhetorical," Janice waved it off, looking reproachfully in Caden's direction. If she wasn't such a bitch, I might have even felt sorry for her.

"You shouldn't get too used to it. You may be in Caden's good graces today, but that could be over tomorrow."

"I take it you speak from experience?" I tried to look as unconcerned as possible, but Janice was the kind of person I could barely contain myself around. She had that *slap-me-for-my-provocations-facial-expression* that those kinds of people always had.

When Caden left his office, I literally jumped up. Luckily, because Janice looked like she almost went for my throat.

"Ready?" Caden asked me with a bright smile.

"More than ready!" I ran around my desk as fast as my heels would allow.

Janice took a deep breath, but Caden held up a finger and slowed her down before she had said a single word.

"Not now, Janice. Email me or stick a Post-it on my desk."

Then he turned to me and angled his arm.

"Shall we?"

"I'd love to," I replied, hooking up with him.

Together we left Janice standing there.

"Thanks for saving me," I whispered to Caden.

"It looked more to me like you put up a pretty good fight."

"Did you hear our conversation?" I asked irritated.

"Janice's voice is not to be missed," he replied, and I thought I saw him roll his eyes.

"You don't like her voice?"

"No."

"But you..." That was all I could bring myself to say.

"I make mistakes, too. It's very, very rare, but it happens."

"Oh, wow."

"Yes, it may come as a shock, but even Caden Saint is not infallible." Caden grinned at me.

"You could also fire Janice if she bugs you."

What I meant to say was: *You could also fire Janice for annoying me*, but I'm sure Caden knew that as well.

"Now that it's getting exciting?" When I snorted, Caden's grin grew even wider.

"Thanks for nothing, Mister Saint."

"How about *thank you for joining me at your sister's wedding*?"

"I could still show up on my own," I said seriously.

"And then the most beautiful woman of the evening is lonely and alone and has to flee from all the bachelors who want to stalk her?"

I frowned. "My sister will be the most beautiful woman of the evening.

Caden looked deep into my eyes and my heart skipped a beat.

"Not in my eyes."

Oh. My. God.

I had not only found the perfect man for the wedding, but the perfect man for life.

Chapter 20 – Caden

Only with difficulty, could I suppress the urge to look at my watch again. The drive to the airport dragged on like cheap chewing gum. Slowly but surely, Aurora noticed that I was hiding something from her, even though she was busy with her very own problems.

Unbelievable. I had made billion-dollar deals without batting an eye, plus there had been no obstacle that were too high or too risky for me. But that little red velvet box in my pocket made me break out in a sweat.

I had planned our trip to Seattle down to the smallest detail and spared no expense or effort to make sure everything went as I intended, yet I could hardly suppress my tension.

"Excited?" I asked as Aurora gave a loud audible sigh.

"And how! I feel like I haven't seen my family in half an eternity. Crazy, right? Yet it's only been a few weeks."

I grabbed her hand, and we intertwined our fingers.

"A lot has happened since you last saw her."

"You can say that again!" Aurora beamed at me and her grip on my hand tightened as the building towered over the horizon. Again and again, my eyes drifted to my smartphone, because any second I was expecting a message that would ruin my plans. My planning had gone off without a hitch, which was never a good sign. I remembered well all the projects that had gone *smoothly* during the planning – every single one of them turned out to be a disaster in retrospect.

"Caden?"

"Huh?"

"What about your family?"

I looked at Aurora, frowning. "What do you mean?"

"Am I ever going to meet her? You've never talked about her before."

And if I could avoid it, I would never talk about her either. Even before Aurora could see my meaningful expression, I turned away from her and stared stubbornly out the window. The hand that had just held Aurora's finger felt strangely empty.

"You know all the important people in my life," I said, waving them off.

"I only know Jackson!" protested Aurora.

"Told you."

"Oh."

Suddenly it became quite quiet in the car. I took a deep breath because my fear that Aurora was looking at me pityingly came true.

"Stop looking at me with pity!" I said in a calm commanding tone.

"I'm not," Aurora replied, shaking her head so significantly that her long, blonde hair whipped in all directions.

"Yes, you were."

"Not at all."

I looked at Aurora seriously.

"I put my past behind me, so you should too."

She frowned. "You want me to leave my past behind? Yeah, mom and I are a little..."

Putting my index finger to her lips, I silenced her.

"I want you to leave *my* past behind. No discussions."

"Yes, sir."

For now, Aurora kept quiet, but I knew her well enough to know that her silence was deceptive. Sooner or later she would bring up the subject again, she couldn't help it.

It wasn't until I saw the gate to the tarmac that I leaned back. Once we were on the jet, Aurora was sure to have other things to do than poke around in my fucked-up past.

At the rolling gate that led directly to one of the runways, a security guard stopped us. But instead of checking our personal details, as they usually did, he gave us the signal to turn around.

What the hell? Okay, maybe I had conjured it up with my cynical thoughts that there was still a problem shortly before departure, but I hadn't expected that.

With the push of a button, I had the window lowered halfway so I could talk to the guard.

"Is there a problem?" I asked. The last time I was denied onward travel here, there had been a false alarm because of an abandoned suitcase – including a four-hour delay for all flights.

"No problem, sir. But the access road is closed."

I put on my most charming smile and held up my smartphone that had the flight number of my booked jet.

"When I booked the jet, they said there would be no problems."

"Possibly. But because of impromptu remodeling at one of the gates, there are new security protocols."

Sighing, I pointed to a white, brightly polished machine not a hundred yards from us.

"I'm Caden Saint, and that's my private jet over there."

"The rule applies to you, too, Mister Saint."

The guy pronounced my name as if he had no idea who I was, which made me even angrier. Aurora noticed my tension and put her delicate hand on my clenched fist.

"Stay calm, Caden," she whispered to me, and I nodded. Then I turned back to the guard.

"How long will this remodeling work take?"

"I don't know, a couple of weeks probably." Shrugging his shoulders, the guard let his gaze roam over my sedan. "Nice car, by the way."

"The car is yours if you let me go to my flight now," I offered him with a serious face.

For a second, the security guard wanted to accept my offer, but then, unfortunately, he thought better of it.

"I'll get fired if I let a car through that doesn't have a siren."

With that, the security guard's willingness to talk was so far spent that he simply turned around and sauntered back into his little bunker.

Fuck.

"We'll still get there on time, right?" asked Aurora anxiously.

"Don't worry. As I said, the jet won't leave until we're on board."

My chauffeur brought us as close as he could to the main entrance and then took care of our luggage.

It was hard enough not to lose Aurora in this turmoil, I couldn't worry about our suitcases as well.

While Aurora and I squeezed through the crowds, my hand kept feeling for the little box in my pocket. Everything stood or fell with this little box.

"I never realized how busy this place is," I grumbled as I pushed my way through a group of tourists, all wearing colorful turtlenecks, flower necklaces and Hawaiian shirts.

"It's all part of flying, isn't it?" replied Aurora, beaming from ear to ear. "I love that great vibe. People flying to their long-awaited vacation, waiting for their best friends, or traveling to their great love."

While I perceived only noise and chaos, Aurora saw things that remained hidden from me. Perhaps I could have looked at the world through her eyes if I had been here as a child with my family?

As soon as we reached our gate, the scraps of words blurred and things quieted down. Not long and we were seated in my booked private jet and took off.

"Look how small everything is getting," Aurora said, lost in thought, as her fingers wiped the window.

"Small and insignificant," I added. The steep approach gently pressed our bodies into the upholstered genuine leather chairs.

Aurora looked at me. "When the world down there becomes unimportant, that makes us special."

"You're special," I said, nodding.

"*We* are special," Aurora corrected me.

I brushed a blond strand from her face because I didn't know what else to say. Her words were true, but I didn't dare think about it. All I felt right now was the fact that the crushing earth's gravity was getting lighter and lighter.

"What are you thinking about?" Aurora asked me as the force that plastered us into the seats slowly diminished.

"Nothing," I answered too quickly for *nothing*. Nevertheless, my look made it unmistakably clear to her that she should not inquire further. As usual, she turned a deaf ear to my warnings.

"Stop thinking so much, Caden. With every second, we're getting further away from Saint Industries, New York, and all the problems we left behind there."

"You're talking about Janice, right?" I asked with a teasing grin, which elicited an eye roll from Aurora.

"Yes, I'm talking about Janice. But also about your projects, which are dragging a bit right now, and about your annoying PR department."

If only Aurora knew that I couldn't leave my main problem in New York because it was sitting right next to me, interrogating me.

"You're right, I should get other ideas. Do you have any suggestions?"

Something sparkled in Aurora's eyes that I could not describe in detail, but it promised to be interesting.

"I actually have an idea." Aurora bit her lower lip lasciviously and looked at me seductively. "But I'm not sure we can be *undisturbed* long enough. If you know what I mean."

"No, I don't," I said dryly.

I knew exactly what Aurora meant, but I wanted to hear it from her mouth.

"How about we join the *Mile-High Club*?"

Grinning, I had to acknowledge her ingenuity, with which she managed to become unambiguous without any clear words at all. But she forgot that we were playing a game according to my rules – a game I had never lost.

"And how do we become members?" My voice became rough and dark, just like my thoughts. Aurora didn't know my real problem, but she had found a solution anyway.

"You know exactly how we become members," Aurora replied with a grin. "But you don't know how you're going to make me beg for anything today."

Had Aurora just challenged me? Too bad I didn't have any clamps or other tools with me that could elicit the most beautiful screams from Aurora.

As if timed, a short tone sounded, signaling that we could undo the straps. Aurora loosened her belt, winked at me and pushed past me. As she did so, she deliberately rubbed her bottom provocatively over my thighs and my throbbing hardness.

With seductive steps Aurora disappeared in the direction of the toilet and I could not help but comply with her request. I followed her. If only to teach her a lesson.

Damn, just the thought of me driving Aurora crazy until she spoke her dirtiest thoughts almost made me lose control.

Aurora leaned elegantly against the open door and let her index finger wander over her lower lip.

"May I introduce you to the *Mile-High Club*, Mister Saint?" asked Aurora with a phenomenal flutter of her eyelashes, extending her hand to me.

Grinning, I took her hand and let her pull me into the toilet, which was not much bigger than in airliners. Fortunately, I had recently tested extensively how flexible my sub could be.

As I closed the door behind me, Aurora fell onto me. Our lips met and merged until we both struggled for breath. Our hands wandered over our bodies, and I had to keep turning so that Aurora didn't accidentally feel the little box in my pants. The timing was still inappropriate, but I just could not separate from this little thing.

"Why not on the spacious armchairs, by the way?" I asked, between kisses.

"Because that's part of the club," Aurora gasped, smothering my next question with another kiss. In this cramped cabin we could barely turn on our axis, but I didn't mind knowing her body was between me and the wall. This way Aurora could not escape me in any case,

"And it has nothing to do with you being jealous and wanting me all to yourself?" I asked, with a wry grin.

Aurora winced briefly. *You got me, beautiful.*

"I like having my fiancé to myself, there's nothing wrong with that," she answered honestly. There was nothing else she could do, because the looks she gave the attractive stewardess who had greeted us were impossible to miss. Admittedly, I liked the fact that Aurora was jealous – and how she acted out her jealousy even more.

"Wouldn't it be better if she caught us in this chair?" I echoed with a grin. Of course, I provoked her anger, but that's exactly what I wanted to see. I loved it when Aurora's eyes lit up like that and her cheeks reddened.

"No." We continued to kiss. Fiercely, wildly, endlessly. Then she pulled me close and whispered in my ear, "I think it's much more exciting when she might catch us."

I knew exactly what she meant and agreed with her. The charm of *getting* caught went out as soon as it was inevitable to get caught. We should save that for another time.

Greedily, I pushed aside the fabric that covered Aurora's most intimate parts before I turned her around and pressed her upper body against the wall to kiss her neck from behind. Because her hands kept brushing dangerously close to my pants pocket, I grabbed her wrists and pressed them against the wall above her head.

Aurora moaned enthusiastically and pressed herself against me. I opened my pants and rubbed my throbbing erection over her wetness. Aurora was ready for me, and I loved her for it. She made me furious;

she made me break my own rules, and she made me forget my restlessness.

Aurora looked at me expectantly and I knew exactly what she was thinking.

"Not until you ask me to!" I demanded softly.

"Not today," Aurora replied with a mischievous grin.

"You know I'll have to punish you for this," I threatened, but Aurora was unimpressed.

"Do whatever you think is necessary, but today I'm not going to beg for anything."

"We'll see about that."

Actually, I should have just put Aurora over my knee, and if the cabin hadn't been so cramped, I probably would have, but now she had awakened my play instinct. I was determined to find out whether I could elicit a quiet *please, sir* from her.

Aurora knew exactly with which looks she could flip my switches. Everything she did worked – I reacted to her every move, every breath. Damn, I had underestimated her. But that didn't change the fact that I knew Aurora, too, and knew what made her tick.

My breath triggered tingling goose bumps that soon stretched over Aurora's entire body. Every single one of my touches had only one purpose now – I wanted to bring Aurora to her knees. But the fact that she resisted me stunned me, because slowly my pressure became so strong that I had to give in. There was no way my pride could allow that.

With an energetic movement, I grabbed Aurora's hips and turned her toward me until our lips met.

I went down on my knees in front of her and Aurora looked at me in surprise. Maybe she thought I would give up, but I made one last attempt.

"You know how wild it drove me the first time you demonstrated how limber you are?"

Aurora's balancing act during her spontaneous strip show had impressed me quite a bit, and it played a role in almost all my fantasies with her.

"You mean like this?" asked Aurora, resting her leg on my shoulder.

I nodded, stood up and held her ankle so it wouldn't slip off my shoulder.

"Just like that," I murmured.

Aurora stared expectantly at my erection. I could see her begging to be fucked. I hoped she gave up sooner than I did, because I couldn't take it much longer.

"I'm not going to fuck you until you beg for it."

Aurora licked her lips. "Then we have a problem."

Fuck! When had my sub gotten so out of control? And why couldn't I deny how much I liked her making new rules?

"Damn you, for that action I will never let you leave the playroom again." My voice quivered with anger and excitement in equal measure.

"It was worth it for that," Aurora said, smiling beatifically.

"Did you get what you want now?"

I pressed my erection harder against her entrance. With every heartbeat I found it harder to hold back – and my heart raced like mad.

"Almost."

Aurora really made me forget my good manners.

"What more do you want?"

"I want you to remember me."

When I looked into her eyes, which reflected the sincerity of her words, I was about to throw my plans overboard, but then I reconsidered. I couldn't throw away my plans just because my feelings were going crazy.

"You will," I replied.

If I could have, I would have torn my heart out of my chest to prove to her that it beat only for her. It was amazing that this gesture seemed easier to me than saying three little words. *I love you.*

Without thinking further about the fact that I wasn't ready for those words to leave my mouth, I thrust hard, eliciting a sigh from Aurora.

Because the cabin was so narrow that neither Aurora nor I could fall over, I devoted myself to her beautiful breasts, which bobbed along with every thrust. I freed her upper body from the annoying fabric that took away my view of her shapely body.

Aurora was tough, yet her buds were so sensitive that my breath was enough to make them even tougher.

With pleasure I took both of her tips between my fingers and kept applying varying degrees of pressure on them, which resulted in Aurora closing tighter and tighter around my hardness. It was unfortunate that I had no clamps with me, her breasts were made for it.

As the stewardess's footsteps grew louder, Aurora held her breath.

"What is it?" I asked. "I thought you were trying to make her jealous?"

Aurora looked at me reproachfully. "But she doesn't have to hear everything we do!"

"Well, in that case, you'd better keep quiet now," I said, unconcerned. The next moment I pinched her buds so hard that Aurora gasped.

"Caden!"

"Aurora?"

"Stop it!"

"You could ask for it."

I could tell that she had hundreds of insults and curses on the tip of her tongue, all of which she swallowed bravely. Her facial expressions, every time I changed the pressure or pushed deep into her, were delicious. And only when the stewardess's footsteps could no longer be heard did Aurora dare to breathe again.

For the fact that I had not made it easy for her, Aurora had put up a brave fight. But in order not to offer her more rules against which she could rebel, I decided to be *gracious*.

"You may come now," I allowed her, knowing Aurora wouldn't miss an orgasm.

"Thank you, sir," she replied. But anger sparkled in her eyes. What a fucking satisfaction! And I was serious about the playroom thing, too. Not today, maybe not tomorrow, but someday Aurora would have to pay the consequences for her behavior today – and I wasn't going to make it easy for her, that much was certain.

I grabbed Aurora by the hips, pressed her against my hard erection and took her as hard as I could while burying my teeth in her shoulder.

I took what I wanted and what I needed – both I got without resistance – until I pumped my lust into her. Aurora also came and let herself fall against the wall that forced us both to continue standing.

"You lost, by the way," Aurora whispered proudly, because I had fucked her without her begging after all.

"Maybe so," I replied, nodding. "But we're playing a game we can't win."

"If that's the case, losing has never been so much fun."

I looked Aurora in the eyes, and I realized that my life was quite complicated and very simple at the same time. We had both lost our hearts to each other – and emerged as winners together.

Chapter 21 – Aurora

When the private jet finally touched down at Seattle-Tacoma Airport, I jumped out of my seat before it had even taxied out. I just couldn't wait to show Caden my home.

Actually, nothing had changed here in the last few weeks, but now I had someone by my side to whom my world was foreign and together with him I rediscovered the magic of all my favorite places.

"Take it easy, Aurora," Caden admonished me as I pulled him through the airport. I was only half listening because I was looking out for my family. We had agreed that we were going home, but deep down I hoped they were here to welcome me after all, with colorful balloons and giant *welcome-back* banners.

"Hurry up, Caden, we're on a tight schedule!" I pulled Caden, like an impatient child, across the great hall, toward the exit.

Caden looked at me frowning.

"You're on a tight schedule?"

"Yes. You've got to see Seattle," I said seriously. "If you haven't seen the Seattle skyline at night from the Space Needle, you haven't lived."

"You know you're talking to a New Yorker right now?"

I nodded. "Of course, that's why I'm saying it."

Caden's lips had that grin on them again that I usually only saw in the playroom. Heavens, I didn't even want to know what my membership in the *Mile-High Club* had cost me, but at least Caden was now back to his old self.

"Also, you have to try the world's best hot dogs, they're at Terry's, near the park," I continued.

Caden and I theoretically had the rest of the day to ourselves, since Maggy's wedding wasn't until tomorrow.

"And if you ask me nicely, I'll tell you the absolute insider's tip when it comes to waffles and pancakes."

Just thinking about the ice cream filled waffles made my mouth water. There were millions of options, two dozen chocolate sauces alone! The dream of every sweet tooth, as I was one.

"Oh dear," I said with a sigh. "It'll take us about a month to show you everything! And another month until you've tasted everything! But selfless as I am, I'll make the time for you."

Caden squeezed my hand tighter and pulled me to him, forcing me to stop. I expected him to laugh at my joke, but he looked at me with a mixture of regret and his business expression.

"We'll have all the time in the world...just not now."

"No?" My critical eyes wandered up and down his body.

"No."

"Do you have something planned?"

"Possibly."

My whole body was tingling with excitement, because now Caden could no longer deny that he was up to something. Hence his cryptic silence and the worried looks that had increased over the past few days.

No, a trip to the water park or a meal at the world-famous *Royal Gourmet* was probably not a reason for his strange behavior.

"What are you going to do?" I huffed.

"I won't tell you." Caden pulled me close and kissed me. "You know how much I love to keep you on tenterhooks."

"Literally," I replied.

Another kiss followed, taking away some of my fear. Sometimes, when Caden looked at me the way he did, I had the feeling that he was unhappy. Whether with me or the overall situation, I don't know. But sometimes I was afraid of the next words he spoke because I didn't want him to say things I didn't want to hear.

Of course, the circumstances were clearly regulated, via a contract that we had both signed, but I still felt that there was more between us than business clauses and rules. At least that's what I wished.

"You should tell your family we'll be a little late," Caden murmured in my ear.

"Okay." I dug my smartphone out of my purse and cringed when I turned it on. Oh!"

"What is it?"

"About tens of millions of calls from mom."

And Maggy. Even Dad had tried it, not a good sign. I had expected my mom to go completely nuts so close to the wedding, but my sis and dad joining in was unusual and made me think something had happened that went beyond the wedding drama.

"Are you okay?" asked Caden with concern as my face grew paler.

"I hope so!"

Immediately, I dialed Mom's speed dial and sent a push prayer to heaven. Shortly after the first beep, my mother answered the call.

"Jesus, kid! Finally you answer your phone!"

Through the buzz of voices, gate announcements, and radios of the cafes and restaurants we passed, I had a hard time hearing my mother.

"I was on the plane," I explained tersely. "What happened? Is everyone okay?"

"Nothing is good! Absolutely nothing!" I heard how hotter her voice was, without a doubt, something was absolutely not okay.

"Mom, just tell me what's going on!" My voice was shaking. Caden was silent, but he squeezed my hand tightly to signal that he was there for me – and for that, I was immensely grateful.

"Mom! Plain talk please!"

But from the plain text became nothing more than a heart-rending sob I did not bring out of her.

"What happened?" By now I was close to tears, too. That is, until I heard Dad's voice in the background. There was a brief crackle, then my dad was on the other end of the line.

"Dad, what happened, for God's sake?"

He sighed loudly. "We're all fine."

"Thank goodness! You guys really scared me."

I exhaled in relief because I had already feared the worst.

"Your mom is a little stressed."

"A little stressed?" she protested in the background loud enough for me to hear. "I don't even know where to start!"

Now I also heard the angry voices of my sister and her fiancé in the background.

"Dad?"

"There are some difficulties regarding Maggy's wedding."

"The whole wedding is in danger of crashing!" my mother bellowed in high soprano.

I took the receiver from my ear, pressed it against my chest, put my head back and groaned loudly. Could you believe it? I caught myself staring at the display boards of the upcoming flights for a brief moment and would have loved to get on the next plane – no matter where.

"Is everything okay?" asked Caden.

"No, now everyone in my family has lost their minds."

I suppressed the impulse to end the call but listened to what my father had to say.

"What's wrong?"

"There are difficulties, but we also find solutions!" My father tried unsuccessfully to appease my mother.

We wouldn't get anywhere like this on the phone.

"We'll be quick, okay?"

I hung up before Dad could even answer so I wouldn't change my mind. Of course I loved my family, but this wedding was the worst thing that had ever happened to us. If it went on like this, I would get married quietly, with no drama at all!

"I guess we're postponing my plans?" asked Caden, frowning.

"Would that work?"

I didn't know exactly why Caden had a bad relationship with his family, but I hoped that he understood that my family was important to me despite everything.

"Of course." He didn't seem entirely convinced, but we both had no choice. It hurt my heart to have to destroy Caden's plans, but I couldn't abandon my family to madness.

We got into the rented SUV, including chauffeur, that Caden had arranged, and sped across Seattle until we reached my parents' house in a quiet suburb.

"Idyllic," Caden said, spinning around once for a panoramic view.

"Deceptive idyll. Don't let it fool you. And whatever my parents are going to say, don't take it to heart, okay? I don't know why, but there's a curse on my sister's wedding that brings out the worst in people."

Caden grinned at me. "If it weren't for that curse, we wouldn't be engaged right now. So I should thank your mother."

I giggled, because he was right. If my mom hadn't mutated into a wedding monster, I would never have made my escape to New York, let alone accepted a proposal from a complete stranger!

I took one last deep breath before ringing the doorbell of our family home.

"Get ready for something," I whispered in a warning tone.

"I think you're exaggerating," Caden replied.

"Yes! It runs in our family!"

The door was yanked open and Caden and I were pulled inside by my mother. Nothing had changed on the outside, but inside the house it looked like a wedding bomb had hit. There were lace scarves, silver beads, white feathers, and other decorative stuff everywhere that I definitely did not want to see at my own wedding. All I needed was a little mountain lodge, fairy lights, and a whole lot of snow!

A crisis meeting had formed in the living room, consisting of my family and Ben's family, who had split into two opposing fronts.

On the one hand, the *normies, of* which I counted myself, with mid-range cars, denim pants, and easygoing sayings, and on the other, the *high society of the world* with tailored suits, glossy spray-fixed hairstyles, and deprecating posture. I gave Caden a grateful look that he hadn't become a snob despite his fat paychecks.

Dad gave me a kiss on the forehead and somewhat awkwardly shook Caden's hand. Fortunately, the details of my engagement were overshadowed by the drama of unknown proportions.

Conspiratorially, my dad looked at me and I nodded, but also indicated that right now was not a good time for me to feed him details.

When Maggy saw me, she stood up and fell around my arms.

"Thanks for being here!"

"But of course, you are my favorite sister," I replied.

"I'm your *only* sister," Maggy replied, yet a smile flitted across her lips.

I deliberately sat down next to my sister because I didn't want to incite my mom any further. She was almost bursting with anger and the last time. It had been years since my mom had been this upset. The last time she had such a high pulse was when Dad and I had unscrewed the heating coil from her two-hundred-dollar hair dryer. Our experiment went horribly wrong, but it was still an afternoon I would never forget. It was burned into my memory...literally.

"Are you going to tell me what's going on?" I asked Maggy.

"My wedding is falling through." My sister was close to tears but tried to remain brave.

"Why? What happened?"

"The villa, the one with the beautiful garden and the big foyer, has a burst water pipe. It will take days to dry everything out again."

"Oh no."

I suppressed a groan, but my mom gave free rein to her emotions and howled again and again. So it was official, I was definitely getting married in a lonely little mountain cabin. Our family could not survive a second, pompous wedding.

Caden cleared his throat. "Would twice as many workmen solve the problem twice as fast?"

Normally I would have rolled my eyes, but in this case Caden was right. This was a problem hole that could be plugged with money.

Ben spoke up because Maggy just shook her head dully.

"No chance. We did everything we could."

"Oh, the beautiful mansion!" howled my mother. "The beautiful wedding!"

Ben's father sat stunned and shook his head.

"We put a deposit on the villa, we should have drama."

Oh no. Maggy and Ben had always made sure for the last few years that our parents didn't run into each other because the gap between them was just too big. But on high feast days and holidays and of course a wedding they met each other and it never went well.

Even before there was a Winter-Goldberg small war, I jumped up and bravely stood in the middle.

"What about another place?" I asked, shrugging my shoulders. "You've looked at dozens of places, surely there was something else."

Discouraging silence.

"All booked up," Maggy replied with a sigh.

"There must be something free!" I insisted.

My sister buried her face in her hands.

"I don't want to get married in a gym!"

"No way!" mom replied in a protesting tone.

"There's no question about that, of course," Mrs. Goldberg said in a calm tone.

At least something we all agreed on.

However, I had started a new discussion regarding the selection of the wedding location.

Caden, who was still standing at the edge of the living room and letting his gaze wander around, sighed softly. I took advantage of the time when the others were engrossed in their conversations and went to him.

"So, did I promise too much?"

"Your family is definitely memorable."

"I'm so sorry to put you through this. When there aren't weddings going on, my family is pretty normal, really!"

I really wish I could have introduced Caden to my normal family and not to this crazy woman whose problem drama had reached the level of *The Bachelor*.

"Your family is lovely," Caden said seriously.

"Oh, stop it," I waved it off, thinking it was a joke. But Caden continued to look at me seriously.

"I've been through a lot of different things. Believe me, you can be thankful for having a family like this."

The pain was written all over his face. I had racked my brain endlessly about it, even googled it unsuccessfully in the end, but I just didn't know why Caden was so closed off in this respect. Whatever had happened in the past, it still tormented him.

Maggy's loud sigh silenced everyone else.

"Ben, it's no use, we have to celebrate in a gym. Almost all the guests are already at the hotel and the rest will come tonight at the latest. We can't call anything off now!"

Ben, who also seemed quite tired, shook his head.

"I promised you on the Space Needle that you would get the wedding you deserve!"

Caden's ears perked up.

"He proposed to you on the Space Needle?"

Maggy nodded and reflexively demonstrated her engagement ring.

"We met at the Space Needle."

"So the place has significance to you?"

Again Maggy nodded, while Ben waved off.

"We should get back to our problem."

Caden pulled his smartphone out of his pocket as he stood in the middle of the living room.

"Then you just get married in the Space Needle."

Silence. Then murmurs ensued until finally everyone agreed that it was impossible to get married there in one day. I agreed with them, but Caden seemed so confident that I wondered if he really had that much clout to hog Seattle's biggest landmark for a day.

"Excuse me, please," Caden said politely, pointing to his cell phone, then disappeared from the room.

"Is he really serious?" asked Mr. Goldberg.

"Of course he means it, Aurora's fiancé is a billionaire," my mom pointed out with exaggerated pride. It was a satisfaction for her to be able to rub the senior lawyer's nose in the fact that he was no longer the richest man in the room.

"First and foremost, he is a good businessman with many connections," I corrected my mother.

"Good businessmen are a dime a dozen. For a fortune like that, you have to be damn good, or have the right contacts," Mrs. Goldberg said.

"Mother!" Ben stood up full of indignation.

I wasn't sure if it was praise or an insult, but based on Ben's reaction, it had clearly been an insult.

"You can't accuse Aurora's fiancé of corruption," Ben said in a calmer tone.

"Saint Industries is changing the world and many people's lives with technology." There was defiance in my voice. I wish I could have defended Caden adequately, but I didn't know how.

"See, no corruption," Ben grumbled, his eyes rolling. Mrs. Goldberg didn't seem all that convinced, even though she nodded.

My dad, who had been holding back until now, cleared his throat.

"I'll bet you a dinner that Aurora's fiancé will make it."

"I'll see you and raise you my famous *Apple Honey Pie*." Ever since I was little, my family and I would have little contests where we would bet on homemade pies or laundry service.

"I bet against it," Maggy said with a pessimistic grumble.

"Hey, you're the bride, you need to stay optimistic!" I reprimanded her with a raised finger.

"But there is no reason for optimism! The only thing left now..."

"Stop! We're not going to conjure things up, you know how things like that ended."

Not that I was superstitious, but I certainly didn't want the situation to get worse with bad mojo.

When Caden entered the living room with a smile on his lips, I already knew what he was going to say.

Mister Universe had saved my sister's wedding.

"There is good news and bad news," he began, and immediately there was silence. I held my breath in anticipation.

"The good news is, you can get married on the Space Needle."

My sister fell into my arms, cheering, and even the Goldbergs let themselves be carried away by a little howl of victory and clapped their hands. Mom looked like she was about to have a heart attack until she digested the good news and cheered as well.

"I told you nothing was impossible for Caden." I couldn't help but pierce Maggy's future in-laws in particular with a meaningful look.

"Contacts," muttered Mrs. Goldberg. "It's all a matter of contacts."

Ben and Maggy fell into each other's arms and I was so happy for my sister.

I tugged on Caden's sleeve to draw attention to myself.

"I don't know how you did it, but you're amazing."

I didn't even want to imagine what would have happened if Maggy's wedding had actually fallen through. Then all those chaotic weeks would have been for nothing – or worse, my mother would mutate into a wedding monster for a second time!

"And what about the bad news?" I echoed after the mood had settled a bit.

"The wedding ceremony must take place today."

Immediately, the mood swung from unrestrained euphoria to absolute chaotic panic.

Heavens, what a day!

Chapter 22 – Aurora

As the first bridesmaid, it was my duty to accompany the bride on the day of the wedding. By now, almost everyone had broken out in a panic and Mom no longer stood out from the crowd. Dozens of guests, including our favorite aunt Amelia who had traveled all the way from Texas, pitched in to help move the boxes containing decorations, tablecloths, dishes and other *essential* stuff to the Space Needle, which was sweaty work in this record-breaking summer.

Fortunately, most of the invited out-of-town guests were already in town and the rest lived nearby anyway, so it didn't take long for many to show up to help.

Interestingly, with all the helpers, you could immediately see which side of the bride and groom they belonged to, but this moderately severe disaster had welded both different halves together - basically a small miracle.

"I don't know how your fiancé did it, but I'll be forever grateful," Maggy said, panting, as the two of us balanced two boxes each to the cart across the way. "To come up with the idea of renting the entire Space Needle on your own is insane. I didn't even know that was possible!"

I chuckled. "I don't think anything is impossible for Caden."

Not because he was a billionaire, but because he was *Mister Universe*, whom no one could slow down.

With a jerk, I threw the boxes, which contained only tablecloths, into the van. I couldn't believe how much stuff my sister had accumulated for the wedding. That had to be thousands of dollars just for the fabrics!

As I set off again to get more boxes, Maggy put her hand on my shoulder and slowed me down.

"I haven't really congratulated you yet, Aurora. Congratulations on your engagement!"

"Thank you! But today is your day, let's rather talk about how beautiful you look," I said smiling.

Maggy laughed out loud and patted me on the back like a quarterback would do to his teammate.

"You're a bad liar. Save the compliments until I'm standing at the altar."

"But don't claim later that I didn't try," I replied with a grin. Admittedly, just then my sister didn't have much in common with a radiant bride. Her makeup was only half done, and her hair had dozens of crooked curlers hanging in it, slipping further and further the more boxes she lugged.

We grabbed the next boxes and when Maggy had balance problems, I took one of the boxes back from her.

"Wait, I'll carry this," I said when I had already taken the box from her.

"You better tell me how you and Caden met."

"Today is *your* day!" I repeated rolling my eyes. I didn't want to push myself to the fore, but even less did I want to lie to my family, but because of the contract I had no other choice.

"About Max," I replied curtly. "Nothing special."

"Like you said, today is *my* day, everything dances to my tune. So go ahead, dance!"

"When did you get so bossy?" I asked in amazement.

"Since you left me alone with Mom," Maggy replied with a reproachful look that I barely saw behind her cardboard wall.

"All right, all right." As we hauled more and more boxes into the van, I told Maggy the part of the story I didn't have to hide, namely that I had mixed up the apartments and called Caden a burglar. I also told about the foam party in detail, although Maggy had already learned everything from the newspaper and from my e-mails.

"That's so incredible, isn't it? You flee Seattle for a wedding and come back even with an engagement ring."

I nodded and hid my naked ring finger, which didn't have an engagement ring on it that was officially still being fitted. The frustration, however, in no way diminished the way I pined for Caden. For the better part of an hour, he'd been hanging on the phone while casually leaning against his SUV. He was quite the cool businessman whom everyone envied for his authoritarian composure.

"Hello, Earth to Aurora!" my sister called out, waving her hands in front of my face.

"Yes, we really do live in crazy times," I replied without taking my eyes off Caden.

When Caden caught me gawking just a few seconds later, he grinned at me before pointing at his wrist and then at the car. After a glance at my watch, I yelped. "Maggy, we have to go! You need to get your dress on, get ready, and ritualize all these wedding rituals I have no idea about."

Breathing heavily, Maggy looked at the remaining boxes that needed to be moved.

"We have to finish packing the boxes!"

I shook my head significantly and pushed Maggy into the SUV that Caden and I had arrived in from the airport.

"Your wedding can do without glitter at worst, but not without a bride! Mom, Dad, Aunt Amelia and all the Goldberg snobs will take care of the rest!"

"Aurora! Ben's relatives are just...as strange as our family. Only different strange. Or are you worried that our differences are too great after all?"

"I was kidding," I reassured my sister. "You and Ben are a perfect match, that's the most important thing. No, wait, it's the second most important thing. The most important thing is that you finally get in the car now so you're not late for your own wedding!"

With protests, I finally managed to drag my little sister into the SUV. Although the interior was huge, Maggy, me and her wedding dress needed all the space, so Caden made himself comfortable in the passenger seat.

Just a moment ago, my fiancé had seemed quite busy, but now he was just staring dumbly at his smartphone. At first I wanted to ask if there were any problems, but then I decided against it. One more problem and my sister would go AWOL, and I couldn't let that happen under any circumstances.

I grabbed Maggy's shaking hands and tried to calm her down.

"I'm as excited as I was when we went to Disneyland. Do you still remember that?" I asked.

"How could I ever forget that trip?"

We had never made it to Disneyland, yet it was one of the best family trips we had ever taken.

"I still get laughing fits when I think about those horrible tourist shirts we all wore."

"And the shield caps."

"And the socks! Wait, didn't we also have cups and pens?"

"Don't forget the Christmas tree balls," I grumbled, grinning.

Heavens, I could still see the broadly grinning beavers that were the heraldic animal of Hill Creek before me. Sometimes the grimaces haunted my nightmares! I don't know how this little village on the lake with all the giant beaver statues slept soundly at night.

"And the raccoon attack!" said Maggy, before bursting into peals of laughter.

Giggling, we once again recounted the highlights of our trip, which ended in a memorable disaster thanks to a broken-down car in the middle of nowhere.

In fact, it was the best family vacation ever.

"Don't worry about it, Maggy. Worst case scenario, we'll remember your wedding the same way we remember our trip to Hill Creek."

"Thank you. Without you I would have really despaired," Maggy said to Caden and me.

"It's a matter of honor," I waved it off.

"No, it's not." Maggy put on a serious face. "Mom's been treating you so unfairly lately that I would have understood if you'd stayed away longer."

"And miss your wedding? Never!" I insisted.

For the rest of the ride, Maggy instructed me on super important things she wanted me to do while she prepared for the ceremony. I listened intently, even though I knew for a fact that Mom was already setting everything in motion. Maybe her wedding mania was a good thing after all?

By the time we arrived at the Space Needle, our helpers had already moved some of the essentials upstairs, which calmed Maggy down a bit. She marched ahead with Caden, me, and the hundred yards of tulle wrapped around her wedding dress, which Caden and I wore together.

At the top, there was already atmospheric light and part of the floor was strewn with rose petals. The railings of the stairs and the balconies above us were decorated with rose vines.

"Wow, you guys really spared no expense or effort, huh?" I asked in amazement. Admittedly, I was envious. The delicate, rose-colored rose petals impregnated the room with a pleasant, sweet scent, and it looked fantastic. Rose petals were definitely going on my wedding checklist.

"It must be from Mom, I had no idea," Maggy replied, shrugging her shoulders. I hugged Caden from the side.

"What do you think, Caden? Isn't it totally romantic here already?"

"Totally romantic," he repeated my words. I didn't know what, but somehow Caden seemed dissatisfied.

"I mean it!" Secretly, I even wished Caden would go to the same lengths for me. I wanted to be the woman who was worth this rose petal romance to him.

When the stylist met us, suddenly everything happened very quickly. Maggy was led into a windowless room where she could change, and in the meantime the guests, the preacher and almost the entire orchestra arrived, all of whom pitched in until the last moment.

I had also changed and was delighted that the dress fit perfectly. I had faith in Max, but not in a tailor who only took measurements and otherwise demanded a free hand. Even more nervous had been the fact that Caden had taken care of picking up the dress.

As I pushed my way through the formed groups to Caden in the orchid-colored dress, my dad waved at me.

"Aurora, we haven't had time to talk yet."

"Unfortunately," I replied with a sigh. "Yet we have so much to talk about."

Dad leaned forward. "Did you bring the plans?"

I nodded and pointed to my purse. "But I can't show it to you here."

"Understood." Apparently we had different definitions of *understood,* because he grabbed me by the wrist, pulled me into the scullery, and asked the baffled kitchen help to clear the field for a moment. My dad was so confident about this that they actually listened to him.

The hot air coming from the dishwashers and the steam immediately brought beads of sweat to my forehead.

"Dad, we can do that later! Maggy is about to get married, and I definitely don't want to miss it."

"We already don't, don't worry. But I'm dying to see your plans. Let me just take a little peek, will you?"

"All right." I admitted defeat and dug out folded copies of the blueprints. I really felt like a criminal because, strictly speaking, I was a criminal.

"Phew, difficult," my dad mumbled into his hand, which he rubbed thoughtfully over his mouth.

"Yep." That's all I said, so as not to upset Dad. Even though he was *just* an auto mechanic, he had an incredibly good grasp of engineering. A few admissions and some more college money in his youth, and Dad would be a rocket scientist by now.

We went over the technical details and the notes I had so far. Of course, I had also talked to my father on the phone, but without the blueprints it had been difficult for him to imagine the problem.

"The problem kind of reminds me of Skippy's car. But drones and cars are not the same thing," I said. Skippy was from the neighborhood and was actually one of those crazy motorcyclists who rode around in death spheres at fairs, but then under the name *Death Destroyer*. Dad had modified a car for him to do a stunt. My dad had fiddled around for weeks until the car actually flew as far as intended.

Dad looked at me, frowning. "How did you get Skippy's car?"

"Because the problem is stability, just like the flying car."

Something flashed in my father's eyes, he flipped frantically through the pages, searching the lines for some of my notes, and then nodded in satisfaction.

"I think you're on to the solution."

"Really?"

"Yes!" Dad waved one of the papers around so wildly I couldn't tell which one it was. "Think again about Skippy's car. That's where I solved the problem by rebuilding the car to give the weight of the engine a different center of gravity."

Then the penny dropped. Finally. I had known that I was only a hair's breadth away from a possible solution! The saddest thing was that I had already learned all the information I needed to solve the problem – at least theoretically – in my undergraduate studies. That was absolute beginner knowledge! Heavens, how had I been able to grope in the dark for so long?

"The weight is not the problem, only the surface on which it is distributed! Brilliant! Thanks Dad, you're the best!"

My dad smiled at me proudly. "You solved that all by yourself."

"No, you put me up to it, Dad!"

He shook his head vehemently and leaned against one of the large industrial dishwashers that was steaming lightly. "That was you all by yourself. I can't even see what these drawings are supposed to represent without my reading glasses."

"You were bluffing?" I asked, stunned.

"Worked, didn't it?"

"What if it had gone wrong?"

Dad shrugged his shoulders. "Well, then the problem would still be unsolved, and I would have looked at it when I got my reading glasses back. You seemed so confident on the phone that I was sure you actually already knew the solution. Now you just have to see if your solution is workable."

"It is, my gut is definitely saying *yes!*"

I was so flooded with adrenaline and endorphins that I could hardly stand still. It was as if I had solved a millennium problem but had to keep it to myself until I could prove my theory. What a shame, I would have loved to surprise Caden with the good news right away.

But when I felt the first drops of sweat running down my back, I shuddered.

"Dad, we should go before we smell like cheap dish soap and sweat."

"Right, now we enjoy Maggy's big day. Tomorrow we'll see."

"But before we do, we bathe ourselves in Aunt Amelia's perfume, which kills every olfactory nerve, ergo no one finds out about our secret scullery chat, with which we may have changed the world."

"Lead the way," Dad said, opening the door for me.

As unobtrusively as possible, Dad and I mingled with the crowd again. While he stuck with Uncle Ted and Bob from the neighborhood, I continued to roam the crowd until I spotted Caden, who let his gaze slide thoughtfully over the guests. When he saw me, his eyes began to sparkle, and I curtsied.

"You look beautiful," he said reverently, rather his eyes kept roaming over my outfit. To give him a better view, I turned on my axis, which made my floor-length dress flutter. It was tightly cut at the torso, but not too seductive, so that everyone only had eyes for the bride.

All except Caden, he only had eyes for me, which made the butterflies in my stomach dance.

"You can be seen, too," I said, hooking up with him. His black suit fit perfectly and emphasized his broad shoulders. He did without a tie, which made him look even more charismatic.

"Have I told you how grateful I am to you for this, Caden?" I asked as we strolled through the company. It took all my strength not to rub his nose in the latest news, but somehow I managed to keep my mouth shut.

"About twenty times already," Caden replied with a smile.

"You'll probably hear it from me another twenty times."

We stopped at the large archway made of roses, leaves and different colored fabrics. In less than half an hour, Maggy and Ben would be standing here to confess their love. Perfectly timed with the approaching sunset, which made everything inside glow with warm light.

At the thought of how beautiful the wedding ceremony would be, a single tear of joy ran down my cheek.

"Sorry, it's the hormones."

To demonstrate how serious I was about hormones, I waved my handkerchief, which I had handy.

"There's nothing to apologize for."

I fought with more tears. Everything was so perfect. Caden was perfect. The rose petal floor was perfect. The entire setting was perfect. There was only one thing that wasn't quite perfect. As if on cue, one of the smartly dressed waiters came and offered us non-alcoholic fruit juices in champagne glasses.

"Say, did you happen to have your fingers in the pie because both the catering service and the restaurants in the Space Needle don't stock alcohol?"

Caden nodded. "I did, yes."

I had not expected this honesty.

"Why? Basically, my family is your business partner if we look at our contract soberly."

"No." Caden took my hand and intertwined his fingers with mine. "Today is a happy day. I don't want it to have a stale taste because guests overdo it on the alcohol and crash later."

I had never thought of it that way before. Silently, I stared out the panoramic glass at Lake Union, which was teeming with yachts and sailboats in the summer months. From here, the boats looked like ants from distant dots on the horizon.

"It's a very important issue for you, isn't it?"

"I don't want to talk about it."

I suppressed a sigh. Yes, he had his secrets and many of them Caden was allowed to keep for all I cared, but on this particular subject I felt it was eating him up.

"Sometimes, though, talking can do you good."

"I. Will. Not. Talk. About. It." He emphasized each word emphatically. "Especially not today."

My heart absorbed the pain of his eyes, and we silently shared his pain.

"Do you trust me so little?" I asked, close to tears.

"Trust is not the problem, Aurora."

"What then?"

Caden averted his eyes from me and took a step closer to the window.

"I couldn't take it if you looked at me the same way as the people I told what you wanted to know."

"Fine, then don't tell me. But you should know that I'm already looking at you the same way. Every time you stare out the window, lost in thought, and every time you silence me, I see the pain in your eyes and wonder what happened to you."

Caden was about to say something, but was interrupted by the preacher, who had tapped his fingers briefly on the microphone to get the attention of everyone present.

"Would you please take your seats? The ceremony is about to take place."

"That was your sign," Caden said. I nodded silently and was about to leave when he grabbed my hand and gave me a passionate kiss.

"Someday, Aurora, but not today."

"Thank you," I whispered and gave him another kiss.

While the guests took their places on the chairs or railings in the upstairs open floor, I went to the bride's room.

Swinging, I opened the door, causing Mom and Maggy alike to squeal. The rest of the bridesmaids, consisting of Maggy's best friends, also went into a brief panic frenzy.

"It's okay, it's just me," I said in a calm tone, as if trying to calm a frightened horse.

"You gave us a scare!" Mom straightened Maggy's bridal veil one last time. For about an hour, she felt like she was doing nothing else.

"Relax, Ben's already seen you today," I said dryly, joking.

"Aurora!" Maggy and Mom reprimanded me in the same tone of voice, but also knew I wasn't serious.

"I'm going to go find your dad now," Mom said, hugging Maggy. "I'm so proud of you!"

As she walked past me, she also gave me a kiss on the cheek. "And on you, too! But you keep your mouth shut now until Maggy says *yes*. Don't put any ideas in her head!"

"I won't, I promise mom."

When my mother had closed the door behind her, I said loudly audibly:

"Last chance to elope!"

"Aurora, you are terrible, mom has been through too much for these jokes."

"No, I've been through too much because of this wedding!" I corrected my sister. "It's about time we finally got it over with."

As if on cue, the first notes of the string orchestra kicked in, playing a beautiful version of Pachelbel's *Canon in D*. Maggy fidgeted restlessly with her dress, while her breathing became faster and faster.

"Ready?" I asked with a smile and Maggy nodded.

"Ready!"

"Well, here we go!" I cheered euphorically, grabbing one of the bouquets, which were a small version of the bridal bouquet, and running ahead.

First, we bridesmaids walked down the rose petal floor to the altar, one by one. I imagined how it would feel if I were the bride and Caden was waiting for me at the other end of this carpet of flowers, smiling with pride and with tears in his eyes.

Even though it wasn't our wedding, I had to fight back tears because Caden looked at me the same way a groom should look at his bride.

When we were all in our place at the altar of flowers, the music changed, and the wedding march started. When Maggy walked across the flower carpet in her beautiful white wedding dress, everyone held their breath. It was like magic, and everything was perfect from start to finish. The preacher's speech was beautiful, as were the vows they had both prepared for each other. Matching the last rays of the sunset, they kissed. Not a dry eye was left until the ceremony was over and the wedding dance continued. My sister was beaming with happiness and slowly but surely the madness disappeared from my mother's eyes.

"May I ask the most beautiful woman of the evening to dance?" asked Caden as the bride and groom's dance ended.

"Yes, I would be honored to dance with the most handsome man of the evening," I replied with a smile and took his hand. Actually, I couldn't dance at all and had a talent for ramming the heels of my shoes into the feet of my dance partners, but Caden led me around the dance floor so well that I felt like I was flying.

"The wedding was beautiful, wasn't it?" I asked Caden dreamily.

"Yes, it was," he replied.

"I hope I didn't cause you too much trouble."

Only now did I remember that Caden had actually planned something else for us – his plan certainly hadn't looked like this.

Caden shook his head as his hand slid a little further down my back.

"That's okay. I'm just glad we were spared the boring part of all weddings."

"Oh yes! I know exactly what you mean."

The day had been entertaining from start to finish, but still relaxed. Caden had really been able to organize everything a real wedding needed on the fly.

"I still think it's unfortunate that I threw all your plans out the window."

"The evening is not over yet."

Caden had that twinkle in his eye again that I found equally seductive and frightening. Whatever he had planned, it had to be something phenomenal, as dark as his eyes were getting.

Chapter 23 – Caden

Slowly, but surely, I led Aurora further and further to the edge of the dance floor. It would have been rude to elope so soon after the ceremony, but I still had a few appointments to keep.

"What are you up to?" asked Aurora with wide eyes as I continued to lead her around the dance floor.

"It's a secret," I murmured in her ear. Inside, I counted the steps. I was a good dancer, but Aurora had been getting my blood pumping all day. Heck, I was almost inclined to say I felt more alive than when I was free-running in Paris. In hindsight, Jacks and I had overdone it beyond measure, we were too reckless and too naive, but it was the thrill of my life. Until now. Now Aurora's emerald eyes and that little box in my back pocket were nearly driving me crazy. My heart never beat as loud as it did today.

"I'm very good at keeping secrets," Aurora replied with a charming smile.

"So, so. So you're good at keeping secrets?"

"Yes!" Aurora's eyes grew big, and she could hardly hide her victorious expression from me.

"Me too," I replied with a grin. I almost fell for her innocent expression, but only almost. I had done nothing else in the last few days but set everything in motion so that my plan would work. And I thought I had thought of everything. Stupidly, I had disregarded the fact that there were higher powers that had nothing to do with traffic jams or delays – family.

Actually, it was a stupid mistake that should not have happened to me, but it did. Because the variable *family* did not exist in my plans.

"Then will you at least tell me how you managed to hijack the Space Needle for us?"

"Fine, I'll tell you, but you should know that it would diminish some of my *Mister Universe* charm."

Aurora winced when I mentioned her nickname for me.

"How do you know about that?" she asked me irritated. At the same time her cheeks reddened, which made her look even more charming.

"You're not exactly holding back your conversation with Maxine," I explained. Then I leaned forward to kiss her cheek. "There are worse nicknames than *Mister Universe*."

In fact, I was flattered. What man wouldn't when he was declared the center of his own universe?

"Back on topic, how did you snag the Space Needle?"

I sighed softly. "Do you really, *really* want to know? Once the magic trick is explained, the magic disappears forever."

"You still have enough magic for a thousand more magic tricks," Aurora replied grimly.

"All right. I had already rented the Space Needle before the wedding."

Aurora's eyes grew huge. Then she burst out laughing. So loud that couples standing around and dancing briefly looked over at us.

"Stop teasing me, Caden."

"I wasn't kidding." My dry, toneless voice underscored my seriousness.

Aurora's laughter died away instantly.

"Are you serious?"

"I told you it would destroy the magic. But you wouldn't listen," I said in a reproving tone.

"It still seems almost impossible," Aurora murmured, lost in thought.

I was Caden Saint, I had the world at my feet – and when the world bowed to you, almost nothing was impossible. Interestingly, though, I found myself at a point where I realized I didn't need the world at all. Aurora was my world.

"As you can see, it was possible after all." I winked at her as we continued to dance to the beat of the music.

"What did you have in mind?" continued Aurora.

"I'm not going to answer that question for you."

Aurora shook her head. "You can't just rent the Seattle landmark like that and then not tell me what it's for."

I kept silent, and Aurora punished me with serious looks that bounced off my facade. Although I loved her honesty, I still had to get used to someone looking at me like that. No one, neither my co-workers nor my subs had ever thought of looking at me that way. But Aurora wasn't just my personal assistant, she wasn't just my sub, she was my fiancée.

The orchestra sang an upbeat version of Bonnie Buckley's *My Heart Is Yours*.

Just this one more song, then we had to go. A few bars lay between now and what could change both our lives forever.

"Enjoy this song, Aurora. After this, we have to go."

"Go? Go where?"

"Secret," I growled softly. My voice sent a shiver down Aurora's spine. Good. Maybe it was selfish, but I found it relieving to know that Aurora was just as tense as I was. She, because she had absolutely no idea what was coming, and I, because I knew all too well.

"Will I like this secret?"

"Possibly," I answered as cryptically as I could. I loved it when her body was so electrified and every muscle tensed. Nevertheless, Aurora let me lead her across the dance floor as light as a feather.

It was like a small but satisfying trip to the playroom. Just the thought of Aurora kneeling on the floor, naked – wearing nothing but a collar and *that* ring – made my member swell.

No matter what anyone else said, she stole the show even from the bride with her radiant smile and sparkling eyes. I wish everyone could see that Aurora was mine. Mine. For me alone!

"Tell me again who you belong to," I whispered in her ear just before our last song ended. I just couldn't help but hear it over and over again.

"I am yours," Aurora replied. We were equally proud of this fact.

"Good girl." I kissed her temple, then reluctantly let go of her waist. "Now go say goodbye to your sister."

"We're not going to come back?"

"Yes, but not today."

Aurora looked at me puzzled. "I'm dying to find out what you're up to!"

"You'll be on fire."

With a broad grin, Aurora flitted through the crowd while her beguiling scent stayed with me. I watched as she and her sister beamed, giggled, and finally fell into each other's arms.

If things had gone differently... I pushed the thought aside, because I couldn't change things. The damned world was at my feet, yes. But that didn't mean I could change it. I don't know why I was suddenly struggling with sentimentality, but the feeling that Aurora must know my past was growing stronger.

I fought it as best I could, but I already knew how this battle, in which I could never emerge victorious, would end.

Thoughtfully, I let my gaze wander over Seattle at night. The colorful lights of the city were interrupted again and again because darkness had settled over the rivers that ran through the entire city. A few individual ferries provided some comforting light in this blackness.

"I'm ready," Aurora said. She could hardly stand still with excitement. "But for what?"

I shook my head. "No, nothing."

Instead of the exit, I led Aurora back to the room where the bride and her bridesmaids had changed.

"Take off your clothes!" I commanded.

"Here, now?"

"As inviting as your contradiction is, I'm not going to spank you now." I noted the spankings in the back of my mind anyway.

To spare Aurora further questions, I took the garment bag from the wall, which contained another dress. If I could believe my two advisors, it would be perfect for my project.

Hesitantly, Aurora accepted the hanger along with the dress. "Should I put this on now?"

Aurora seemed visibly confused, although she should know me well enough to know that I led a rather unconventional life in some respects.

"I asked for you to," I replied, turning around like a gentleman so I wouldn't destroy the magic of this intimate moment. From now on we played by my rules again, I had planned every second of our evening so that I could give Aurora what she deserved.

"Caden? Would you help me?" asked Aurora, looking over the mirror she was standing in front of at me.

"I'd love to." I answered. Slowly I pulled the zipper at the back together, my fingers touched her tender skin and Aurora inhaled audibly. A kiss on her neck strengthened her reaction even more.

As I took a step back, Aurora meticulously scrutinized herself in the mirror until she finally came to a conclusion I already knew. The white, strapless dress reached Aurora's knees, where it shimmered with several layers of tulle and sequined silk.

She looked like a swan lake ballerina, only much, much more beautiful.

"It's perfect," she informed me, beaming, before her expression turned a bit more serious again. "But what did I do to deserve this?"

I wrapped myself in deceptive silence and winked at her. Aurora would find out soon enough why I wanted a perfect evening for her or what the small, all-important velvet box, whose existence she didn't know, had to do with it.

As we opened the door and snuck out behind the backs of the rest of the wedding party, Aurora giggled the entire time.

"This is so exciting!"

"I promise you that running away from your family was not the most exciting thing today."

Aurora looked at me knowingly. "Of course not, my sister's wedding was the most eventful thing today!"

"No." I growled softly, leaving a meaningful pause. "Even if the wedding came as a surprise, it won't be the most memorable thing today."

Aurora tilted her head. "What do you have planned? I'll burst with excitement if you don't tell me right now!"

"Not telling you is one of the most memorable moments of this evening for me."

Smiling, but with a devilish look, Aurora wrapped her arms around me.

"Sometimes I really feel like I know exactly what you're thinking or feeling or up to. And then, every single time, you convince me that..."

Aurora faltered as the horse-drawn carriage pulling up and stopped directly in front of us.

"You were going to say something else," I said, amused, because Aurora couldn't take her eyes off the white-painted carriage.

"You always surprise me."

"Maybe I live for just that look in your eyes?"

Almost touched, Aurora grabbed her heart and looked at me seriously.

"You really love to drive me crazy."

"You can't get to paradise without madness."

I opened the small door to the carriage and held out my hand to Aurora.

"Do you mind?"

"Only too happy to."

The interior of the open carriage was covered in white, velvety faux fur, and around the edges were strings of lights that reflected in Aurora's emerald eyes.

At my signal, the coachman drove off and we rode through the streets of Seattle with characteristic clattering hooves until we turned into the park.

"I feel like a princess," Aurora gushed.

"You look like one too," I replied with a smile.

She grabbed my hand and clasped it with her dainty fingers.

"Thank you, I know you're not a romantic, so I appreciate it even more."

I squeezed her hand as I let my eyes wander over the trees and lakes of the park. There were still a few blocks between us and the actual surprise, but I didn't want to whip Aurora up anymore, because she was supposed to enjoy the ride. I certainly didn't want Aurora to just keel over with excitement at the crucial moment.

"How about a little stop at Terry's?" I asked.

"Yes!" replied Aurora, as if shot out of a pistol.

"The hot dogs must be really damn good if you answer without thinking."

"They are the very best hot dogs!"

For a second it looked like there was some madness glimmering in Aurora's eyes, but when I let my gaze wander for a second, the expression was gone again.

Smiling to know Aurora's specialness, I took her in my arms and pulled her to me.

"It's perfect," Aurora said with a sigh. "But you know what else is missing?"

I looked at her questioningly. "What?"

"Snow!"

"Snow?"

"Everything is more romantic when it snows!"

"It's summer," I said dryly. Then I pointed to Aurora's bare arms, the green trees, and the shimmering lakes where swans, ducks, and other waterfowl splashed.

"I know," Aurora replied with a smile. "But when it snows, even you can't mistake the romance behind it."

"That remains to be seen," I replied with a wink.

Just before the end of the park, Terry's mobile hot dog stand appeared, which Aurora recognized from a distance.

"There's Terry up ahead!" Aurora looked around suspiciously. "But he's not usually standing here."

"I know," I agreed with Aurora. That most of my phone time earlier went to even being able to contact Terry, I kept to myself. "He's waiting for us there."

"Oh. My. God." Aurora gasped as her nails clawed so hard into my hand that I had to take a deep breath myself.

Right in front of the hot dog stand, the coachman stopped.

"Good evening, Miss Winter, Mister Saint," Terry greeted us with a bright smile. Admittedly, I had pictured the hot dog vendor as a short, somewhat rotund fellow, with a full beard, tousled, graying hair, and huge glasses. But standing in front of me was a well-trained athlete who was about my height and build.

"What would you like?" asked Terry.

"The usual – twice," Aurora replied. She slid around in her seat in anticipation, like a child on Christmas Eve.

"Two hot dogs with everything, special sauce and extra onions coming right up."

"Extra onions?" I asked after Terry was already getting to work. Yes, it was Aurora's night, but extra onions were pretty unromantic for special occasions. I didn't put much stock in romance, but I knew

Aurora did. Somehow I had to dissuade her from her unromantic endeavor.

"Extra onions!" replied Aurora firmly.

"Are you sure?"

"Yeah, don't worry about it. You're eating the onions too, so I don't have to worry about you not wanting to kiss me anymore." Aurora giggled.

"And if we have anything else romantic in mind?" I asked bluntly.

"Trust me, whatever it is, the extra onions are worth it!"

I sighed and Terry grinned broadly at me.

"I can only agree with Aurora. The young lady has taste."

Aurora giggled even louder, then looked at me. "Yeah, I guess I do."

"Fine, fine by me. Extra onions it is, but don't say I didn't warn you."

I gave in, albeit reluctantly, which delighted Aurora.

Beaming, she accepted her hot dog and passed the second one to me.

"Enjoy your meal," Terry wished us. While Aurora took a hearty bite of her hot dog, I balanced the overloaded milk roll back and forth between my hands, not knowing how to take a bite without ruining my suit.

"I love New York," Aurora began, taking a bite and then continuing to speak. "But I love these hot dogs even more."

While Aurora took one bite after another, I could do nothing but watch her. As seductively as Aurora ate, I almost had to take it as an invitation to fuck her on the spot. The special sauce ran down her fingers, which, without thinking about it, she put in her mouth and licked off. Not just like that, but moaning and to the hilt.

Damn, if Aurora always ate her hot dogs like that, she must have turned dozens of guys' heads. Fantasies involving fruit, cream, and some of Aurora's delicate dance moves overwhelmed me. I wish I had been prepared, but by now I should have realized that Aurora was still good for surprises.

Although I suppressed the reflex of wanting to wipe some sauce from the corner of Aurora's mouth, I couldn't resist the urge. With gentle pressure, I pushed her chin in my direction and ran my thumb over the corner of her mouth.

Gratefully, Aurora licked the tip of my thumb and looked deep into my eyes.

Her emerald eyes made a heart that was thought dead beat.

Her words tempted me to break my own rules.

Her scent alone awakened in me the desire to lay the world at her feet.

I don't know how Aurora had done it, but she had turned my head. She was more than a sub, more than the signature on a paper. Without meaning to, she had crept into my heart and now we were branded with each other's love forever.

I had warned Aurora about me, but foolhardy as she was, she turned all warnings against the wind. At first I had been afraid for Aurora, that she was a naive little girl who didn't know any better. But now I knew better.

If Aurora was thrown into a black, dark, never-ending hole, she would simply become light herself. And I would protect that light, at all costs!

When I didn't say anything, but just continued to stare at her, Aurora poked her elbow into my side.

"Taste it already!" she urged me resolutely.

Reluctantly, I complied with her request and after one small bite, I realized that it was ridiculous to resist this hotdog. Aurora hadn't lied, it was the best hotdog I had ever eaten. It was almost as if I could taste all the park trips Aurora had taken as a child. It almost felt like I had had a carefree childhood myself.

This hotdog that Aurora had more or less forced on me triggered feelings in me that made me shudder. Never before had I felt the desire for a family, but now nothing seemed more important.

"So, did I promise too much?" asked Aurora, snapping me out of my thoughts.

"No." I shook my head. "You're right, they are excellent."

"Very good, otherwise that would be grounds for divorce!"

"What?" My heart contracted painfully.

"It was a joke, Caden. You're allowed to laugh!"

I didn't feel like laughing. Not with jokes like that. Not when Aurora talked about divorce.

"Tomorrow you will sign a contract that will forbid you to make such jokes," I said dryly. Aurora grinned from ear to ear.

"There you go, I knew you had a sense of humor too!"

Actually, my statement was meant seriously, but I let Aurora believe that it was just a joke.

"Ready for our next destination?" I asked when we had finished eating.

"Ready!"

After Terry had cracked a few more of his jokes, the coachman spurred his horses until they fell back into a steady trot.

As soon as we left the park, my heartbeat got louder again. It wasn't far now. So I pulled a white silk ribbon from my pants pocket and presented it to Aurora.

"Is that really necessary?" she asked with a pained look.

I pulled Aurora to me and kissed her.

"This time I'll make sure that nothing can interfere with the magic," I murmured before placing my lips on hers one more time in a demanding manner. My tongue forced her soft, full lips apart and only reluctantly did we separate again.

Aurora was gasping for breath while I was struggling to control myself. Sometimes I just couldn't help digging my hand into her hair and pulling her against me, as if the laws of the world demanded it of me.

"It's not far now," I promised as I blindfolded Aurora.

It was only a few minutes from here, yet it felt like we were moving in slow motion while the rest of the world stood still. Silence – through which only the clatter of hooves and my loud heartbeat penetrated.

"Aurora?"

"Yes?" A gentle smile rested on her lips.

I didn't know exactly how to put it, but suddenly I felt that Aurora should know the whole truth about me. I had been toying with the idea ever since our conversation on the Space Needle. After all, I knew everything about Aurora, every little detail of her life, which was unfair, because she knew of me exclusively what I showed her. In this respect I had always been damn stingy.

"Do you have a secret?" I asked, trying to make the transition.

Aurora winced. "What do you mean?"

"Something that no one knows about. Like a treasure you're guarding or a beast you're trying to hide. And if someone knew about it, it would shake the worldview."

"Wow, the mood has turned quickly," Aurora muttered in irritation.

I took her hand and gently stroked the back of her hand to reassure her.

"Oh, forget it, it's okay. It was a stupid question."

"No, not at all, Caden. In fact, I'm grateful to you for finally bringing it up!"

Damn. How long had Aurora been waiting for an explanation from me? And why was my voice failing me now that I had the opportunity to show her my darkest side as well? I could do nothing but swallow the pain that was soaked with anger.

Aurora took a deep breath. "Caden, I have something to tell you."

Now it was I who was irritated. Had she not spoken of my secrecy, but of one of her secrets?

"Shh." I put my finger to her lips. "Let's talk about this later."

"No!" Aurora's expression was so determined that I saw it even under the white blindfold. "It's been on my mind for a long time, and it has to come out or my heart will explode! Caden. I know it wasn't meant to be and you didn't mean for it to come to this, but there's nothing I can do about it. I'm powerless against what you're doing to me and the feelings you're causing in me." Was Aurora just doing what I suspected? "Caden Saint, I've fallen in love with you."

I didn't know what to say to that, because Aurora had run me over with it. My heart was beating painfully against my chest and faster than ever before. I felt like I was balancing on the top of the Empire State Building without a safety line.

Damn! I had never felt so good, so alive. I had never felt so much.

Chapter 24 – Aurora

Silence. Silence that almost tore my heart apart. I pondered whether it had been a mistake to confess my feelings to Caden. Yes, it was contractually agreed that there was no love. But honestly? I didn't care about the contract, because love didn't care about rules, rights, or responsibilities. I had taken Caden into my heart and I couldn't keep it to myself any longer.

"Caden?" I asked as the silence grew more stifling. "Say something!"

There was no mistaking my exasperation, but even so, Caden didn't seem to think it appropriate to say anything in response.

I was about to pull off my blindfold, but Caden stopped me by gripping my wrists tightly.

"We're here," he said, pretending I hadn't said anything.

Heavens, he couldn't just ignore my words!

"So are we going to pretend I didn't say anything?" I asked irritably. Anger was the only thing that could protect me from the burgeoning pain.

"No. But you'll have to wait a little while for my answer," he said.

"Why not here and now?" I became more and more indignant; at the same time, Caden became calmer and calmer.

"You will understand as soon as you see it, Aurora," he answered me and got out of the carriage.

I found it difficult to analyze the situation. I confessed my true feelings to Caden, and he answered nothing. Absolutely nothing.

"Why does everything always have to be a big mystery?" I asked.

Caden inhaled audibly as he thought about a response.

"Because some things are not easy to explain."

"And some things are," I protested, pulling a pout.

"This is one of the more complicated things," Caden replied. I was far from satisfied with his explanation. In fact, it only confused me more.

What am I even doing here?

Only hope kept me from taking off the blindfold and disappearing into the night. I clung to the fact that my hopes were justified. Caden would never have gone to such lengths if he didn't care about me. He had rented the Space Needle, arranged for a carriage, and had the most beautiful dress in the world made for me.

And when he started talking about secrets, I thought it was about our feelings for each other, which we had kept secret for so long. Perhaps I was mistaken.

Anyway, I couldn't keep sulking in that carriage until Caden finally gave me his pending answer. I stood up and immediately Caden grabbed my waist and gently lifted me down from the carriage.

"Caden?" I asked, getting his attention. I just had to confess to him how I felt. "I'm afraid you're going to leave me."

Immediately Caden pulled me close to his chest. A statement that needed no more words.

"I won't leave you," Caden whispered, stroking my hair.

"Then why these secrets?"

"In a few minutes, you'll understand. Trust me."

Although that wasn't an answer, and I was standing blindfolded somewhere near the park, with my heart open and more questions than answers, I realized I trusted Caden.

He led me away from the horses, but I balked.

"Aurora?" I felt questioning looks resting on me.

"Can I still pet the horses?" Possibly it was childish, but I really wanted to stroke the soft, shiny coat of the gray horses that had led us through the night.

Caden gently pushed me in another direction. Just before we reached the horses, he took my hand and stretched it forward until I touched the soft nostrils of the carriage horses. One of the horses snorted and blew its hot, tickling breath at me and I giggled. I had almost forgotten again that Caden still owed me answers.

"It's kind of romantic," I murmured, lost in thought. Meanwhile, Caden continued to guide my hand over the soft fur.

Only after a full dose of horse cuddling, I was able to detach myself from the magnificent animals.

With calm, Caden led me further into the unknown. I counted the steps, but I had no idea why. Neither did I know where we were, nor how much further it was.

I heard a door open, but before we went through, Caden put something warm and soft around my shoulders.

"You'll need these," he explained, and I frowned. Even at night, temperatures on the West Coast never dropped below twenty degrees in the summer.

But after a few more steps I no longer trusted my own perception, because it was getting cold. Quite cold even, and without the fluffy jacket, I would have certainly froze.

After a few more feet we stopped.

"Where are we?" I asked, rubbing my forearms to demonstrate the cold. Not only cold enveloped me, but also the scent of coniferous trees, which confused me even more. The ground beneath me was hard and firm, but there was a carpet between the soles of my shoes and the solid ground.

"We're in your best dreams," Caden replied. Then he tampered with my blindfold, before removing it, he said urgently, "Keep your eyes closed for now."

Something began to buzz softly, then a cold drop hit my skin, followed by another. The drops were cold and so gentle that they tickled my skin.

"Wait ... is that snow?" I asked, stunned. I couldn't help but open my eyes, so stunned was I by snow in mid-summer.

I had to blink a few times to let my eyes adjust to the light shining around us.

"Did I promise you too much?" asked Caden.

"Wow." That was all I could say as I spun around. I now knew we were in Seattle's largest rink, but it looked nothing like our rink!

Caden and I stood at the edge of the ice rink, and around us were hundreds of coniferous trees draped with strings of lights and smelling wonderful. The same fairy lights stretched across the rink and almost looked like a starry sky.

My heart sank because Caden had gone to so much trouble. Now it slowly dawned on me that the rose petals in the Space Needle were actually from him. I was worth this rose petal romance to him!

I let my eyes wander further over the hall, which Caden had arranged like a winter wonderland. In the center of the hall was an open, completely snow-covered area, to which a red carpet led. To the left and right, the ground was completely covered with snow, as were the tops of the coniferous trees.

A quietly humming snow machine was also now blowing small snowflakes into the air around us.

"I don't know what to say," I said, looking at Caden. Exactly two things popped into my head.

First, I felt terribly guilty for snapping at Caden about his secrets and second, I had eaten a ton of onions!

Caden took my hand and led me across the carpet.

"Caden, I want to apologize, I was a real monster earlier."

"It's okay, it was an emotional day full of unplanned surprises."

Before I could say anything back, Caden pushed me off the carpet and onto the snowy ice. To my surprise, it was not slippery. At the same moment, *I Can't Help Falling in Love* by Elvis Presley began to play, and I thought for a second that I was about to faint. Before my body could decide to do anything stupid in its stupor, Caden kissed me.

Everything was perfect and at that moment I was the happiest woman in the world.

"Do you like it?" asked Caden after he grabbed me, and we danced the first steps. In the snow. To my very favorite song. Mister Universe had made the impossible possible by making it snow in the summer.

"It's wonderful." I snuggled against his warm body and fought the tears.

"You are special, Aurora. I know it was mean not to tell any of this, but I thought it best."

I nodded vigorously. "Oh, yes. In retrospect, I'm still ashamed of it."

Caden began to grin. "It's okay, Maxine gave me a heads up."

"I see. Yeah, Max knows me pretty well," I replied. It wasn't until a second after that that his answer struck through my body like a bolt of lightning and I winced. "Wait, Maxine knew about this?"

"Yes, she helped me."

Caden and Maxine must have been corresponding behind my back days, maybe weeks ago. Unbelievable that I had not noticed anything about it. Even because of Caden's strange behavior, I hadn't had the slightest suspicion!

"I can't believe Maxine put you up to all this," I said, stunned.

"No." Caden shook his head and looked so deeply into my eyes that I held my breath. "I asked her for help."

Even better. For a second I was afraid that my best friend had coerced him into all of this, because when Maxine wanted to, she could be quite intimidating.

"Why?" I asked.

"Because she's your best friend and knows dreams and desires that you haven't shared with me yet."

Jesus. My heart thumped wildly in my chest, for desire glittered in his eyes. Caden wanted to know my desires so he could fulfill them.

"I want to know your desires, too," I whispered.

"Most of them you already know. And you'll get to know the rest."

Caden hugged me tighter to his chest as he hummed along to the tune.

I couldn't help but grin from ear to ear. It was like a fairy tale, only it was real, and that made it even more precious.

"I still can't believe you pulled all this together in such a short time," I said as we danced past the decorated, fragrant fir trees.

"Everything didn't work out either," Caden said thoughtfully. I didn't even ask at first, knowing he was keeping quiet about what we'd lost focus on because of Maggy's flash wedding. Instead, I continued to nestle against his trained body, letting him lead me across the dance floor, sucking in the winter scent that mingled with Caden's incomparable musk.

"I was impossible, and even though you planned *this*. How can I ever make it up to you?" I asked, lost in thought, when the song ended.

"By accepting this ring," Caden replied, getting down on his knees at the same time. Caden opened a small velvet box containing a ring with a shimmering diamond.

"It's sudden, but I just couldn't leave our lightning engagement like that, Aurora. You're special, and you deserve better than a bare finger. You deserve a fiancé who knows exactly what you're thinking, what you're feeling, what you need, and also what you deserve. Aurora Winter, would you say *yes one* more time so that someday, maybe not today or tomorrow, but someday we can really get married?"

My breath caught in my throat, and I didn't know how to respond. Caden had staged everything exactly as I had imagined my engagement. Only in one thing the reality differed from my dreams – Caden exceeded all my fantasies.

"Yes!" I finally answered. The proposal was perfect, a *no* had not been an option!

Caden put the ring on my finger; it was light as a feather, yet weighed heavy.

So it was official, I was *Mrs. Aurora Dawn Winter-Saint-Universe.*

I was moved to tears, which did not go unnoticed in front of Caden. Actually, I didn't want to cry, but I was so incredibly relieved that I couldn't help it. Caden's change of heart the last few days had to do with our engagement, not with a breakup, as I had feared.

The more Caden had withdrawn, the greater the fear had become that he was giving up on us, now all that fear fell away from me at once.

"You make me the happiest woman in the world," I said in awe, looking at the ring. The set diamond sparkled as beautifully as the snowflakes around us.

"You make me happy, too," Caden replied, standing up. "Because I finally figured out how to capture your heart."

"Oh yes, Caden Saint, you are the official owner of my heart," I reinforced his statement. He didn't like romance, he probably didn't like any of this, and yet here he was, just for me!

When a snowflake blew right into the back of my neck, I shuddered briefly.

"Are you cold?" asked Caden.

"No. I would like to stay," I answered resolutely and clung to Caden's arm. I would have loved to stay forever. Far away from all the chaos, drama, and other stuff that was waiting for me in the outside world. Not to mention my flash stalkers who followed my every move.

"How about some hot cocoa then?" asked Caden.

"Sounds tempting," I replied, rubbing my hands together to warm them.

Caden led me to the edge of the skating rink, where there was a wooden picnic table with hot cocoa steaming with marshmallows. Pastries dusted with powdered sugar and macarons rounded out the presentation.

"Can we stay forever?" I asked dreamily.

Caden grinned at me conspiratorially. "Could be arranged."

"That would be quite magical," I whispered. For a brief moment, I allowed myself to indulge in the illusion that we really were staying here forever.

We sat down, and I wrapped my fingers around the warm porcelain of the cup while inhaling the delicious chocolate scent. After a few short sips, I looked at Caden, who was still watching me.

"The day was beautiful."

Caden accepted the compliment with a smile but looked like another *but* was coming as he de-skinned a muffin and dipped one half into the cocoa.

"I just wish you could have shown your family the engagement ring," he replied with great regret.

I waved him off, grabbed the other half and did the same.

"You saved my sister's wedding, that was a much bigger sign than this ring."

The cocoa, marshmallows, and cake created a sweet taste explosion in my mouth, causing me to groan softly.

"Caden, the day was absolutely perfect," I emphasized again. "And so is this cocoa!"

To clarify, I sipped cocoa again loudly and Caden grinned at me. He conceded defeat. He didn't do that often, which I gave him credit for.

"Good, because I'm tired of being silent on questions like this," Caden grumbled.

"Does that mean we'll be working more closely with PR in the future?" I asked cautiously.

"Hell, no." He looked at me with surprise before understanding why I had even considered PR. "We have a couple of press appointments in the near future that you'll be accompanying me on."

I exhaled a calming breath and immediately put the Janice drama out of my mind. Caden had just proposed to me, a real proposal. There was no more charade to play, we were really together, with real feelings.

Now only Caden's secrets stood between us, and I was slowly getting to the bottom of them.

"Earlier, when I first confessed my feelings to you, there was something else you wanted to say," I began, then looked intently at Caden. "What's on your mind?"

"Nothing more, I was a little sentimental, that's all."

Caden waved it off, with a charming smile and a sadness in his eyes that almost tore my heart apart.

"I know I'm a bad liar, but you know who's pretty bad at it, too? You!" I insisted. Why did he hesitate? I had given him my heart, and I was willing to take good care of his, too, if he let me. But his dark nightmares had dug their claws so deep into Caden that I couldn't reach him.

"I wanted to tell you what was bothering me. I wanted to give you answers to the questions that are still outstanding, but I can't. Not today." Caden sighed, then caressed my cheek and looked deep into my eyes. "You're happy, your eyes shine like diamonds, and I can hear how wildly your heart is still beating. I don't want to ruin this moment."

Attentively, I listened to Caden as I drank my hot cocoa.

"You wouldn't. On the contrary, your show of trust would make me happy. I want you to be happy too," I defended my position, but Caden remained adamant.

"No, my demons would overshadow this experience, and I can't let that happen. But I promise you that I will answer you tomorrow."

"If after midnight, the spell fades?" I asked and Caden nodded.

"Exactly. But luckily I've already found my princess."

"Actually, you had already found me before I could even lose my shoe," I replied with a grin and immediately stole two macarons from the plate.

"The main thing is that you know you belong with your prince," Caden murmured.

He was truly my Prince Charming, my perfect prince with dark, bittersweet secrets he shared with me and mysteries I had yet to crack. His kingdom was vast, and the world was his oyster, in some places more than others. And I was his princess, only too happy to get down on my knees before him.

Admittedly, I adored his dominant side, but I didn't misjudge the sensitive gentleman slumbering inside him either.

We sat in our winter wonderland, holding hands, kissing, sharing endearments and whispering until a call on Caden's cell phone put a damper on the romance. No, actually, that call had shredded the romance to the core, I read that from Caden's face as he took the call.

On the other end of the line was Jackson, and although the speaker wasn't on, I heard his excited voice and siren wailing. This could not be good.

"Fuck! I'm coming as fast as I can!" replied Caden. The fact that he was cursing was another sign of my theory, and if he really wanted to get back to New York right away, something terrible must have happened.

"Is everything all right with Jackson?" I asked quietly. Actually, I hardly dared to ask, just in case.

"No," Caden replied, and I winced in shock. "Yes, it is. It's...complicated."

Caden jumped up, and I followed him. As I walked, I took another handful of macarons – I was a monster, but I was just a monster with fragile blood sugar.

"I'll have someone take you to the hotel," Caden said as we left the winter wonderland.

"I want to be with you!" I protested.

"I can't expect you to leave your family in the middle of the night, without notice, because there's a fire in New York – literally. I've booked the penthouse suite at the *Golden Palace*. Tomorrow, massages, chocolate desserts and everything else you crave await you there."

Granted, it was a tempting offer, but I didn't think to take it.

"Sounds tempting, but if you're so big on massages, you can do that and treat me to your chocolate mousse before, after, *and* during."

Caden looked at me, stunned. "You want to trade a week at *Golden Palace* for terrible jet lag and a fragile Jackson?"

"Yep!" I replied rock solid.

"And what about your family?" echoed Caden.

Maggy was finally married, and I could be there for her most beautiful day. My family would party the night away and not get up until the afternoon. Probably even hungover, depending on whether someone could find alcohol after all. So it made little difference whether I was in Seattle or New York waiting for a sign of life from my family.

I took Caden's hand and squeezed it tightly.

"You're family too, and Jackson is your family. So don't argue, I'm coming with you."

Now it was Caden who was moved to tears after my short speech.

"Fine, but the price for *Mile-High* members is higher than the standard prices," Caden said with a grin.

I waved it off, stuck my nose up in the air, displayed my engagement ring and replied, "Caden Saint is my fiancé, so I can afford anything I want, and no price is too expensive. His words."

"Nice try, Aurora. But you should also know that I will call in your debts without mercy. And you owe me a staggering amount of money."

Caden had my butterflies fluttering again, and I couldn't wait for Caden to call in my debt. But first we had to take care of the fire that was raging in Jackson.

Chapter 25 – Caden

Restlessly, I drummed my fingertips on my knee as we headed toward *South Memorial Hospital*. At Aurora's request, we made a small detour to pick up Maxine Lancester, who was already eagerly waiting for us.

"The fire was really bad," Maxine gushed after she got in. She immediately held her smartphone in front of Aurora's nose, then mine. On it, you could see a high-rise building that was ablaze.

When Aurora's best friend had found out what was going on, she had insisted on standing by Aurora, which was just fine with me. Aurora would never have agreed to just go home.

"How awful!" replied Aurora, snatching the phone from Maxine's hand to skim the article. Her eyes kept darting from left to right until her posture relaxed a bit.

"But everyone made it out. Unbelievable! Jackson is a real hero!"

I took the phone from Aurora to read the article myself. The pictures were shocking, but the fact that not a word was mentioned about the equipment failure was more shocking.

Unbelievably, my best friend had thrown himself death-defyingly into those flames despite everything. He was a real hero.

The closer we got to the hospital, the more my muscles tensed. Jacks had survived but had escaped death by a hair's breadth. I didn't know the details but knew enough to know that I really had to do something. There was no way I wanted the Twenty-third's corruption-induced budget cuts to have my best friend on my conscience.

Sighing, I rubbed my temples. I had the jet lag of death, and the morning light struggling over the horizon burned my eyes like battery acid. I hadn't slept a wink the entire flight, and Aurora lacked sleep as well.

"Can I have my smartphone back?" asked Maxine, looking at me expectantly.

"Sure," I replied, shaking my head. In my anger, I had just kept looking at the flames on the huge display. Jackson had called me when he was still in the field, but I hadn't heard from him since. No idea if he was at the hospital to assist comrades or if he needed to be patched up himself. I guessed both, because Jackson literally went through fire for his people.

"Um, Caden? Can I have my phone now?"

"Sorry," I muttered, passing the smartphone to Aurora, who sat between us and handed it to Maxine.

At this, Maxine cast a meaningful glance at the engagement ring. She was so convincing that one could really have believed that she had never seen this ring before.

"Wow, what a ring! Are you guys engaged? Really?" she asked excitedly.

Aurora giggled. "As if you didn't already know."

"Me? I don't know anything!" Maxine defended herself innocently and grabbed Aurora's hand for a closer inspection. Granted, she was a passable liar, but that didn't help her because I had betrayed her. Still, I gave Maxine credit for acting surprised, as a best friend should.

"Oh, so Caden, all by himself and by chance, one hundred percent set up the engagement I wanted? With snow, cocoa, and mini marshmallows?" asked Aurora, tilting her head.

"Well, sure, Caden is just your perfect soulmate! It's a rare thing, but it happens."

"And he finds the perfect dress, too?"

Maxine eyed Aurora from top to bottom. "This has nothing to do with me or Caden, but with Brando's super ability."

Aurora giggled louder. "You're cute. But Caden has long since revealed to me that you've helped him with a thing or two."

Immediately Maxine pierced me with reproachful looks. "You are a traitor!"

Aurora laughed louder and louder as she grabbed my hand and Maxine's at the same time.

"Max, you are the best friend I could ask for. And Caden is the very best fiancé in the world. I love you both for making yesterday unforgettable."

Aurora's eyes sparkled, and I knew immediately that I would do anything just to maintain that smile. *My smile.* Aurora dedicated this heartwarming laugh only to me.

"So everything was perfect?" echoed Maxine.

"Absolutely."

Aurora gushed on the fly about our engagement and also shared a detail or two about Maggy's wedding, which I happened to be able to save. It did me good to listen to her tales, because they distracted me from the shit that was going on around us right now.

"If I'd known how much hustle and bustle there was in Seattle, I might have let myself be persuaded to come along," Maxine said half-seriously. I understood her fear of flying better than I would have liked, because it had taken half an eternity to get back into a car.

"It would have been magical," Aurora replied. "But we can arrange a little after-engagement party for you."

Maxine snorted loudly. "If I do, I'm throwing the after-engagement party!"

"Shall I order the snow cannons already?" I asked with a grin. But my joke backfired, because two pairs of beaming eyes sparkled at me.

"I was joking," I grumbled. But I fell on deaf ears.

Well, now the milk is spilled ...

"We could also go to *Hazlenut Temptation*. I owe you a visit there anyway!"

I brightened up and looked at Aurora urgently.

"I thought you ate the quote-unquote world's best hazelnut cake ever there. I even remember seeing a Facebook post."

"We did," Aurora replied sheepishly. "But in the car, because of all the press people who waylaid us." She bit her lips and looked down, embarrassed. "Because of the Facebook post."

Maxine clicked her tongue to get attention.

"But without Aurora's superpowers, we never would have made it to Chocolate Hazelnut Paradise."

"Superpowers?" I asked. I didn't deny that Aurora had superpowers in some ways, but I doubted that we were talking about the same superpowers.

"Oh, never mind," Aurora waved it off. "Let's get back to talking about my engagement."

Unlike Maxine, Aurora was a bad liar. I could tell at first glance that my fiancée was trying to hide something.

Maxine shook her head. "You didn't tell Caden about your heroic rescue? That was so cool!"

"No, I didn't say anything because she wasn't cool or heroic. It was something normal, okay? Besides, Caden doesn't care anyway," Aurora denied everything.

"Yes, I'm very interested in what Maxine has to tell," I said in a serious voice while looking at Aurora even more seriously. She didn't dare to look me in the eye, while Maxine didn't ask twice to confess Aurora's secret to me.

"As we were driving Dad's Rolls Royce down the expressway, there was a short *bang,* and ... "

Aurora interrupted Maxine.

"It was more of a quiet scratching."

Cute how Aurora tried to downplay the story, but was almost certain Maxine had more to tell. And the way Aurora tried to talk everything down, Aurora and I had some things to work out later. In the playroom. Without rules.

"Anyway, panic broke out, only Aurora kept her nerve. Nerves of steel!"

"It wasn't a panic either, but maybe a brief restlessness until everyone got used to the situation," Aurora continued to placate.

"And what was this situation that you had to get *used to*?" I probed further.

"Jonathan, the chauffeur, couldn't shift gears anymore, half bad," Aurora replied, giving Maxine a definite look. But it didn't help, her best friend was so busy talking that she didn't notice Aurora's *please-shut-up* looks, but I noticed.

"Half-bad? I'd say speeding down the expressway at full throttle while the gas pedal is stuck isn't half-bad. It's like a bad action movie!"

I thought I had misheard, so I repeated Maxine's words.

"You were in a car you couldn't brake?"

"No!" protested Aurora.

"Yep," Maxine overruled my fiancée.

Aurora was close to despair, as was I. While Aurora was talking everything harmless, Maxine was describing horror scenarios and I had no idea where on the scale of *nothing* to *we all die!* the incident really lay. In any case, it reinforced all the more my view that I needed to watch out for Aurora.

"Then what happened?" I asked.

Aurora talked over Maxine before she could answer.

"Jonathan pulled the car onto the hard shoulder and no one was in danger at any time. End of story."

"Oh come on, Aurora. Why are you leaving out the coolest part of the story?" asked Maxine in wonder.

"The end!" Aurora repeated her words, but Maxine got so lost in her excitement that she just kept talking, which was fine with me. I wanted to know all the details that Aurora had withheld from me.

"Aurora fixed the car in no time," Maxine said proudly.

I frowned and looked at Aurora. "You fixed the car?"

"Yes, I did. But that was a piece of cake." Aurora waved sheepishly and her cheeks reddened within a second.

I knew her dad had a garage and she had started an engineering degree, but that Aurora was capable of fixing a car on the expressway was something I hadn't been aware of. Aurora had never said much about her father's workshop or what they did there.

"With a shoelace!" added Maxine so emphatically that we had finally reached the punch line of her long story.

I summarized the situation once again in disbelief.

"You drove around New York in a broken car that was fixed with a shoelace? And you don't think it's necessary to tell me because you think it's not worth mentioning?" I looked at Aurora expectantly.

Aurora sighed softly. "Of course, when you put it that way, it sounds a little different."

"Indeed." I didn't say it out loud, but my looks were enough to make Aurora realize that we were going to have a long talk about this later. A very long talk – in the playroom.

Only now did Maxine notice the serious mood that had spread over us.

"Oh. Maybe I exaggerated a little," she admitted grudgingly, but Aurora waved it off.

"Let it go."

Aurora knew exactly what was in store for her later. Good. But now I had to concentrate on other things. Like stopping my best friend from burning down the twenty-third firehouse himself.

The closer we got to the hospital, the more anxious I became because I had no idea what kind of condition I would find Jacks in or how I could help him. I was not good in such situations, but I was the only friend Jackson had.

When we arrived at the hospital, I stroked Aurora's thigh.

"I'll see you at home."

But my silent, telling look made it more than clear to Aurora that she should wait for me in the playroom.

"See you later, Caden."

I leaned in and robbed her of a kiss so intense that Maxine turned away in shame.

"Don't keep me waiting," I murmured.

"No, I won't," she replied softly.

"And not one more ride in that death vehicle, understand?" I looked at both Aurora and Maxine with stern looks.

"That's not a death vehicle, it's Dad's Rolls Royce!" protested Maxine.

"Besides, it's a classic car, it's perfectly normal for classic cars to sometimes have little things that need fixing," Aurora added.

"All the more reason to stay away from that thing," I grumbled and got out. I should keep a better eye on her and Maxine in the future. Just the thought of Aurora sitting in that death trap made my heart race.

As I walked, Aurora grabbed my hand and pulled me to her once again.

"Take care of yourself, will you?"

I smiled, then nodded. "I will, I promise."

"You will stay away from tall buildings!" demanded Aurora firmly. Normally I didn't let anyone tell me what I should or shouldn't do, but I was too tired to argue. And if I was too tired to do that, I was too tired to free run.

"We'll stay on the ground," I assured Aurora. "Now, enjoy your coffee and gossip."

"Hey!" cried Maxine. "We're not gossiping, we're just stating!"

"Well, have fun *finding out*," I replied with a wink.

"See you later, Caden."

"See you later, Aurora."

With a heavy heart, I parted ways with my fiancée, grabbed a duffel bag from the trunk, and made my way to the ER entrance.

"And watch out for Jackson!" she called after me through the open window before the car disappeared down the next main road.

All hell broke loose in front of the emergency room. Ambulances and fire trucks were everywhere, sirens and blue lights irritated my senses and again and again I had to dodge doctors and nurses who crossed my path with supplies and other medical equipment.

For a second, I stopped and hesitated. It had been ages since I had last seen the inside of a hospital. My heart contracted, but I overcame the pain and shook off the memories.

There was a state of emergency in the hospital, everywhere sat soot-covered firefighters with bandages on various parts of the body, many of them wearing breathing masks. Among them there were also house residents in bathrobes and pajamas, who were surprised by the sudden fire in their sleep.

Everywhere people were coughing or crying, machines were beeping, doctors were giving instructions.

I felt sick to think that these injuries could have been prevented. A cross hung above the entrance, and I wondered what kind of world we lived in, where there was a God who allowed so many tragedies that could have been prevented.

No matter what Jackson would say, I was hell-bent on doing something about it, whether he wanted to or not.

Slowly, I made my way through the crowded emergency room, shaking off fragments of memory that kept stubbornly biting, until I heard Jackson's unmistakable growl. He wasn't making it easy for a nurse to dress the burn on his arm. He was sitting on a hospital bed in an alcove that could be partitioned off with bright blue curtains.

"Jacks!" I shouted, walking purposefully towards him.

"Caden, finally!" Jackson tried to get up, but the nurse emphatically pushed him back onto the cot.

"Sir, you have to hold still, or I won't be able to treat this!" she admonished him.

"Good, there are more important emergencies than me," Jackson growled.

The nurse didn't reply at first, probably they had been discussing with each other the whole time. My best friend could be a real stubborn person when he wanted to be.

"The sooner you get fixed up, the sooner you'll get out of here," I said, shrugging my shoulders.

"Fine by me." Jackson exhaled heavily but dropped back onto the gurney and continued to be treated. The nurse gave me a grateful look. "Thank you!"

"If it were up to me, I'd still be helping with the fire," Jackson said. He looked tense, his jaws grinding on each other, and his entire body electrified.

The nurse, who was having every trouble keeping Jackson's arm in place, snorted.

"And if it were up to me, you would have been treated long ago. These are first- and second-degree burns! They are not only painful, but also dangerous if infection occurs."

The burn on his arm looked painful, but Jacks didn't make a face, either when the wound was dabbed with alcohol or after it was treated with a burn ointment.

"What are you even doing here?" Jackson asked me.

"You called," I answered, as if it were a matter of course. Even though I knew what he actually meant.

"You could have waited outside." I smiled gratefully because my best friend gave me a chance for a retreat, but I stayed.

"Now I'm here," I said in a firm voice.

Two months ago, I wouldn't have had the strength to stand here with all the medical equipment, smells and sounds around me, but Aurora's scent still enveloping me made me get through it all. Jackson nodded at me gratefully, then watched closely what the young nurse was doing.

"What happened?" I asked.

"I'm sure there's everything you need in the *Morning Post*." Jackson clenched his hands into fists.

I sat down next to him on a free chair and shook my head.

"Not really. Only the fire is mentioned, nothing else."

"Fuck," Jackson cursed softly. "But I kind of knew they wouldn't say a word about the fucking aerial ladder."

I frowned. "What happened?"

"The aerial ladder went on strike while three people were stuck."

Jackson recounted at length, and with a hell of a lot of cursing, how they finally did get the firefighters out of the basket, which was hanging at a height of around twenty-five feet.

"Well, and the end of the story is that two of my colleagues and a civilian are lying around here with broken bones."

I was stunned and couldn't say anything back, but I didn't have to, Jacks had just warmed up. Even the nurse listened spellbound.

"Because the damn vehicle blocked the way for so long, fire trucks couldn't follow, so the building is now ready for demolition."

"You still did a good job," I replied. Of course, that was no consolation, but it was reality. "According to the newspaper, there were no deaths, so you made it in spite of everything."

"No deaths, but at what cost? Damn budget cuts," Jacks muttered.

"Tell me about it. Our board just voted through austerity measures that will cost lives, too," the nurse replied, patting Jackson's thigh comfortingly.

If it wasn't so unfortunate, I would have found it interesting that the world was all about money. My world had never revolved around money because I always had enough of it.

"Ready?" asked Jackson, holding up his bandaged arm.

"Done," the nurse replied. But she slowed him down before he could get up. "But I'll see you again tomorrow for a checkup, all right?"

"Sure," Jackson lied without blushing, and I looked at him admonishingly.

The nurse wrote something on a card she gave Jackson.

"Tomorrow at four o'clock I would be free. Just ask for me at the front desk, I'm Katy."

"You got it, Katy." Jackson winked at her, and I got the impression that Katy almost fainted when he said her name. Poor girl. She was beautiful, no question, but Jackson wasn't interested. He lived for his job, our broken hobby, and nothing else.

Katy gave Jackson a second paper.

"This is a prescription for painkillers."

"Don't need it, thanks."

Jacks jumped up from the cot, grabbed his gear, and we left the ER.

"What now?" I asked.

"Like you don't know," Jackson replied with a grin, pointing to my duffel bag.

"Are you sure?" I echoed. "We've never been in worse shape."

"That's exactly why we need this now." Damn, I couldn't counter an argument like that. So we went to the bathroom and changed. Before we went outside, Jacks bunkered the duffel bag with a colleague who was still waiting for his treatment.

Once outside, the morning summer sun was a relief to my eyes. The white, cold halogen light inside, the stench of disinfectant and the green vinyl floors triggered a migraine in me.

"How about a race?" asked Jackson.

"You're hurt," I replied.

"No big deal, it's equal opportunity now." Jackson grinned challengingly at me. He could still smile away his anger, but I could see it bubbling under his surface.

"Fine, fine by me. But we'll stay on the ground."

"Coward," Jacks taunted, but I was not deterred.

"I'm overtired, my jet lag is nearly killing me, and you, you've had second-degree burns and a hell of a mission. Under other circumstances, I wouldn't have promised Aurora anything, but in this case, she's right."

Jackson looked at me frowning as he stretched his body, preparing it for the rigors ahead. "So Aurora didn't run away when you tried to put a ring on her?"

"No!" I replied proudly, puffing out my chest like a noble rooster.

"Congratulations, buddy." Jackson patted me on the back. "Aurora is really lovely."

"Yes, she is," I confirmed and returned to my own training preparations. "But you know who else wouldn't run away from you?"

"Who?" asked Jackson.

"Katy, the nurse."

Jackson started laughing. "Stop messing with me."

I shook my head and looked at him seriously to demonstrate that I was not teasing him.

"She was flirting with you the whole time. Subtly, with her eyes, but still clearly enough that even a sentimental idiot like you should pick up on it."

"She treated me, that's all," Jackson continued to deny the obvious.

"Don't be so picky. You should go out again, have a drink, be in company."

"I am and I do."

I grinned at him. "I'm talking about a very specific form of *society*."

"Me too." Jacks didn't let up, but I was persistent, too.

"If I win, you'll take Katy out on a date – on me."

Jackson gave me the middle finger before giving himself up to starting position.

"You are so going to lose, you scumbag."

"I won't, which is why I'll cede whatever you want. So where do you want to go?"

Jackson gave me a serious look. "Good, then I'm about to be the proud owner of a VIP table at *Italian Gourmet*."

"So you can take Nurse Katy there?" I asked with a grin.

Jackson cracked his knuckles. "You must be out of your mind. You know I don't want dates, much less relationships."

I noted his answer and smiled knowingly because I had been thinking the same thing recently. Damn how stupid I had been all this time. I hoped Jacks also realized one day that there was no way he could let his Mrs. Right go as soon as he met her.

"What's our goal?" I asked and got into starting position as well.

"Hmm." Jackson considered for a moment. "How about Rockefeller Center?"

I suppressed my groan because Jackson was not suggesting a race, but a marathon. Rockefeller Center was several miles away from us and we had to cross Central Park and 5th Avenue.

"Fine by me."

I agreed, but only because I knew Aurora's café was on the way, and I absolutely had to make a secret detour to see her. Because earlier, when I was standing in the emergency room, I realized two things.

First, Aurora had made me realize that I hadn't breathed in far too long – meeting her was like taking a life-saving breath just before drowning.

And secondly, I could no longer let myself be consumed by the secrets I kept hidden deep inside. I had to let them go, they had to disappear. Immediately!

I pulled a coin out of my pocket and placed it on my thumb.

"On your mark, get set ... "

Ping.

Chapter 26 – Aurora

"You know what I really enjoyed about Seattle?" I asked rhetorically, sipping my hot cocoa. After Caden texted me that Jackson was doing well under the circumstances, I could finally sit back.

"No, but you're about to tell me," Maxine replied with a grin. She spooned the frothed milk from her cocoa macchiato and winked at me.

"The silence!" Maxine giggled, though I was absolutely serious. Without press hype, the *Hazlenut Temptation* tasted like it used to. The cocoa was sweet as sin and the hazelnut cake brought back memories. So far, the reporters hadn't figured out that Caden and I were back in New York, and that was just fine with me.

"*Silence,* she said, after fleeing to New York from her chaotic family."

"Yeah, yeah, hold that over me," I muttered. "But I'm serious about this. I had never in my life believed that reporters could be so pushy."

Sometimes the press people came so close to my face with their microphones that I was afraid of a lobotomy.

"Well, it's not every day that Mr. Universe gets engaged," Maxine replied, grabbing my hand. "That ring really looks great on you."

"Probably because you made sure of it," I replied with a grin.

"No." Maxine pricked a slice of strawberry shortcake on her fork. "I was in on it, but Caden picked out the ring himself. He thought the ring captured the sparkle of your eyes."

"Really?" I asked incredulously, while my heart almost jumped out of my chest.

"Yep. And if you weren't my best friend, I would have grabbed him!"

We both giggled, knowing that Caden was absolutely not Maxine's type of booty call.

"Caden is really perfect," I gushed.

"Absolutely," Max confirmed. "By now, do you know what Caden and Jackson do secretly when they go around the houses? Shady speakeasies, illegal boxing matches in Hells Kitchen, or a billionaire secret club after all?"

"Max, your imagination is running away with you again!" I finished my cocoa and immediately ordered a second one. With extra cream, extra chocolate syrup and extra cookies. Then I leaned forward conspiratorially toward Maxine. "And you should know if there are any secret billionaire secret clubs, right?"

"I'm sorry, I can't tell you about *my* secret club, which of course doesn't exist!" replied Maxine with a diabolical laugh. "What are Caden and Jackson up to now?"

"Free-running," I said, grabbing my temples. Just the thought of Caden climbing around on skyscrapers, eaves, and construction cranes made me dizzy. At least he had promised me today that he wasn't doing anything dangerous.

"Free-running?" Maxine frowned. "In any climbing gyms?"

I shook my head. "No. On top of the Empire State Building. Without a safety line."

"Oh." Now Max understood why I was so worried. "When did he tell you about this? And more importantly, how? *Hey honey, by the way, I'm polka dancing at a dizzying height.*"

Although the subject was serious, I had to suppress my grin when Maxine imitated Caden's deep voice.

"No, Jackson told me," I replied, turning my attention to my walnut cookie that I had ordered. "If it weren't for Jackson, I'd still be in the dark."

"You met Jackson? When?" asked Maxine between sips of cocoa.

"When he had dinner at our house," I said, shrugging my shoulders, and took a hearty bite out of my cookie.

"He had dinner at your place?" Maxine jumped up from her seat, stunned, which got us the attention of all the other patrons in the café. She cleared her throat sheepishly, sat back down in her seat, and looked at me seriously. "Why don't I know about this?"

"Well," I said, acting as unconcerned as possible. "You'd have known by now if you'd taken my calls more often!"

"Oh, Aurora. I just couldn't risk spilling the beans."

With a conciliatory smile, Max slid me a raspberry macaron.

"Because you were in cahoots with my fiancé?"

I grabbed the French cookie but continued to give Maxine a serious look.

"I feel terrible for ignoring you for so long. Okay? Is that what you want to hear?"

"At least that's a start. And next time you'll let me in on it when you're in cahoots with Caden!" I demanded. I hadn't told anyone about the extra onions yet, but if Max didn't relent, I was going to have to share that detail willy-nilly. Otherwise, Maxine knew every single detail, both about Maggy's wedding and about my engagement. I hadn't told her about the *Mile-High Club,* but my best friend could figure that out for herself when two lovers flew to the other side of the States in a private jet.

"Forget it, then it's no longer a surprise. Besides, these are promises of honor that you have to keep. Period." Maxine waved it off in disagreement. I sighed, having to play the onion card.

"Then at least tell me when not to order extra onions!"

Maxine's brows lifted questioningly. "Huh?"

"Just before Caden's proposal, I insisted – and very clearly – that we eat hot dogs with extra onions."

"No!" Maxine's jaw dropped.

"Yes, he did," I replied in anguish, rolling my eyes. "He ate onions, too, but still. I should have smelled like roses when he proposed, not hot dogs."

I expected Maxine to start laughing at me, but instead she cocked her head to the side and let out an *Awww,* like she was looking at a clumsy baby kitten.

"That's so cute!"

"No, it's not!" I protested. But I had lost Maxine to her crushes.

"Yes it is, it makes your engagement *imperfect in* the perfect way. And believable! It's so sweet!"

Thoughtfully, I scraped together the last crumbs on my plate.

"I never thought of it that way."

"But that's exactly how you have to look at it! Man, I would have loved to have seen Caden's face when you ordered the onions."

Now, in retrospect, the sheer panic on Caden's face had been impossible to miss, but sometimes, especially when I was hungry, I had no sense of anything.

"Caden has tried to dissuade me several times," I said, chuckling.

"Then you should listen to him the next time he advises you to do something."

"I should. Although I have to admit, I'd order Terry's hot dogs again with extra onions."

Maxine suppressed her laughter by covering her mouth.

"That's so typical Aurora."

"I just have principles that I'm not going to throw overboard for Caden."

"Then you'll just have to prepare yourself for the next extra onion incident, because it's sure to come."

I acted shocked and pointed the forks in Maxine's direction.

"Thank you for your optimism."

"Always at your service," she replied, indicating a curtsy.

Shaking my head, I looked out the window. The higher the sun moved, the busier the city became. Pedestrians crowded close together at the red lights, while hundreds of cars rolled along the streets. The crowd grew larger and larger until the traffic light finally turned green.

While I spooned cream from my cocoa, and Max devoted herself to her second piece of cake, I continued to watch the colorful goings-on.

When startled pigeons flew by right outside our window, I curiously searched for the cause.

I first recognized Jackson sprinting across the sidewalk, closely followed by Caden. Just before the crosswalk, however, Caden slowed down, and I had the feeling that he was intent on arriving only when the light turned red.

To my surprise, Caden really did stop at the red light. When our eyes met, my heart leapt, and when Caden waved me outside, it leapt again.

"Excuse me a minute," I said, pointing at Caden.

"Wow, so Caden doesn't just look this good in suits," Maxine stated matter-of-factly.

She was right. Caden cut a fine figure even in this sweat-soaked shirt.

As I walked through the store door, Caden pulled me around the corner breathing heavily and demanded a kiss, which I was only too happy to give him.

"What are you doing here?" I asked. Of course, I didn't mean the side alley where we were hiding behind stacked boxes and wooden pallets.

"Losing," Caden replied more proudly than befitted a winning guy.

"To make Jackson feel better?" I asked and Caden nodded.

"Yes. He was pretty angry, but by the time he got to the Empire State Building, he had calmed down."

My eyes grew huge, and I stared at Caden in disbelief.

"You're running all the way to the Empire State Building? From the hospital?"

"No big deal," Caden waved it off. He really seemed like it was no big deal to him. "We're staying grounded, after all."

"At least something," I replied with relief.

Caden grabbed my chin between his thumb and forefinger.

"When I promise something, I deliver."

"I know," I replied with a smile. "Still, I worry when you act so recklessly."

Caden demanded another kiss from me before responding.

"I'll be careful. I promise."

"Good, then I guess you should be careful now that Jackson doesn't find out you're letting him win," I said, nudging my index finger against his chest.

"He won't." Caden pressed me against the brick wall behind me. "I'm going to take the car to just before 5th Avenue and resume the race from there."

"Clever," I replied with a grin. "How much time do we have left?"

"A few minutes," Caden murmured. "Time I want to spend with you."

I moaned softly as Caden pressed me even harder between himself and the wall.

"Caden! What if someone sees us?" I protested half-heartedly. Basically, I didn't care if anyone saw us or not. For all I cared, the whole world could know what Caden and I were doing. Still, I held back because Caden's good reputation was important.

"I don't care," Caden growled. Nevertheless, he broke away from me to look deep into my eyes.

He was giving me millennial looks, whatever he was about to say had meaning. I clearly felt that Caden was about to show me how profound his soul really was.

"I'm not going to let Jackson win for no reason. He needs this, he needs a win after this lousy loss."

I nodded in understanding. It would never occur to me to try to drive a wedge between Jackson and Caden. Even though I couldn't deny that I would rather they pursued a hobby that was less life-threatening.

Caden took a breath to say something.

"Jacks did the same thing for me back when we met."

"Sounds like he's as good a friend as you are."

I smiled, because I was very fortunate to have a similar deep connection with Maxine.

"He is," Caden replied, staring thoughtfully at the floor. When he returned my gaze, the pain in his eyes almost broke my heart. "If I hadn't met him then..."

He didn't dare say the next words and I didn't dare think them.

Instead, I soothingly placed my hand on his chest.

"You don't have to do this, Caden. Not now. Your promise that you'll do it eventually is fully enough for me."

Caden fought his way to a smile before swallowing down the lump in his throat.

"I want to tell you, now. I realized that earlier in the ER."

My brow furrowed as I looked around.

"Here, now? In the middle of a back alley?"

"It's pretty hard to ruin romantic vibes around here," Caden replied with a shoulder shrug. He was right, there really was no romance to be found amidst containers, wooden pallets, and trash.

"Okay," I finally replied so that Caden could say what was so heavy on his mind. Caden took a deep breath as he revealed the deepest part of his soul to me.

"Everyone who knows my story still looks at me today with pity and regret."

"All except Jackson," I said thoughtfully.

"Right," Caden confirmed. "He just said *fuck*, and then dragged me to the nearest rooftop he could find."

There was a nostalgic, pained smile on his lips that almost broke my heart. Whatever Caden was telling me now, it was not a story with a happy ending.

"How did you two meet?" I asked. The smile on his lips disappeared, and I felt his hands clench into fists, which he used to support himself to the left and right of my head. I still wondered if a back alley was the right place for a soul striptease, but Caden seemed so convinced that I wasn't going to dissuade him.

"In a support group that Child Protective Services ordered us to go to."

Oh, a shiver ran down my spine. Until now, I had suspected that Caden might have had a fight with his family, but not that the bond with his family had really been cut. Just the thought of living without my messy family made me nauseous.

"What happened?"

"Too much." Caden sighed. In his mind's eye, all the horrible events he had to go through must be playing out. I put my hand on his chest, a simple but significant gesture that signaled I was there for him.

"If I had been smarter, if I had been stronger and faster, maybe my parents would still be alive."

My heart broke at the realization that Caden's family ties were not only cut but shredded.

"I'm so sorry I burdened you with my family drama, Caden," I said in a weak voice. "If I had known..."

Caden put an index finger to my lips to stop me.

"There's nothing to apologize for. A family has ups and downs. What I experienced was a low – but it's followed by highs that I definitely don't want to miss."

Incredibly, Caden just showed me his traumatized, hurt side and still managed to smile so adorably that I fell in love with him all over again.

"You are part of the family! You will experience all the ups and downs, whether you like it or not."

Caden stroked my hair and looked at me thoughtfully.

"My mom would have loved you. You and your messy family."

"I would have liked to have met her," I replied with a smile.

His features hardened again, and I didn't dare breathe. Around us it became icy cold, as if the sun lacked any warmth, although it was shining.

"My mother would still be alive if she had left my father earlier." Caden's voice quivered with anger and his soul seemed conflicted. I was sure that some of his anger was directed at himself.

Understanding, I took Caden's clenched fist and opened his hand, which also took some tension off the rest of his body.

"What did your father do?" I asked.

The pain in Caden's eyes seemed almost too real to grasp.

"He took her with him to her death when he drove the car into a guardrail in a drunken stupor."

My heart contracted as Caden's words flowed viscously from his lips. I gasped for air but was unable to breathe and waited for Caden to continue speaking.

"My father was a drunk, I don't remember ever seeing him without a bottle of beer. Before noon he was drunk and stayed that way until at one point he collapsed comatose outside the hallway in the living room. Mom wanted to leave him, but stayed for my sake, because of the image of the *perfect* family. I was too young to understand it all."

I buried my face in Caden's shirt because I didn't want him to see me cry. I didn't want to cry, I wanted to be strong for him, but his story took me away because I could hardly imagine what it must be like to have to live in such a fragile family.

"And when I finally understood what was going on, it was too late."

"You were a child," I took Caden's side because he couldn't do it himself. His self-doubt forced him to do so.

"I could have stopped it! If I had refused to get in the damn car...or if I had called the police, the fire department, anyone!"

I wish I could have said something to him that eased his pain, but there was nothing. No words in the world could make up for what Caden had lost. I squeezed his hand and looked at him intently, showing him that I was there for him and willing to share his pain.

Caden looked at me in pain, me reflected in his gleaming eyes, revealing all the sadness Caden had ignored over the past years and decades.

"The damn guilt is still eating away at me."

"Have you ever told anyone that?" I asked.

Caden shook his head. "There are a few people who know about the accident. The ones from Child Protective Services, distant relatives – who didn't want to know about me – and others from a support group. Jackson." When Jackson's name came up, Caden's features softened a bit. I didn't know that's how they had met, and my guilty conscience for calling them both idiots grew. Yes, they were dumb jerks, but now that I knew the background, I understood them much, much better.

"But you never told them about your accusations?" I echoed.

Caden took a deep breath. "No."

"That must have been hard."

"You have no idea how hard," Caden replied with a sigh. "And Erica was going to make a PR show out of it. I don't know how she figured it out, but she did."

My eyes grew wide. "Wow, how heartless."

"Yes, heartless is an apt word for it, even though Erica is basically just doing her job."

"You can also advertise without breaking or tearing out hearts," I replied seriously. "That's why the contract?"

Caden nodded. "Yes. She even knew the details that no one else knew. That I was in the accident. That my father was killed instantly, the cowardly scumbag." Every time Caden spoke of his father, his voice quivered with anger. Understandably so. Silently, I thanked God that my father was the exact opposite of what Caden had endured.

"You asked me why I insist you ride in my car, with my chauffeurs." I nodded. "These SUVs are statistically the safest cars in the world. And the drivers are trained paramedics."

"Oh." That's all I said. On the one hand, I was touched that Caden wanted me to be safe, but on the other hand, he still had to be panicked that something would happen to me if he wasn't with me.

"If the paramedics had gotten to the scene earlier, they could have saved my mom. But they were late because the cell phone didn't have reception, they were late because they didn't know exactly where we were."

"That's terrible."

"Yes, it was terrible," Caden said thoughtfully. "That's why I funded satellites that can receive emergency calls from difficult areas. Smartphones that will survive any crash. Smart braking systems designed to prevent accidents. And if my engineers don't screw up, there will soon be drones monitoring all roads."

"That's very noble of you."

Caden waved it off. "No, it's the least I can do so other kids don't have to go through what I went through. Saint Industries only exists so I can sleep more soundly."

Wow. That took some digesting. Even though Caden invested billions to make the world a little safer, he thought he was being selfish. If I could, I'd pay his father a visit and give him a good telling off. Caden was so magical, such a good man, and his father had nothing better to do than ruin his perfect family, his perfect son.

"Can you sleep more soundly?" I asked.

Caden's dark eyes brightened a little. "Since you lay beside me, Aurora. You are the light in the eternal twilight. You have dispelled the darkness."

Smiling, I kissed his lips.

"The price was not small, it cost you your heart."

"Everything has a price," Caden replied. He often said these words, but now they had a completely different meaning.

Caden kissed me again and exhaled in relief.

"It was good to talk about it."

"Anytime," I offered him sincerely. "I'm always here for you."

Caden had done nothing less for me than I had needed him. That was how it was in a real partnership, in a real engagement. You helped each other, stood by each other in good times, but especially the bad times, and shared everything. Joy. Pain. Sadness. Love. All of this was only available as a complete package, completely or not at all.

Thoughtfully, I bit my lips. Now that I knew Caden's story, I understood much better what was going on inside him. It was as if his layer of ice had simply melted. The truth had simply shattered the granite protective wall around his heart.

"Caden, I want to apologize to you," I finally said.

Caden eyed me with irritation. "For what?"

"If I had known why you demonize alcohol so much, I would have..."

Again Caden put his finger on my lips.

"You couldn't have known, Aurora."

"But now that I know, I swear to you I will never touch another drop of alcohol."

I was serious. So really *for-always-and-ever-seriously*.

Caden smiled mildly at me. "That means a lot to me."

"You mean everything to me."

A smile flitted across Caden's lips. The darkness disappeared from his eyes, the oppressiveness between us fizzled out within seconds.

I glanced to the right and left in the side alley. This place was remote, unromantic and also a bit dirty, but now it meant the world to me.

Caden pulled me to him, demanding my mouth, and I opened it willingly. Our kisses tasted of sweet love and freedom.

After an eternity, we detached from each other, reluctantly, but it had to be done.

"I hate to say it, but I have to go. I just want to lose without offending Jackson."

Giggling, I pulled Caden to me one last time to enjoy the togetherness, because now nothing – absolutely nothing – stood between us and that was good!

"Why do you want Jackson to win, anyway?" I asked, frowning. Caden was a winner, an alpha. Jackson was too, but I didn't believe in making him feel better by winning, but by competing with Caden himself. What the two of them were doing wasn't about winning, it was about the path to victory.

"Because I'm a good friend," Caden replied with a shrug. His poker face was good, but I had gotten better at seeing through him.

"So, you're a good friend? It has nothing whatsoever to do with you wanting to lose something on purpose?"

Caden looked at me in surprise, though he should have realized that I knew about their bets.

"Clever girl," he finally admitted, thus confessing everything.

"Thank you, for your sincerity," I said with a smile. "It means a lot to me that you shared your thoughts and feelings with me."

And that's without a declaration of silence! This proved to me twice that Caden had really earned my heart.

"It wasn't easy, but I feel much better." Caden cleared his throat and left a meaningful pause. "I love you, Aurora Dawn Winter."

I suppressed a snort because Caden, from wherever, had picked up my full name.

"I love you, too, Caden. But don't ever say my full name again!" With a raised index finger and a serious face, I looked at Caden.

"Is that a threat?" asked Caden, amused.

"You betcha!" I fired back with a grin.

"So, I'm going to lose to Jacks now, so we won't be kept from more important things on our honeymoon by broken aerial ladders or melted shoe soles. If I lose, it will never be altruistically."

Caden winked at me, then ducked into the bustling streets of New York, leaving me with a wildly beating heart.

Wow. The day was just *wow*. Caden's honesty had blown me away and the fact that he had this strength and this calmness in him despite these experiences was admirable. Caden had shared his biggest secret with me and now I could take some of his pain away.

I am Miss Universe.

Chapter 27 – Caden

I intertwined my fingers in Aurora's hand as the elevator doors closed and we continued our ride to the executive floor. Nothing had changed for the outside world, but everything was different for us. The spectacle we had put on for the whole world had become real love. Our fiction had become reality, which pleased me quite a bit.

But not only that had changed, it was also the way Aurora looked at me that had changed. So full of love, full of pride and also a little teasing, which elicited a grin from me. The fact that Aurora was still looking at me like that was almost a miracle to me and was definitely a sign that we belonged together. All the others who knew about my past still gave me pitying looks.

Actually, today was a normal morning for me, for Aurora, and for the whole world, yet the day felt significant. This was every day that I could hold Aurora's hand.

"What's on the agenda today?" asked Aurora, yawning.

"You could have stayed home," I said with a warning look.

"What kind of personal assistant would I be if she just left her boss hanging like that?" asked Aurora rhetorically, giving me a *no-discussion look*. I loved everything about Aurora, but the fact that she had her own opinion and that, in some circumstances, she got her way with claws extended, was something I particularly appreciated.

"You'd make a good wife who sleeps in to her marital duties," I said dryly. Actually, we were still supposed to be lying in the king size bed, eating chocolate covered fruit and doing depraved things with each other. Instead, I had called a special board meeting to help Jackson with his problem. Neither Aurora nor I had slept much that night because I had some things to prepare. If I was lucky, I'd kill two birds with one stone - Jackson's problem was history and the PR department would leave me alone.

Aurora waved it off, shaking her head.

"Come on, your jet lag is at least as bad as mine. If I slept in and you worked through the day, you probably wouldn't..."

I interrupted Aurora with a meaningful expression on my face.

"Think carefully about what you want to say about me, perseverance, and the Playroom."

"Do you feel your honor has been insulted?" asked Aurora, giggling.

Okay, that was enough. Before Aurora could realize what was happening, I had her pressed between me and the wall. I buried my face in the crook of her neck while my hands secured her wrists to the side of her body.

"Caden! We'll be right there!"

I let go of one wrist, bent over to the elevator's control panel and pressed the emergency stop. With a whirring sound, the elevator stopped.

"No, we won't," I corrected Aurora.

"But the board is waiting!" Aurora tried to get out of it one more time. But it was too late for that now. She had wanted it that way, so now she had to live with the consequences.

"Right. And he'll wait until I show up."

I continued with what I had started with, sucking in Aurora's scent deeply and tasting it on my tongue at the same time. *Cinnamon.* I would love to do nothing all day but bury Aurora under me, feel her, taste her, hear her moan.

When my hand slid between her legs, Aurora opened her thighs as far as it would go with her tight skirt to make it easier for me. Against my better judgment, Aurora was wearing panties.

I held my open palm upward, prompting her to remove her panties.

"Really?"

"Do I look like I'm joking?"

Aurora gave me a pained expression while her eyes shone provocatively.

"I'm almost out of panties at home!"

"Good," I answered curtly and waited for Aurora to give me her red lace panties. She was right, my drawer now contained a hodgepodge of Aurora's underwear.

"Will I get them back someday?" asked Aurora, snapping the panties emphatically onto my hand.

"With that tone of voice, rather not."

Aurora remained rather unimpressed by my answer, leaning back against the wall and folding her arms.

"Luckily, I have a gold credit card and can buy hundreds, heck, thousands of panties!"

Remarkable how Aurora tried to beat me with my own weapons, but also foolhardy. After all, it was *my* game we were playing.

My hand slid between her legs one more time, this time without any disturbing fabric and I moaned softly when I felt her wetness. With my free hand I massaged her breasts until their tips pressed through the fabric of her blouse.

For a moment I forgot the appointments, the obligations and all the shit around us. There was only us and our unbridled desire for each other.

"I wish I had something with me to drive you crazy with," I murmured in her ear. Then I claimed her mouth, robbed her breath and stopped only when I myself ran out of breath.

"Your promises are quite enough for me," Aurora replied with a sigh. She pressed her hips against me, ready for more, but she was right. My promises, but especially my threats, were more effective than any vibrators or love balls I could muster.

I detached myself from her, set the elevator in motion again, and watched from the corner of my eye, amused, how astonished Aurora was. There was that fire in her eyes again that made me want to grab her immediately and put her over my knee, but I controlled myself. Watching Aurora become more and more stunned was delicious.

"Don't you have anything else to say?" asked Aurora challengingly.

I suppressed my grin and put on my business-like face.

"A gentleman keeps silent and enjoys."

Aurora could not respond to that. Basically I was right, I was a gentleman. One who held open the door to the playroom before spanking the woman. I gave sincere compliments on makeup and hairstyles before trashing both. I probably belonged to the rare group of *gentle-doms* who could rein in their dominance.

As befitted a gentleman, I let Aurora go first when the elevator doors opened. Perhaps not entirely unselfishly, Aurora's bottom had a particularly nice shape in the gray, tight-fitting dress. Besides, I loved how her walk seemed when her lower body throbbed with pleasure – and it did, I had made sure of that!

We found ourselves in the board meeting room, a sparse space with a long oak table, leather chairs for each board member, and a horribly oppressive painting that could be attributed to modern art. Most of the board members were already in their seats, chatting with their seatmates to the left or right.

"Wow, pretty sparse," Aurora muttered as we walked along the table.

"Exactly as it should be," I replied.

I had done my utmost to make this room as uncomfortable as possible. I owned most of the company shares and therefore had the power to vote. Regardless of whether the board wanted it or not, I decided where things went, and that was just fine with me. The fact that I called meetings was more a sign of politeness.

When I took my seat in my chair, the conversations immediately fell silent. All eyes were on me while Aurora stood behind me and distributed some papers we had prepared.

My eyes roamed over the room, some people were still missing. Checking my watch, I frowned and realized that I was already ten minutes late.

"Where is the PR department?" I asked.

Shoulder shrug. Silence. Impassive expressions. *Thank you, team.*

"Fine, we'll start without them."

This would have been Erica's chance to push through her plans, but if she didn't show up at all, that was fine with me. I took advantage of the board members' undivided attention and roughly explained what today's meeting was all about for me. At first, my explanation remained fairly factual, but the more I told about conditions in the Twenty-third, the more fiery and emotional my speech became. It was no longer about a possible PR stunt; it was just about the fact that tomorrow's heroes needed support today.

"In summary, I can say that the media impact will continue to reinforce our positive trend, the fire station can finally be renovated in principle, and we can thus distract from the prototype chaos and the impending stock market slump."

Shrugging shoulders, silence and impassive expressions - again. If the stability of Saint Industries wasn't so essential these days, I would have fired the entire board.

"Objections?" I asked more precisely. Out of friendliness, because I had already initiated everything necessary.

A clearing of the throat went through the room, which I could trace to Coleman, my chief engineer.

"Yes?" I asked.

Coleman adjusted his glasses before folding his hands together and looking at me seriously. From the way the other board members looked at him, he was the poor devil sent to the front to deliver bad news to me.

"We need more budget for drone development."

I furrowed my brow. "More?"

In the last days and weeks, the development had applied for – and been granted – more and more funds. Our deadline was getting dangerously close.

"There are still bugs we need to fix!"

Sighing, I leaned back in my chair.

"How much money are we talking about? And what is the magnitude if the bugs are not fixed?"

Oppressive silence. Then another board member intervened. Joe Alastair, who also took care of some of the finances and kept bringing in good, new contacts.

"More money? Maybe we'd better bring in more capable employees!"

"Impudence!" protested Coleman angrily.

Sighing, I pulled my smartphone out of my pocket and leaned back. Since no one objected to my plans for the firehouse, I allowed them this caboodle. That being said, Alastair was so on top of things that he was going to beat Coleman up in the hallway after the meeting if the matter wasn't resolved.

Aurora watched the action at the table intently as she bit down on her lower lip. For her, the business world was new and exciting and probably very different from how Hollywood portrayed such meetings on TV. I opened our chat history and typed away.

What are you thinking right now?

Aurora's cell phone buzzed softly; she looked at me in surprise. Only when I nodded my agreement did she pull her smartphone out of the small side pocket of her gray outfit and type something.

I think your job is very demanding. Shouldn't you be a little more attentive?

Grinning, I sent back a laughing smiley face.

You still have a lot to learn, Aurora.

Aurora gave me a meaningful look.

What, for example?

Admittedly, I had wished that Aurora would ask this very question, even though hundreds of answers popped into my head at the same time. There was still so much I wanted to experience or try with Aurora. Just the thought that her fantasies and desires overlapped perfectly with mine made my anticipation of the future grow even more.

I was lost in my thoughts for a moment, until Aurora conspicuously cleared her throat inconspicuously, demanding an answer.

That board meetings are boring, and you should use the time to think about other things.

Restlessly, Aurora shifted her weight from one leg to the other. She wore forbidden high heels, which she tamed effortlessly.

What do you think should be thought about?

I wondered what Aurora was thinking about right now. Did she know that I could hardly restrain myself?

You. Naked. Bent forward on this table.

When my message was sent, Aurora gasped softly. In shock, she put her hand over her mouth, but the discussion at the table was so heated that no one paid any attention to Aurora. Good thing, because otherwise they would have seen her cheeks reddening more and more and her posture changing.

Caden.

When I read her message and knew the tone in which she had phrased it, I had to grin.

I'd rather fuck you right now than continue to deal with these brawlers.

Again, Aurora took a loud audible breath, but instead of answering, she pocketed her phone again and tried to put on a professional face.

Bad girl.

Her cell phone vibrated, but she showed no reaction. Aurora's gaze remained fixed on the events in front of me, which I had completely blanked out.

I still preferred that Aurora slept off her jet lag, but I was grateful to her for making the board meeting more bearable. Just the sight of her rosy cheeks was worth all the drama.

Aren't you curious what else I'm thinking about?

Aurora still didn't move a muscle, but I could still see her struggling inside. The curiosity inside her was fighting for dominance and would win sooner or later. It was only thanks to her curiosity that we were here today.

I want you. Now. The thought alone drives me crazy.

Aurora continued to be brave, but I was getting impatient. It's a good thing we were playing my game, where I set the rules.

I looked at Aurora and beckoned her to me with my index finger until she leaned down to me.

"For every unread message, I will withhold an orgasm from you," I whispered urgently in her ear. My threat bore fruit, because Aurora grabbed her smartphone and read the messages.

Good girl.

Chapter 28 – Aurora

While the board was having heated discussions in front of us, Caden and I were having an equally fiery conversation. I don't know how he always managed to make me blush. Sometimes I thought that was one of his favorite things to do.

Welcome to the latest episode of: How quickly can Aurora's cheeks redden?

My middle throbbed violently, but I had no choice but to continue reading Caden's news, because the consequences were clearly worse.

Knowing Caden, he would have brought me close to orgasm dozens of times, only to steal it from me. *I'm not playing along!*

Caden was busily typing into his smartphone while he kept giving me seductive looks that led me to conclude that his message must be quite salacious. My treacherous body could hardly wait for his message, while a small, weak part of my consciousness tried to listen to the conversations around the table. Any bit of information could be a breakthrough for me, too. After all, Dad and I had some theoretical progress to make for Caden's drones, too.

When we get home, you will freshen up and then wait for me in my playroom.

Smiling, I read his message. Clear and yet without facts.

Yes, sir.

Caden looked at me.

Wishes?

Thoughtfully, I wiped off the fingerprints on the display.

No.

Quietly, Caden clicked his tongue.

That was a question for you to ask me.

As I read his words, it was as if I heard his reproving tone in my head. Goosebumps prickled over my body just thinking about all that was associated with Caden's harsh, animalistic voice.

Wishes, sir? I typed with anticipation.

Again and again, my gaze slid over the board, which paid no attention to us while our smartphones vibrated like washing machines in spin cycle.

Surprise me. Two simple words that made me sweat, because that included a wide range of where to put my foot in my mouth. And if there was one thing I was good at, it was putting my foot in my mouth!

Just as I was about to answer Caden, the chief engineer's voice caught my attention. Unfortunately, the discussions were never about anything concrete that I could relate to. One thing was certain, they weren't getting anywhere. Somewhere in the implementation, the engineers were stuck, and things were neither moving forward nor backward.

Caden tried to stay calm, but I could see that the problems weren't just rolling off him. Understandable! His reputation, his entire business, probably depended on the drones, not to mention thousands of potential lives he could save.

Perhaps it was time to share my very own findings with the scientists. A new perspective could get the project rolling again. Of course, I wouldn't get any credit, but I didn't care as long as Caden could sleep soundly at night.

I would like to help solve this problem.

Caden looked at me in surprise.

Let the engineers do it.

I suppressed an annoyed groan because I had heard that answer too many times before. Not just from Caden, but all my life. Sometimes it was just unfair that I was reduced to my feminine features.

I see how well they are progressing.

My answer was cynical, and I hoped it would secure Caden's undivided attention.

Don't worry your pretty little head. It only gives you worry lines.

Caden meant well and I understood his good intention behind it, but it also made me terribly angry.

I can help!

I typed so energetically that the display cracked menacingly under my fingers. Caden then put his smartphone aside and eyed me with interest, while the rest of the board members continued to argue against the wall.

With a gesture, Caden indicated that I should lean down to him.

"You seem pretty confident that you have a solution."

Jesus! He looked at me as if he was about to spank me. Granted, I'd rather be in our playroom right now than here, but I had to pull myself together! I finally had the chance to stand my ground.

"Yes! I'm pretty sure!" I answered firmly, before rowing back a notch after all. "Well, I don't have a solution, but I think I'm close."

"Says Coleman for about three months, too," Caden growled sullenly. He gave his chief engineer a brief but scowling look.

"But unlike your chief engineer, I know exactly what the problem is!" I continued to assert myself.

"Oh yeah?"

Startled, I winced, knowing what question was coming next.

"How do you know about this problem, Aurora?"

I found myself at a crossroads. Either I told him the truth and hoped it would bring us all closer to solving the problem, or I kept my secret and hoped the engineers could do the same. The truth was tempting, but it also brought dangers, because I was also admitting to having stolen plans.

Out of the corner of my eye, I watched Coleman, who was arguing so wildly that his glasses kept sliding down the bridge of his nose.

"I saw the blueprints," I confessed truthfully, hoping my answer would suffice. Caden rubbed his chin thoughtfully.

"Where did you get the blueprints?"

"They were lying around like that," I replied with a shrug. But I was a bad liar and Caden knew it. A single, stern look was all it took for me to correct my answer. "Okay, they were lying around in a filing cabinet. Behind a locked door. In a department where I really have no business being."

After I had hastily spoken the words, I felt better. Much better, in fact, almost as if a weight weighing a ton had fallen from my shoulders. I hadn't known how much this secret had been weighing me down until I finally shared it with Caden.

"You broke into my company?" Caden's expression remained rigid. I had no idea what was going on behind his facade, because he didn't let on.

"Broke in is a pretty strong word," I whispered as I fiddled with the hem of my dress to avoid looking Caden in the eye. "You just never gave me a chance to prove myself."

"And you can't let up," Caden murmured.

Yes, I was sometimes dogged, but that was not a bad thing, on the contrary! I had convictions and stood up for them, just as any person should.

"I didn't think you had that much criminal energy."

I yelped as Caden's raspy voice reached me.

"I'm not a criminal!" I protested loudly enough that some of the board members looked up at me. Embarrassed, I stared at the floor and cleared my throat until everyone refocused on the heated discussion between Coleman and the finance guy whose name I had forgotten.

"I should have known you were attracted to circumventing prohibitions and breaking rules ever since you entered my playroom." There was a challenging grin on Caden's lips. On the one hand, I was relieved that he wasn't mad at me, but on the other hand, I didn't think his teasing was very nice either.

"That was something completely different!"

Of course, I knew Caden was out to upset me, but he just knew me too well. He knew which buttons to push to provoke the reactions he wanted.

"Sometimes I hate you," I said, pouting.

"Then you look especially cute," Caden replied with a grin. Then his face turned serious again. "The fact that you bypassed all the security protocols at Saint Industries is something we'll talk about later."

I already knew exactly where and in which context this *meeting* would take place. Actually, I should not be happy about it...but I was happy about it.

"And now you have a chance to point Coleman in the right direction," Caden prompted me. "I'm curious."

"Now? Here?"

Excited, I pushed the same strand of hair behind my ear twice. I didn't have any documents, nor was I prepared for a presentation to the company's board of directors.

"Now. Here," Caden confirmed, nodding.

I wish I could have prepared myself better, but life was not a wish-fulfillment concert. Sometimes life handed out opportunities, though, and this was mine!

"Um, excuse me," I said, raising my hand in a vain attempt to get everyone's attention.

"Hello!" I tried a second time. Again, no response. Seeking help, I looked to Caden, hoping he would tame the pack for me, but he did nothing but look at me expectantly.

"Stop it!" I yelled angrily as the board continued to discuss money. Finally, I had their undivided attention. "If you'll listen to me for a minute, I may have a solution to both problems."

Death glances shot in my direction. The anger that had just been directed at the development or finance department was now channeled at me. I swallowed hard, because I had not expected this.

The courage that had just inspired me was gone and I plunged unchecked into the depths. My flight of fancy was abruptly over.

All the words that were running around in my head got stuck in my throat at the latest, and I closed my eyes for a moment.

This is the wrong time for stage fright!

"The problem..." I began, but then faltered again.

What a bummer! That was one of those discussions where I later thought of three quick-witted phrases in the shower that I could have used to improve the situation. Unfortunately, I couldn't think of any of the imaginary shower discussions I'd had in the past.

"What's the solution now?" asked Coleman impatiently.

"The exterior..." I tried again. "The calculations are right, but..."

This time it wasn't my sudden, unnerving insecurity, but Coleman interrupting me.

"Of course the calculations are right!" He looked angrily at Caden. "Mr. Saint, we don't have time for these shenanigans!"

My jaw dropped. Board member or not, running his mouth while pretending I wasn't here was too much. I couldn't take any more and the tightness constricting my throat was becoming more and more uncomfortable.

"So my fiancée's constructive suggestions aren't even being heard?" Caden defended me when I was at a loss for words. I looked at him gratefully before looking defiantly at Coleman. I didn't care if I had to play the *I'm-the-fiancée card* or not, as long as he finally heard me out!

"All right, I'm listening," Coleman said, without a word of apology. Presumably, as head of the engineering department, he was used to never having to apologize, even for his own mistakes.

Just as I had recovered some of my words, the door was torn open and Erica rushed in, closely followed by Janice, who gave me icy looks. Just now the room had been heated up by the heated discussions and now temperatures felt below freezing.

Crap. I tried to force my body to say the words that almost made my head explode, but I couldn't do it. My body had betrayed me.

"What is it now?" asked Coleman demandingly.

"Oh, nothing," I whispered, symbolically taking a step back.

"Good, because we have some things to talk about!" Erica launched into.

Caden looked at me in surprise and was about to veto it, but I shook my head, slowing him down.

Erica demonstratively stood in front of the board and no one dared interrupt her while she talked about her plans that Caden had rejected.

I was still two steps behind Caden, actually I wanted to stand next to him again, but my lead-heavy legs didn't move an inch. Not even when Janice stood right next to me. I was clearly one of those people who would fall victim to natural selection because the flight reflex was prevented by shock rigidity.

"Back already?" asked Janice quietly, but with a diabolical grin.

"Family emergency," I replied curtly. My brain and tongue were still at war.

"Caden doesn't have a family," Janice replied victoriously, thinking she had caught me in a lie.

"None that you know of," I countered angrily.

I wish Caden had overheard the conversation, but we were too quiet for that, and he was too busy with Erica, who accused him for the third time of trying to ruin his business by not leaving PR to the professionals.

It was unwise to add fuel to the fire, but I couldn't help but adjust my perfectly placed hair so Janice couldn't miss the sparkle of my high-profile engagement ring. My plan worked, for a second Janice's features derailed, and I thought I had victory on my side, but I was wrong.

"I wonder if that ring would still be on your finger if Caden knew about your *revealing* secret."

Janice had had to dig long and deep into my past to know that I had financed my undergraduate studies in a strip club.

"You should stop searching my past, you won't find anything," I coolly advised. But truthfully. I had no skeletons in my closet and no shocking secrets to discredit me. My college job had been my biggest secret ever. I don't know how Janice had found out, but she definitely couldn't disarm me with that.

"So this is nothing?" countered Janice with an aggressive smile.

I took a deep breath and looked at Janice seriously.

"Caden knows," I replied dryly.

"Caden knows about this?" Janice hadn't counted on that, and that was my ace in the hole, with which I might be able to shut down Janice for good. Maybe Janice would finally give up now.

"Yes. Caden knows everything about me," I said confidently. "Just like I know everything about him."

My answer gave me strength because it was merciless. There was nothing left to stand between us. My last secret – the stolen blueprints – was also revealed.

I wondered if Janice's silence was some kind of white flag, or if it was a calm before the storm. Probably I should be prepared for anything, until she really accepted that the love between Caden and me was real.

Although the buzz of voices and discussion continued, Caden suddenly jumped up from his seat. His posture alone forced everyone to quiet down within the blink of an eye. Caden was absolutely aware of his strength, his energy, and his power. Heavens, he was not the boss of a multi-billion company for nothing!

"Talk out what you need to discuss. But my fiancée and I are going to the Twenty-third now."

"What?" Erica and I asked as if from the same mouth.

"Twenty-third is getting new equipment today," Caden replied, grabbing my hand and pulling me outside. "And the PR department can come along, make videos and cut any campaigns from them, or not. I don't care."

Janice and Erica followed us in a rush, and I immediately felt two pairs of death-eyes on my back.

This could be fun. Not.

Chapter 29 – Caden

When we were only a few houses away from Station Twenty-three, a few reporters were already lurking in their vans on the sidewalk, but otherwise there was still no sign of the chaos I was about to conjure up.

Leaning against one of the cars was Jelinda Cherry, who had basically started everything that had happened since my interview with her. As we drove past her, she waved at us. Her eyes were shining with sensationalism, and I'll be damned if I couldn't satisfy that today. I owed it to the reporter after she had portrayed me in the Times as better than I actually was.

"You called the press?" asked Aurora, frowning, as she pointed to a Channel Three vehicle parked between that of the Times and one of the Morning News.

"Yes. And Miss Cherry at the Times has called in a colleague or two as well. The more attention it gets, the better," I replied. "Won't please Jacks, but it's necessary."

Normally, I could do without the press and the associated media hype, but the public needed to know about the abuses in the fire department so that corruption could finally be put to an end.

Aurora nodded as her eyes continued to be glued to the Channel Three vehicle. "If there's anyone worse at accepting help than you are, it's Jackson."

"I'll take that as a compliment," I replied, straightening my cufflinks.

"No, that wasn't a compliment!" replied Aurora sharply. Only now did her eyes detach themselves from the vehicles and find their way back to me.

"Okay, okay. Possibly there are some weak points, but you're not free of mistakes either."

"Oh yeah?" Aurora tilted her head while crossing her arms. A gesture that clearly signaled I was on thin ice. "Like what?"

"You snore when you sleep," I replied with a grin. Aurora slept like an angel, beautiful and innocent, but in fact sometimes it happened that she gurgled or snored very softly.

"I don't!" protested Aurora immediately.

"Yes, you do." My dry, uninvolved manner upset Aurora even more.

"No, I don't snore!"

"And how you snore. Want me to record you snoring like a walrus?" I teased her further. Her reaction was just too cute not to savor it further.

"Caden Saint! I wish you had a middle name, so you'd realize how pissed off I really am!"

"Take it as a compliment, I always do with criticism too," I advised her with a laugh, but meant it quite seriously. Still grinning, I patted her thigh and waited for Aurora to calm down.

"Maybe you snore like a walrus." Aurora pulled a pout and looked at me with her big moon eyes, which seemed even bigger in such situations.

"If I snored, you would have rubbed it in my face by now," I speculated.

"You also waited until today to inform me of my *alleged* snoring."

"Touché."

"You should never argue with a winter," Aurora replied with satisfaction. She stretched her head upwards.

"And you should never feel safe with a Saint," I murmured.

We didn't have more time for teasing discussions, because we reached the fire station, in front of which scattered uniforms were standing, staring critically at the avalanche of reporters that was creeping ever closer.

Jackson was among them and by far the one staring most menacingly in the direction of the press. When he saw me getting out of the car and helping Aurora out, he marched straight toward me.

"What did you do?" Jackson was quite upset, understandably, but sooner or later even he knew that my action was right.

"You have a good day too, Jacks, thank you," I replied calmly. My voice didn't seem quite as reassuring to Jackson when the PR department, led by Erica, was positioning a pack of cameramen at various corners. My PR boss would never admit it, but she was on fire for the project, the only thing that made her seem rather uninvolved was the fact that she hadn't thought of it herself.

"I guess the day is going to be anything but pretty," Jacks grumbled sullenly. "If I'm lucky, I'll *just* get fired."

"Good thing I happen to have a fire safety job left over at my company," I joked.

"You could have just lured me in with a good starting salary," Jackson replied. He even forgot for a moment that he was actually mad at me.

Another firefighter, wearing an identical uniform to Jackson, joined us.

"Do you want to introduce us to each other, Washington?"

Jackson crossed his arms in front of his chest, which made his muscles look even bigger.

"This is the guy who's going to be responsible for everything that happens today," Jackson introduced me cynically.

"Guilty," I said with a grin, because I took it as a compliment. "Caden Saint."

"Hunter Porter," the firefighter replied, shaking my hand. "What's going to happen today?"

"I wish I knew," Jackson growled.

"I'll solve your problems. All of them."

They both looked at me in equal disbelief, then Hunter called his people over.

"Hey, come on everybody!"

While I basked in the attention of Jackson's colleagues, he seemed to have only the demise of the entire Twenty-third in mind. I patted him on the back and smiled at him confidently.

"Trust me, Jacks. I know what I'm doing."

"Didn't seem that way to me last run," Jackson said half-seriously. Slowly, ever so slowly, his anger boiled away, so I swallowed my burgeoning.

Admittedly, Jacks was rubbing salt into a still-aching wound. He wasn't talking about our race through the streets of midtown Manhattan, but about our last *real* run. The one where I suddenly couldn't lift a foot in front of the other, let alone jump to the roof of the next building.

"It's business, so it's something completely different," I countered nonchalantly.

Aurora looked tensely back and forth between me and Jackson.

"What happened during your last run?" she asked. I don't know how Aurora had managed to sound curious, worried, and even a little accusatory at the same time, but she had.

I pulled her closer to me so that only she could hear me.

"That's when I first realized how much I love you."

Aurora's eyes sparkled as my words reached her heart.

"You're cute." Aurora smiled at me. "I guess that was also the moment when I couldn't deny how much I love you. Only the perspective was a little different."

Regardless of the fact that dozens of pairs of eyes rested on us, I pulled Aurora to me for a passionate kiss. Our love was real, the world could know that quietly and everyone who had ever been in love understood us.

"Are you going to tell us your master plan now?" asked Jackson impatiently.

As if on cue, the captain of the firehouse came thundering toward us. Now, at the latest, it became clear to me that Jackson had not exaggerated a word. The captain appeared slick even at first glance. His close-set eyes had that twinkle that only con men had, the kind that robbed poor grandmothers of their hard-saved money. The literal crowning glory was his slicked-back hair, which screamed *I'm really corrupt*.

"What the hell is the commotion out there?" he asked, taking stock of the situation.

"You'll see in a moment, Captain," I said, not bothering to introduce myself.

I cued Erica and Janice, who were on the sidelines giving instructions to their own cameramen.

A pedestal I had made was dragged in from the left and Erica made sure it was at the perfect angle to the fire station while the captain scowled at us.

"Keep the way clear!" he blared, pointing at the podium and the press pack that was inching closer and closer. "Washington, Porter, get these people off the property!"

Even before Jacks or his colleague could act - or veto - I was leaning against the firehouse captain.

"I'm asking you, captain. There is no operational vehicle. Or do you want the broken down vehicle shunted to the nearest repair shop?" I asked with a knowing smile. "I think it would be more appropriate for Washington, Porter, and the rest of the firehouse to get into their fine uniforms."

He didn't like my answer at all, but he couldn't say anything back. In contrast to the media, I had inside knowledge, because until now not a single word had been mentioned about the defective aerial ladder. The captain stepped closer to me.

"Think carefully about what you are doing. I have powerful friends," he threatened. "Besides, it's Captain Kinnley for you!"

I remained unimpressed, because I heard such threats all the time. Besides, I doubted that Captain Kinnley's contacts were any better than mine.

"Relax, captain. Everything I do benefits the firehouse, which is in your best interest."

I could tell by the look on the captain's face that he would have loved to punch me in the face, but the press standing around prevented him from doing so. Even without the press, I was superior to the guy in all respects. I was bigger, stronger, and more determined! Whether the captain wanted it or not, I had everything under control, unlike him.

"Good, then we're all in agreement that we're all here to support the fire station!" said Aurora hastily, squeezing in between me and Captain Kinnley to further de-escalate the situation.

"That's right," I replied with a smile. At the same time I gave Aurora a meaningful look that everything was all right and I felt her muscles slowly relax.

Reluctantly, Captain Kinnley gave the order to don the uniforms that were usually only worn for honors, parades or funerals. For most of the firehouse, my appearance was definitely a cause for celebration, but for a few, it felt like a funeral.

When the platform was set up, and the entire firehouse was dressed up, I looked to Erica, who nodded at me. *Very good.* Then I could finally get started.

I grabbed Aurora, walked to the podium and waited for both the Firefighters and the press to gather around me. My eyes swept over reporters from Channel Two, Three, Four and Five, plus reporters from the Times and other, major newspapers. This was not only going to make waves, it was going to be a tsunami!

"Damn, this is going to be an even bigger thing than my engagement," I murmured to Jackson, who was standing representatively to my left as one of the lieutenants, right next to the captain.

"Am I supposed to feel honored now?" Jacks pressed out from behind clenched teeth.

"Yes, *honey.*" Staying serious was now even harder for Jackson than it was for me, but we pulled ourselves together and presented ourselves from our best side.

I tapped on the microphone to make sure it was working. I wasn't actually a guy who liked to stand at podiums, but there were hashtags listed on the front for citizens to show solidarity with. For that alone, the podium was worth the impact.

When I saw Jelinda Cherry in the crowd, I winked at her and waited for her to ask me the first question.

"Mr. Saint? What do you have planned today?" she asked impatiently. Unlike the other press people, she had already known about the press appointment last night and since then she had been burning for details that I had withheld from her.

"Good question, Miss Cherry," I replied with a smile. "And with that, I can get right to the heart of what I want to do." I would have liked to cover everything, as I always did during speeches, but I forced myself to stop and clasped my fingers to the lectern.

"The New York Firefighters are true heroes, often reported. They are heroes who are appreciated by us because they are the ones who bravely jump into the flames to save us." Approving nods and scattered applause followed. I then cast a sharp sideways glance at the captain of the Twenty-third Fire Station, who knew exactly what was happening now.

"These heroes risk their lives for us. They are not just fighting fires, they are fathers, mothers, brothers and sisters, they have family and friends. They are brave heroes who risk their own lives every day." Again, I left a meaningful pause, allowing time for a round of applause that the Firefighters got far too infrequently.

"They're risking their lives! The job is damn hard and even more dangerous. And that's why it's a shame our heroes are so neglected." Murmurs, murmurs, and possible speculation again forced me to pause. Aurora, standing next to me, looked at me with pride, even though I knew how uncomfortable she must feel in this pack.

"Fire is dangerous, there's no denying that, but what if the heroes of the fire station suddenly have to deal with melting shoe soles because there's no money for safe equipment? How can we justify people dying in flames because the helpers can't walk another step? What if they run out of oxygen halfway across?" Again I looked at Captain Kinnley, who was anything but happy. This time I kept talking while my gaze continued to rest on his slick face.

"What if there are casualties because the aerial ladder fails, like in the recent high-rise fire in the Bronx?"

Immediately, dozens of questions poured in on me and the captain of the fire station. I listened to every single one of them so that I could answer them afterwards.

Heck, if looks could kill, Kinnley would have killed me three times in a row. Jackson didn't let on on the outside, but I knew my best friend was doing happy dances on the inside.

But because there were still questions to be answered, and I had not yet said everything that was on my mind, I continued to pour oil on the fire.

"The money for new equipment is there, it comes from the city, the state and donations. But the money isn't getting to where it's needed, which is the men and women of the firehouse."

Captain Kinnley was bursting with rage as the reporters bombarded him with the corruption charges I had given them ammunition for.

"No comment." That was all the firehouse captain had to say before he marched back inside the firehouse, his head high. No matter what the captain might say in his defense, his career was over. Tomorrow, the day after tomorrow at the latest, he would be the face of the corruption affair at Station Twenty-three.

"We will take the allegations seriously and investigate them immediately," Jackson replied, taking a step forward and bravely facing the reporters. As a lieutenant, he ran the risk of being confronted with the same accusations, but his honest face, reflecting his equally pure heart, protected him from hostility.

I cleared my throat to bring my speech to a close.

"Since such investigations can take months, sometimes even years, Saint Industries has decided to make sure today that the heroes can protect us well."

The next moment, a whole fleet of brightly polished fire engines with blue lights and sirens came around the corner. Followed by smaller vehicles containing brand new equipment.

The press couldn't get their heads around it when the vehicles stopped in front of the fire station.

"I hope I was able to answer your question, Miss Cherry," I finished, and she gave me a cheeky grin. Then I turned to the rest of the reporters. "I'm sure Lieutenant Washington will give you an exclusive look inside the firehouse if you ask nicely."

"Fuck you, Caden!" growled Jacks so low that only I could hear him.

"You're welcome," I replied, patting Jackson on the shoulder and leaving the lectern. I didn't let it show, but the adrenaline was pumping violently through my body, almost as violently as it had back in France.

"Wow, you were amazing! The reporters are blown away by you – and so am I!" Aurora adored me when we had retreated from the spotlight.

"Well, that's just the magic of Mr. Universe," I replied, smiling charmingly.

Sighing, Aurora blew a blond strand off her forehead.

"You're never going to let me forget calling you that, are you?"

Aurora's cheeks reddened because she was still embarrassed that I had overheard some of her phone calls with Maxine. Until now, she had not dared to ask which conversations I knew exactly about.

"Absolutely not."

Giggling in love, Aurora grabbed my arm and nestled her cheek against my shoulder.

"It's really great what you've done for Jackson."

"Jackson will undoubtedly hate me for this," I said seriously, while still being a little amused at how Jackson tried to brush off the horde of reporters.

"And that's exactly why you're such a good friend," Aurora replied softly.

From a distance, Aurora and I continued to watch as Jackson made a quick exit and pushed forward his colleague Hunter, who was feeding stories to the sensation-hungry reporters. But before Jackson was even halfway to us, he was slowed down by another group of reporters.

"Jackson will be busy for quite a while," Aurora said thoughtfully.

"I hope so," I replied with a cryptic grin. Then I pulled Aurora inside the firehouse.

"Caden, what are you up to?" asked Aurora. From the looks I gave her, she knew exactly what I was up to.

Yes, damn it. Here and now!

Chapter 30 – Aurora

Caden marched across the firehouse with me in tow.

"Where are we going?" I asked, trying to duck under somehow. My cheeks were burning with heat, and you could still see how embarrassed I felt at a distance of over one hundred feet.

"Somewhere quiet," Caden replied. He opened the first door we passed and immediately closed it again.

"Have you been here before?" I asked further.

"No. Otherwise I probably wouldn't have to look for a suitable room," Caden replied. Unbelievable! He just walked around here and acted like he owned the place. That's probably why no one stopped us from sneaking around. Not to mention that most of the firefighters were still busy with the press. Almost all of them were giving interviews or leading reporters to the new vehicles. Only there was no sign of the captain. Presumably he had retreated to lick his wounds.

Caden pulled me to the next door, then the one after that.

Growling in dissatisfaction, Caden peered at the farthest door of the firehouse and peered inside.

"Perfect," he said, pushing me into the room where the heavy uniforms were stored on hooks and equipment in boxes.

Immediately after the door slammed shut, Caden grabbed my shoulders and pressed my back against the closed door. I felt how fast his heart was beating - in the same beat as mine. His hands dug into my hair and his lips claimed a passionate kiss. When his tongue licked across my lips, I opened them willingly and let him explore my mouth. Caden tasted deliciously of man, dominance and wild desire. He demanded everything from me, and I was ready to give it to him.

"I haven't kissed you like this in far too long," Caden murmured as we pulled away from each other, breathing heavily.

"That's right," I whispered breathlessly.

It was forbidden that we were here alone doing lewd things, but it felt so good that I couldn't resist.

The entire fire station was swarming with lurking press, plus there could be an emergency call at any moment that would require the entire station to storm that room. And yet, the only thing I could think about was how exciting *it* was.

When I was with Caden, all boundaries blurred and forbidden was as seductive as the pleasure-pain just before orgasm.

"How long do you think we can stay here before they miss us?" asked Caden between kisses.

"Two, maybe three orgasms," I replied, biting my lower lip lasciviously.

Caden kissed my cheeks and neck until he reached my collarbone and I groaned softly.

"Good answer," Caden replied with a grin. Then he pushed my skirt up, exposing my womanhood and kissing my most sensitive spot.

Alternately, he drove me crazy with his tongue and lips. Every time Caden sucked on my clit, he elicited a louder moan than I would have liked. At the same time, I buried my hands in his full, dark hair. The fact that I had destroyed his perfectly fitting hairstyle didn't matter to either of us. Our love took its toll, or to put it in Caden's words, *everything has its price.*

To bring me even closer to my climax, Caden penetrated me with one finger to massage me inside. With the other hand he pressed me against the wall, because my legs were trembling menacingly, as always when my climax was within reach.

When Caden dove back up to me, he pressed his lips to mine with desire. I tasted my own pleasure and couldn't wait to taste Caden's as well. But Caden wasted no time in unbuttoning his pants. He grabbed me, lifted me upward, pressed me firmly against the door, and penetrated me before I knew what hit me.

"Oh God!" I groaned. It was just too good to hold back. Luckily, Caden was strong enough to hold me with one hand while he covered my mouth with the other to muffle my moans a bit.

The harder his thrusts became, the tighter I wrapped my legs around his hips. I moved my pelvis against his movements so that he could penetrate me even deeper.

"I love you," Caden gasped. His words triggered an intense tingling in my body that wouldn't subside.

"I love you too." Our words were still unspent and triggered the most beautiful emotions a person could feel, and I hoped it stayed that way forever.

Caden put his head on my shoulder and his hot breath brushed my neck. As long as I could, I still delayed my climax, but eventually I couldn't hold back any longer. I tightened tightly around Caden's hardness, which grew even harder in response. Thousands of endorphin butterflies danced through my body and I felt wonderful as Caden filled me with his gold.

Breathless, we sank to the floor together and recovered from our flight of fancy. Caden stroked my hair while my fingers ran over his striking features. The tender moments were as important to me as our games. Pain and pleasure were like the air to breathe, but Caden's tenderness was the lungs that breathed the air.

"We should get back with the others, it's getting noticeable," Caden said, tapping my thigh.

"One more minute!" I begged softly as I enjoyed his fingers on my skin. "I don't want it to be over already."

"I have something against that," Caden said with a grin, because my request had probably created the perfect segue for his scheme.

"Oh yeah?" Although I looked at him curiously and promptly, Caden wrapped himself in silence. He stood up, buttoned his pants, and finally helped me back to my feet. Walking in those killer heels was one thing, but standing up in them seemed absolutely impossible.

Looking down at my wrinkled, knee-length dress, I tried desperately to brush the wrinkles out of the fabric. Those wrinkles were literally screaming what we had done. Of course I didn't regret anything, but I also didn't want our *locker room affair* to be on the evening news. Caden grabbed my hands to steady me.

"You're beautiful, no one will even notice the wrinkles."

"I'm your fiancée, the whole world will look for wrinkles that aren't there," I replied.

"Good thing the only opinion you should care about is mine," Caden replied dryly.

I tilted my head to look Caden up and down. He was planning something, I could see it in his eyes.

"And what is your opinion?" I asked.

"That with this outfit, these two pieces of jewelry would look great on you." Caden rummaged around in his pants pocket until he pulled out two – familiar to me – nipple clamps. They were slightly smaller than the ones I wore the first time we met, but certainly no less devilish. Surprised, I raised my index finger and poked it several times against Caden's chest as if my finger were a gun.

"I knew you were up to something!"

Caden raised both hands upward to demonstrate to my finger gun that he was unarmed.

"Guilty."

"Caden Saint." I crossed my arms demonstratively in front of my chest. "You plead guilty a little too often for my taste."

"And I told you that I am definitely not a saint, even though my name suggests I am."

"True." Caden had warned me often enough, but I had thrown every one of his warnings to the wind – and I would have done it again without hesitation. Nowhere else, I could fly as high as in Caden's abysses.

"Now what about these two accessories?" Caden held them up and jingled the little beads on them.

I chewed thoughtfully on my lower lip until Caden looked at me admonishingly.

"Last time, they pushed me pretty close to my limits," I confessed.

Caden nodded. "But since the first time, your boundaries have shifted."

Smiling, I had to admit that Caden was right. We had not only crossed dozens of my borders together but had blown them into thousands of pieces.

But boundaries or not, I had no idea how long we were going to be at the firehouse and when I was going to find the opportunity to get rid of these little buggers.

"I don't know, Caden."

Thoughtfully, he put the clamps back in his pants pocket and looked at me with understanding.

"I figured the price of the *Mile-High Club* would be too high for you."

Caden, I hate you!

He just knew exactly how to trigger me and my anger. Caden had the rare gift of being able to convince me of things I thought were impossible, even if it was just out of spite to prove something to him.

"Give it to me!" I urged Caden with outstretched hands.

"No, you're right, the brackets are more for the playroom."

His hands continued to rest in his pants pockets.

Caden played with unfair means, but that was not a problem, because it was his game - I was just a piece moving on his dangerous playing field.

Snorting, I put my head back.

"Sometimes I really hate flying high," I said, pulling a pout.

"These are the moments when I think you're especially cute."

"Great, you don't even take my anger seriously," I replied, still pouting.

"Good, you've convinced me, here are the nipple clamps."

Caden presented them to me with a triumphant smile because he had managed to turn the tables. Not even a minute ago I had been against the little toys, now I was literally begging to be allowed to wear them.

I bared my torso and Caden pounced on my womanly curves, causing me to stagger back to the door I was propped against. He kneaded my breasts, alternately sucking on my tips and pinching my more sensitive buds with his thumb and forefinger.

As Caden fastened the clamps to my buds, I inhaled sharply. It wasn't pain, but pure anticipation of the arousal that followed – and hopefully, release.

As I suspected, they were a smaller model with less clamping force. With this I could stand it for some time.

After my breasts were back in place and the thick fabric of bra and dress covered our secret, Caden wanted to retreat. He already had his hand on the door handle when I grabbed his arm and pulled back.

"Just a minute!" I grabbed two of the fire helmets, put one on me and the other on Caden. "A photo for Max!"

Before Caden could fight back, I pulled him close for a selfie.

At the same moment, the door behind us was ripped open and Jackson burst into the middle of our selfie session.

"Caden, bringing the press down on me is one thing, but here..." Jackson paused, and when he realized we were both no longer naked, he exhaled in relief.

"But what, Jacks?" asked Caden with a grin. Jackson had indeed caught us, but a few minutes too late.

"Oh, never mind," Jackson waved it off. "Still, you shouldn't be snooping around here by yourselves."

"In theory, this is *my* firehouse," Caden replied businesslike as he spread his arms and grinned. I held my breath. Could Caden really buy a fire station? My knowledge was limited to the fact that fire trucks were red, and I could reach them at *911* in an emergency, but I knew nothing of what else was going on.

"Even you can't buy government facilities," Jackson said with a laugh, answering my mute question.

"Is that a bet?" Caden looked challengingly at Jackson, and I slid in between them.

"Must there be constant competition between you?"

"Where's the fun in that?" they both replied as if from the same mouth.

I could only think of one thing to say about that – *men*. I wondered what my friendship with Maxine would be like if we acted like Caden and Jackson and had to giggle when I thought of us having high-heel races through the mall or rummaging through the junk boxes for the best bargain.

After Jackson took our helmets off, he pushed us back into the commotion.

"Wow, it's still pretty busy," I muttered, and Caden nudged me in the side with his elbow.

"This won't get any quieter before the evening. By now, even the last reporters have caught on to what's going on."

My eyes roamed over the fire station, where there were hundreds of people packed with cameras, microphones, or both, standing in front of well-dressed reporters smiling at the camera.

We strolled together towards the new fire truck, which had a huge, folded aerial ladder on it.

"How did you manage to wrest the vehicles from the Twelfth, anyway?" asked Jackson, frowning. For the first time since the vehicles had been driven into the station, I noticed that it didn't say twenty-three on the vehicles, but twelve.

"They're renovating the entire station right now, so emergencies are being split up among other stations. And until the station gets a new look, they have new vehicles, too."

"Clever," Jackson said, looking impressed.

Admittedly, until now I hadn't even thought about how or where Caden got the vehicles. In his presence, I permanently had the feeling that nothing was impossible anymore.

While Jackson and Caden continued to banter amicably, as they did most of the time, I let my eyes continue to wander over the hustle and bustle. I got stuck on Erica, from the PR department. She delegated a dozen cameramen and seemed to have very precise ideas about everything.

"I've never seen Erica so happy," I said half-jokingly. Actually I was serious, Erica seemed fully in her element. I giggled softly, but the pain that shot through my sensitive buds from the movement slowed me down. I almost forgot about those beasts, but only almost. And I was sure that they demanded even more attention with every breath.

"Yeah, she does a pretty good job when she's not bugging me," Caden replied with a sigh. "I have no idea why she wants to drag my face in front of the camera all the time."

"Speak of the devil," Jackson said with amusement.

"Sorry," I apologized sheepishly. "I didn't mean to bring anything up."

Because almost as if Erica sensed that we were talking about her, her head rang toward us. She beckoned two cameramen and a sound technician to join her, then they marched toward us. Janice, who was talking to a firefighter, abruptly ended the conversation and trotted after Erica.

Caden waved it off. "It's okay, they'll want to go to Jack's."

"If I have to give even one more damn interview, I'm going to set the Twenty-third on fire myself," Jackson threatened.

Because I understood Jackson all too well, I put my hand on his shoulder encouragingly.

"Hang in there." My cheeks still hurt when I thought about how often I had to demonstrate my big smile in front of the paparazzi.

"We're already gone," Caden said, probably more out of reflex, when Erica showed up with appendages.

Compassionately, he patted Jacks shoulder as well before grabbing me and pulling me away. I was only too happy to follow him willingly, away from Janice.

"Stop, not so fast! We need another interview from you."

Caden shook his head without turning around. "Later."

Erica persisted and overtook us. "I'm talking about Miss Winter."

We both stood rooted to the spot when my name came up.

"An interview with me?" I asked incredulously.

"Yes, about the engagement. Slowly, but surely, we need details."

Without warning, Erica grabbed my hand and held it up so that my engagement ring shimmered demonstratively in the midday sun.

I shook my head and withdrew my hand. "But not now. All that matters today is that firehouses all over New York need more help."

Erica vehemently denied it, while Janice, who had just caught up with us, nodded.

Who would have thought that we once agreed on something?

"Sure, the firehouse gets Saint Industries enough PR. But as soon as the ads go down, we'll have to refire." Erica grinned briefly at her little fire pun. "And that's with details of your engagement. That'll get another PR for the Twenty-third *and* for Saint Industries. And then everyone's happy, it's that simple."

I looked at Caden, who was thoughtfully crossing his chin. *No.* Caden couldn't really be thinking about accepting her offer! I had no idea what I was allowed to say, what I wasn't. Not to mention, in Janice's presence, I had to be careful to always show my best side. I was dead certain that she took every opportunity to photograph me with a crooked smile and unflattering poses.

"So, what do you say?"

"I agree," Caden replied thoughtfully.

"What?" I yelped, grabbing him by the arm. "Please excuse us for a moment."

After putting distance between us and the PR, I looked at Caden in despair.

"I've never done an interview before!"

"Just tell the truth and leave out a few unimportant details. You can do it," Caden said, encouraging me.

Sighing, I let it go through my mind again until I gave my heart a jolt.

"Okay, I'll do it. But only because you care so much about Jacks and the firehouse."

"Thank you, that means a lot to me."

Caden pulled me against him as if he had forgotten that my buds were quite sensitive. But the way he pressed me against him, Caden knew very well that they were there. Also because he could feel them.

"My *Mile-High* debt is paid off for that," I demanded in a serious business tone.

"You're playing your hand pretty high," Caden said, raising a brow. He looked insistently at my nipple piercings, which quickened my heartbeat.

"Luckily, I have my fiancé's gold credit card. I can afford it," I replied with a wink, not letting my excitement show. "My demands are non-negotiable."

"Good, that pays off *those* debts," Caden conceded, and I faltered.

"What do you mean by *those debts*? Are there other debts?"

In my mind I went over the last days and weeks but was not aware of any mistakes that could punish Caden in the playroom. Then I remembered that I had confessed to stealing the blueprints.

"So it came back to you, huh?"

Grinning, Caden pushed me back toward Erica so I couldn't veto it. I was pretty sure Caden was just teasing me, but you never knew with him.

"Have fun," Caden said, kissing my head and pulling away with Jackson.

"Wait, you have to stay here!" I protested in panic. He couldn't just throw me to the wolves!

"I'll be right back," Caden tried to reassure me. But he failed. Only with effort could Caden shake off my hand, with which I had clung to him.

I would have liked to beg him on my knees to stay, but that would have been too much of a good thing. So I turned to Erica, Janice and the cameramen.

"We're good to go," I said uncertainly, actually meaning the opposite. I have no idea how Caden could make speeches out of thin air in front of such a large audience.

While Erica was giving me instructions, I watched Caden walk over to Jelinda Cherry and talk to her.

When Erica clapped her hands joyfully after her speech, which I had completely tuned out, I flinched in shock and pretended I had been listening to her the whole time.

"Great, then the interview with Aurora can start! And don't panic, we'll edit everything to fit Saint Industries."

"Thank you?" I didn't know exactly what Erica's answer was supposed to mean and was wavering between a poor attempt at reassurance or a hidden insult.

After a stylist who had appeared out of nowhere powdered my face, Erica pushed me around the firehouse for an entire twenty minutes to find the perfect angle to give my interview on the *spur of the moment*.

We finally stopped in front of a wild rose hedge that grew next to the fire station and framed a large *Station Twenty-three* sign.

"Perfect!" enthused Erica. "Romantic, but unmistakably firehouse."

Janice watched me with eagle eyes, but otherwise kept a low profile and did what Erica told her to do. So at least here she could do without drama and just do her job.

In my head, I kept going over possible answers while Caden took an alarming amount of time chatting with Jelinda Cherry.

The stylist powdered me one more time, while lamps and microphones were directed at me. It struck me again that the spotlight was absolutely not my world and never would be.

When Caden finally returned with the Times reporter, I clawed my nails into his arm so hard that if he escaped again, he could expect to be cut or lose his arm right away.

"You have a pretty firm grip," Caden said. There was almost something like respect or admiration in his voice.

"Well, if my fiancé commits possible desertion, I'll just extend my claws," I whispered to him as I smiled sugary sweet at the camera.

"Literally."

"Fact, you can't duck this interview any more than I can," I stated matter-of-factly.

Erica looked at Caden and Jelinda Cherry in turn, irritated.

"Miss Cherry will get the exclusive for the first interview," Caden said, and Jelinda nodded at him appreciatively.

It was impossible not to notice how the PR manager's head was smoking when Caden had messed up all the plans again. Admittedly, I was pretty nervous, too. Giving an interview was one thing, but standing up to an interview in front of a seasoned Times reporter was in a whole other league. Kind of like trying to fight the Avengers with a water pistol.

I took a deep breath and tried not to let my inner excitement show. Reporters smelled fear sweat at a hundred feet against the wind.

"Don't worry, Erica. Miss Cherry will wait with the publication until Saint Industries gives its okay," Caden tried to placate his PR manager.

"Yes, that's it. Word of honor," Jelinda supported him.

Erica retreated two steps and grabbed a tablet with all the cameras in miniature.

"Well, get started," Erica urged.

At first, the fear of saying something wrong was huge, but with each word that slid viscously across my lips, it got easier. Not least because I was losing myself more and more in real, genuine crushes. My heart sank just thinking about the snow, the fairy lights, and the hot cocoa. But the thing that really made my heart soar was Caden's looks at me. Full of affection, full of true love.

The sparkling engagement ring I was all too happy to hold up to the camera was further proof that Caden loved me, because I knew full well that he didn't give a damn about such things. But because they were important to me, they took on meaning for Caden as well.

"That sounds quite magical," Jelinda Cherry gushed. She turned to the camera. "Who would be able to say *no* to a proposal like that?"

Even Erica started to gush a bit, even if her sparkle was probably more due to the fact that she would have loved to film our real engagement. Only Janice gave me disdainful looks the more details I included in my story.

Caden also showed his charming side, which often made me giggle. He probably did this on purpose, because every time I had to laugh, I felt the nipple clamps more clearly than I would have liked. Probably a little fit of laughter in combination with these beasts could force me to orgasm as violently as my abdomen quivered.

Fortunately, the interview was over in no time and – surprise – it hadn't hurt me at all, at least not in the way you'd expect. Anyway, I was relieved that it was over. Not only because I was getting rid of the nipple clamps, but also because the details about our engagement were slowly leaking out. So there were no more secrets for the paparazzi to lurk around on our doorstep.

Slowly, but surely, the throng of press at the fire station withdrew and quiet returned. Caden and I strolled to our car, where we planned to wait for Jackson.

"You were gigantic today, Caden, you helped Jackson and the entire Station Twenty-three a lot," I said proudly.

"Yes, today was a good day, we solved several problems at once," Caden replied with a smile.

I agreed with him. Now there was only one problem, well two if I counted Janice, that needed to be solved.

Caden opened the back driver's door for me and let me in so I could undo the clamps without any audience at all. On the opposite side, Caden got in with me and waited for me to expose my upper body.

The windows were sealed opaque on the inside, but I still took a furtive glance left and right before presenting my sensitive tips to Caden.

I took advantage of the brief togetherness we had to address him again about my botched presentation.

"Caden? Can I talk to one of the engineers again tomorrow?"

He looked at me with interest. "Why?"

"Because of the prototype thing."

"You had your chance," Caden said seriously. "And, then you rowed back."

"Because I wasn't prepared, but it won't happen to me a second time!" I promised.

But Caden waved it off. "It wasn't because you weren't prepared, it was because you were too unsure."

"I wasn't at all," I replied disappointedly, wishing Caden was on my side. But I understood that I couldn't just drive the businessman out of him like that.

"Yes you were, but it doesn't matter. You have a job you do well, you're my personal assistant."

I blew a strand of hair out of my face. It wasn't that I didn't enjoy being around Caden, but in those brief moments when I was dealing with Caden's prototypes, I was doing something that really fulfilled me.

"If you let me, your drones will fly soon!" I insisted.

"Your persistence in all honor," Caden began and paused meaningfully. He used the time to wrap his fingers around the clamps. "But you shouldn't make promises you can't keep."

Before I could object, Caden released the clamps, ending the discussion before it had really begun because I had to gasp for air.

Jesus.

I hated him for solving his problems *that way* sometimes and I loved him for it, because it was so much nicer that way than yelling at each other.

"We'll talk about that later!" I pressed out behind clenched teeth.

"Not if I can help it," Caden replied, letting the clamps snap open and shut a few times.

When Jackson reached our truck, Caden tossed him the keys and Jacks got in the driver's seat because he was the only one who knew which bar the firefighters spent their after-work hours.

"That's a pretty big honor to have someone from out of town come to the bar with you," Jackson said reverently, and Caden nodded.

As we drove off, my eyes lingered on Janice, who was talking to press people I hadn't seen at all at the fire station. But today, I had seen hundreds of faces, so it could also be that I just didn't recognize them. Either way, an uneasy gut feeling spread that I couldn't quite shake.

I had the uneasy feeling that the calm before the storm was about to end, and with a very loud bang.

Chapter 31 – Aurora

Outside the Saint Industries building was so busy that Caden and I had to use the back entrance. Even in the lobby, we had to squeeze past reporters whose words were unintelligible in a jumble of shouting and flashing lights.

Only when Caden had pushed me protectively into the elevator could I breathe again.

"Wow, your speech yesterday must have hit like a bomb," I said respectfully. I would never have admitted it, but I was glad it was all over soon. Once the prototype went into mass production, PR wouldn't have to rely on publicity either, which meant the paparazzi could pursue their sensationalism somewhere else.

"We'll see how much we blew up in a minute," Caden replied with a grin. "Erica has certainly already compiled some initial statistics."

Admittedly, we had dawdled this morning, which is why we hadn't looked at the news, or the newspapers.

Yawning, I stretched my arms up in the air and Caden used the moment to grab my hips and pull me against him. I yelped before wrapping my arms around his strong shoulders, holding Caden against me as tightly as he held me against him.

Although I resisted, I yawned a second time, and although makeup hid my dark circles, they hung down on me like heavy weights.

"I didn't know you could get a hangover even when you're sober," I said with a sigh, rubbing my throbbing temples that I had simply forgotten about in the excitement of the lobby. But now they were coming back twice as painful.

I looked at Caden, who didn't show any signs of last night at all, and with no makeup at all.

"How do you manage to look so handsome?" I asked thoughtfully. His full hair sat perfectly, his eyes shone, and his flawless skin made me more envious than I should be.

Caden raised a brow questioningly. "Is that a rhetorical question?"

"No," I answered seriously.

While Caden was thinking, I could tell there was a lot on his mind.

"So now you're accusing me of being attractive?" he echoed as his thoughts came to an end.

"Yes!" it blurted out louder than I had intended.

Caden still seemed confused and each of my responses confused him even more.

"Would you rather I was ugly?"

I shook my head. "No. But I wouldn't feel so awful if the bags under our eyes were the same level."

Grinning, Caden pulled me close and kissed my forehead.

"You look quite enchanting, Aurora."

"Yes, I do. But only thanks to this magic makeup you got me." Then I looked at Caden seriously. "Next time we're going to have a blast with

Jackson and his crew, it'll be in the afternoon. I won't survive another night like that."

Caden's grin turned into a laugh and the more I tried to back up my seriousness, the louder his laughter became. Until I finally gave it up completely and waited with folded arms for Caden's laughing fit to slowly subside.

Halfway to the executive floor, Caden pressed the button to the technical department, where I knew my way around better than I should. I held my breath and hoped that Caden had forgotten about my break-in.

"I need to talk to Coleman for a minute. I don't know how the discussion with Alastair turned out," Caden grumbled. The relaxed mood had faded, and the dry daily work routine had crept back in.

"Whew, have fun," I replied, exhaling in relief. In my mind, he had driven me across the department with nipple clamps, love balls and a whip until I really regretted my transgressions.

Caden scowled at me.

"I'd rather have a root canal."

"Don't say that, Caden. Root canals are terrible!"

Just thinking about the shrill sound of the drill made me dizzy.

"I'm really not keen on that part of my job," Caden repeated to himself.

I grabbed Caden's collar and pulled him to me. Our lips met passionately and hungrily. Caden's taste on my tongue made my heart beat faster, and there was nothing I would rather do now.

His tongue parted my lips and explored my mouth where my own tongue welcomed him.

Caden pressed me against the wall of the elevator so I could feel how hard his erection was getting when I kissed him *like this.* Breathing heavily and extremely reluctantly, I detached myself from him.

"That's more in line with my expectations for the workday," Caden murmured.

"Then we should get on with it as soon as you get back," I replied with a wink.

I took a step to the side, straightened my favorite gray and newly named dress, and when the doors opened, I pretended nothing happened.

"Count on it," Caden said in a throaty voice. He gave me that wicked look that announced pretty depraved, magical things.

As the elevator doors closed and I continued my way alone to the executive floor, I leaned against the wall, sighing.

Hopefully every day with Caden will be just like this.

Basically, I still couldn't believe my luck. I, Aurora Winter, a chaotic woman with a chaotic family, had the greatest man in the world by my side. *Miss Chaos meets Mr. Universe.*

Again and again my fingers unconsciously grabbed the engagement ring, simply because I couldn't believe that it was really true.

All hell broke loose on the executive floor. Nothing new, but the serious looks that hit me triggered an uneasy gut feeling in me. It didn't take long for me to realize that something was wrong. No, that was too mild, something major seemed to have blown up.

Without exception, all the people were waiting for Caden and none of them looked happy about it.

Arriving at my desk, I saw Erica pacing up and down Caden's office while Janice stood in front of her with her arms crossed. As our eyes met, she came toward me.

I had an uneasy feeling that Janice had something to do with the chaos, because unlike the others, she seemed pretty happy about the situation.

"What's going on here?" I asked Janice.

"You," Janice replied with a wide grin as she swung her coffee-to-go cup through the air.

Uh oh. I didn't like that at all.

"What do you want me to do with the mess here?" I asked, shrugging my shoulders and dropping into my chair, demonstratively bored.

"You're the talk of the town. Haven't you been reading the papers? Or watched the news?"

I shook my head. "Caden and I have been busy with other things."

Janice twisted the corners of her mouth for a second before her devilish smile returned. She walked over to the next table, grabbed one of the morning papers, and slammed it down on the table.

When I saw the cover, I immediately shot up out of my seat.

"Oh, damn," I muttered, catching myself actually cursing for the first time in my life. But one *Oh Crap!* just hadn't been enough.

"You can say that again. Caden's not going to be very happy about this, no matter what he personally thinks."

I would have loved to shoot Janice a death glare, but I just couldn't turn away from the cover, which featured me. In my underwear, on a pole.

"You must have dug pretty deep to find pictures like that," I said softly. Shock blocked the raging anger inside me. Now I understood the looks on the others' faces. They had imagined me with no clothes on! *Heavens!* My cheeks turned so red against my will that they burned.

"Me?" asked Janice, feigned innocence, clutching her chest, "I washed my hands of it."

Any blind person could tell at first glance how dirty Janice's fingers were.

I finally managed to loosen my glued gaze.

"Couldn't you have waited another two weeks to do that?" I asked, hurt. Not only because I felt embarrassed, but also because she had destroyed Caden's plans. The intended publicity to draw attention to the grievances of the fire department had fallen flat.

My heart broke at the thought of how bad Caden must have felt once he found out.

Janice rubbed her nails together as if to dig out non-existent dirt from under her designer fingernails.

"As I said, I had nothing to do with it. But I personally think the timing couldn't be better."

"You really think that's how you're going to get Caden back?" I asked, shaking my head. "Caden is way too good for you."

"And even more so for you," Janice hissed.

Slowly, my shock thawed, and I struggled to control my anger. But I didn't want to make a scene. I was to blame for the problem, and I now understood why all eyes were on me. For that reason alone, I had to prove to the others that I had the situation under control.

"Caden put so much heart into the firehouse, Janice. He'll never forgive you for that," I said, not responding to her counter. I could do without these *but-yes-but-no* discussions.

"Am I mistaken, or is it your face that is on the front pages of all the newspapers?"

Wow. Janice just couldn't help rubbing it in that the entire East Coast had seen me in my underwear.

Frustration, anger and pain mixed together, and I found it difficult to hold back my tears. Where were the holes in the floor when they were needed?

Sighing, I put my head back.

"Let's just wait for Caden and see what Caden thinks of this," I struggled out in a firm voice. Of course, I was sure that Caden was on my side, but I was still afraid of the confrontation.

"No need, here he comes." Janice emphatically set her coffee mug down on my table. "He looks pretty pissed, but don't worry, PR will fix everything." Janice gave me a fake smile she could do without and tossed her dyed hair over her shoulder to strut back to Erica. The PR head was about to leave a trail in Caden's office.

His looks did not bode well. He marched straight toward me while a flock of employees circled him like hungry vultures.

"Get out!" growled Caden. Everyone paused, but no one felt addressed. "Get the hell out!"

Reluctantly, his coworkers backed down; no one dared to contradict him. Caden wasn't just sour, he was really sour-milk-sour. On a scale of one to ten, he was somewhere around one hundred and thirty. Although he was trying to be calm, I could see his tense muscles shaking. I had no idea what was next, but I knew I couldn't solve Caden's anger with any play-room thing. I had to bring out other guns, which is why I wrote Jackson a note, just in the off chance that Jackson hadn't seen any messages.

SOS. Caden needs a man talk. But don't kill yourselves doing it, wherever you're climbing!

I still wasn't comfortable with the fact that Caden and Jackson were dancing around on facades, but I knew them both well enough to know that they knew what they were doing. And once Caden got his frustration off his chest, I could make sure the last of it fell off.

Everyone had left the department, all except Erica and Janice, who continued to lurk in his office. I followed Caden to his desk but stopped two steps away from him. A symbolic demonstration that I was there – and there for him – but at the same time I gave him enough breathing room not to crowd him.

"How could this debacle happen?" asked Caden without mincing words.

Erica shrugged her shoulders. "We have no idea."

As if. Maybe Erica really was in the dark, but Janice certainly wasn't.

"Do you have a solution?"

"Not yet, but we're working on it."

"Get out of here, Erica," Caden pressed out from behind clenched teeth. He rubbed his temples, which were throbbing violently. Yesterday everything had been fine and today it was blowing up in our faces. I couldn't imagine how bad it must be for Caden, who, in addition to my exposed dignity, had to deal with the entire exposure of Saint Industries.

Erica wanted to protest, but when Caden's sharp eyes met her, she changed her mind.

"Aurora, escort PR outside to the elevator," he asked me wearily.

Nodding, I complied with his request and opened the door.

"Great save," I whispered to Janice as she walked past me. She had probably hoped for a different reaction. Probably a whole bunch of employees had imagined something different.

As we walked, Janice grabbed her half-empty coffee mug that she had set down on my table and said nothing. While Erica trailed off ahead of us in a hurry, muttering unintelligible things, Janice slowed down suspiciously.

Just as I turned to check on things, I was met with a large gush of lukewarm coffee brew that smelled suspiciously like it had a generous shot of whiskey in it.

"Oops," Janice apologized, grabbing her forehead. "How thoughtless of me."

Janice had so exposed me with her press report on my study job that a little coffee stain on my gray dress was nothing in comparison.

And a teensy consolation prize on top of that was that Janice's red, immaculate dress had gotten a much bigger stain.

"I hope you solve your problems better than you can walk in those shoes." That was all I said to that.

"I'm just getting the biggest problem out of the way," Janice answered unequivocally. And with that, she had finally exceeded the limit of my tolerance. Either Caden had to transfer Janice or me, but I couldn't stand another day with this woman and her chronic prickliness.

After they both disappeared into the elevator, I went back to Caden's office. The air was thick enough to cut and I had no idea how to help Caden.

Where the hell was Jackson? Hopefully Caden's best friend wasn't on any missions, because there was a worshipful conflagration to put out here.

"Caden?" I asked, knocking on the open door. "Can we talk?"

"Come in," Caden replied without looking up. His eyes lingered on the pile of newspapers in front of him.

I hardly dared to ask, but I had to, there was no way around it. The situation was too serious to be denied.

"How bad is it?"

Caden looked at me, and his eyes spoke volumes.

"That bad, huh?"

"Damn bad."

Caden sighed before continuing to massage his temples. Although he had looked dewy-eyed earlier, he now looked so exhausted that I was worried he would just collapse.

"I'm so sorry that nothing is being reported about the firehouse. You worked so hard for it."

"I'm sorry, too," Caden growled. "Shit, why now of all times?"

I took a breath to respond but changed my mind. Caden was far too upset to tell him my suspicion that it was Janice's fault.

"This is a fucking disaster that could cost us everything," Caden said more to himself than to me. I really wish there was something I could do to help him. But when I tried to put my arms around his torso, he blocked, and I backed away. He had probably never experienced such affection as a child and knew nothing about the comforting effects of closeness and tenderness. Another thing I regretted but could not undo. Nevertheless, I vowed to do everything in my power to help Caden.

"What can we do?" I asked, driven by my desire to pull Caden out of this hole he was falling into, and into which I would gladly fall myself, as my face – and especially my breasts – were being abused for this mess.

"Nothing at all."

It hurt my heart to see Caden so destroyed.

"And what can *I* do?" I emphasized my question.

"Even less."

"Ouch." The words came over my lips before I could stop myself and Caden growled softly.

"Sorry Aurora, I didn't mean it that way."

Caden took my hand and kissed it. I couldn't help but notice how much strength this tenderness cost Caden.

"It's okay." I swallowed the frustration. "Is there really nothing we can do about it?"

"I don't know. That's Erica's job."

"She's not going to be boss of the year," I blurted out. I managed to elicit a smile from Caden for a second.

"I guess not, no," Caden replied.

I leaned against the desk to take the weight off my feet. Those high heels looked really fancy, but must have been forged in hell, the way my calves were burning.

After taking a deep breath, I confronted the snapshots that were on all the covers.

"Will I ever be able to show my face in public again?"

Caden waved it off. "Sure. That's not the problem."

"What?" I almost choked as my brain processed Caden's response. "Then what, please, is the problem if not my half-naked body billboarded in half of New York?"

For the first time, I thought about the fact that the waves could even hit Seattle. *Jesus.* I felt terrible because I had betrayed my family one more time. This was the second time they had learned about me from a newspaper. No one had known that I had worked in that strip joint, only Dad, who had covered for me. Officially I had financed my studies by working in the shop, but unofficially he had never been able to afford my salary, so I had needed a second job.

"Jesus, my mom is going to freak out when she finds out I used to be a stripper!"

I got all dizzy because I only gradually realized the extent of Janice's *prank*. My reputation was gone, my dignity was stuck to one of the pole dance bars and my family was haunted by the next drama.

Caden shook his head significantly. "Don't worry, they're just little things that we'll get back on track quickly."

My jaw dropped.

"What?" I repeated myself. "Are you even taking what I just said seriously?"

"Yeah." Caden stood up, walked to the window, and let his gaze wander over the morning skyline.

"The whole East Coast has seen me half naked, possibly even all of New York!" I explained to Caden the short version of our huge problem. How could I have reacted so calmly and level-headedly when Janice had confronted me earlier? With my current mood, I probably would have rolled up the newspaper without comment and beaten Janice with it until she bled – and then some more!

Caden wordlessly returned to the table and spread out one of the newspapers, which also had a photo of me emblazoned on it, but the lurid headline went in a different direction. I grabbed the paper and skimmed the article, which suggested that I had been hired to whitewash the impending bankruptcy of Saint Industries.

"Wow." That was all I could say.

"You said it."

"Then we'll just have to prove to the world that's not the case."

"Easier said than done. The stock has tanked and continues to fall into the bottomless pit. If we don't get the damn prototypes done, that's it."

The finality of his words was merciless and painful. And all of this was Janice's fault. Unbelievable how motivated a single woman could be when jealousy drove her insane. Basically, she had single-handedly dismantled a billion-dollar company, just like that.

"Do you know what Saint Industries' real problem is?" I asked.

Caden gave me a serious look. "Now I'm curious."

"Janice." Before I could strike out, Caden rebuffed me.

"Aurora. This is the wrong time to talk about your issue with Janice."

"No, it's the perfect time! Because without Janice, this whole mess wouldn't even exist!" I persistently maintained my point. The issue was far too important to back down. No matter how much Caden could threaten me, I decided not to stop until every single word was said.

"What would Janice have to do with this?"

"She dug up the photos and gave them to the press!" I yelled louder than I had intended.

When I glanced over my shoulder, I saw that dozens of people were standing outside the door again. Probably because there was a fire in every single department.

I cleared my throat sheepishly and continued in a calmer tone.

"She was still talking to press yesterday when everyone else had left," I continued to explain.

"Of course she talks to the press people, she works in the PR department."

I was speechless when Caden continued to defend her. He should know me well enough to know that I don't just denounce people like that. But he obviously didn't know Janice well enough to realize what kind of a show she was putting on.

"Caden, listen to me! She released the pictures, I'm sure of it!"

"Just as sure as your solution to the prototype problem?" asked Caden cynically. Of course, I knew the anger was speaking from him, but it still broke my heart.

"Janice hates me, Caden. You have no idea how much."

Caden stood up and paced around his office.

"If it's Janice's fault, then is it also Janice's fault that you reek of alcohol?"

Caden wrinkled his nose disdainfully as he eyed me sharply.

"Yes!" I yelled angrily.

What the hell had just happened? And why were we fighting in the first place? Did Caden not trust me at all?

"I didn't drink anything! Not a drop!" I affirmed. Then I shook my head in bewilderment as Caden continued to eye me critically.

"Thank you for your confidence," I muttered, miffed.

Instead of apologizing, Caden remained silent and continued pacing.

If he listened very carefully, he could hear my heart shattering into a thousand pieces at that moment.

"Don't you have anything to say?" I asked, wishing he would say something. Anything, any *I'm sorry* or at least a *let's not argue,* but nothing happened.

"I thought we were above these things, Caden. And I also thought you really loved me, but maybe those newspaper articles are right. Maybe I'm just the fake fiancée for PR reasons."

Tears obscured my vision and the lump in my throat swelled more and more.

"You know that's not true," Caden replied. He rubbed his chin thoughtfully and cowardly avoided my gaze.

Slowly but surely, the feeling crept over me that not only Saint Industries was in ruins, even if I didn't want to admit it.

"Then you should also react as if you were standing by me," I whispered. Although I was almost bursting with anger, my voice had no strength left.

"I'm sticking by you," Caden replied a little too matter-of-factly for my taste.

"If that's *sticking by me*, I don't want to know what happens if you ever don't stick by me."

Where had his passion gone? The fire in his eyes when he drove me crazy? Had it ever existed, or had it all been imagination?

"What does that mean?" echoed Caden. "You know I can't do anything with these cryptic half-messages."

"It means you should trust me, even if the facts are against me. And you should have fired Janice much sooner, at the latest when you realized that I was really uncomfortable with her arguments." Actually, I was still going to accuse Caden of being more supportive at the last board meeting, but he cut me off.

"You're wanting Janice fired? After the way you stood up for her after the transfer? Fine. Then she's fired. Are you happy now? Or do you want me to fire Coleman, too? Are there more people you've clashed with that you want me to fire?"

Caden had been talking himself into a frenzy, and I didn't dare interrupt him because the only way I could have stopped him was by yelling over him, and I didn't want to yell.

"No way." I buried my face behind my hands. It took all my willpower not to sob as my little New York bubble burst. "I don't want you to just fire someone like that, I want you to understand why!"

"Because of silly arguments that I don't understand and don't have time for. In case you haven't noticed, we're in deep shit with this monster problem," Caden growled.

It was too much. Caden had not only shattered my heart, now he was dancing around on the broken pieces.

"You forget that I am the face of this monster problem." I took a deep breath. "No, I was that face. The press is right, and whether I want to admit it or not, even Janice is right. We are fundamentally different."

Caden looked at me, frowning. "There's a problem, and the first thing you think of is escape?"

"No, the first thing I thought was that you must be feeling terrible! But I'm probably only playing a minor role in your thoughts."

Admittedly, the past spoke against me. After all, we had met while fleeing from another problem. But this wasn't an escape, but a tactical retreat so that nothing more would happen to the heart shards.

"Aurora, you misunderstand me," Caden began, and I abruptly interrupted him.

"No, I'm afraid I understand exactly what you mean and feel."

It hurt terribly and I wished I was falling, but I was too realistic to fall for false hopes.

"You broke my heart, Caden, and you have no idea how much it hurts."

"Because I didn't fire Janice? Come on, Aurora. That's not fair!"

Was he really that obtuse or was he just pretending? Either way, Caden made me furious with his questions and I surrendered to the rage that wrapped itself protectively around my heart. As long as my blood boiled, it distracted from the pain that had eaten into my heart.

"It's not fair that you have no idea what I'm even talking about!" I yelled at him.

I pulled the engagement ring off my finger and threw it at Caden's feet. It felt like a body part was missing, but I ignored the feeling.

"Aurora! You will listen to me!" said Caden in a commanding tone.

"We're not in the playroom, you can't order me around!"

Without letting Caden get a word in edgewise, I stormed out of the office, past dozens of coworkers who looked after me, puzzled, while Caden stood haphazardly in the office.

The fact that he didn't follow me, even though I wanted nothing more, was another sign that we were both chasing a utopia.

Maybe it was premature, and certainly it was pretty stupid to just leave Caden here. But the decision was made, I had to leave. Caden and I hadn't built a castle in the air after all but had merely made a brief stopover on cloud nine before we came crashing back down to earth.

Well, that was the way it was. I had bet my heart...and lost.

Chapter 32 – Caden

It took me a while to realize the situation, but it took too long. When my legs finally moved again, Aurora had long since disappeared into the elevator.

Fuck. Had she really just broken up with me? The engagement ring at my feet screamed *yes,* but the rest of my mind refused to acknowledge the fact as such.

Full of disdain, I stared at the damn tabloids that had gotten me into all this trouble in the first place. Not only had Aurora left, but when things went badly, I lost Saint Industries.

Of course, the rumors were nothing but rumors, but if sown in the wrong places, they could still cause massive damage.

Thoughtfully, I leaned against my desk and pondered what to do next with Aurora. Yes, probably as a businessman I should have thought about my company first, but Aurora's escape just didn't give me any peace. But I couldn't just pick up the ring and run after her either.

"Hmm," I mumbled thoughtfully. For a brief but painful second, it occurred to me that our relationship was not as strong as I had assumed. If we couldn't cope with such a trivial argument, how could we survive a real problem?

My fingers drummed restlessly on the oak table until I jumped up and picked up the ring from the floor, weighing a ton in my hand. But I couldn't just leave the token of our love on the floor.

Even though it seemed hopeless, I refused to just give up. I was a Saint; I didn't fucking give up when things got tough!

If there was one thing I had learned about women, it was that you should definitely not follow them when they made their escape – that only led to more problems. It was hard for me, but I resisted the urge to immediately search the entire city for Aurora.

She probably buried herself in the four-poster bed of our apartment and waited for me to come into the bedroom with flowers, chocolates and an apology.

I placed Aurora's engagement ring on my desk and went to Aurora's desk, regardless of all the people waiting for me. Although Aurora was not there, the scent of her hair hung in the air, which I inhaled with pleasure.

The bottom drawer of her desk was half open and I irritably pulled out a stack of papers that reminded me suspiciously of the blueprints my engineers had presented to me months ago.

On some of the papers there was only a single word, on others there were line-long explanations. Although I ran a tech company, I didn't understand anything about all the technical stuff; my qualities definitely lay elsewhere. But from the looks of it, Aurora had a hidden talent here. Okay, hidden it wasn't, she had pointed out to me several times that she might be able to help.

If only I had listened to her better. Now it was perhaps too late to listen.

Again and again, the waiting staff sent some poor sap forward to address the floor to me, but a single glance was enough to make them turn around. I was definitely not in the mood for any more negative headlines.

I still couldn't believe that Aurora had run away – she had left me, just like that.

My fingers glided over Aurora's finely curved handwriting, even the paper smelled of cinnamon.

A large shadow that divided the waiting crowd caught my attention.

"Caden, what the hell is going on?" asked Jackson.

"And what the hell are you doing here?" I asked a counter question.

I grabbed Aurora's papers, ran to my office, and gestured for my best friend to follow me.

Admittedly, I was surprised, but definitely glad that he was here. For whatever reason.

"Aurora let me know," Jackson said with a shrug, looking around, "Where is she?"

"Not here," I growled, not yet ready to admit defeat. I closed the door behind Jackson, staining the wall a milky color. My coworkers really didn't need to see me in a crisis meeting with Jacks.

"So what's going on here?" asked Jackson a second time.

"On the off chance you haven't read the paper today."

I pushed the stack of newspapers in his direction, and he ran his hand thoughtfully over his chin.

"Shit." My best friend rifled through the newspapers. "Not a single report on the firehouse?"

I shook my head in displeasure. "Not a single item."

"Oh shit."

Jackson dropped into one of the armchairs that stood in front of my desk.

"You can say that again." I followed suit and threw myself into my chair. "Has anything happened to you yet?"

"Yep." Jackson nodded and rubbed his knuckles. Only at second glance did I notice that his entire right hand was swollen. When Jackson saw my critical look, he unconcernedly covered the right with his other hand and waved it off. Now I also noticed that his cheek looked suspiciously as if his face had run into a fist.

"Captain Kinnley is gone, that's the main thing."

"You beat him up," I stated matter-of-factly, though I was seething inside. Damn, now if my best friend started another major fire, I was screwed. I could maybe still handle two big problems, but if Jacks maneuvered himself into trouble too, I couldn't guarantee anything.

"And what about you?" I echoed.

Jacks shrugged quietly. "Nothing more." He left a very, very long pause before meekly adding, "Probably."

"Don't tell me I could have saved myself all this mess."

Immediately Jackson jumped up. "No! The vehicles will definitely save lives whether I'm in it or not."

I nodded thoughtfully.

"Reassuring, but still not the answer I wanted to hear," I replied. Was I a bad person for enjoying Jackson distracting me from Aurora with his problems?

"They're not going to suspend me or drag me into court," Jackson affirmed.

"And what makes you so sure?" I asked, already rattling off my lawyers in my head.

"Because Kinnley struck first," Jackson replied. He didn't even try to hide his big grin, and I couldn't blame Jacks. Kinnley deserved to have someone read him the riot act.

It was unfortunate that there was no one to hold accountable for my problems.

Whereby...Aurora's words came back to my mind. She suspected Janice, and even though I had no idea why Janice would do such a thing, I couldn't just accuse Aurora of lying either – why should I? Aurora had always been sincere.

"Caden!" Jackson snapped me out of my thoughts.

"Sorry, what?" I shook the thoughts from me like water from the ends of my hair.

"I said my problems are solved, by fisticuffs and plugging holes with money, just as advertised."

I was far from in a good mood, yet I had to smile when I thought back to that crisis conversation. There, Jacks had also given me the idea of making Aurora my fiancée. Possibly I realized it too late, but that was the best decision I had ever made.

"I'm not sure I can really plug every problem hole with money anymore," I said dejectedly.

Jackson flipped through the top newspaper that was on the table.

"Oh, come on. Once the competition realizes how much media exposure there is, it won't be long before even more revealing photos of other women end up in the news," Jackson tried to placate me.

I shook my head. "It's not about the company."

Admittedly, Saint Industries' reputation was hanging by a thread and my engineers had succumbed to gridlock, causing us to slide even further in the stock market. A downward spiral that was bound to end in doom if I couldn't stop it.

"And what problem are we talking about then?" Jackson eyed me closely before nodding knowingly. "Aurora."

I nodded as well, repeating the answer he had deduced for himself. "Aurora."

"Don't tell me you fucked up, Caden."

"Well, what can I say? I fucked up."

Jackson looked at me, stunned. "How the hell?"

"I'd like to know that, too," I murmured. Because I couldn't answer the question myself.

"And how bad is it?" Out came the lieutenant in him, who immediately wanted to get an overview of the danger situation.

Silently, I pointed to the engagement ring that was on my desk.

"Fuck," Jackson cursed. His shocked eyes pierced me. "You want her back?"

I punched him hard on the upper arm. "What do you think, you idiot? Of course I want her back!"

Sighing, Jackson rubbed the spot I had hit.

"What are you still doing here?" asked Jackson energetically, almost in a commanding tone. *Good question.* He cleared his throat briefly. "I mean, you should make a plan before you start running. But you should definitely make your way to the starting line."

Just like Jacks did as a lieutenant, I had to get an overview of the fire before I could put it out. Rushing headlong into the fire never ended well.

"What do you want me to say?" I asked Jackson.

"Did you say something you regret?" he asked me a counter question.

I thought about it for a moment and was glad that neither Aurora nor I had been impulsive enough to hurl insults at each other.

"No," I answered in a firm voice.

"Very good, then everything is still salvageable." Jackson's confidence awakened tender hopes in me.

"But there are things I should have said but didn't."

Jackson's initial euphoria had faded.

"That's almost as bad. If you want it back, you need something really, really big!"

"Thank you for your optimism, best friend." I exhaled loudly audibly.

Jackson raised his arms as if I were threatening him with a pistol. At the same time, he took a step back.

"I'm just being realistic." Jackson let his gaze roam the room until it lingered on the newspaper articles. "And what about this problem? Is there a solution to that yet?"

"No."

"Man, you must have really accumulated a lot of bad karma," Jackson grumbled.

Now that Jacks brought it up, I really wondered what I had done wrong in my last life for all the shit that had happened. On the other hand, there were not only low points in my life, but also bright spots – like Aurora – and friendships that I no longer wanted to do without. But when things went bad, my ray of hope was gone, and I was wandering around in the dark again. And why? Because I was an idiot!

"Aurora is mad at me for not believing her," I said lost in thought, more to myself than to Jackson.

"But now you know she's telling the truth?"

I shook my head.

"Not yet, but we're about to find out."

"I'm ready for any outrage. Good cop, bad cop, seductive cop, multiple personality cop, whatever cop you need, I'm it." Jackson pulled his Firefighter badge out of his pants pocket and waved it around. "And if you didn't look closely, you'd really think I was a cop."

"Thanks," I said with a grin, because Jacks never lost his sense of humor even in serious situations.

Then I cleared the glass, and I roamed over the gaggle of employees lurking outside the door. My eyes remained glued to Janice, why wasn't I surprised she was here again? Now that I thought about it, it all made more sense, and I was officially the world's dumbest idiot. Mr. Idiot-of-the-Universe.

I opened the door and immediately I was met by a flood of people waiting for answers.

"Janice, in my office," I prompted my former personal assistant without mincing words. I released the door behind my back and marched back to my desk. As I made myself comfortable in my chair, Janice entered, looking irritably at Jackson.

"Jacks? Would you make sure no one disturbs us?" I asked my best friend. He didn't object but looked at me in irritation.

Janice took a seat across from me, with a smile that for the first time I exposed as fake.

"What is it, sir?"

"You should tell me," I replied seriously.

"I don't know what you mean, Mr. Saint."

Janice pretended to be innocent, but she forgot that she had been my sub. I heard it when arousal resonated in her voice, and I recognized the demanding looks she gave me.

"Aurora." That's all I said, but that was enough to get me started.

Janice looked at the table and couldn't help but see the engagement ring. Affected, but with a beaming smile, she grabbed her chest.

"Did you guys break up?"

"What does it look like to you?" I asked. It took all my strength to remain calm on the outside. The thing was not yet final, but something close to it.

"I'm so sorry, sir!"

Janice jumped up from her chair, tossed her hair over her shoulder, and strutted unabashedly toward me, leaving nothing to the imagination for the staff behind the glass windows.

"Is there any particular reason you're wearing this exact dress?" I asked as my fingers gripped the red hem of her skirt.

"I felt like it," she replied with a smile.

This little beast knew exactly that I loved red dresses. And I had not infrequently received Janice in this dress in the playroom. One part of her dress was darker than the others. As if she had tried to wash out a stain.

A deep breath was enough to smell out the whiskey that clung to her dress.

Damn. Aurora had really been right, and I had lost her because I had thought Janice was a better person than she was.

"What happens now, sir?" asked Janice expectantly. Presumably she already saw herself in the role of the woman who was to console me over Aurora and as a later *fiancée 2.0*.

"You're fired," I replied dryly.

"That sounds ... " Janice began and faltered. I don't know what she had wanted to hear at first, but when she realized the meaning of my words, she gasped. "Why?"

"Because you exposed my fiancée, and you did it more than once."

Janice began to giggle shrilly. God, how I hated her voice; it raged in my head, sharp and painful.

"Aurora doesn't deserve you at all!"

Her response was tantamount to a confession. Although I had good reason to yell at Janice, I remained calm. Janice should feel how indifferent she was to me.

"That's not for you to decide. You also don't get to decide that everyone knows about Aurora's past – which, by the way, is no problem for me if you didn't know. Still, it's not for you to decide who finds out about it."

Even when Aurora first told me about her work at the strip club, I wasn't particularly impressed or intimidated. We were in the twenty-first fucking century, it should take more to create a scandal these days than a dance on the pole.

Janice went pale, another indication that she was to blame for all my problems without exception and that her day was not going at all as she had planned.

"You're fired, pack your bags," I repeated to myself emphatically.

"But Caden! That was special with us, we shouldn't just throw that away!"

"To you, I'm *Mr. Saint*, and there was absolutely nothing going on between us, understand? And speaking of which, I swear to you by God and the devil that you're not working anywhere since you've taken Aurora away from me forever with your action."

Janice's eyes grew as big as moons and wet with tears. She had been my personal assistant; she knew that I only had to make one phone call to permanently destroy a career. No one would hire Janice if they knew her background.

"That's unfair!" grumbled Janice. If I hadn't seen through her game, I would almost feel sorry for her.

"Do I really need to repeat myself?" I frowned and pointed toward the exit. "Get out of here before I forget myself! And if I see you one more time, I'll make your life a living hell! You mean nothing to me.

I love Aurora, she'll be my bride someday. Get it the hell out of your head that there was anything going on between you and me, because there wasn't. It was just sex."

After a short, hysterical scream that drew all eyes outside to her, Janice took a quick breath.

"You don't deserve me anyway," she hissed before retreating. Finally. She stormed past Jackson, who looked after her in confusion before returning to me.

"What just happened there?" asked Jacks, crossing his arms in front of his chest.

"I'm an idiot, that's what happened."

Jackson waved it off with a grin. "You've always been a jerk, Caden, nothing new."

"Possibly," I replied thoughtfully. "I understood far too late what kind of game Janice was playing."

Jack's eyebrows drew together as he put one and one together.

"She did that?"

"She did everything," I corrected him sullenly. "She manipulated me and Aurora, messed up the PR for the Twenty-third, and slipped pictures of Aurora to the reporters. I wouldn't be surprised if she was to blame for famines and plague outbreaks, either."

"Me neither," Jackson said. "But even though you're rid of the evil now, it still doesn't solve your other problems."

"Right."

Silence fell over us, because we had no idea where to even begin. Damn, could it be so hard to know how to win back the woman you loved? Hell yeah. My entire future was hinged on a single decision, the pressure was huge, and I was in danger of breaking under the weight. But I stayed strong – for Aurora. She deserved to be happy, and I knew exactly that I was the man who could make her happy!

"Come with me!" I ordered Jackson and jumped up from my seat. But before I could take another step, Coleman stormed into my office. It had been he who had told me the bad news earlier. It wasn't just about the rumors and speculation, but also about the fact that the damn drones were still crashing, if they made it into the air at all.

"What else?" I growled impatiently.

"We need some kind of strategy, Mr. Saint!"

I waved it off. "That's not my job, it's the engineering department's job!"

Annoyed, I pushed Coleman aside as he blocked my way. As he did so, he noticed the copied blueprints of Aurora, which he grabbed and flipped through critically.

"I didn't know anything about an independent expert," Coleman muttered without looking up. For the first time in months, my chief engineer's expression softened.

"That wasn't an independent expert. That was my fiancée," I replied, watching Coleman's head rattle.

"Yes, the very fiancée you cut off yesterday."

Coleman's features derailed within a second. "Oh."

Still dismayed, he spread the plans out on my desk, kept mumbling something, nodding, shaking his head, leaving a fat question mark on my head and Jack's.

"Well?" I asked impatiently.

"Some testing would have to be done, but with the 3-D printer, it won't take long. The equations are flawed, but they're on a good path. If we integrate them into our own calculations, it could potentially make a difference."

My chief engineer pinned one cryptic message to the next without me being able to make any sense of it.

"Out with the language, can that help? I have other problems to solve!" I demanded.

"I don't want to get too far out on a limb, sir, but potentially this could solve our problem."

Unbelievable. How could I have overlooked Aurora's brilliance? No, I had not only overlooked it. I had even tried to convince Aurora of the opposite.

I swore by all that was sacred to me that nothing like this would ever happen again if Aurora forgave me.

"How soon will you know if it's working or not?"

"Two, three hours tops, then the calculations are done."

"Good, then let's get to work!" I said in a commanding tone. Immediately, Coleman grabbed Aurora's papers and ran toward the engineering department.

"Good, and you and I are going to my apartment now so I can convince Aurora that I'm not the ass I've been acting like."

"I can tell you don't want me to play any kind of cop. But sure, I'll just be the sidekick who holds doors for you, closes them, or guards them."

"Those are the main sidekicks," I replied with a grin.

Then we marched out of my office, ignoring the crowd of employees we had to fight our way through, and got on the elevator.

I laid out several plans in my head and was confident that I could change Aurora's mind if I didn't act as stupidly as I had earlier. On the other hand, I had hurt Aurora pretty badly. Not only had I insinuated that she was exaggerating, but I had also insinuated that she reeked of alcohol. Hell, Janice knew my red rags, but she had left one thing out – Aurora had thawed my ice-cold heart and now it only beat for her.

Hopefully it's not too late.

Chapter 33 – Caden

Actually, it should have been clear to me that I would find our apartment empty, yet hope had driven me through every single room. Everything looked exactly as it had when we had left the apartment. A pair of Aurora's heels stood in front of the closet, right next to the dress I had torn off her yesterday.

The entire bedroom was filled with her cinnamon scent, and I thought I could feel her warmth on my skin.

Driven by hope, I dialed Aurora's speed dial again, but was again routed directly to voicemail. Wherever Aurora was, she didn't want to be disturbed, and I couldn't blame her.

Damn. Fate had played us a dirty trick. No, not fate, it had been Janice. If I had just trusted Aurora, none of this would have happened. The self-reproaches I tormented myself with grew stronger and stronger, as did the fear that I had done something that was irreparable.

Sighing, I started to retreat, I couldn't stay here, surrounded by her scent, her warmth and all the memories that tightened my throat. I was not the sentimental type, but when it came to Aurora, I became so.

My restless feet carried me back to the lobby where Jacks was waiting for me.

Before I even turned the corner, I heard Jackson start laughing and Sebastian joined in. Sebastian, the guy from the lobby who must have decided decades ago never to have fun again, was laughing at the top of his lungs. Until a few seconds ago, I had always thought Jacks was teasing me when he claimed Sebastian was a funny guy.

As soon as I appeared in their field of vision, the laughter died away.

"Well?" asked Jacks expectantly. Sebastian, meanwhile, cleared his throat as if ashamed of his laughter, even though I could barely make out anything in his opaque expression.

Disgruntled, I shook my head and continued my way into the underground garage. Jackson said a quick goodbye to the mute receptionist and caught up with me within a few steps.

Neither of us dared say anything until we were sitting in my SUV, and I slammed the driver's door shut and banged the steering wheel.

"Fuck!"

"Aurora wasn't there, I guess," Jackson said cautiously. So far, he had no idea what had happened in the apartment.

"No," I replied. "She wasn't here."

"Hm," Jackson murmured, sounding almost relieved, which I couldn't understand at all. But before I could demand an answer, he continued himself. "She's staying out of your way. That's a good sign."

Now my facial features completely slipped away.

"Since when?" I asked, frowning.

"If she had wanted to leave you, you would have found her packing suitcases in the bedroom while throwing shoes, hangers and insults at you."

"Sounds reasonable," I replied.

"Or she hates you so much she took off without packing," Jackson added, patting me on the back.

"Thank you," I growled, shaking my head.

"I was joking!" Jacks immediately defended himself. Still, I couldn't laugh at my best friend's joke. Hell, I didn't feel like joking at all, but rather like beating the crap out of everything. Only the fact that my mother had raised me to be a better person kept me from putting my plan into action.

"Let's better figure out how to get Aurora back!" I grumbled.

Jackson leaned back in the passenger seat, holding his fingertips together and looking like Sherlock Holmes through his thinker's expression.

"Sure can, but we have to find her first."

I pulled my smartphone out of my pocket while I thought.

"When I'm really pissed off, I bug my best friend about it. Probably Aurora won't feel any different," I concluded. Of course, I could have just called Maxine, but I realized that she was sticking up for Aurora and that automatically made me the enemy.

"So we're going to her best friend's house?" asked Jackson.

"Hold on," I muttered as I continued to swipe across the display. "Max has about twenty apartments, we have to find out which one she's in first."

"And how the hell are we going to do that?" I saw Jackson's brain rattle as he thought about Maxine's living arrangements.

"Luckily, Max gives quite a few updates on her projects," I explained. Thanks to social media, it didn't take me long to get a good overview. On her most recent post, I could even tell which neighborhood it was in.

Fuck. I wish Max would stay in another apartment, somewhere other than Brooklyn.

"What's wrong?" Jacks asked when he saw my scowling face. I held out the display with the photo, which made me feel sick all of a sudden.

"This is Brooklyn," Jackson stated matter-of-factly. Unlike me, he had not yet realized where exactly the apartment was.

"Take a closer look," I prompted him.

Jacks grabbed the smartphone, zoomed in, and then the penny dropped.

"Oh. So there it is."

"Yeah, right there." I clutched the steering wheel of my SUV to think.

"Is that a problem?" asked Jackson cautiously.

"What do you think?" I said to my best friend more sharply than I really wanted to.

Ironically, Aurora was right where I first became aware of my feelings for her.

I knew exactly where Aurora was, yet my fear slowed me down. Not the fear of the abyss over which I could not jump, but fear of Aurora's possible rejection that would destroy me.

Fuck it.

I started the engine and put it in gear.

Jackson looked at me with a raised eyebrow.

"Do you have a plan?"

"No," I replied calmly.

"Love doesn't stick to plans anyway. Whatever you're up to, I'm in."

"True words."

We made slow progress in New York's midday traffic, and the bigger Brooklyn became on the horizon, the more conflicted I became. On the one hand, I wanted nothing more than to confess my love to Aurora, but on the other hand, I wanted to delay the trip endlessly because there was a chance that Aurora would no longer return my love.

This insecurity was cruel, and I hated Aurora for exposing me to this feeling.

When we reached the street where I assumed Maxine's apartment was, my gaze slid restlessly back and forth. Except for a cab that was driving away, it was pretty quiet. Too quiet for a beautiful summer day. No birds chirping, no children playing, no happy dogs – dragging their owners through the streets – it was as if there was no love left.

In front of the building where I thought Maxine and Aurora were, I stopped the car and sighed softly.

"Ready?" asked Jacks as I unbuckled my seatbelt.

"No," I answered honestly. But I only had this one chance, and I'd be damned if I didn't take it.

"If you need backup, I'm here, buddy," Jackson let me know of his support.

"Thank you, Jacks."

I crossed the street and perused the name tags on the doorbell. When I found the name *Lancester* on one of the signs, the lump in my throat grew thicker. With all my might, I swallowed the feeling and rang the bell.

"Yes?" Although the PA system was rushing and scratching, I recognized Maxine's voice immediately.

"I need to talk to Aurora," I said without mincing words; it was self-explanatory who I was.

"She's not here."

"It's important! Come on, I know Aurora is with you!" I demanded one more time.

Noise. Crackling. It took what felt like an eternity before I got an answer.

"Aurora really isn't here, Caden."

"I don't believe a word you say!" I growled. "I know you hate me, that's your duty as Aurora's best friend, but I want to make it up to you. I love Aurora and Aurora loves me."

Silence.

Of course, I understood their reaction. Jacks and I would probably act the same way, but I had only the best intentions. Aurora was within reach, and yet she was out of reach.

"I believe you, and I swear we're on the same page," Maxine began, and I guessed which way the conversation was going. Before she even spoke further, I lost my temper and punched the intercom. Another *Aurora is not here*, I couldn't take.

"Fuck!" I cursed, rubbing my aching knuckles after my hand crashed into the wall. The speaker buzzed one last distorted time, then there was silence.

I had disassembled the entire intercom; a deep crack ran right through the device and it was obvious that it had done its service.

I marched back to the car and opened the trunk. Jackson, who had heard nothing of the entire conversation, looked at me questioningly.

"Aurora is in that damn apartment," I answered his silent question.

"But?"

"But they won't let me in." I opened the duffel bag that was in the trunk and began to change clothes in the open street. I didn't cut a good figure on rooftops in a tailored suit and designer shoes. When Jacks noticed what I was up to, he jumped up from his passenger seat.

"And that's why you're going to break in, or what?"

"Leave *or what* out of it."

I was hell-bent on winning Aurora back. And if I had to break into Maxine's apartment to convince Aurora that we belonged together, then I'd break the hell into the damn apartment! Come what may.

"Do you think that's a good idea?" cautiously echoed Jackson.

"No, but it's the only plan I have."

After I moved, I looked at the house where Aurora was located. Maxine's apartment was on the top floor and had a connection to the fire escape on the west wall. Unfortunately, the way to the fire escape from below was completely blocked, so I had to break in from above.

"If I run along our standard route to the corner of West Avenue and then turn toward Pacifica, I should theoretically make it," I shared my plan with Jacks. He thought about it for a moment and ran through the route in his mind's eye.

"But to do that, we'd practically have to go past the *place to* get to the house with the worn graffiti. That would be the only way that would begin to go in that direction."

"No," I shook my head.

"What, how else are we going to get here?"

Jackson leaned against the body and crossed his arms.

"I have to do this, Jackson. Alone."

My best friend eyed me carefully. It was not an easy decision, but it was the right one.

"You sure?" Jackson eyed me from top to bottom.

"Sure."

My heart was racing, but I had made my decision. It was the only chance I had, so I took it. Not to mention, Jacks didn't have any gym clothes with him – there was no way Jackson could keep up in jeans and worn-out sneakers.

"Good, I'll wait here that long in case Aurora leaves the house," Jackson said.

I patted him gratefully on the shoulder because I could rely on my best friend.

To prepare my body for the following exertions, I sprinted through the cross streets. At the alley where I had lost my courage last time, I stopped. From below, with both feet firmly on the ground, the gap between the two houses did not look very dangerous, almost ridiculous. Nevertheless, I could hardly ignore the uneasy feeling that was spreading in my stomach area.

Sighing, I jogged on, for I had no time to lose. As quickly as I could, I reached the hotel from which Jacks and I usually started. Most of the staff, all the way up to the assistant director, had been greased by me so that we could use the fire escape without any problems.

Never before had I felt so queasy about going up on the roof. Not only because Jackson was always there for my daredevil hobby, but also because my entire future depended on this one run.

The first, short jumps felt strange, but the closer I got to Aurora, the more I pushed myself. And before I knew it, the world was flying by. Every step was sure, every grip purposeful, every jump perfect.

My heart was hammering like a jackhammer against my ribs and my shallow, rapid breathing was barely keeping up. But I pushed myself further and further, almost to my limits – I had to save a few reserves so that I could really go beyond my limits.

Only when I arrived at the infamous spot where I had lost my invulnerability did I take a little breather.

To those who saw me, I was just some guy on the roof, yet I was about to fearlessly face the abyss.

I allowed neither fear nor anger to take over but stared unconcerned and cool at the abyss below me.

A small, insignificant alley made me aware of my vulnerability. I could still only shake my head in bewilderment.

This abyss had made me realize last time how important Aurora was to me, and today it reinforced the feeling even more.

But there was a significant difference. Last time, this realization had slowed me down; now it propelled me forward.

I took three steps back and concentrated entirely on my breathing. In my head I went through the entire jump, from takeoff to landing. Then I took a running start and took off.

As I leapt over the precipice at breakneck speed, I briefly thought I could fly, which was an incredible feeling.

My hands gripped the wall ledge of the opposite house and I effortlessly pulled myself up.

Grinning, I faced the abyss I had conquered and from which I had emerged stronger than ever before. Who would have thought that it was so easy to face one's fears?

Damn. I had really done it.

After the hardest hurdle was cleared, I sprinted from obstacle to obstacle as light as a feather to close the distance between Aurora and me. It was wrong for us to be apart, we belonged together. Period.

Now there was no stopping me; I went full throttle and set a new course record that could never be topped. Earlier, I had thought that there was nothing that pushed me forward more than the escape from my past, which I had finally faced with Aurora's help. I was wrong. No escape in the world could propel me forward as quickly as the motivation to see Aurora again.

I had run away from my past long enough, now it was time to sprint to my future.

Chapter 34 – Aurora

With a worried face, Max handed me another pack of tissues.

"Stop crying already, Aurora, otherwise I'll have to cry along with you!" she urged me with a tortured face.

"I'm sorry," I apologized, sobbing, and grabbed the tissues. So far, I hadn't been able to get a word past my lips, but from my naked ring finger, my best friend knew immediately what was going on.

Maxine put her hands to her face and snorted.

"Oh God, I'm such a bad friend! Of course you can cry, Aurora. Actually, I just wanted to say that it breaks my heart to see you so sad."

"I know," I muttered, sniffling. It took all the strength in the world, but I fought off a smile.

"Let it all out, you'll feel better afterwards."

Maxine threw a cuddly blanket around my shoulders and pressed a hot cup of cocoa into my hand. Around us was a huge battlefield of tissues, empty Ben & Jerrys cups, and nibbled-on chocolate bars. But in the renovation chaos, the exploded heartbreak starter kit didn't stand out at all. Some furniture was covered in foil, individual wall sections were covered in paint, and there were paint buckets, ladders, and old rugs everywhere. When I stood tearfully in front of her door earlier, Max had given the workers a day off and unceremoniously kicked them out.

"I'm not so sure about that, Max. I don't know if I'll ever be okay again."

It felt like my heart was no longer there, just the aching emptiness eating me up from the inside.

Max screwed up her face. "But of course, Aurora. Don't hang your head. I'm here for you – a sorrow shared is a sorrow halved."

"Not true."

I shook my head vehemently and buried my face in a ball of tissue again.

"I guess so!" protested Maxine, biting off an entire row of a strawberry-cream chocolate bar with gusto.

"No. A sorrow shared is a sorrow doubled," I argued logically. For a brief moment, in my belligerence, I even forgot why we were fighting in the first place, and that really felt good.

"Not at all!" Max continued to counter.

I sipped my hot cocoa briefly before resuming the discussion.

"Yes you do, you said it yourself, it breaks your heart to see me like this. Ergo, we both suffer. So it's double suffering."

Maxine snorted but remained silent. My best friend couldn't do anything about it, I had checkmated her. At least that's what I thought until she thought of something after a while. After another bite of chocolate, Maxine looked at me seriously.

"Yes, your theory is correct, but only in theory. In practice, of course, I feel worse for a short time, but that's okay because it massively shortens the time when you feel bad. And so it becomes half suffering.

Logical calculation, right? And as your best friend, of course I'm happy to share your pain if it makes you feel better."

Maxine grinned at me, knowing full well that she was right, while my heart sank because her words were so moving.

"I would do the same for you," I replied, touched.

"Yep, I know. You already did. You remember the first time you went to that apartment in Central Park?"

"How could I forget?" I replied. "I've never eaten so much ice cream in my entire life!"

"Oh, we had that danced away in no time!" waved Maxine off and we both giggled.

A lot had happened in the apartment since Max and I had gotten over her heartbreak at the time, and my mood became more serious again when I thought about how much had happened. Caden had happened.

"What's behind the door, anyway?" asked Maxine curiously.

"Behind which door?" I asked.

"The one at the end of the hall. Did you figure it out?" Max went into detail and my cheeks immediately turned deep red. I had no idea how to answer that. When I remained silent, Maxine probed.

"A superhero base? A forbidden secret laboratory housing a weather machine? Or just some boring storage room?"

"I'd say kind of like a second bedroom," I replied with a gasp, hoping Max was content with my answer.

Maxine flopped down on the couch with a loud sigh. "How disappointing. Every cool guy needs a secret, otherwise it's totally boring."

"Caden is not boring!" I immediately defended him. It was a reflex I couldn't suppress, even if it hurt.

"Maybe not, but he's definitely stupid if he just lets you go."

It was more like I was running away from him, but I didn't answer because I was focused on not crying my head off again.

"Do we hate him?" asked Maxine specifically.

"No." I shook my head, then nodded again, only to shake my head again right after. "Oh, I don't know."

"What happened?"

"Too much," I sobbed. Then I forced my body to calm down and told Maxine everything that had happened. I didn't leave a good hair on Janice's head, and Maxine's eyes got bigger and bigger the more I told. I was actually talking in a rage because of the rising anger, and in the heat of the moment almost all my tears evaporated.

"That's unbelievable!" Max blurted out, stunned, when I had told the whole story.

"I have no idea how it got to this point," I said. Then I grabbed a half-full tub of chocolate ice cream and shoveled the comfort food into my mouth one spoonful at a time.

"How exactly did Caden react?" Max inquired.

"Not at all." Frustrated, I blew a strand out of my face.

"Okay. Kind of dumb." Unlike me, Maxine didn't seem as outraged by this as I would have liked.

"Kind of dumb? It's the absolute horror! Instead of sticking by me, he just threw me to the wind!"

"Did he?" Maxine shrugged. "Or did you read more into his silence than you should have?"

I faltered, briefly, before demonstratively spooning chocolate ice cream. "No, I didn't read anything more into it. Janice sabotaged me from day one, period."

Max slid a little closer and tried to catch some of my chocolate ice cream.

"I never denied that either. You still remember our mission, *Towerqueen*?"

I chuckled softly. "How could I forget, *Watchman*?" Then I got pretty serious again. "You know what the worst part is? Our mission was successful. I think I found a solution to the drones' flight problem, but I didn't have time to show Caden."

"Oh, Aurora." Max looked at me like I was a totally cute but blind puppy dog. "Is it really, really over between you two?"

"What do you think I'm doing here?" I asked, my tone snippy.

"Recovering from a teeny tiny fight you guys had?" Max put her thumb and forefinger as close together as if she were holding the head of a pin.

"I wish." I sighed heavily. "I threw my engagement ring at Caden, I'm sure he's pissed off and hurt. Besides, he's got other problems to deal with right now."

"Yeah, I've heard about that," Maxine said so unconcerned that it sounded suspicious.

"So you've seen the headlines too?" It was more of a rhetorical question, because my best friend's reactions were clear.

"Possibly," Max replied diplomatically, swiping my sundae from my hands.

"You don't have to go easy on me," I offered because I was dying to know what my best friend thought about it.

"Really?" echoed Maxine.

"Really," I replied, because I could tell she was about to burst. Whatever was on the tip of her tongue, it had to come out.

Max jumped up and pulled out from behind the sofa cushions a copy of the Daily News with me on the cover.

"Actually, I always get the Times, but you're way too dressed on the cover!" said Max with a grin, tossing me the article by Jelinda Cherry, who was reporting on the abuses of the firehouse. At least I had a reporter who hadn't stuck a knife in my back. Actually, the situation was no laughing matter, but I had to laugh at Max's stupid line.

"You got yourself a different paper specifically?" I echoed.

"Sure, after all, my best friend isn't on the cover every day."

I grabbed my temples. "And I hope that will never happen again either!"

Max dropped down next to me on the couch and unfolded the newspaper, which showed me in my underwear.

"Well, my first reaction was, *what the hell!* and when I recognized you, there was just pure envy! Could have been that the photos are fake or you got mixed up."

I looked at my best friend, frowning. "What?"

Max held the cover so close to my face that I could smell the printer's ink.

"Have you ever seen your flawless, perfectly toned body? I'd kill for hips like that!"

"You have an incredible body, Max! And you know how to stage it much better than I do," I admitted grudgingly. When it came to fashion, Max was worlds more suave than I would ever be. Max waved me off.

"Anyway, if you ask me, Janice didn't do herself any favors by doing that," Max finished her presentation.

"I'm gone – exactly what she planned," I objected.

"Nope. Caden is pissed for sure, and I guarantee you he's going to find out that it was Janice who sabotaged his last PR stunt. Not to mention, now all of New York knows how hot Caden Saint's fiancée is – hot as hell, that is!"

"I'm not his fiancée anymore."

My heart grew heavy as I thought of all I had lost. It was hard for me to accept that the left half of the bed would be empty when I woke up or that Caden's calm gaze would rest on me while I tried in vain to concentrate. But what I would miss most were his touches on my skin, sometimes tender, sometimes demanding, but always passionate.

"I didn't know you were that pessimistic, cheer up!" Max demanded of me and pressed the almost empty sundae against my chest.

"I've never been so sad either," I defended my doom and gloom. "My fiancé is gone, I've been exposed in front of the entire East Coast, and I lost my job. Soberly, I have the right to hang my head."

"It's a good thing we don't have to look at this thing sober. How about a cabernet?"

Max jumped up before I could answer.

"Another sundae for me," I replied, tossing the empty cup onto the pile of cups that was growing ever higher. I was in absolutely no mood for alcohol, even though there was now no contract binding me to abstinence, only my promise to Caden continued to hold.

"So where do we go from here?" asked Max after she thrust a Strawberry Cheesecake cup into my hand.

"I'm going to go back to Seattle first to help Dad in the garage."

All was still well in the workshop. There was only the smell of diesel, the purr of the engine and the warmth of my dad, because he had put all his heart and soul into the workshop.

"Are you sure?" asked Maxine, frowning.

"Yes. There's nothing here to hold me anymore," I whispered sadly. "Thank you, *best friend*."

I gave Maxine a quick hug before conciliatory handing her the sundae.

"You know how I meant it. I can't stay here now, not when everything reminds me of Caden. I wouldn't survive."

"I still think you guys belong together," Maxine said, pulling a pout.

I had hoped so, too, and that's why I now felt the way I did – miserable and devastated. I had been foolish enough to believe that our feelings went beyond a contract, but I was wrong. For Caden, our love continued to be just a signature on a piece of paper.

"It was doomed from the start," I replied.

"You could just stay here with me. We'll binge-watch our very favorite shows until you're back on your feet!"

I was genuinely touched by her offer, but I couldn't be in the same city as Caden, or I would only risk making a fool of myself by having my heart trampled a second time.

"My flight leaves today," I said with an apologetic smile.

"So early?" Maxine looked rather disappointed but returned my smile with understanding.

The fact that I had already ordered a cab so that I would arrive on time I preferred to conceal so that Max could digest one shock after the other.

"The sooner the better," I explained. "Shared misery and all that. I can let off steam in Dad's workshop until I'm well again."

Maxine thought about it for a moment while we both fought over the last crumbs of cheesecake in the strawberry ice cream.

"Fine, fine by me." Then Max raised her index finger threateningly. "But don't you dare let me catch you holed up in your bed instead of fixing cars, like MacGyver, with shoelaces and duct tape!"

I couldn't help but laugh out loud. "You got it."

"Good, and when you come back, you show me how to contort myself just like you," Maxine demanded.

"I promise," I replied with a smile.

The situation was still awful, my heart ached with every beat and my tears lurked behind the next memory, but still I felt a little lighter. My best friend had cushioned my fall and for that I was infinitely grateful to her.

We giggled, destroyed Maxine's last stash of Ben & Jerrys, and devoted ourselves to the first season of our absolute favorite show.

For a moment I forgot the heartbreak, there was only Max, me and the anticipation of Seattle. Until the doorbell rang and my heart skipped a beat.

Jesus.

I gave Maxine warning looks that she should not move. Although it was impossible to know from outside whether we were here, I hardly dared to breathe.

On the one hand, my heart leapt for joy because Caden was fighting for me after all, but on the other hand, I couldn't let that blind me. Because if the man who had stolen my heart stood in front of me, I had lost even before the fight began. I would forgive him, simply because I couldn't help it. But I couldn't forgive him, not if he didn't trust me and even less if he didn't love me.

And after today, it was clear where Caden's priorities lay – very far from my own.

I loved him more than anything, but my love was not enough for both of us if his heart did not beat for me.

Max did what I lacked the strength to do – she went to the intercom – for which I loved and hated her at the same time.

"Don't panic, Supermax saves the day!"

"That's exactly why I'm scared!"

Oh God, oh God, oh God!

Chapter 35 – Caden

The biggest challenge of today's course was to figure out which window actually belonged to Maxine's apartment on whose roof I was standing. If I knocked on the wrong window, I might get arrested before I even had a chance to explain myself.

In fact, it had happened to me once shortly after college, and that's when I had learned in a painful way that you couldn't bribe cops as easily as the people who called them.

Carefully, I jumped onto the fire escape, which definitely needed repair, the way the enclosed grates swayed under my movements.

My gaze briefly wandered over the deserted street, and I became suspicious. Wasn't Jacks supposed to be my lookout in case Aurora made a run for it? Once my fiancée could run away from me, but twice? No way – I was not a man to play such games.

I waved it off and settled for the assumption that Jacks was waiting in the car, trying to look less like a loitering criminal.

Slowly, I brushed past the windows and peeked inside until I found the room cluttered with moving boxes, paint buckets, and foil. Behind it was a bright green wall that I knew from Maxine's social media posts.

"That must be it!" I said aloud to myself to convince myself once again that it was. After all, I had the intention of breaking in right away, breaking in being a pretty harsh word. Actually, I just wanted to convince my fiancée that I couldn't live without her.

The window opened more easily than I thought appropriate for Maxine's safety, and I climbed in. In a clumsy move, I knocked over a vase that bounced ominously on the dresser until it finally shattered on the floor with a crash and a clatter.

Fuck.

Not a second later, Maxine was standing at the open door, looking at me in confusion.

"Caden? What are you doing?"

"What does it look like? I'm not going to let you take away my chance to win Aurora back!"

I straightened up, smoothed out my shirt, and straightened my chest. Instead of answering me, Maxine put her head back exactly like Aurora and snorted. Inevitably, I had to wonder which of them had copied it from the other.

I took the chance, with Maxine still searching for words, to get mine off my chest – so loudly that it was heard throughout the apartment.

"I'm human, and humans make mistakes. Especially when insecurity has a firm grip on them." I took a quick breath. Feelings had never been my strong suit, and expressing them seemed almost a thing of infinity. "But I'm damn sure of one thing, and that's that Aurora and I belong together. She charmed me from the first second I saw her, and I love her with all my heart."

The words just slipped from my lips, and I wondered why it had been so hard all those years before? The answer was close, it was only because of Aurora.

"Caden..." Maxine began, but I interrupted her again.

"I'm not done yet!"

Aurora's best friend gave me a defiantly angry look, but silently crossed her arms in front of her chest so I could continue. Hopefully Aurora did not doubt the sincerity of my words.

"I fired Janice, she will never sabotage us again. And I'll tell you again, you shouldn't be ashamed of being on the front pages of the most important newspapers in the country. Besides, you will be again soon – because you saved my engineers' asses with your plans. I apologize for not trusting you when it mattered. That mistake will never happen to me again. And I'm sorry for not taking you seriously and supporting you. But most of all, I regret what a huge idiot I am for only now realizing how much I love you. I can't live without you, Aurora. I can't."

Without Aurora, I lacked the air to breathe. If she didn't take me back now, it was like a death sentence.

"Can I finally say something?" asked Maxine, annoyed.

"Please, go ahead," I replied after I had finally said everything. Actually, I would have liked a reaction from Aurora, but she remained silent.

"That was a beautiful, heartwarming speech – and Aurora would take you back in a heartbeat if she heard that, but Aurora really isn't here!"

"I understand that she's hurting and that you want to protect her, but Aurora just needs to look me in the eye and say that she forgives me." I paused for a moment. "Or that it's over for good."

Forgetting my good manners for a moment, I squeezed past Maxine into the living room where I suspected Aurora was. I skimmed the battlefield, consisting of renovation utensils and sundaes, and when my gaze lingered on Jackson, my breath caught.

"How the hell did you get in here?" I asked.

"Maxine was lovely enough to invite me in after you broke the intercom. Actually, she wanted to talk to you, but you were already gone," Jackson replied, shrugging his shoulders.

Maxine nodded before looking at me.

"You know what, Caden? You're really right about one thing. You're a huge jerk, and if you'd let me finish earlier-or before-I could have told you at the door that Aurora got into a cab headed for JFK Airport thirty seconds before you arrived."

"Damn," I muttered.

"You can say it out loud, buddy. What now?"

"What now?" Maxine slapped the flat of her hand against her forehead. "Well what do you think, you guys take up pursuit and intercept Aurora outside the airport!"

"Easier said than done," Jackson replied what I was thinking.

"You're Caden Saint, come up with something!" Maxine urged me angrily. It was strange to know that my fiancée's best friend was on my side.

I pulled my smartphone out of my pocket. First, I researched the flight Aurora had probably booked and quickly found it. There was only one flight from JFK Airport to Seattle today, and it left earlier than I would have liked.

Then I followed Maxine's instruction and responded in usual Caden Saint fashion by calling the number of the airline Aurora was flying with.

Before the person on the other end of the line could say anything, I cut him off.

"I'm Caden Saint, CEO of Saint Industries, and I'm buying all the airline tickets for today's flight to Seattle."

Actually, I didn't like the plan, but it was a lifeline in case I couldn't find Aurora in the vast airport area.

"I'm very sorry, sir, but the flight is fully booked," the woman on the other end of the line said without regret.

"Then I'll just buy all the tickets – whatever the price, I'll buy every single seat!"

She hesitated briefly, then regained her composure.

"I'm afraid I can't do that, Mr. Saint, some guests have already checked in."

Damn! I was up to my neck in water and no longer had a lifeline.

"Then I'll just buy the whole plane," I replied indignantly.

Now the woman hesitated longer before declining again. "You'd better talk to the managing director about that."

"Then connect me. If I have to, I'll buy out the whole damn airline!"

Short keyboard clatter, quiet voices.

"Our executive director will get back to you."

After fobbing me off, she hung up and left me stunned.

"Looks like we need another plan," I growled.

"So what's plan B?" asked Maxine curiously. As if I could always pull plans from A to Z out of my sleeve.

"Well, at the Fire station, we would now say that this is a classic *O'Riley.*"

Maxine and I looked at Jacks, questions obviously on my mind.

"What's a classic *O'Riley*?" asked Maxine. "Is that real firefighter slang, like cops have an *eight-fifty-three* or a *nine-twenty-eight*?"

Jackson shook his head. "No, more like an insider on Twenty-third. Long story."

While Jackson and Maxine were talking about the fire insider, I was thinking about the fire department itself. The situation was dicey, and I wondered why there wasn't a 911 call for situations like this. Existences were at stake, hearts at risk of breaking.

Then I remembered that I had my very own firefighter by my side who still owed me a favor.

"I have a plan B!"

Jackson raised his eyebrow. "Your face tells me I'm not going to like this plan."

"True," I answered honestly. "But you're my best friend, and besides, you still owe me a favor, and I need to call it in now."

"Shit, I knew it all along," Jackson cursed, leaning forward as Maxine clapped her hands in glee.

"I have no idea what it's about, but I'm pretty sure it's going to be just as cool as when Aurora and I stole the blueprints!"

Only when I looked at her seriously did Maxine cover her mouth in horror, "Oh, whoops."

"You were there?" I asked.

"Sure I was in on it. I might even have put Aurora up to it," Maxine confessed.

"Aurora never told me how exactly she got the plans," I said thoughtfully. Then I thought back to our real problem. "We'll talk about that in more detail later, but first we have more important things to take care of."

"You got it," Maxine replied. Jacks also nodded sullenly. Although he didn't know my plan yet, he guessed how much he would dislike our next big thing. But I played the *you-dealt-me-that card*, so as best friend, he had no choice but to keep his word and pay his debt.

Maxine threw herself on the sofa after listening to my plan.

"Complicated, dramatic and almost impossible. I like it! This is going to be super spectacular. Operation *Save the Towerqueen is going into overdrive*!"

Aurora's best friend was right, it was complicated, dramatic and almost impossible, but it was my only chance to win Aurora back. Once she left New York, all was lost. Aurora's flight to Seattle destroyed both of our hearts – I couldn't let that happen!

Chapter 36 – Aurora

I couldn't believe I was really going through with my escape to Seattle, and even less could I believe that no one was looking at me funny. The entire John F Kennedy Airport was plastered with juicy headlines from my past and no one cared.

Silently, I stared at the screen of my deactivated smartphone, wondering if I should listen to any messages Caden might have left for me. But the fear that there were no messages almost broke my heart.

It was no secret that I had fled to Max and Caden had had the chance to dissuade me from my decision. He hadn't, proving to me that I was just a signature to him after all.

Sighing, I put my smartphone back in my purse and waited for my flight to be cleared for check in.

Leaving New York felt wrong, but it was the only thing I could do. Everything here reminded me of Caden, if only because he could be lurking around every corner.

When my flight was called, I jumped out of my seat and marched quickly to the gate before I could change my mind. Sitting around had worn down my spirit and my sad, broken heart longed for comfort – in Caden's arms, of all places. Yet he was the reason I felt this way!

Because the flight was as good as fully booked, check-in took an eternity. An eternity in which I was again in danger of listening to my naive heart.

But my mind switched to survival mode and forced my body to walk step by step down the gate until I was sitting in my seat.

In front of me sat a group of cheerleaders who were literally in each other's hair because they all wanted the window seat. Behind me an elderly lady was discussing with the stewardess that there was no way she could sit next to the man next to her because he listened to the *devil's music* and wore black, long hair. I rolled my eyes and wondered if I really hadn't suffered enough today. *Obviously not.*

At least the chaos in front of and behind me distracted me from my heartbreak. Nevertheless, the question of whether I was doing the right thing remained omnipresent. Caden had undoubtedly been the love of my life. The one, great love that you only find once in a lifetime – if you were very lucky.

Well, but Caden had other plans, my head told me cynically. But the more distance I gained, the longer I thought about it, the clearer it became to me that this problem was not Caden's fault alone. A relationship always consisted of two people, just like conflicts.

And grudgingly, I had to admit that I hadn't been entirely fair either. I had blindsided him with my problems because I was far too angry to tell my findings about Janice in a matter-of-fact way.

Even his doubts that I had smelled of alcohol I could understand. Every person who had to go through such terrible things as Caden did bore scars that never healed properly. Yet Caden had never given up. When had I reached the point where I had given up?

Melancholy, I stared out the window and watched as we slowly drove away from the gate. Then the realization that I wasn't supposed to be here hit me like a slap in the face.

I shouldn't have given up! Never, ever would I get over Caden – if I chickened out now, I'd never forgive myself for the rest of my life.

"Stop, I have to get out of here!" I shouted, jumping up and running down the corridor towards the emergency exit.

"Great," the woman behind me began to jeer. "I'm surrounded by devil worshippers and devil-possessed people! If that's not an omen!"

I paused and suppressed the urge to give that awful woman a piece of my mind. I lost the battle and turned to the old woman whose discontent had been chiseled into her face over the years.

"Only the devil recognizes his peers at first sight."

That left the woman speechless, while the *devil worshipper* grinned gratefully at me. Then I continued to aim for my own destination – the emergency exit.

Focusing, I blanked out the fact that all eyes were on me until a stewardess intercepted me. She had a perfectly fitting hairstyle, perfectly fitting makeup, and a perfect smile, but underneath all her perfection, she couldn't hide the fact that I was crowning the chaos of today's flight.

"Please sit back down, miss," she said in typical stewardess singsong.

"No! I have to go back to the airport!" I protested and pointed to the gate we were taxiing away from.

"I'm sorry, but we're already on our way to the tarmac. We can't just abort now. So sit back down and calm down, please!"

That was no longer a request, but an annoyed command that I didn't care about. It was about my future! It was about my entire world. It was about Mr. Universe!

We engaged in an unprecedented death stare duel until the captain made an announcement and the *seatbelt lights* began to glow.

Again and again, my gaze lingered on the emergency exit, which could be opened manually. The stewardess then blocked my view and looked at me urgently.

"That's twenty-five thousand dollars or two years in jail. I know that look!"

Obviously she knew that look! Frustratingly, Caden's solution to the problem would have worked magnificently by simply charging the twenty-five thousand dollars to his gold Mastercard, stupidly I didn't have that kind of money. Caden's credit card was in the apartment. And two years in prison was certainly not an option!

I would have loved to jump out of the plane, but there was no escape. My pride-driven attempt to escape had backed me into a corner from which I could not get out again.

"All right, all right," I said, raising my arms disarmingly.

The plane accelerated more and more, and there was nothing I could do but defiantly sit back in my seat and hope that Caden would forgive me for my stupid action when I boarded the next plane back to New York.

Please forgive me, Caden.

Chapter 37 – Caden

"I can't believe I'm actually doing this," Jackson said, shaking his head as he drove the fire truck out of the station. "I'm so getting fired."

"No shit." I waved it off and gave my best friend an encouraging pat on the back. "And if you do, I'll just buy you your own firehouse."

Jackson grinned, even though we both knew I was absolutely serious.

"Let's just hope no one notices," Jackson grumbled.

Because the new vehicles still had to be repainted and inspected according to regulations, they were not yet officially in use. So we didn't steal an active car that was needed in an emergency, which was good, because I couldn't have reconciled anything else with my conscience.

Although we were driving without blue lights, we got through New York City traffic quickly.

"I don't think I've ever gotten through Brooklyn that fast," I said, impressed, as the streets just flew by.

"One of the advantages of being willing to climb into burning buildings," Jackson replied. Then he looked at his watch.

"It's going to be a pretty close call."

I shook my head. "No, we'll make it!"

My determination could not be ignored. Everything depended on the next few minutes, which I still could not quite realize. In the blink of an eye, my life could change from the ground up, almost like it did back then ... only this time I could take fate into my own hands! I had a plan, I had allies, and I had the courage to go through with it.

"Caden, even if we don't get past any red lights, the plane will be in the air before we even get close to the airport."

Jackson in no way meant to dampen my spirits, he was just afraid I would crash to the hard ground of reality unprepared.

"Don't worry, the plane won't take off," I replied confidently. I certainly hadn't overcome my fear of jumping to then see Aurora fly away – no chance.

"And what makes you so sure? Your faith in all honor, but I'm afraid that's not enough".

I grinned briefly because neither Jacks nor I were believers, but damn often swore at the devil.

"Of course, that's not enough, so I create distractions."

"Oh yeah?"

As if on cue, my smartphone vibrated and I immediately picked up the phone.

The loud engine noise made it difficult for me to hear Coleman.

"Coleman? I hope there's good news."

That was not a hollow phrase, but a real threat. Basically, it was the last chance to save my company.

"There is, sir," Coleman replied ecstatically. This was the first good news in months!

"All right, how many drones can you get in the air?" I continued.

"A good dozen. We're working flat out to finish another dozen."

"Good, send everything you have to the coordinates I'm going to send you."

Jackson looked at me frowningly while my engineer rattled off more technical data that I barely understood until the connection finally broke off completely. Satisfied, I put my smartphone in my pocket because everything important had been clarified.

"What exactly do you have in mind?" asked Jackson. I could tell he was hoping he had misunderstood me, but I was going to have to disappoint him.

"Exactly what you think," I replied.

"Damn, I was afraid of this. If anything goes wrong, we'll both go to jail for a long time."

"There would be worse cellmates than you," I replied, smiling with one corner of my mouth.

"Not the answer I wanted to hear, Caden!" growled Jackson. "I don't know how you can stay so calm. I certainly can't."

"Neither do I, I'm just better at hiding it," I confessed. Only Aurora had brought down my facade, which had suppressed my feelings for decades.

"I really hope you know what you're doing," Jackson said as his gaze continued down the road.

"I know exactly what I'm doing," I replied seriously. And deep down, Jackson knew it too, otherwise we wouldn't be sitting in a fire station aerial ladder truck, heading for the airport.

The drive through Brooklyn didn't take long, and when the tower of JFK Airport appeared on the horizon, I barely dared to breathe. All the words I had prepared for Aurora fell by the wayside – disconcerting, but I was brave enough to try without prepared speeches.

"Ready?" I asked Jackson, offering him one last chance to get out after all.

"Absolutely not, but here's the thing," Jackson said. Then he turned on the siren and blue lights.

When Jacks stopped in front of the locked gate I had failed at the other day, I recognized the security guy from last time exactly. To remain unrecognized, I buried my face deep in the borrowed helmet that disguised me as a firefighter.

Jackson turned off the siren again because it was impossible to understand a word under the howling.

"What's up?" the guard asked, irritated.

"What's up?" repeated Jacks, horrified, his question. "What do you think there is?"

The guard shrugged his shoulders. "I don't know, I didn't get a report."

"Well, we did. We were called to a potential ten-ninety-two," Jackson stated matter-of-factly.

"Um," the guard began, but then faltered. He probably didn't know the meaning of the code any more than I did. Then he turned around and spoke something into his radio.

"Please, don't be in a hurry," Jackson noted cynically, which elicited only a shake of the guard's head.

Meanwhile, my eyes roamed the runway. I did something I hadn't done in decades, I spoke to God and pleaded with Him that Aurora was still on New York soil. We truly didn't have the best relationship, but I was ready for a second chance.

When my gaze lingered on a deep blue aircraft standing in the middle of the tarmac, my heart stopped for a moment.

Damn. Aurora was really still here! Fortunately, the airline that Aurora had chosen had made it a trademark to paint all of their planes deep blue.

"Hurry up, Jacks! Aurora's plane could take off any second," I quietly ordered him.

"What do you think I'm trying to do?"

If Aurora's plane took off now, I could no longer guarantee anything. I hadn't taken all this on myself just so that fate could trip me up so close to the finish line!

"And where are the damn drones?" I muttered so quietly that no one else understood me. Actually, the prototypes should have been buzzing around somewhere on the tarmac a long time ago, interfering with operations for the short term.

The plane, in which Aurora had to be, rolled slowly over the starting field and then became faster and faster.

Damn, damn, damn!

I didn't know the guy guarding the gate, but I officially declared him a mortal enemy from now on. It was the second time he stood between me and my goal.

Now he also had the audacity to just march back to his cottage while we were waiting for a damn answer!

I would have liked to smash everything to bits, because Aurora flew away before my eyes without me being able to do anything. The realization that I was powerless almost killed me.

I was officially at my lowest point ever, falling even lower than I had many, many years ago when my father had decided to destroy my family in a drunken stupor.

At that time, I had been a frightened boy who could have done nothing. But today? Today I could have done something if my pride had not stood in my way.

Paradoxically, part of my burden fell from my shoulders because I finally realized that I could not help the accident that had cost my parents their lives. But the fact that I had lost Aurora – and could have prevented it – weighed three times as heavily on my shoulders.

I knew Aurora would never forgive me for not stopping her and now there was nothing I could do about it. The plane kept accelerating, shredding my heart at breakneck speed.

Then, all of a sudden, the plane braked again, and I leaned forward to get a better view of what was happening. At the same moment, the gate opened.

Jacks and I looked at each other in equal amazement, but neither of us dared to say anything. The guard – my mortal enemy – trotted out of his box again and waved us through.

"Looks like there really is an emergency. Something about aviation security, there seems to be a problem."

Jackson nodded, then stepped on the gas. A short jolt went through the vehicle, and we rolled off at walking pace. The security guard walked a few more steps along the open window.

"I have no idea what's wrong here, but something stinks big time!"

"I can assure you that this really is an emergency," Jackson tried to placate the guy. Basically, he was speaking the truth, it was an emergency.

I only caught the conversation in passing, however, because I was still scanning the skies for my drones, which were undoubtedly related to the problem in aviation security.

"Hey, wait a minute. Haven't we met before?" the guard asked, looking at me seriously.

"Step on the gas, Jacks!" I commanded before the guard could place my face.

"The pedal is down," my best friend replied. "But it just takes a little time to get several tons of steel moving."

Slowly but surely we rolled away from the security guard before he could really remember my face. By now, not a single plane was moving because my drones were flying all over the place.

Jackson headed for the deep blue plane parked in the middle of the tarmac.

"What is a ten ninety-two, anyway?" I asked curiously.

"A false alarm," Jackson replied with a grin. "But if you lay it out generously, we're heading straight for a ten-sixty. That's code for needing to rescue a missing team member."

"I hope Aurora will let me save her," I replied softly. My heart was in my throat.

"She'll be so blown away after doing this that she won't let you miss a single prison visitation date for the next five years!"

"Don't worry, my PR department will figure out something to keep us out of jail."

I patted my best friend on the shoulder while he eyed me critically.

"Are we talking about the same PR department that got us into this mess, and that we're single-handedly scooping up?"

"Yeah, that's the one," I replied seriously. "Minus Janice, who is probably flying on her broomstick right now to the next company she wants to ruin."

Grinning, Jackson brought the fire truck to a stop directly in front of the plane.

"Now what?" I asked as I stared upwards. "Can you get close enough to the plane with the aerial ladder?"

Jackson growled thoughtfully to himself until he shook his head.

"I hardly think the pilots would let themselves get highjacked. If they keep the doors locked and just roll along, we can't get in." Instead,

Jackson picked up a radio and held it in front of my face. "This is loud enough to reach Aurora."

"Okay, let's do it," I said, signaling for Jackson to turn on the speaker that was connected to the integrated radio.

"Aurora," I began, faltering because I had no idea what to say. "I know you're angry with me, and you have every reason to be, but I'm asking you to listen to me anyway."

I paused meaningfully to buy myself time until my heart took control, shaking my head and also a little ashamed.

"I love you. I love you so much that I broke into your best friend's apartment because I thought I would find you there. I love you so much that I broke into the airport with a hijacked fire truck. And I love you so much that I use drones – which were only completed thanks to you – to shut down all of New York's air traffic."

I waited for a reaction, but nothing happened. Nevertheless, I continued to cling to hope, no matter how much it hurt.

"I'm an idiot and I'm sorry I didn't realize it until now. I need you, Aurora. You are the love of my life, and I would do anything to have you take me back."

Again I waited, again nothing happened.

I had to face the fact that this game was over, and over for good.

Disgruntled, I pulled my smartphone out of my pocket and dialed Coleman's number.

"The drones can leave again," I grumbled into the phone and hung up. New York air traffic didn't need to be at a standstill any longer than necessary.

"Man, I really would have liked a happy ending for you guys. I'm really sorry, buddy," Jackson said softly.

"Me too," I growled. "Let's get out of here."

As Jackson drove off, I grabbed the radio one last time.

"Janice got kicked out in a big way, by the way – you were absolutely right."

Now I had really said everything that needed to be said and, even if Aurora didn't take me back, she wasn't going to leave feeling like she had lost something to Janice.

With a loud hiss, the front door of the plane opened, the next moment the emergency slide shot out, and not a second later Aurora was struggling down. Behind her was an indignant stewardess, who grabbed her perfectly fitting hairstyle in bewilderment.

"Caden! Wait for me!" shouted Aurora, struggling to her feet. She ran so fast toward the fire truck that she even stumbled.

Surprised, I rubbed my eyes to make sure I wasn't dreaming.

"What are you waiting for?" asked Jackson, elbowing me in the side.

I did not need to be told twice and left the vehicle. Aurora rushed toward me, and I took her in my arms.

"I'm so sorry, Caden!" apologized Aurora, her face streaming with tears.

"Me too!" I replied, pulling Aurora even tighter to me. "I can't live without you."

"And I can't without you!"

Relieved, I buried my face in Aurora's hair and sucked in her scent, which I had missed.

"So your drones are flying now?" asked Aurora when we had broken away from each other.

I nodded and scanned the horizon for one of the prototypes. "Coleman was able to correct the mistakes thanks to your plans."

"How cool. I've outshone a few chief engineers," Aurora said proudly.

"No, you did a lot more than that. You saved Saint Industries from a pretty big loss."

"Really?" echoed Aurora, and I nodded.

I would never have said it out loud, but the bad PR, combined with the failure of my engineers could have been the end.

"You should look over the engineers' shoulders more often," I suggested.

"Is that a job offer?" Aurora eyed me carefully. "Because I already have a job as a personal assistant. It's pretty fulfilling and often demanding, but I love it anyway."

"Are you talking about your job or your employer?" I echoed with a grin.

"Both," Aurora replied. Then her face turned serious again, and she looked conspiratorially in the direction of the plane from which she had fled. "Do you happen to have your credit card with you?"

Aurora had that innocent look again, which clearly signaled that she had cooked up something.

"What did you do?" I asked with a raised eyebrow.

Aurora bit her lips and hardly dared to look me in the eye.

"It may have cost me twenty-five thousand dollars to open the airplane door behind me."

"What?" Amused, I looked back and forth between Aurora and the plane. "You opened the emergency exit just like that, without any emergency?"

Outraged, Aurora put her hands on her hips. "It was an emergency, okay? Besides, I feel terrible about it."

Sometimes Aurora was sweeter than was good for her. Grinning, I pulled her to me and gave her a kiss on the forehead.

"The stewardess told me more than once how many laws I was breaking while she defended the door tooth and nail," Aurora added meekly.

"And I was beginning to think Janice's resignation had been the main argument for you to forgive me," I said with a grin. Of course, I knew that I had won Aurora's heart in a different way and that Janice had nothing to do with all this.

"Caden!" Aurora hit my chest with the flat of her hand, and I disarmed her by simply pulling her back to my chest.

"Anyway, it sounds like a good story for our eventual grandchildren," I murmured into her hair, smiling.

"No! Our grandchildren will never know about this!" Aurora threatened with a serious look and her index finger. "And Maxine won't hear a word of it either, or she'll hold it against me forever."

"Oh, come on Aurora, are you really going to put our grandkids to sleep with boring stuff?" I teased her, hitting a sore spot.

"Okay, fine. But then before that, you tell our hypothetical grandchildren about your adventure in Paris."

Touché. Aurora dominated this game better than expected, which only made our game more exciting.

"We should go now," I said, eyeing the tarmac out of the corner of my eye. Slowly but surely, security should have gotten wind of my action.

Aurora nodded and followed me toward Jackson's aerial ladder truck.

"Thank you," Aurora said as I helped her get into the tall vehicle.

"Not for that," I waved it off.

"For fighting for me," Aurora replied with a smile.

I did not dare to let go of her hand. At that moment, I swore to myself that I would never let Aurora go again. I didn't care where we went, as long as we were together.

"I love you," I murmured.

"I love you too," Aurora replied, beaming. Her emerald eyes triggered something in me that I couldn't put into words and that I never had before. *Home.* There was no other way I could describe the feeling Aurora triggered in me at that moment. I was home and my heart was in its place – beating close to hers. *Forever.*

Epilogue – Aurora

Take a breath, Aurora.

All morning I tried to calm myself down, but no matter how deeply I breathed, I felt like I couldn't get enough air. I was sick, actually sick as a dog and today should actually be the most beautiful day of my life!

Everything was perfect. Outside, big, thick snowflakes fell from the sky and covered the tops of the fir trees with white crowns, in front of me crackled a forest-scented fireplace and just one room away stood the man with whom I wanted to spend my life.

It was all exactly as I had wished, but still I did not feel as I was supposed to feel. Did I?

Heavens, what's the matter with me?

I took another deep breath as I stared out at the snowy winter landscape.

Admittedly, I knew exactly what was wrong with me, but I didn't want to admit it to myself under any circumstances. I missed my family. I missed my absolutely chaotic family, whose chaos would have upset the magical idyll. I hadn't even let Maxine in on it, all she knew was that Caden and I were vacationing in Aspen.

Nervously, I paced back and forth, hoping to somehow shake off my insecurity, but I just couldn't do it.

"Aurora?" asked Caden through the closed door.

"Caden? Stay outside!" I ordered Caden in a panic. "It's bad luck to see the bride before the wedding!"

Inevitably, I wondered if that was just for *seeing*, or if one conversation was enough to attract bad karma. I hope not! We had really gone through enough in the last few months and worked off bad karma for three lifetimes.

"It's okay, it's okay. I'll stop right here," Caden placated me in a calm voice.

"What is it, anyway?" I asked.

"That's what I'm asking you," Caden replied with a counter question.

"Nothing," I replied more quickly than was good for my credibility.

"Is that why you've been running in circles for ages?"

Caden shamelessly drilled into my problems, which almost made me angry if I didn't melt because he could be so sensitive.

"I'm not running, I'm walking," I corrected him, stalling for time.

"Oh, I see. Well, if you're just *running around* in circles in a panic, then everything's fine," Caden joked, eliciting a loud sigh from me.

"Okay, I might be a little shaken up," I finally admitted to myself.

Caden was silent for an endless moment.

"Do you want it..." Again he was silent and before he could finish his sentence, I interrupted him.

"No, no way! I want to marry you, with all my heart." I meant it; my feelings for Caden had actually intensified over the past few months. He was the one. *He is the one!*

"I have a feeling there's another *but* coming," Caden said expectantly.

"Possibly." Although he couldn't see me, I nodded with a shrug.

"What's the problem?"

Silently, I continued my panic march from one end of the room to the other while convincing myself that everything was perfect – and that was exactly the problem.

"Caden? I need you to hold me. Now!" I ordered him in a commanding tone that was due to my panic.

"And what about superstition?"

"Superstition or not, this is an emergency! As long as you keep your eyes closed, no major disaster should happen." *Hopefully.*

Caden pushed the door handle down and I reflexively held the door shut.

"Are your eyes really closed?" I asked seriously.

"Yes, they are. I swear to you by everything I hold sacred," Caden replied in a firm voice.

"Almost nothing is sacred to you," I muttered.

"And precisely because *almost* nothing is sacred to me, you should know how sacred my sacred things are to me." He paused meaningfully before finishing his sentence. "Very sacred."

"Okay." Carefully, I released the door handle so Caden could enter.

When I saw him, I was speechless. His hairstyle was perfect, as always, and I could imagine how the dark suit accentuated his bright amber eyes, which he kept closed, as promised.

I pressed myself tightly against his chest, and as his scent enveloped me, I felt like I could breathe again for the first time. Caden just held me until I was ready to let him go again. I stole a kiss and Caden demanded a second one in response.

"Are you feeling better?" Caden asked me worriedly as we broke away from each other.

"Yes," I replied. "And no."

Caden stroked my cheek.

"What's the matter, Aurora? Talk to me."

"I think I made a mistake not letting my family in on it," I said with a sigh.

"Told you so." There was a satisfied smile on Caden's face that seemed almost smug to me.

"Really?" I asked, stunned. Could Caden think of nothing else to do but laugh?

"Yeah, really," Caden fired back with a grin.

"Couldn't you have told me more clearly that I missed my family?" I asked, pouting.

"Something like: Aurora, you're going to regret not letting your family in on this? Or on the hundred other comments in the last four weeks?"

"Yeah, just like that." I sighed because Caden was right. He'd been going on and on about this for the past few weeks, and I'd brushed him off – every single time.

"You just wouldn't change your mind," Caden replied, shrugging his shoulders.

"You could've beat that out of me in the playroom!"

Caden shook his head. "*That's* not an issue we can settle in the playroom."

Although I was grateful to him that we never discussed important decisions in that room, but at eye level, in retrospect I wish he had anyway.

"What are we going to do now?" I asked.

"We'll find a solution," Caden tried to placate me. He sensed my desperation and pulled me tightly to his chest.

In my fantasy, it had been really magical to get married alone and all romantic, but now I knew I wanted my family by my side. Dad should have walked me down the aisle while Mom cheered so loudly that she even overruled the small orchestra. Maggy and Max would have been the perfect bridesmaids and Jackson the perfect best man.

Oh dear, when had I mutated into such a selfish monster? Had the curse that turned all winters into wedding monsters also hit me without realizing it?

Obviously it has, my mind screamed.

"How are we going to find a solution to this problem?" I asked.

"By working the famous *Mr. Universe magic,*" Caden replied confidently.

Caden broke away from me and took three steps back. Frowning, I watched his every step.

"Did you ... No! You didn't. Did you?" I stammered to myself when I had possibly debunked his plan.

"Did I what?" Caden demanded specific details, which was a clear sign that I was on the right track.

"Did you let my family in on this without my permission?" I asked cautiously. Not because I was afraid of him saying *yes,* but because I was afraid of saying *no*.

"I'm not only marrying you, Aurora. But also your messy, crazy, adorable family. I want them there for our most important moment, and I knew from the beginning that deep down, you wanted it too."

There was a huge rattling in my head. "So you really let my entire family in on this, smuggled them into Aspen without me suspecting anything or anyone spilling the beans?"

As if on cue, my entire family including Maxine stormed the room, shouting in unison:

"Surprise!"

Mom rushed forward, hugged me to her and looked at me reproachfully.

"A wedding without your family? Child, where did you get that harebrained idea?"

I shrugged apologetically. "I had insight after all."

"Thank goodness your husband has insight much sooner!" blurted out Max, causing the rest of my family to giggle.

"Husband-to-be," Caden improved. "The *word 'yes'* hasn't been said yet."

"Oh come on, formalities," Maxine waved it off.

Maggy, who had been holding back until now, looked at me with tears in her eyes.

"You look beautiful, Aurora!"

"Shh! Caden mustn't see me," I whispered and put my index finger to my lips.

Caden, still standing with narrowed eyes amid the commotion, cleared his throat.

"I suppose that was my cue. I'll see you in a bit."

"See you in a minute, Caden!" Maxine didn't miss a beat, pushed Caden back even further and closed the door before I could say anything.

With all the chaos that my family suddenly brought, all the tension fell off my shoulders.

While Mom and Maggy nibbled on my wedding dress, my dad looked at me with pride.

"Dad?" I asked, looking over my shoulder at him because I wanted to look him straight in the eye. "Would you walk me down the aisle?"

"I would be honored to walk you down the aisle."

"Thank you," I whispered close to tears of joy.

Now everything was perfect. Maggy and Max's bridesmaid dresses were small, simple versions of my beaded and diamond wedding dress, and Mom wore an even more well-behaved version of it. So Caden had left nothing to chance - hopefully without seeing my wedding dress first.

"Well, let's get it over with, I'm hungry!" demanded Maxine, grinning.

"Max!" I replied indignantly, before laughing as my best friend's stomach began to grumble.

"What?" she asked, rubbing her stomach. "I had a thirty-hour drive and all there was to chow down on was motel chips and highway hot dogs."

"And don't forget the vegetable muffins," Maggy interjected, to which Max immediately screwed up her face. "Vegetable muffins don't count! Vegetables simply have no place in muffins, absolutely no place!"

Confused, I looked back and forth between Max and Maggy. My sister – after her fit of laughter – agreed to finally enlighten me.

"Maxine mistook a vegetable muffin for a slightly burnt vanilla muffin. The look on her face when she realized the muffin was filled with cauliflower and celery...just divine!"

"Yeah yeah, just make fun of my suffering," Maxine replied, rolling her eyes.

Delicate violin notes came to us from the main room, whereupon everyone abruptly fell silent. Everyone stared at me expectantly, which confused me.

"Is that my sign?"

"What do you think?" mom asked, chuckling as she fiddled with my veil one last time. "I'll go ahead."

My sister and best friend were also getting ready for the short march outside, while Dad joined me and I hooked myself in his arm.

"Ready?" he asked when it was just us in the room.

"Ready!" I replied after a deep, liberating breath.

"I couldn't be prouder of who you chose to be your husband," Dad whispered and I nodded.

"Caden is perfect," I gushed.

"So are you."

My heart sank when Dad led me outside to the decorated main room.

The entire room was alive with the scent of pine needles, cinnamon, and firewood, and the panoramic glass offered a wonderful view of the snow-covered forest and the huge, snow-capped mountain peaks beyond.

But when my gaze lingered on Caden, who had tears in his eyes when he saw me, I was speechless. That one look said everything I needed to know – he loved me at least as much as I loved him. Finally, Caden was no longer hiding his heart behind book-thick contracts and that thick, impermeable wall of ice.

Step by step I got closer to Caden, and I wished that the quintet would start a faster rhythm because I couldn't wait to be with Caden again.

"You look beautiful," was the first thing Caden said when we were finally eye-to-eye. I smiled gratefully at him before we both turned to the preacher who was marrying us. To my left stood Maxine and Maggy, to Caden's right stood Jackson, who was having quite a hard time not revealing how touched he was by the scenery.

The preacher gave a short, beautiful speech before prompting us to ask the question of all questions that we were so impatiently waiting for.

"Aurora Winter, do you vow to love and honor Caden Saint as your husband - for better, for worse?"

"Yes," I replied, suppressing a quiet sob. "Yes, I do!"

Then the preacher turned to Caden.

"And do you, Caden Saint, vow to love and honor Aurora Winter as your wife, for better, for worse?"

My heart stopped until Caden finally said the redeeming words that got my heart beating again.

"Yes, I do."

"Then you may kiss the bride now."

Caden didn't let him tell him twice. He pulled me to him, pressed his lips to mine and sealed our vow with the most passionate kiss he had ever given me. It took what felt like an eternity before we broke away from each other again, but this was *our* moment where neither time nor space had any meaning. All that mattered was our sincere love for each other.

"I love you," Caden whispered to me as he looked at me with a mixture of affection and pride. I knew how difficult it had been for Caden to say those three words at first, so I was all the happier that they slipped so easily from his lips now.

"And I love you," I replied.

With that, I was officially the happiest woman in the universe, because I had Mr. Universe by my side – forever.

Epilogue – Caden

I was still speechless when Aurora smiled at me as lovingly as she was doing right now. Her eyes were shining, and her heart was beating so loudly that I could hear it, because it was beating in the same rhythm as my own heart.

"I love you," I said and took her hand. I couldn't tell Aurora enough how much I loved her. Ever since the day she almost traveled back to Seattle, I had vowed to never let Aurora go. And I was hell-bent on proving to her every day that our love was special.

"I love you too," Aurora replied with a smile, intertwining our fingers.

Along with her engagement ring, our wedding ring now adorned her ring finger, showing the whole world that Aurora was mine alone. *To me alone.*

Drunk with bliss, we strolled through Aspen's snowy winter wonderland, enjoying our togetherness at dusk.

With her white wedding dress she looked like a real ice princess in the snowy landscape.

"I can't tell you how grateful I am to you for letting my family in on this. I was going to thank you earlier, but then everything became so..."

"Chaotic," I finished Aurora's sentence with a grin.

Aurora nodded significantly, shaking a few snowflakes out of her blonde hair.

"You hit it right on the head."

I was damn happy that Aurora was happy, because she made me happy, too. On the outside, I was still the ruthless, notorious boss of Saint Industries, but deep inside I was a completely different person. Aurora had made my stunted heart beat again, and for that I was eternally grateful to her.

And not to mention, Aurora's senses had saved Saint Industries from a huge mess, which is why she did not accompany a special post in the engineering department for nothing, and became a valued member, especially by Coleman. Of course, Aurora continued to take care of her duties as my personal assistant, which added a pleasant spice to our daily work routine.

Aurora blew her condensed breath into the air, blowing in the direction of the North Star, already visible in the sky, bringing me back from my thoughts.

"Are you cold?" I asked, automatically pulling her closer to me. Her cheeks, and even the tip of her nose began to turn red.

"No," Aurora replied, but at the same time rubbed her arms as if she were shivering.

I raised a brow questioningly, making it clear to Aurora that I had seen through her lie.

"Okay, yeah. I'm freezing a little bit. But not so much to go back inside just yet. It's way too beautiful in the snow for that! I couldn't think of a single place I'd rather be right now."

Aspen had way too dark days and even colder nights for my taste, but there was still no place I would have preferred.

"Any place where I hear your laughter is the most beautiful place in the world," I replied with a smile.

"Oh, Caden," Aurora replied, touched, clutching her heart. "I love it when you're this romantic."

Fortunately, Aurora loved not only my romantic side – which came out only very rarely – but also my dominant side, which I could definitely handle better.

"We should go back slowly," I suggested.

"Okay," Aurora replied before putting on her diplomatic face. "But slowly! I want to hear the snow crunching under our shoes with every step."

I didn't like the idea of Aurora being exposed to the cold any longer and at first I wanted to object, but I immediately realized that Aurora had a mind of her own. If I wanted her not to catch a cold in the next few days here, I had to solve the problem in a more sustainable way – luckily I already knew exactly how.

"As you wish," I also replied in a diplomatic tone and slowed my pace.

"Really?" asked Aurora, surprised, because she had expected resistance.

"Yes, really." To make it clear that I was serious, I walked even slower. Aurora walked slower, but examined me very closely from top to bottom.

"You're up to something, aren't you?" she asked with a critical expression.

"Me? Never," I replied with a telltale grin.

"Come on, spit it out, Caden!" demanded Aurora, but I remained quite the diplomatic businessman she had teased out.

"You know that everything has its price, which I claimed at the appropriate time."

Aurora stuck her chin up and strutted in front of me like a noblewoman.

"As of today, I'm officially Mrs. Universe, which means I'm pretty rich. So I can pay any price with ease."

Aurora pretended to be confident of victory in our little discussion, yet it was her words that I could use against her.

"Not everything that has its price can be paid with money. Your words, dear," I replied with a grin.

"Good move," Aurora grudgingly admitted and picked up the pace a bit again. Probably my little ice princess was freezing more than she wanted to admit.

"You play well, but I've been playing this game a lot longer than you," I said confidently, winking at her. "There's no shame in losing to the best."

Outraged, Aurora put her hands on her hips. "I didn't lose!"

"Of course not," I replied teasingly.

"Stop making fun of me!" complained Aurora, half-seriously.

"I would never allow myself to do that!" I continued to tease.

"You are impossible," Aurora sighed.

"And that's exactly why you love me," I said confidently.

Aurora returned my answer with a grin and finally gave up. No, she didn't give up, she had just decided to make a strategic retreat, which I granted her.

Together we walked back to our small log cabin with panoramic windows, which we had to ourselves. Our guests were accommodated in their own houses so that nothing stood in the way of our wedding night as I had planned it.

At the door, I slowed Aurora down until we both stopped. From my pants pocket I pulled a white silk scarf that fluttered in the gentle evening breeze.

"This doesn't come as a surprise to you, does it?" I asked as I continued to let the silk scarf blow in the wind.

"Not really," Aurora grinned cheekily at me before her expression turned more serious again. "A lot has changed between us. We've changed. But I'm glad some things haven't changed between us."

I knew exactly what Aurora was talking about, and I agreed with her. My dominant side had always been a part of me, just as Aurora's submissive side belonged to her.

"Like a heart without a heartbeat," I whispered, and Aurora nodded.

"Exactly."

I pushed a blond strand behind Aurora's ear and looked at her flawless face between my hands.

"I'm about to make your heart beat faster," I murmured to her, watching a shiver go through her body. Aurora's body reacted violently to my words and admittedly, I loved how I could play her body like an instrument.

I allowed Aurora to look into my eyes one last time, then I blindfolded her with the silk scarf.

Thanks to our endless trust in each other, Aurora allowed herself to be led through the log cabin as easily as a feather until we reached the center of the room.

"I hope there's a hot bubble bath waiting for me at the other end of the room!" said Aurora with a smile, rubbing her shivering arms.

"Would have, but you expressed a desire earlier for us to settle our affairs more often in the Playroom," I replied, brushing her cozy faux fur jacket over her shoulders.

"That was before our wedding ceremony! I was completely out of my mind!" Aurora defended herself.

"And during our walk, you made it impressively clear to me that you were right," I continued, as if I had overheard her last words. My game had long since begun, whether Aurora wanted it to or not. I got rid of my winter jacket and then turned my attention to Aurora, who was standing awkwardly in front of me, waiting for me.

Slowly, I unlaced the corset that had so perfectly accentuated Aurora's figure. But if there was anything that emphasized Aurora's body even more than her wedding dress, it was the flickering light of a fireplace, directly on her naked skin.

Admittedly, I could hardly wait to finally free her from this annoying tulle that prevented me from touching her body. More and more sheaths fell to the floor and where my fingers grazed her skin, she was cool.

I clicked my tongue and pushed Aurora even closer to the fireplace so her body could warm up.

"You should really listen to me when I think you've had enough," I said in a throaty voice. To make clear what I meant, I breathed against her neck, which resulted in goose bumps spreading.

"I haven't had enough," Aurora protested softly.

"So you're not cold?" I echoed. Aurora bit her lower lip thoughtfully, probably because she was weighing her answers. She should know that I would only let one answer pass - the truth.

"Yes, I did freeze," she finally confessed. "Actually, I'm still freezing."

Knowing she wanted to get back to the hot bubble bath, I placed a finger on her lips.

"Fortunately, I can think of a few things to warm your body back up." My friendly, almost caring tone made Aurora shiver. Good thing, because that was exactly what I had intended. *He who will not hear must, as is well known, feel...*

Aurora inhaled sharply when I also took off her panties and she finally stood naked in front of me. I stalked around her, grabbed a chair and placed it in front of Aurora. Expectantly, she took a deep breath, but when nothing happened, she suppressed a disappointed exhale.

Silently I took a seat on the chair in front of her and enjoyed the view and the warmth that the fireplace radiated in front of us. Although Aurora hid it, I could tell she was still cold, so I made short work of grabbing her arm and pulling her onto my lap.

I buried my face in her hair, growled softly and then licked over her neck, down to her sensitive bud, which was getting harder and harder.

My pants were getting tight, but I suppressed my desire to fuck Aurora, because she still had a lesson to learn.

"Don't worry, dear. In a moment you won't be cold anymore," I promised her and turned her with an elegant movement, so that her exposed backside stuck up in the air.

"I could actually get used to this sight," I said with a smile on my lips as my hand rested on her butt.

"You're so quiet," I murmured after Aurora continued to be silent.

"Sometimes it's better if I keep my mouth shut," Aurora replied.

"True, true," I agreed with her. I knew Aurora well enough to know that her level-headed nature didn't last long, especially not when I went for it and tickled the anger out of her.

With my first stroke a jolt went through her entire body, my second one Aurora took with more composure. I enjoyed this intimate position where our bodies were so close.

Alternately, I worked her two sides until her pale skin glowed rosy. With each stroke, my hand hit her tight buttocks a little harder, and although Aurora struggled, she found it increasingly difficult to hold still.

"Don't move!" I ordered her.

"Easier said than done," Aurora gasped.

"So you want motivation," I stated matter-of-factly.

"No!" replied Aurora in a matter of seconds before adding a meek "Sir."

Grinning, I accepted her apology, but that couldn't shake my motivation. I had made my decision.

"How many more strokes can you take?" Thoughtfully I rubbed over the sensitive red skin of her buttocks. My handprints stood out clearly, there was no more beautiful work of art than the expression of our passion for each other.

"Ten," Aurora replied after some consideration. "Maybe more, but ten is at least."

Smiling, I noted Aurora's offer that I had permission to go beyond her limits. I decided to take Aurora up on her offer, but not until later.

"Good, then you should hold still for the next ten strokes." I rubbed her sensitive spots with vigor to show her that I was in control of her pain, and more importantly, her pleasure. "For every stroke you don't hold still, I'll withhold an orgasm from you."

Aurora snorted loudly, which directly earned her a firm slap. Only with effort did she manage to suppress a scream.

"Do you have anything else to say?" I asked.

"No, sir."

"Good girl."

My next blow was a little less firm, but I didn't miss the chance to hit the same spot three times in a row. Aurora bravely controlled her body, but she gave free rein to her voice.

Damn, how I loved her moans. Every time she gasped, my erection got even harder. I couldn't control myself for long, but I didn't have to. Six strokes still separated Aurora and my cock.

Each stroke brought us closer to orgasm, me at least, as Aurora's body quivered menacingly under my hands.

"You really want to show me today, huh?" I asked with a smile.

"Yes, sir," Aurora pressed out between clenched teeth. "I'm going to have the most phenomenal orgasm in the world on my wedding night!"

Grinning because Aurora was so into it, I put my work in front of her. Of course, tonight I gave her the most phenomenal orgasm in the world, and right after that another ... and another, after all, today was the most important day of our lives. But Aurora didn't need to know that yet, because this thrill was part of the game.

While the first strokes were fast and merciless, my strokes now became agonizingly slow and unpredictable. Three more strokes and Aurora had done it.

"I suppose you're warmer now?" I asked, amused.

"Oh, yes," Aurora replied – it was more moan than speech.

The next two blows hit Aurora's butt with full force, yet she didn't move an inch. *Damn.* I really loved how much she provoked me with her obedience. But I could tell she was just as impatient as I was, possibly even more so, which I immediately used against her. I let my hand fall gently on her bottom, caressing her skin and taking all the time in the world to do so.

Minutes passed, during which Aurora became more and more agitated, until she almost exploded.

"Jesus, Caden! Now finish spanking me!" demanded Aurora imperiously.

Again I clicked my tongue to rebuke her impatience, which I myself had provoked and registered with relish.

"Would you like another ten strokes?" I asked challengingly.

"No, sir!" Aurora's voice was still excited, but less provocative, which I almost regretted a little.

"Good."

Aurora took the last blow just as bravely as the previous blows. I had made her angry because her body almost exploded with pleasure, and I knew it well.

"On your knees!" I commanded softly and let Aurora slide down from my thighs.

She made no secret of the fact that she would have preferred it if I had thrown her on the bed and fucked her mercilessly, because that's exactly what she wanted. After all, today was Aurora's big day – but it was also mine, and I was just a man.

Automatically Aurora crossed her arms behind her stretched back and looked at me devotedly.

Damn, I loved this sight that I could feast my eyes on for the rest of my life. Aurora stared expectantly at the bulge in my pants until I finally freed my erection. Lasciviously, as if she couldn't wait, Aurora bit her lips and leaned forward so she could lick over my tip.

I sat back and enjoyed the show that was presented to me. Aurora knew exactly how to drive me crazy, which she shamelessly exploited against me. Her full lips closed around my length while her tongue licked along my shaft.

Piece by piece she slid down until the tip of her nose touched my belly. *Damn!*

Groaning, my head fell back and I reflexively grabbed Aurora's hair so that I could seize control. I thrust deep into her throat, pulling out of her, only to thrust harder shortly after.

One look into Aurora's eyes was enough to know that this was the treatment she had been craving all day. She enjoyed my erection in her throat at least as much as I did.

My thrusts became firmer, more merciless, and my grip kept Aurora exactly where I wanted her – kneeling in front of me while my cock fucked her mouth.

Her moans became louder and louder, and her entire body shook with pleasure. This sight alone was enough to make me come, but I held back, after all we still had all night.

One last time I pressed Aurora tightly against my erection, enjoying the feeling of my erection sliding down her throat as Aurora begged for air with pleading looks, but didn't resist my grip.

After I let her silky hair slip out of my fingers, Aurora gave me a reproachful look because I had withheld my orgasm from her. Grinning, I took note of her defiance, but didn't give her time to provoke me into an orgasm with teasing after all. Instead, I effortlessly threw her feathery body over my shoulder and gently laid her down on the plaid cashmere blanket that lay to the side next to the fireplace.

I spread her legs and knelt between them. Aurora was more than ready for me, yet I didn't miss the chance to indulge in a little taste of her lust.

My hands wandered up her taut thighs until I arrived at her most sensitive spot, eliciting a moan from her. Aurora stretched her hips towards me demanding, I was only too happy to accept this invitation and licked down over her mons veneris until Aurora could hardly control herself. Already my breath directly over her clit was enough to make her come.

"Not yet," I murmured.

"Oh, Caden!" moaned Aurora. "You're driving me crazy!"

"Good," I replied with a grin. Then I tasted her pleasure again, licking over her delicious body and enjoying how Aurora squirmed under my touch.

Her nails dug uncontrollably into my shoulders, her legs trembled more and more, and if I hadn't stopped, Aurora would have come without my permission.

I pulled back, which Aurora punished with reproachful looks, which I skillfully ignored. Instead, I bent over her, kissed her neck, her cheeks, her mouth and rubbed my manhood against her wet entrance.

"Our first orgasm as husband and wife should be together," I whispered in her ear.

"Together?" replied Aurora nodding and reaching for my hand.

"Together. Just like we're going to do everything else together. The two of us against the rest of the world."

Aurora smiled gratefully at me as our fingers intertwined and I entered her. Immediately she wrapped her legs around my hips and her breathing quickened.

The glow of the campfire was reflected in her emerald eyes and on her flawless skin, and it felt to me like she was really on fire. Because of me – and especially with me.

Her tightness was driving me half crazy, and the closer we got to orgasm, the tighter she tightened around my erection. But that in no way prevented me from taking Aurora the way she expected me to. Hard. Deep. Merciless. She was intent on fucking her brains out, and I was only too happy to comply with that request.

Our lips met passionately, our tongues demanded even more passion and neither Aurora nor I had any choice but to give in to this incredible feeling that catapulted us into other spheres.

We came. Wild. Fierce. *Together*.

Breathless, I sank down onto her body and rested my head on her torso, which quickly rose and fell again, over and over. I listened to Aurora's soft sigh that escaped her throat with every breath and stroked her hair out of her face, lost in thought.

When our eyes met, Aurora looked at me, frowning.

"Caden?"

"Aurora?"

"You're staring," she said matter-of-factly.

"I don't stare," I replied businesslike, although Aurora was right.

"You do." Aurora withstood even my *I'm-punishing-you* look that usually silenced her, but this time she insisted on her right to disagree with me, no matter what the consequences.

"Okay, you're right, I was staring," I finally confessed. Of course I had been staring at her, how could I not adore the brightest star in my darkness?

"Why?" echoed Aurora, further furrowing her brow, which I tried to smooth with my index finger.

"Because I just can't take my eyes off you," I tried to explain my feelings. "You're going to have to get used to that, because I'm not going to do anything else for the rest of my life."

"I don't think I'll ever quite get used to the fact that Mr. Universe made me, of all people, the center of his universe," Aurora replied with a smile and kissed me.

"We have a lifetime for that, too," I whispered.

"I love you, Caden."

"And I love you, Aurora."

Get a free copy of my fan-exclusive romance novel *Palace of Pain* over at: https://lana-stone.com/

Printed in Great Britain
by Amazon